P9-CRY-933

A GENTLEMAN OF THE PLAINS

"I want . . ." Faith rolled her head to the side where Luke couldn't see her face. She didn't have the nerve to finish her sentence.

Bending close, he slowly nibbled at her lips, sending fire coursing through her veins. He lightly touched the swell of her breast. "Faith, honey, this is very sweet of you but—"

"It's the only thing I have to give you, Luke," she interrupted. "You've done—"

"Hush," he whispered, as he took her face in his hands and turned it to see into her eyes. "Don't you know I don't want this unless I can have what's *here?*" He tapped softly on both of her temples. "And this, too." He leaned down and kissed the spot where her heart beat wildly in her chest. "It would mean nothing to me without the rest of you."

Other books by Caroline Fyffe:

WHERE THE WIND BLOWS

Montana
Dawn

CAROLINE
FYFFE

LEISURE BOOKS NEW YORK CITY

I dedicate this book about brothers to my sons,
Matthew and Adam.
So different, yet so much alike.
Thank you for giving my life meaning and joy.

A LEISURE BOOK®

August 2010

Published by

Dorchester Publishing Co., Inc.
200 Madison Avenue
New York, NY 10016

Copyright © 2010 by Caroline Fyffe

ISBN 10: 0-8439-6427-8
ISBN 13: 978-0-8439-6427-1
E-ISBN: 978-1-4285-0911-5

The name "Leisure Books" and the stylized "L" with design are trademarks of Dorchester Publishing Co., Inc.

Printed in the United States of America.

10 9 8 7 6 5 4 3 2 1

Visit us online at www.dorchesterpub.com.

Chapter One

An eerie keening echoed through the trees. Luke Mc-Cutcheon straightened in the saddle, and his filly's ears flicked forward, then back. "Easy, girl. Don't dump me now." Not with ten miles to go, he thought as he felt the green-broke filly hesitate. Lightly reining her to the solid side of the slippery embankment, he pressed her forward. Still, she balked at a mud-covered tree stump, snorting and humping her back.

Rain came down in sheets now, drenching them both. Squinting through the darkness, Luke scanned the clearing for any sign of the others he'd split from some three hours before.

A bolt of lightning flashed across the sky, followed by an explosive boom. Chiquita whirled a complete circle and crow-hopped several strides, sending an icy rivulet gushing from the brim of Luke's hat.

"Hell." Luke squeezed with his legs, pushing her onto the bit. "Flighty filly," he said under his breath. "You'd be a great one if you'd ever settle down."

Cresting the rise, Luke searched the horizon through the downpour. Nothing. Nobody in sight. "Long gone." Frustrated, he slapped his gloved hand against his thigh and spun Chiquita in the opposite direction. He'd head back to camp and try again at daybreak.

Suddenly the uncanny cry came again, peculiar in its tone and just as troubling as the first time he'd heard it. "What . . . ?" He'd never heard anything like it in his twenty-six years. He reined up for a moment, listening.

A minute slipped by, then two. Still nothing but the unrelenting storm. A wounded animal? No. That queer sound was totally unfamiliar. He headed in its direction to investigate.

His efforts proved useless, and after several minutes he stopped. As if called, a streak of lightning lit up the landscape, revealing a dilapidated wagon half-hidden in the brush. It listed to one side, the wheels buried up to the axles. As quick as the light came, it vanished, leaving him in darkness.

He dismounted, cursing the jingle of his spurs. His gloved hand dropped to his sidearm and slid the gun from its holster. Another ghostly cry emanated from the wagon, raising the hair on his neck. Silently, he made his way over the uneven ground. With his back to the wagon's side he reached around with his free hand and cautiously pulled back the canvas cover.

"Hello?"

Only the wind answered, whipping a smattering of rain against his face. Not daring to take his eyes from the dark opening, he steeled himself against the chilly water dripping down his neck. He flexed his shoulders, willed himself to relax. Then a sound, like the rustling of a mouse, caught his attention. He held his breath.

"Coming in," Luke warned. He trusted his instincts, and it didn't feel like someone had a gun pointed at him. Cautious, however, his boot on the wheel axle, he lifted himself slowly through the opening. He paused, letting his eyes adjust to the dark interior.

The aroma of musty canvas engulfed him. And the smell of something else. Fear? Bending low he inched slowly through the cramped interior. He winced: a sharp edge. Fire and ice coursed up his leg. He stopped. Something was in the corner.

With his teeth, he pulled his glove from his hand and reached into his inside pocket for a match. He struck it and held it high. It winked brightly for only a moment and was extinguished by a gust of wind. But not before he saw a woman crouched down, her eyes the size of twin harvest moons.

"You're hurt?"

A soft panting was her reply.

"Your lantern. Where is it?" He felt around the rafters. Finding a lamp, he lit it and turned down the wick until a soft light glowed around the cramped area.

He knelt beside the woman. Beads of sweat trickled off her brow and her breath came fast. Eyes wide with fright were riveted on the gun he held. Then he noticed a stick clenched between her teeth. His gaze flew downward. Her knees were drawn up and a blanket covered the lower half of her body. But there was no mistaking what was underneath.

Luke leaned toward her, intending to take the stick from her mouth when excruciating pain exploded in his head and shot down his neck. "What the . . . ?" He turned. Stars danced before his eyes and he fell to the wagon floor. His gun slid from his grasp.

A groan was all Faith could manage before she was overcome by an all-consuming urge to bite down on the stick with all her might. She wanted, needed, to keep her eyes open and on the stranger, the large man who'd climbed into her wagon, sending her heart skittering up her throat. But it was no use. Another contraction began, and it was next to impossible to keep her eyes open; the icy fire gripped her stomach with a grasp as strong as the devil's.

Mentally counting, she wrestled against her impulse to tighten up as burning beads of sweat dripped into her eyes. Eight . . . nine . . . ten. Ten seconds of sheer torture. Then the hurt eased, and Faith lay on her pallet, spent. The stick dropped from her teeth.

Summoning what strength she had she pushed up on her elbow. "Why'd you hit him, Colton?" she asked the wide-eyed boy, a frying pan dangling in his hands. "I hate to think how mad he'll be when he wakes up." Dread rippled within her as she studied the cowboy lying within an arm's reach.

"Thought he was gonna hurt ya, Ma."

Faith drew in a shaky breath. "Quick, give me the gun."

Colton carefully picked up the revolver. Faith took it, feeling its steely cold weight in her hands.

The man moved slightly and his lashes quivered on his darkly whiskered cheek. His face, hard with angles and chapped from the cold, lay flat against the wagon bed. He moaned as his face screwed up in a grimace, which sent Faith's heart careening. The rest of him looked mighty big under his rain slicker and leather chaps.

Overwhelming despair descended. Just today she'd dared to dream that she and Colton had escaped her brother-in-law Ward, and that he'd given up his hunt for them. Horses couldn't drag her back to Nebraska to marry him and subject her children to the cruelty of that family. Their despicable plot framing her for Samuel's accidental fall was evil. Truth didn't matter, though, when they had the law, or lack of it, on their side. She felt like crying every time she thought about it. The Browns wanted her farm in Kearney and would stop at nothing, it seemed, to get it. So far this journey had been extremely difficult—long days and nights full of danger and fear—and one she wasn't ready to see end futilely.

And now this! In her mind she weighed their chances against the man before her. When her gaze moved back up to his face, her heart stopped.

Chapter Two

$\mathcal{T}$HE stranger watched her through narrowed eyes. He struggled to a sitting position and stared at the gun she had pointed at his chest. "Give it . . . to me."

His tone was colder than the weapon she held. Faith shook her head.

He turned and frowned at Colton, whose hair was rumpled, eyes hot and angry. "You're dangerous with that thing," he accused, and reached for the offending object. The small boy reared back, the heavy iron skillet raised high in the air. "Just settle down, kid. I'm one of the good guys."

"Colton, go back to your bed," Faith ordered. The firm grip of a contraction began and would soon move painfully to her back. The boy did as he was told, crawling behind some crates in the opposite corner. "Don't"—Faith panted a few times, the gun wobbling in her hands—"come out till I call."

"Yes, Ma. I just didn't want that sidewinder to hurt ya none."

Even in the darkened interior Faith couldn't miss the stranger's amused expression.

"Sidewinder? The name's Luke. Luke McCutcheon."

"Well, mister, as soon as my ma is finished birthin' my brother, we'll be on our way. Won't we, Ma?"

Faith didn't answer. It was all she could do to hold the gun.

Mr. McCutcheon's face softened, and his gaze touched hers. He reached out and gently took the heavy weapon from her hands. Her fear ebbed slightly. Deep inside she felt this wasn't the kind of man a woman had to fear. Not like Samuel.

He holstered the firearm and stood, a little unsteady. "I'll get help. Someone who's done this before. Our camp cook is always boasting on all his accomplishments. I'm sure delivering a baby is one of 'em. I'll be back as soon as I can."

But, he hesitated. Looked to the wagon opening and back at her, clearly uncertain. Fingered the rim of his hat. "It's best. If you have trouble, Lucky is the man to help."

"Don't go." Even though she didn't know him, his presence was comforting. Something inside her chest—something she hadn't felt in a very long time—ached. She wanted to trust him.

Without warning, hot liquid gushed between her legs. Faith gasped in surprise, cradling her belly for support. Mortified, she pressed some folded towels under the blanket to her body. An unmerciful urge to cry surfaced. She turned her face into the darkness and let the tears fall.

"No, no, don't cry. It's natural. No need to worry." He slowly backed away. "I'm going now. But I'll be back. I promise."

Luke pulled off his hat and let the rain buffet his face. It felt good, cold and clean. He knew weather. He knew rain. He didn't know the mystery of a woman's body in childbirth. Before he could change his mind, he strode over to where Chiquita stood. The filly stuck out her muzzle and nudged him.

"All right. We're going." He looked back at the wagon. Everything was quiet within. Sliding his foot into the stirrup, he swung into the saddle.

He'd faced danger and even death many times. Hell, he'd once killed a cougar with only a knife. He considered himself a brave man. But right now, he was scared to death. Scared by a small woman and a baby.

"Damnation!" He couldn't just ride off and leave her alone. What if it were his little sister out here? He'd sure want someone to help her.

Riding back to the wagon, he dismounted and tied Chiquita to the rear wagon wheel; then he climbed back inside. "We'll get through this together," he announced. "I've delivered my share of calves. It can't be much different."

Without much trouble he found a cloth and held it out in the rain. He stroked the young woman's forehead and cheeks with the cool cotton rag, wiping away drops of beaded moisture and tears. Her face contorted and her shaky hand snaked from under the cover and rubbed her large belly.

"Please," the woman asked. "Can you help me sit up?"

Her plea was a velvety whisper but she watched him closely with distrustful eyes. What was she thinking? Her gaze followed his hand as he reached out to help her. So wary. So *alone*.

Gently, he eased her up, bracing her back against a trunk. "Better?"

She nodded.

Luke went for the canteen on his saddle. Hunching his shoulders against the wind, he inhaled the sweetness of wet earth. It grounded him. He desperately needed that now with the woman in the wagon doing crazy things to his insides. He wanted to help her. To take the pain away. He wanted to be what she needed, though that made no logical sense whatsoever.

Inside, he held the canteen to her dry lips. A blast of wind rocked the wagon, swaying it precariously to one side. She grasped his arm, clinging to him with strength at odds with her size. "Whoa, easy now. Just the wind. This wagon's not going anywhere." Her expression, tight and apologetic, tore at his gut.

Moments ticked by. She rested. What should he do in preparation—boil some water? Not in this storm. He fidgeted with the horsehair clip he kept in his pocket, turning it over and over.

She was watching him again with those big coffee-colored eyes. Her hair, mussed and tangled, lay heavily across her small shoulders, a combination of rich chocolate and flaxen highlights. Mahogany. The exact color of the rocker his ma had in the kitchen at home.

"What's your name?"

"Faith."

"Is someone out there looking for you, Faith? A husband?"

She shook her head and began to pant.

Anxiety burned hot in his belly as he watched her struggle. Taking her hand he fitted it tightly in his. "Go on. Squeeze. It might help."

She did. Luke was astonished again by her strength. Her forehead crinkled and her mouth pursed. Sweat trickled down both temples. Nostrils flared. A series of expressions slid across her face as fast as clouds move in a storm. Then she quieted and her grip eased up, but she didn't let go. Her eyes drifted closed. Minutes crawled by. His thumb stroked softly across her fingers, which were delicate in size, but roughened from hard work. . . .

One hour of torture crept by, then another. Would Roady come looking for him when he didn't make it back to camp? Even if he did, Luke had ridden farther north than he normally would have. He had a slim-to-nothin' chance of getting any help here.

It was dawn, and Luke wondered how she kept on. Her grasp had long since lost its strength. When he'd laid her back onto her pallet she was no stronger than a kitten; he was more or less holding on to her.

She gave a gentle tug. "I think it's coming."

Chapter Three

At her words, Luke took courage. He scooted to her feet, lifting the blanket that covered her body. She was bloody, but if things went right, it wouldn't be too long before this baby was born. He wasn't weary anymore but filled with excitement.

"You're doing fine." He smiled into the expectant mother's

exhausted face and brushed some strands of hair off her forehead. "Next time, you should push a little. Think you can?"

With bleary eyes, she nodded and soon began to whimper and pant.

Luke grasped her hand. "Start bearing down slowly at first, slowly, slowly, good girl, good, good, now . . . *push*." Faith grunted and strained. Her face went from crimson to stark white. "That's it, easy, easy, that's it, good. Keep pushing."

After the contraction eased, she relaxed and her eyes slowly drifted closed. She looked . . . dead. Luke banished the horrible thought from his mind. Within moments she was up and panting again.

"Already?" Luke checked her again. The baby hadn't proceeded any further.

"Something's wrong," Faith said. Fear, stark and vivid, glittered in her eyes.

"No, you're doing fine. He's just taking his own sweet time."

She was limp. Like a rag doll. If she didn't deliver this baby soon, she'd surely run out of steam. And blood. It looked as if she'd lost a bucketful. With barely any force, she pushed again. Nothing. Was the baby turned? He'd seen it in livestock.

A shallow contraction. Then another. Faith was growing weaker by the second; her face was whiter than the first snowfall of winter. Now would be a good time to pray. Luke searched his recollection for any of the prayers his ma had insisted he learn as a boy. Frustrated he realized he'd have to improvise.

Lord, I know you're not used to hearing from me very often, but this girl needs your help, and she needs it now. I don't really know what to do. Any assistance you could send our way would be appreciated. He thought for a moment to see if there was anything he'd left out. *Amen.*

Almost before he could see what was happening, and with no sound at all, Faith gave a weak push and the baby was delivered. Caught off guard, Luke barely had time to catch the infant. Its skin was slick and slippery, its eyes opened wide as if surprised at the new surroundings. Luke grinned up at Faith, unable to hide his excitement.

"A filly!" he laughed. "As pretty as, as . . . as anything I've ever seen. She's beautiful."

"A girl?" Creases lined Faith's tired brow. She looked at the tiny baby he held in his hands. "I never dreamed . . ."

The baby began to shiver and cry as Luke tied off the umbilical cord with some twine he'd found in a box, and then, before he could think about what he was about to do, he made a fast cut. He gently handed the baby to her mother.

"Do you have something to wrap her in? Won't take but a moment for her to catch a chill."

Faith glanced around the wagon. "Yes, but it's all packed away. I wasn't expecting this so soon." Her eyes drifted down. "It all came on so quickly."

Without thought, Luke swiftly unbuttoned his shirt and pulled it off. He yanked his thick undershirt over his head and handed it to Faith. "Here. Wrap her in this." He threaded his arms back into his shirt as she swaddled the baby and snuggled her close. The infant whimpered softly and began rooting around, looking for her first meal.

The next contraction delivered the afterbirth, and Luke set it aside in a towel to be buried later. When he was sure he'd done all that he could for the pair, he donned his coat and went out to check on his horse, giving Faith some privacy. Chiquita stood tied to the wagon, tail tucked, head low. She looked his way when he ran his hand along her sodden neck, then scratched her withers. Her head tipped in pleasure, bringing a smile to his lips.

What should he do now for Faith? He didn't have any supplies with him. After that expenditure of energy, she must be famished. Somehow the boy had slept through the whole thing, but surely he'd be up now that the sun was peeking over the treetops. Luke leaned his weight onto Chiquita and rubbed his hand down his face. This had been the most gut-twisting experience he'd ever been through. Thank God it was over.

The rain had stopped sometime around dawn. Luke rounded up some wood, and after several tries he had a fire burning. First he'd warm some water for her to wash with; then he'd see what she had in the way of food fixin's he could whip up. Right now a cup of strong black coffee would be better than his ma's warm apple pie with a double dollop of sweet ice cream.

"Still here?" The kid who'd hit him with the frying pan climbed from the back of the wagon.

Irritated from lack of sleep and the boy's highfalutin tone, Luke bristled. "Yeah, I'm still here."

"We can manage now."

The cocky little . . . Luke reined in his temper. A boy barely out of short pants shouldn't be able to get his goat. "Sure you can. Still, I'm going to fix something to eat for your ma and then talk to her. I'll be out of your hair soon."

"Good." The boy trotted around the far side of the wagon, his messy brown hair bouncing up and down as he went. Luke heard him relieving himself against a rock. When he returned, he eyed Luke suspiciously.

"You aren't too trusting, are you?" Luke said.

"Got no reason to be."

"I stayed all night, helped your ma deliver, never gave you any reason to mistrust me. Did I? Not even when you bashed me on the head."

"That don't mean you ain't waiting for the right chance."

Luke slowly shook his head. The boy was serious. He was also protecting his mother, a heavy burden for such small shoulders. "I'm not waiting for the right chance. I won't hurt you or your ma." Colton's intense stare never wavered, so Luke changed the subject. "What do you think of the baby?"

"They were asleep, so I didn't get a good look at him yet. But I can't hardly wait to take him froggin'."

"You mean *her*. Take *her* froggin'."

"Her? You mean he's a girl?" Colton screwed up his face in disgust, and it reddened with annoyance. "Ma said it'd be a boy for sure. No, sir, you must be wrong."

"Sorry, Colton." It was hard to hide his delight at having disappointed the kid. "One thing I'm sure about, that's one itsy-bitsy female in that wagon with your ma."

"Whoreson!" Colton kicked the ground, causing a wet clump of mud to fly in Luke's direction. It missed him by inches.

Although surprised that someone so young would use such language and display such anger, Luke hid his astonishment. If he'd talked or acted like that when he was a boy, his skin would have been tanned off his backside right quick. "Your pa let you talk like that?"

"Sure, why not?"

"Because it's not polite. Decent folk don't take kindly to it. I can't believe your ma doesn't care if you sound like a donkey."

"Well, maybe she does, but she can't hear me now."

"I hear you, Colton John," Faith called from within. "If I had any strength, I'd jump up and wash your mouth out with soap. Now, say you're sorry." The baby started crying, and Luke heard Faith trying to comfort her.

The boy glared at Luke, not intimidated at all by his size or age.

Luke grinned anyway. "Say you're sorry."

The boy's face turned bright red. "Sorry," he spat out.

"Apology accepted."

Faith's voice interrupted the scene. "Come in and meet your sister," she called to Colton.

"I don't want to meet no sissy girl." His expression still obstinate, the boy fiddled nervously with a slingshot he'd pulled from his pocket.

It was Luke's turn to glare. He was almost overcome by an all-powerful urge to throttle the mouthy child. Pointing, he silently mouthed the word, "Go."

Colton held his ground.

Stretching to his full height, Luke took one step toward the boy. Colton hurried to the wagon and climbed inside.

Chapter Four

A loud whistle snapped Luke out of his thoughts. *Roady?*

Colton popped his head back out from behind the canvas cover. "What's that?"

"My friend, looking for me." Luke gave an answering whistle and waited for his companion to appear. Moments later, a horse and rider came crashing through the scrub brush, sliding to a halt in camp.

"Luke, you all right? We've been looking for you! Thought maybe that green-broke filly you like so much had her fill and pitched you off some cliff." Roady dismounted. He motioned with his head toward the wagon and the boy. "Whatcha have here?"

At that moment, the baby started crying. Roady's eyes opened wide, and a smile split his lean, tanned face.

"You're never going to believe me." Luke swiped his hand over a day's growth of dark beard and yawned.

"Try me."

After hearing the story, Roady gave a long whistle. "Where's her husband?"

"Not sure. We didn't get a chance for parlor talk."

"Did he tell ya I bashed him on the head with a fry pan?" Colton called triumphantly from inside the wagon. "Knocked him out cold."

"And I'm not forgetting it, boy." Luke reached under his hat to finger the egg-size lump.

"How's the woman?"

"Fine, I think. I haven't checked on her since the baby came, but I hear them in there from time to time."

"Can I see them?" Roady raised his brows and crossed his arms over his whipcord lean body.

"Let's find out."

But as the men approached the wagon, Colton blocked the opening. "You ain't coming back in. My ma ain't no sideshow."

Luke called past him. "Ma'am, would you mind if my friend saw the young'un?"

"That would be fine."

Climbing in as quietly as they could, the two men looked at Faith. The baby was nestled to her mother's side, warm and content.

"Oh, she's a beaut." Roady sighed, a tone of admiration coming from his throat. His dark brown gaze had meandered from the baby to rest on the woman.

In the soft glow of the morning light, Luke was astounded, too. Without pain gripping at her, Faith looked different. Much younger. He'd been so caught up in the delivery he hadn't realized just how pretty she really was. The mountains in springtime paled in comparison. When her gaze was drawn to his, he felt an all-consuming jolt from his heart to his boots. She smiled up at him for the first time since they'd met, revealing straight white teeth and a dimple.

Both men whipped the hats from their heads. "This is Roady Guthrie," Luke said. "He works for us. This is Faith . . ."

"Brown."

"I'm pleased to make your acquaintance, Faith Brown," Roady said in a teasing voice. "And the young'un's, too. She's a sweet little thing."

Faith's cheeks turned a pretty shade of pink at his compliment, and Luke felt a jab of irritation. "Thank you, Mr. Guthrie."

Roady's smile widened.

The infant started whimpering and soon her face was ruby red. Her bottom lip trembled as she opened her mouth to suck in a mouthful of air. Turning, both men scrambled to get out of the wagon.

Luke followed Roady over to where his horse was tied. Roady opened his saddlebag and handed him a strip of beef jerky. They chewed in silence for a good two minutes.

"Well, Luke." Roady swallowed his mouthful. "Your brothers will be right pleased to learn we were all successful in rounding up strays last night." He playfully slapped Luke on the back. "But I have to admit. Yours are a darn sight prettier than ours."

Chapter Five

FAITH bathed her daughter with the warm water Mr. Mc-Cutcheon had so kindly provided. As she did, she listened to the low tones of the conversation from the campfire where the men were going about mixing up some biscuits and making coffee.

With trembling hands she gently rolled the baby from her back to her tummy and wiped a soft cloth across the child's bottom and down her pumping legs. She marveled at the perfect shape of each tiny toe, the wispy soft hair, the beautiful blue eyes. Wonder, warm and rich, spread through Faith, filling her with such happiness she could hardly repress her joy. How could something so perfect, so precious, so unbelievably wonderful come from the horror of her life with Samuel? It seemed impossible.

"They look like frog legs to me," Colton said from his perch on a box. He hadn't said one nice thing about his half sister since he'd come in to see her.

The baby let out a protesting wail as Faith pulled over her head the little sack she'd made out of soft yellow flannel. She maneuvered until the garment was on, then pulled the drawstring at the bottom. Picking up the baby, Faith held her to her shoulder. Reaching for the warm shirt Mr. McCutcheon had given her, she wrapped her daughter snugly and then worked the row of worn ivory buttons on the bodice of her dress, being careful not to expose herself to Colton. The baby stopped crying immediately, nestling close to nurse.

"Yours looked like frog legs, too. But, much bigger. You were so strong when you were born that your mama and me had to be careful not to let you kick us." She glanced at Colton to see if he'd caught her exaggeration. "I remember when Beatrice brought you over for the first time to my house to show you off. She was so proud of you."

Her stepson eyed her with a look of disbelief. Colton used to be so trusting and sweet-natured. Since his father had come back into his life he'd changed so much she sometimes couldn't believe he was the same little boy.

Blasted Samuel! He'd been so cruel and heavy-handed with him. Colton had transformed right before her eyes. Nothing she did or said seemed to make a difference.

Faith placed the now-sleeping baby in a small wooden box she'd fashioned into a tiny bed. She knew she needed to get up and take care of Colton, see that he was fed, but knowing and doing were two different things. Dredging up the energy seemed next to impossible. She'd cleaned up the best she could after the birth, but that still left much that needed doing.

"Come here, honey," she said.

Colton reluctantly climbed off the box, eyeing the infant distastefully, and came to her. She wrapped him in her arms and drew him to her chest. The dusty smell of little-boy hair tickled her nose.

"You're such a good son, Colton. I couldn't have made this trip without your help. I love you, you know."

"I ain't done much." His response was sullen, but he didn't move from her embrace. "Because of me, the horses are gone. I'm good for nothin'."

"That's not true. Don't you ever say that again. I'm the one to blame for that."

He shrugged his small shoulders.

"You always help me cook and even lend a hand with the cleanup when we're done." She rubbed his back. "That's more than most grown men know how to do, willing or not."

Vivid memories of Samuel pawing her made Faith shiver. She'd had her fill of such horrors. The only things men were good for were drinking, sleeping, and turning a woman's life to pure misery. She chastised herself again for blindly falling for the man's charms after Bea's death. Lies and deception was all he knew. She should have looked after Colton, as she'd promised her friend she would do, without marrying his father. But, sadly enough, there was no changing the past.

Now that her daughter was born, resting would be a welcome luxury—but one she couldn't afford just yet. Samuel was dead but Ward wasn't. He was pure meanness and made Samuel look like a saint. Shuddering, she remembered the night he'd been visiting and beat his dog to death with a shovel. Drunk and laughing he'd said he'd stopped the bitch's barking for good. It was awful. When she realized what was happening she'd tried to protect Colton, and covered his ears as they hid in his bedroom.

She hugged Colton tightly, eliciting a small cry of protest from him. Loosening her hold, she gazed at her sleeping babe. She was done being scared. Done trying to keep the peace. Done taking orders, and doing things she hated. Done, done, done!

"Ma, I'm hungry."

"You must be," she replied. "There was no supper last night with the birthing and all. The men probably have the biscuits almost done." She kissed the top of his head. "Let's go see."

Summoning strength from within, she headed for the back of the wagon. She held the wagon ribs for support as she started to climb out. Halfway down, a buzzing swirled in her head and the landscape wavered before her eyes. Panicked voices called her name. Everything went black.

A few moments later, Faith opened her eyes. She was lying on the ground. Three faces stared worriedly into hers. Pain radiated everywhere in her body, and a small moan escaped her.

"Ma'am, are you all right?"

"Of course she's not all right, Roady. She just fell from a wagon after having a baby. What kind of a fool question is that? I'm putting you back to bed." For all his gruffness, Luke McCutcheon handled her as if she were made of spun glass. He gathered her in his arms and stood. "What were you thinking, woman, trying to get up so soon?"

She bristled at his scolding. "Put me down so I can help Colton. He's hungry."

"Not on your life. You're going back to bed and staying there. I'll see to it that the boy gets something to eat. And you, too. I was just about to bring you a plate."

He climbed easily into the wagon with her in his arms. She felt no bigger than a mite as he carried her in his embrace. A niggle of fear slipped down her spine at the close contact. She pushed at his chest with the palm of her hand, testing her boundaries. He looked down questioningly.

"Please." She avoided his gaze. "Put me down."

The baby started to cry no sooner than he laid Faith on her mat, so she picked the child up. "Mr. McCutcheon, I'm much obliged for your kindness. Truly, I am. But I'm well aware that you must be a busy man with important things to do. I'm sure here with us is not where you need to be."

His large frame shrank the already small interior of the wagon, cramping its occupants unmercifully together. He took off his hat and held it in his hands. "And just what am I supposed to do with you?" Aggravation laced his words as he stared at the canvas overhead. "Leave you out here with no way to make it to the next town? Do you even know how far that is? Or its name?"

She had no response.

His brows tented over his eyes as his expression softened. "Pine Grove, Montana," he said flatly. "From there, if you go due west a day and a half you'll come to Y Knot, Montana, where the McCutcheon ranch is located. Due north a week from Pine Grove is Priest's Crossing. You have a team of horses somewhere?"

She didn't want to answer, he sounded so accusing. But the same common sense that had kept her alive this long whispered she couldn't make it alone. "When my labor progressed to the point where I couldn't go on, we stopped to make camp. I guess I should have known better than to try to stake them out on such a night because the thunder spooked them and they ran off."

"Your husband?"

This was the question she'd been waiting for. And dreading. "He . . ." Her voice cracked and the baby started. "Shhh." She kissed her daughter's temple. "He's dead."

Chapter Six

DEAD?" His serious expression held hers. "How long?"

"Three months tomorrow." Not long enough to suit her, to be honest.

"And where are you headed?"

"I've"—she paused for a moment—"secured employment in Priest's Crossing. We're on our way there." When had lying become so easy? "My aunt is quite wealthy and has a big house. My mother's sister."

He looked extremely skeptical. "Alone? Frankly, I'm amazed. In your condition it was a dangerous and somewhat stupid idea."

Faith patted her daughter's back, reining in her temper. Did he know anything about her? Who she was and the life she'd left behind? No! "I understand why you'd think that," she said, steadying her voice. "But I hired someone to come along and help with the horses and driving, all the heavy things I couldn't do. Unfortunately, he canceled at the last minute." One more tiny lie. How much could it hurt? "I had to try. Once the baby came, traveling would be much more difficult. My only chance was to leave on schedule and make good time. If it weren't for the storm—and my daughter coming early—we would have made it."

Luke cleared his throat. "If you say so." There it was again. That tone. She watched as he made his way to the back of the wagon. "I'll send some men back with horses. They'll hitch up and dig you out of the mud. Pine Grove's the next town on your route to Priest's Crossing. We're going there now. If you want, you can join our drive and travel with us."

She'd had a year of practice appeasing Samuel, and Faith knew when not to look a gift horse in the mouth. "Thank you. That's very kind of you." She smiled, hoping to soften Luke up a little. "How long will it take us to reach Pine Grove?"

"With the size of our herd, about a week. That is"—he settled his hat back on his head and turned to leave—"if the men don't get jelly-brained over silly distractions. Colton!" he shouted. "Bring your ma a plate of food." Then he climbed out of the wagon without giving her a chance to respond.

Silly distractions? Was he referring to her? His attitude hurt. She picked up her daughter, who'd begun to cry, and patted her back. She wouldn't distract his men, not on her life. She planned to stay as far away from them as possible.

Faith lay back and closed her eyes. A week following Mr.

McCutcheon's herd would be dirty and slow, but maybe this was just the miracle she'd been praying for. It would be impossible for Ward to track them in a cattle drive.

For the first time in weeks, Faith felt just maybe she could relax a little. The likelihood of actual escape from this nightmare was becoming a possibility. The chance of starting fresh, just her and the children. She'd yet find a place to settle and put down roots.

The sun had moved from one side of the wagon to the other as morning passed into late afternoon. The baby still slept, so Faith quietly scooted away from her upon awakening, cautious not to wake her.

She climbed out the back of the wagon, being careful this time to hang on tight. Colton sat around a small fire with two strangers, his small arms moving as he recounted a story.

Both men stood as she approached, and one offered his seat on the log. He was a big man with dusty clothes. His face was kind and thoughtful. "Sit here, ma'am." He gestured toward the log. When she was seated he continued. "My name's Jonathan Burg. Luke sent Smokey and me to hitch you up and bring you over to our campsite. How soon can you be ready to go?"

Faith hesitated. Was she supposed to just ride off with them without a by-your-leave? It went against everything she knew.

As if he sensed her reluctance, the cowboy fetched his horse over to where she sat. "See here, that's the McCutcheon brand." He pointed to the horse's muscular hip where a mark, a mountain enclosed within a heart, was easily identifiable. "You won't find finer horseflesh in the country. The McCutcheons are good, honorable men, ma'am. Well respected. No one here is going to hurt you or the children."

It was just what she wanted. But was it true?

* * *

The herd was enormous when they joined it. In every direction it stretched as far as the eye could see, a rippling brown-and-white wave of dusty, bawling cattle. From her bed in the wagon, Faith watched Colton up front, next to the wrangler named Smokey. The boy's small hands gripped the seat tightly to keep from being tossed off, for the wagon bounced over rough, damp ground. The cowboy named John rode alongside.

It was wonderful to see Colton so happy. The corners of Faith's mouth curled up as she listened to his high-pitched voice. The conversation kept the two men chuckling.

"How many are there?" Colton asked in excitement.

"Better side of two thousand, I reckon."

Colton pinched his nose. "Whew. They sure smell awful."

Smokey grinned. He untied the bright red bandanna around his neck and handed it over. "Put this 'round your nose."

Faith closed her eyes and held the baby close. The men's deep voices reminded her of Luke, and his image came unbidden into her thoughts. When she'd first seen him, half hidden in the darkness, she'd been petrified with fear. She'd expected cruelty akin to Samuel's or Ward's. But he'd been nothing like them, nothing of what she knew men to be. Snuggling deeper into her blanket she relished the warmth. She could almost feel his thumb softly caressing her hand.

"Look!" Colton shouted. "A bull! He's fatter than a ton a lard inna molasses can."

Faith opened her eyes in time to see Smokey send a long string of tobacco juice streaking from his mouth. He wiped his face with the back of his hand, removing a few stray drops that clung to his whiskers. It was all Faith could do not to gag.

Colton, however, declared with boyish admiration, "I'd like to learn to spit like that. Will ya teach me? I never seen anyone who could spit so far!"

In the late afternoon Luke gave direction to make camp and settle the cattle even though Faith's wagon still hadn't joined the drive. The warm temperatures, mixed with moisture from the storm the day before, made it muggy and hot. Now, an hour later, Luke watched the approach of Faith's rickety wagon from the middle of the herd. He was looking for a heifer the men had reported had an infection, probably conjunctivitis. So far, all he'd found were unruly cattle, flies and cow pies.

His oldest brother, Matt, whistled sharply, a signal they'd used since childhood, and pointed to the wagon. Luke waved back. Both Matt and Mark mounted up and rode over.

"Here she comes," Mark, the second oldest McCutcheon brother, drawled. "Can't wait to see her. From Roady's description, she's a real beaut."

Luke sighed, resigned to the fact that he'd never hear the end of this. His brothers were champion teasers from way back. They wouldn't forget this episode for years to come, him having delivered the baby of a woman on the road, all alone, and in a storm. It was the kind of fodder they lived for. "She's comely. But I wouldn't go so far to call her beautiful." Not so, his conscience whispered.

Matt winked at Mark. "We'll be the judge of that."

"That's enough," Luke stressed a little too harshly. "She's just lost her husband, and I don't want you two embarrassing her." Luke eyed them seriously, feeling the strain of his responsibilities, and walking a fine line. He was in charge of the family's yearly cattle drive for the first time, and his brothers were respectful of that fact. But he had to be careful not to step on too many toes.

"Damn it, Luke," Mark snapped back. "Quit being so cross. The past two months have been long and dirty. Anything to take our minds off those surly bovines."

"Anything? I wonder if your wife would feel the same."

Instantly Luke was sorry. Mark's face went dark. He spun his horse around and galloped off.

"That was uncalled for." Matt shook his head. "What's gotten into you, anyway? You're touchier than a cornered rattler."

Luke inhaled deeply, ignoring the comment. He *was* testy, and he knew it. Gazing at the nearing wagon wasn't helping.

What a difference a day made. How, exactly—and why—was this chance encounter with Faith and the birth of the baby girl occupying his every thought? Where the devil was the Luke McCutcheon of yesterday, the man focused only on getting this herd to its destination, the son proving to his father that he was up to the job? The half-breed proving to himself that his blood was the same as the other McCutcheon brothers. Maybe not exactly, but pretty damn close. As hard as he tried to convince himself something extraordinary hadn't happened, his heart kept telling him different.

"We're nine days overdue as it is. Now, after this storm . . . I just don't want to lose any more time over this woman."

It was horse manure, and Matt's expression said he knew that, but the lines around Luke's older brother's eyes and mouth softened. He leaned close, eyes beseeching. "We've all got ghosts, Luke. But don't go thinking you're so different from the rest of us that you can walk around with a chip on your shoulder just begging for someone to knock it off." He was using the brother-to-brother voice that Luke was intimately familiar with. Matt was the peacekeeper in the family, whereas Luke, or so everyone believed, looked for confrontation. "Frankly," Matt continued, "we're all gettin' pretty damn sick of it."

Faith's wagon had stopped, and men crowded anxiously around. Mark was already there, sitting his horse next to Roady.

Luke snorted, feeling a sharp pang of jealousy, though he didn't approve of the feeling. "Let's get over there before they smother her with their curiosity. You'd think she was the only woman in the world to have a baby." He rode toward the wagon.

Pushing his way through the cluster, Luke could hear

Colton's high-pitched exclamations: the little scrapper wasn't afraid of anything. Then, a soft sigh of appreciation rippled through the men, and it grew so quiet you could have heard an ant sneeze. The boy's mother had appeared.

Chapter Seven

ℋOLDING her baby close, Faith stepped slowly from behind the canvas and carefully settled herself on the wagon seat. The men's conversations hushed until all was completely quiet.

Luke rode up alongside and pulled off his hat. All the other hands reached to do the same.

"Mrs. Brown," he said.

"Mr. McCutcheon." She nodded politely to him.

A moment of uncomfortable silence passed until Matt rode up next to Luke and smiled at her, forcing Luke's hand. Luke said, "This is my oldest brother, Matthew McCutcheon."

"I'm very pleased to make your acquaintance," she offered.

Matt's smile grew broader as she looked his way. "The pleasure is all ours, Mrs. Brown."

Luke pointed to the right and then rested his palms on his saddle horn. "Mark, my second oldest brother, is over there next to Roady, who you've already met."

"Ma'am," both men said in unison.

In the soft evening light, Luke couldn't help but notice both his brothers' damp, hat-creased chestnut brown hair. Mindful that his own was raven black, he ran his fingers through it, then put his hat back on. "You've met John and Smokey. This is Chance, Bob, Uncle Pete, Earl and Ike. The old goat in back is Lucky, our cook." Laughter trickled through the men. "Six more are out riding watch."

Faith's eyes grew wider and her free hand came up to touch her child. She seemed a bit bewildered, but she nonetheless gifted them all with a beautiful smile.

"Ma, did you see how many cattle they have?" Colton spoke up, breaking the awkward moment. He waved in the direction of the herd. "More than the stars in the sky!" The men chuckled good-heartedly again, clearly enjoying him.

"I did," she replied.

Faith's cheeks were now the color of their mother's summer roses that would be in full bloom when they reached the ranch. Luke shifted his weight in his saddle, agitated more than he wanted to be by the men's obvious approval. "All right, back to work!" he called. "John, take the wagon and settle it under those pine trees. Whatever Mrs. Brown needs, take care of it."

"Sure thing, boss." The wrangler stepped forward and took the horses. "Hang on up there."

Faith bent over her sleeping infant, pretending to check her. Twelve men? And six more out with the herd. The thought was unsettling, to say the least.

Daring a glance from the corner of her eye, she watched the men milling around, talking and laughing, apparently glad she and the children would be joining them for a short while. One man she hadn't noticed before stood apart from the rest. Why hadn't Luke introduced him? His pants were tucked into tall black boots, and his red vest hugged his upper body snugly. Long hair, unfettered by a hat, moved slightly with the breeze. He must have suffered some sort of horrible accident, because his left cheek was disfigured by a nasty scar. His expression frightened her, too. Their gazes locked, and he grinned in a nasty way.

When the wagon was settled, Faith waited for an opportunity to talk with John, a man who looked to be her father's age if he'd still been alive. "Mr. Burg," she began, until she saw his beseeching expression. "*John*," she corrected, "who was the gentleman over there? The one with the red vest?"

"Red vest? I don't recall seeing anyone wearing red, Mrs. Brown." The cowboy securely locked the wagon's hand brake and then carefully lifted her down.

"You didn't see him? Mr. McCutcheon failed to introduce him with the rest of the men." She didn't want to seem indelicate, but she needed to know whom she was up against if that vile look had been in fact directed at her. "An awful scar marred his left cheek."

John turned abruptly from unhitching the horses. "He ain't no gentleman. You best stay clear of him." His tone was upsetting.

"Why? Who is he?"

John draped a blanket over Faith's shoulders. "His name's Will Dickson. He works for the Broken T, another outfit a hundred miles southeast or so. He's a bad hombre. Delivered a bull the McCutcheons are buying from his ranch and has been hanging around."

Faith scanned the campsite, finding Colton still busy in the wagon.

"But don't worry none," John continued in a fatherly way. "Just you stay away from him, and with all of us here watching over you, he's 'bout as dangerous as a bee in butter."

She ran her hands down the fabric of her old blue dress, thin from continual use, and hoped that were true.

Chapter Eight

CHIRPING crickets, hushed voices and the crackle of burning wood drifted over to Faith's haven, where she was nestled beneath a grouping of ponderosa pines. A light breeze lifted her hem gently and rustled the leaves. Barely audible were the strains of a harmonica. The song being played suggested the musician was missing a sweetheart.

Pulling her shawl tighter around her shoulders, Faith sat gingerly on a blanket laid out on the grass, enjoying a moment of solitude. Colton was over with the men in camp and the baby dozed. The peace was heavenly.

John completed all her camp chores with a minimum of effort and a smile on his face. He unhitched the horses and took them off somewhere to be with the others, she'd presumed. Whistling cheerfully, he'd gathered armfuls of wood needed for a fire, then worked diligently until he had a nice blaze burning. He even brought her a bucket of water from the chuck wagon.

"Grub will be ready soon," he'd told her before leaving. "Just listen for the bell."

She might hear the bell, but she had no intention of eating with all those men, regardless of their politeness. No, she'd fix something for herself here at her own wagon. There was flour for biscuits and a little apple cake left. She'd make do.

The aroma of meat and something else—possibly gravy—drifted over on the breeze. Her mouth watered and her stomach rumbled loudly. She was starving. She'd never experienced anything like it before in her life. The baby was nursing now almost every hour on the hour. Thankfully, regardless of their scant rations of late, she seemed to have plenty of sustenance to satisfy her. For the time being.

A bell clanged hollowly in camp, the racket going on for a full minute. Men materialized out of nowhere, ambling toward the chuck wagon. Clearly still curious, one by one they glanced in her direction.

Faith set about gathering her cooking supplies, her stomach grumbling in protest all the while. Colton could eat with the men if he wanted, but she'd eat here. That was that. She'd be fine. It was for the best.

After measuring a cup of flour into her bowl, she carefully poured some water into a small well she'd formed in the center.

"Aren't ya comin' to dinner, ma'am?"

Faith's hands jerked, spilling water onto her skirt.

"Sorry." Smokey blushed sheepishly as she brushed the water off as best she could.

"No harm done." Faith forced a smile. "I'm just fixing some supper for myself. You go on back and eat before it's all gone."

His look was one of sheer disbelief. "But Lucky will be awful disappointed if you don't come and eat. He's rustled up a fine supper with all the fixin's just for you."

She glanced over at the chuck wagon. All the men stared in her direction. No one was eating.

"They aren't waiting for me, are they?" she asked in alarm. Puffs of flour landed here and there as she mixed the batter vigorously, her gaze riveted on the other camp.

"Of course they're waiting."

She stopped mixing and looked up into Smokey's face. "Tell them to start."

"Lucky won't let 'em, ma'am."

Like it or not, she'd have to take supper with the cowboys. And, she'd best hurry. A passel of hungry, disgruntled men wasn't her cup of tea.

Luke sat apart from the rest of the men as the object of his frustration slowly made her way into camp. A braid as thick as his wrist hung down her back, swinging from side to side as she walked. A few maverick wisps of hair had pulled free from their bonds and danced freely in the breeze, caressing her pretty face. In her arms, nestled protectively against her chest, was the baby. Quiet. Sleeping. Wrapped snuggly in his shirt.

He was about to get up when Matthew went forward and met Faith and Smokey. Luke's brother usurped Smokey's position and escorted the woman over to the chuck wagon, where Lucky was happy to take charge.

The cook forked a thick slab of roast beef onto an enormous plate and ladled on a spoonful of potatoes. He smothered everything with thick brown gravy then added a cob of yellow corn and wedge of red cabbage. Finally, with practiced skill Luke recognized from years of friendship, Lucky squeezed two sourdough biscuits onto the rim of her plate and a heaping dollop of freshly churned butter.

The men all waited patiently as she took the seat that was offered her.

"I'll take the baby, missy." Lucky handed Faith's dinner to John and reached for the baby. "I've had lots of experience tendin' to young'uns. Don't you be worryin' none."

Faith looked uncertain.

"Ya can't eat and hold her at the same time. I'll jist sit right here till you're done." The cook took the infant from Faith's arms and nodded. "And don't stop till ya cleaned your plate. A few extra pounds will do ya good."

When Faith picked up her fork, a deafening clamor ensued. Quiet until now, the men scooped and swallowed as if in a race and cleanup duty would fall to the loser.

"Ain't it good, Ma?" Colton called from across the campfire. "Best I ever ate." Without seeming to breathe, he shoveled in another enormous mouthful, confirming Luke's suspicion it had been some time since they'd eaten anything substantial.

As the eating commenced, so did the conversation, with laughing and joking between bites. Every once in awhile, someone would glance in Faith's direction. Luke sat off to the side. He didn't feel much like talking, and his appetite wasn't what it usually was.

He sipped his strong black coffee. Faith was struggling to eat slowly, but she looked like she wanted to dive headfirst into her plate. She paused, taking her gaze off her food long enough to check Lucky and the infant. She scanned the area, eyeing each and every man. When she reached Luke, their gazes locked. Her cheeks turned a deep rosy hue obvious enough to cause Matt to seek out what had caught her attention.

"Looky here," Lucky said, standing and making his way around, showing the baby to each man. "She ain't no bigger than my hand. Ain't she about the tiniest little thin' you ever seen?"

"She sure 'nuf is," Ike agreed over a mouthful of potatoes.

"Bring her over this way, Lucky," Chance called from the other side of the fire.

"What's her name?" someone else asked.

Faith glanced up as everyone grew quiet. They were all looking at her. What had they just asked? She'd been concentrating on the butter melting down onto her meat and hadn't heard.

"What's the little one's name, ma'am?" the one named Uncle Pete said from his spot on the camp bench.

"I haven't decided."

"I've always been partial to Rose," offered Jeb, a newcomer who'd just gotten back from riding patrol. "What do you think of that?"

Faith swallowed a bite of potatoes and gravy. "I think that's a very pretty name, actually."

Roady winked at Chance. "What about Francis?"

A whoop of laughter rocked the camp that instantly had the baby crying. Lucky danced around with her in his arms, trying to comfort her.

Faith didn't get the joke. She looked from face to face until Roady got her attention. He said, "That, over there, is the youngest cowhand in our outfit. Francis, stand up and take a bow!" A boy of about fourteen shyly ducked his head and kicked the dirt.

Someone threw out, "Jane's pretty. She looks like a Jane to me."

Bob scoffed. "She ain't no Jane. She has light hair, like sunshine. A Jane has to have black hair. I know, because I used to be sweet on one."

Smokey shook his head. "I wouldn't trust him if I were you. That's the most I've heard him say in two months."

The men all laughed again, and Faith felt a gentle sweetness warming her heart. It was impossible not to like this group, and surprisingly she found herself laughing, too—a much easier feat now that her tummy was full.

She watched as Luke stood and took his cup over to the wagon, put it in the wash kettle. Ambling over to where Lucky held the now-quiet newborn, he pushed close. With his finger he gently moved his shirt aside and softly stroked the child's cheek.

"She fought her way into this world at dawn," he said so softly that everyone quieted. Faith was instantly reminded of the special experience they'd so recently shared. "And, she's pink and golden like the Rockies before sunup. Dawn."

Faith held her breath. Luke was devastatingly handsome as he looked down at her daughter. There was wildness in him that didn't apply to his brothers. Her heart fluttered in her breast as if it had wings, and when he glanced her way, his gaze went straight to her soul.

"Dawn." She tested the name on her lips. "That's beautiful."

For the first time since she'd arrived in camp, Luke looked pleased.

"Yes, I like it," she said softly. "Dawn, it is."

The men let out a resounding cheer that sent the sleeping child into a third fit of crying. Faith stood and anxiously reached for her daughter. The baby's eyes were large and glittered brightly with unshed tears. The lump in Faith's throat made it difficult to speak.

She looked to Lucky to break her runaway emotions. "Can I help you clean up?" she asked as most of the cowhands dispersed to their bedrolls. It was then that Will and Earl came into camp.

"Oh, no," the cook said. "I have help. The McCutcheon boys always make sure of it. You jist get on back to yer wagon and git some rest. You're plum wore out."

She was. And sore. What she wouldn't give for a hot bath.

"Go on now." He gave her a little nudge. "Rest up. Tomorrow comes early on the trail."

"Ain't no woman I know can get her lazy backside up afore noon," Earl said, and nudged Will. He was tall and skinny and his laughter set Faith's nerves on edge. He and Will, whose scar was vivid in the bright light from the lantern, were looking at her, trying to catch her eye.

"Hush your mouth, Earl!" Lucky ordered. "It's a good thing Luke or another of the McCutcheons, or anyone, ain't around to here you talk like that in Mrs. Brown's presence." The cook's admonishment only made the two laugh harder.

Chapter Nine

LUKE waited at the edge of the main campfire to walk Faith back to her wagon.

She approached leisurely, holding her baby as she gazed at the stars. A hot, unsettling feeling sank lower into the pit of his stomach with each step she took. When she reached his side, her unassuming smile hit him like a double-barrel blast from a shotgun.

"Mr. McCutcheon," she said in hushed tones.

"Don't you think you could call me Luke?" He looked over her head to see who might be watching them. "We've another week at least together. It just seems like the logical thing to do."

"All right then, Luke." As she said his name, those long lashes encasing her coffee-colored eyes lowered shyly.

"I'll walk you to your wagon, bank your fire," he offered.

"You don't need to bother yourself . . . Luke. I wouldn't want to be *a distraction*."

Concentrating completely on the husky way she said his name, it took a moment for her meaning to sink in. He fought embarrassment. "You're not a distraction to *me*. It's my men I'm worried about."

Side by side, they fell into stride. At the wagon he went about the things he'd said he'd do, checked inside it to make her feel safe, looked underneath and all around on the ground for snakes. When he finished he hunkered down in front of the fire and looked into the flames.

"If you'd like, Lucky could heat you some water for a bath," Luke said over his shoulder as he put another log on the fire. He stirred the coals with a stick and sparks danced into the sky. "That is, if you don't mind using the tub Lucky has in the chuck wagon. Rest assured, it doesn't get much use."

"A bath." The word came out as a caress. Faith's eyes closed as if in ecstasy, and a little smile tipped the corners of her mouth. "Yes, that would be more than wonderful. I'd like it very much." She smiled again, and Luke had to drag his gaze away. "Thank you."

With her newly named daughter fed and tucked away in her makeshift cradle, Faith relaxed in the hot, steamy water. She was tender, but after the first excruciating seconds the soak eased away the hurt and pain caused by childbirth. Dawn was a beautiful name, so fitting for her perfect little girl. Even more so since it was Luke who'd thought of it. And now the bath, too. Such luxury! Samuel used to get so angry when she spent more than a little time soaking. He'd scream and get worked up and . . .

Faith slammed her eyes closed, blocking out the memories. What on earth drove a man to such heartlessness?

Scuffling footsteps brought her out of her thoughts. "Ma, I'm back."

"Shh, don't wake Dawn," she called to Colton from behind a tarp and two blankets she and Luke had set up using one side of the wagon and a tree. She wasn't ready to leave this blissful warmth just yet.

"What're ya doin' back there?" Colton's tone was tinged with apprehension.

"I'm soaking in a nice, hot bath. Would you like to be next?"

His reply was instantaneous. "No, ma'am!"

"Why aren't I surprised?" Faith brought her hand out of the balmy water to swat at a mosquito that was buzzing around her face.

"Where'd the *tub* come from?" He said the word as if it were something dirty.

"Luke had it sent over. Wasn't that kind of him?" Faith took the clump of soap and lathered it up. Enjoying every second, she slowly worked her way up her arm and around her neck.

"Real neighborly," Colton returned.

"And just what is that tone supposed to mean?" She repeated the washing process with her other arm then sank into the water up to her chin.

"Just that he ain't needin' to be so nosy about you and the baby. Every time I look at him, he's staring at you like he ain't never seen a girl before."

"Is that so?" Luke was staring at her? Butterflies fluttered around in her tummy as she thought of him. Disconcerted, she reminded herself promptly that she'd sworn off men. Luke was just another of the same. One moment they could be kind and caring, like he indeed seemed to be, but that didn't mean he wouldn't change. Samuel's death had been a gift and she would not forget that. Life wasn't long enough for a repeat of her last mistake.

"You wash up and get into bed. I'll be in shortly."

Colton's reply surprised her. "I was hoping I could sleep over at the main campfire. You know, with Smokey and the other men."

"You won't be scared?"

"Ma! Of course I won't be scared. I'm not a kid no more." He was growing up. He was almost nine.

"*Any. Anymore,*" she corrected.

"That's what I said. Well, can I?"

Another lump formed in her throat. He'd been depending on her for the past three years, ever since Bea's death. He'd been five and had clung to her through thick and thin. Now it seemed he was spreading his wings.

Gratitude to the men for befriending Colton threatened to overwhelm her already raw emotions. It brought another round of maternal sentiment to her heart, making her eyes sting. This was a happy group, a good group—which seemed to be just the medicine her stepson needed. It was only Luke who brought out the worst in him. But that was natural. Luke was an authority figure, like Samuel had been.

"Well?"

"I suppose it's all right. Be polite and don't get in anyone's way."

"I will. I mean, I won't," he called excitedly.

"Colton?"

"Yes, Ma?"

"Please don't yell. It'll wake your sister."

* * *

Around sunrise Luke ambled in from his watch, hungry, tired and testy, two days' worth of beard black on his face. He took a blue-speckled cup, wrapped a towel around the coffeepot handle and poured himself some brew. The men who'd had the watch just before his were still in their bedrolls; the rest were heading out to be with the cattle. Lucky was up, the fresh coffee attested to that, but for now the cook was off doing something else.

With a sigh, Luke lowered his tired body onto the camp bench and stretched out his legs. Damn! This would prove to be a long day. Before his watch last night he'd lain in his bedroll, sleep completely eluding him. No matter how he circled it, Faith's story didn't add up. It sounded like a lie—or at least like she was covering up for something. Her being that far from civilization, all alone, just didn't feel right. And her agitated reaction to his questions was surprising, being what they'd just gone through together. He couldn't put his finger on it, but there was definitely something that gave him pause. Before he'd known it, Jeb was shaking his shoulder, rousing him to take watch.

Luke gulped a swallow of hot coffee and glanced around camp. Colton was there, his bedroll squished between Francis and Pedro, his scruffy hair the only thing showing.

"You look 'bout as sociable as a festering back tooth," Lucky rasped, carrying a long side of bacon around the back of the wagon. "What's eatin' ya?" The cook had smashed his foot as a young man and because of it walked with a limp. He'd been preparing food for the wranglers ever since. Luke had been a boy no older than Colton at the time.

"Just tired. Didn't get much sleep."

"Hmm." Lucky went about stoking the fire. Laying the bacon in it first, he placed a large cast-iron griddle atop the heat.

"Mornin'," Roady called, making a beeline to the coffeepot.

"Goin' somewhere?" Luke asked. His friend was shaved and shined like he were off to a Sunday church meeting.

"No. Why?"

Luke took another swallow and shook his head. "Just wondered. You look mighty gussied up."

"Can't a man shave without being set upon?"

Roady's stance was defensive, so Luke knew to back off. But this was exactly what he'd worried about: the men couldn't help but be attracted to Faith. It was natural. It wouldn't be long before they were fighting over her. Moving cattle was a dangerous business. A wandering mind could get a man killed.

Quiet conversation sounded. Chance and Bob strode by purposefully, hair slicked back and clean-shaven for the first time this month. Luke snorted.

"Look at you boys," Lucky guffawed as he eyed them. "I ain't never seen such a pretty-faced lot. You look about as soft as the butt of that baby sleeping over yonder." He took a long whiff. "Good-smelling, too."

The men ignored the cook and went about filling their plates with slices of ham and spoonfuls of potatoes mixed with onions. They forked plentiful flapjacks from a big white plate. When they tried for the bacon that wasn't quite done, Lucky swiped at their hands with a spatula. Safety in numbers, Luke thought.

Colton, now up, filled his plate with gusto. He struggled to find room between his potatoes, ham and flapjacks for a handful of biscuits left over from supper. Before Faith knew it, the kid would be grown and gone with the next cattle drive. Wanderlust was bright in his eyes.

"What're you staring at?" the boy said as he passed Luke. The wranglers' conversations quieted, and all eating stopped.

"You," Luke said.

The boy's impudence was incredible. "Well, knock it off. I don't like you drilling me with them black eyes."

Chapter Ten

$\mathcal{A}$ strained quiet hovered around the camp. Lucky, who'd been scraping some leftover potatoes into bacon grease, gaped. "Boy, that ain't no way to be talking to the head man. I'd walk softly if I was you."

Luke knew the others were waiting to see how he would handle this smart-mouthed pup. From the edge of camp, his two brothers turned from cinching up their saddles, amused grins on their faces.

Two long strides took him to Colton's side. The boy cringed, eyes large with surprise and plate of food forgotten. Luke took a firm hold of his arm and led him through camp. Colton, kicking and fighting for all his worth, painfully connected with Luke's shin.

"Enough." Luke sidestepped, narrowly missing another attack. "Settle down."

Colton stopped his wild struggling. They were now well beyond the trees, all alone. The birds had quieted, and the stillness of the forest amplified the boy's heavy breathing. Luke could almost smell his fear.

"You surprise me, Colton," he said, still holding the boy. "I thought you had some sense."

Several seconds ticked by before Colton answered. "I do."

"Really? Well, why don't you act like it?"

Colton didn't answer. He stood firm. As still as a statue. He seemed to be waiting for something to happen.

Luke followed Colton's gaze and shamefully realized the boy was staring at the fist he had clenched by his side. Uncurling his fingers, he sighed. He'd seen Colton's reaction to him in camp, felt it hum like a tightly strung bow. This boy's pa must have been mighty heavy-handed with him. He didn't like the notion of someone treating a child that way—or a woman. He wondered about Faith.

Disciplining Colton was not high on his priority list for early morning activities, but if the boy needed some male influence, someone to straighten him out, he'd take the job. Faith surely didn't keep a tight enough rein on him.

"Colton," he said, getting the boy's attention. "Men don't treat other men disrespectfully. Even if they don't like them." He hunkered down so he could look Colton in the face. "I don't take back talk from the men who work for me, and I'm sure not going to take it from you. If you can't keep your sassy mouth quiet, you'll have to stay in your ma's wagon until we get to town. I'm warning you now. I won't be warning you again. Do you understand?"

The boy stood for several seconds without answering. "Yes, sir."

"Good." Luke let go and straightened up.

"That don't mean I have to like ya or your meddlin' ways."

"That's so," Luke agreed. "You can't help how you feel about someone—but you can help how you treat them."

Colton scuffed his boot toe through the dirt and looked around. "Can I go back to camp now before all the food is gone?"

Luke nodded. "You best hurry."

Faith lay in her blankets inside the wagon. She could hear the men now. They were eating and carrying on by the campfire.

She closed her eyes, enjoying the semiquiet. She hoped Colton had made it through the night without being frightened. She'd half expected to wake up and find him back in the wagon with her.

Dawn. She said the name again to herself, smiling and thinking about the man who'd named her daughter. She knew she was being silly, fostering these daydreams about Luke.

Against her better judgment she found herself yearning for him, waiting to hear his voice. It's natural to feel this, she told herself. He delivered Dawn. We're connected because of that.

As if such thoughts could wake her, the child stirred. She began rooting around in her cradle, and soon let out a cry that would curl toes.

"Oh my poor baby, you're soaking." Faith rose, picked Dawn up and laid her on her blanket. She was ill prepared for motherhood. She didn't have near enough swaddling blankets and only a handful of diapering cloths, the majority of which had been used last night. She'd have to wash first thing this morning or else run out.

"Shhh, sweet thing," she said as she changed the baby, then held her to her breast. She winced and breathed deeply as her daughter took hold. Oh, she was sore. Did all mothers experience this? After the first few painful seconds, feeding time turned pleasant. Until then, it was pure misery, like shards of glass slicing to and fro across her swollen nipple.

Pulling a corner of the canvas aside, Faith peeked out at the camp. All the cowboys were eating or saddling up. "My, my, they all look so nice," she noted to the suckling infant. Minutes ticked by and the tautness of her breast reduced, bringing relief. She switched the baby to her other breast and continued her perusal of the camp.

Colton came running in. He'd been somewhere outside the camp. Faith said, "There's your brother. He thinks he's all grown up now." She blew gently at the baby's silky soft hair, watching it shimmer.

Luke followed Colton. He looked tired and grumpy. Still, he stood out. Faith liked his fluid, catlike walk and his quiet assurance. It was hard for her to tear her gaze away.

Lucky said something to some of the men, and in unison they turned and looked in her direction. Quick as lightning Faith dropped the canvas and held her hand to her racing heart. They'd been talking about her. Had they seen her watching them?

She straightened. "Well, just let them." Dredging up her newfound courage, she pulled open the canvas. "I'm a widow now. Doesn't hurt to look. Or be looked at."

The words were meant to strengthen her, to bolster her flagging confidence, and actually it seemed like it might just be working. Regardless of if she still felt anxious as she had three months ago, she was going to hold her head high. She hoped if she talked big enough, maybe she could fool herself into belief.

After changing Dawn's bedding, she placed the sleepy infant back in her bed and covered her with a blanket. Fretting about the washing, Faith climbed out the back of the wagon.

The youth named Francis squatted by her cold campfire, building up the flame. He blushed when he saw her. "I was sent with food, ma'am," he said, pointing to a plate covered with a red-checkered cloth. He looked painfully shy, red splotches burning his cheeks.

"Thank you," she said, imagining what wonderful delicacies Lucky had sent over.

"I'm to hitch your wagon, too."

Panic filled her. "When will we be leaving?"

"Right soon, ma'am."

She had to wash. The baby couldn't go without wrappings, even in this warm August weather. Would they let her stay behind and then catch up? But, what about Ward? She didn't want to be left behind where her brother-in-law might find her.

Francis hitched the team and left. Faith put water on to boil and set upon her food like a tiger.

Oh, it was good! Huge, fluffy flapjacks smothered in fresh butter and maple syrup tickled her tongue. A mound of spicy potatoes nestled beside crisp, juicy bacon. And to top it off, coffee laced with sweet milk and sugar. Why, these men ate better than anyone she'd ever known. If she were a man, she'd take a job with this outfit just for the food.

Faith avoided taking her plate back to camp as long as possible, but the baby's things were now soaking in the bucket of water John had provided yesterday and she'd freshened herself up. There was no delaying any longer. Walking into camp, she tipped her chin up and plastered a smile on her face. She knew the men couldn't see her heart beating wild like a bird's.

"Mornin', missy," Lucky called as he watched her approach. "How was the flapjacks?"

"So delicious, Lucky, I ate every morsel. How soon will Mr. McCutcheon want to leave?" she asked.

"Almost anytime, I'd reckon. It's near six now. Most the men are gettin' ready ta pull out."

Faith sat gingerly on the bench to wait. She was deep in thought when Luke approached.

"Problem?"

Faith stood quickly, stars bursting before her eyes. She swayed.

"Easy now." He steadied her with his hand.

"I . . . um." She didn't want to ask for another favor. It seemed to her that was all she ever did. But she couldn't leave just yet. The baby had to have clean things.

Luke waited patiently. His face, strong with angles and rough from not shaving, looked down into her own. What would it feel like if she were bold enough to reach up and touch it? She tried with all her might to stop the smile she felt forming at the ridiculous thought.

His eyes, dark with question, took on a hint of softness. "Out with it."

"Well, uh, I need to do some wash. Almost everything of the baby's was soiled and if I don't do it this morning they won't be dry when I need them."

Luke turned. "Francis, you stay with Mrs. Brown's wagon. You, too, Lucky. When she's ready the two wagons can travel together and help her catch up." He looked back. "How long will you need?"

"Just an hour or two, I think. I'll hang the things in the wagon to dry as we go." She was relieved. He didn't seem angry at all.

Earl, close in proximity, grumbled into his cup. "I knew that woman would hold us up. Females are always whinin' about somethin'." He paused for a moment, then added slyly, "Did ya whip the boy good, boss?"

Luke's brows drew together in an angry frown. His jaw clenched several times before he looked at Faith. He said nothing.

"Whip him? *The boy?* What did he mean?" she asked, her tone rising two octaves. Anxiously she searched the camp. She felt her face heat from a mixture of hot anger and fear. "Where is Colton?"

"Get out on the trail," Luke commanded Earl, his voice low and dangerous. The man smirked, giving Faith one last look as he threw the remainder of his coffee into the fire, and stalked away.

She turned on Luke with the same ferocity she'd felt whenever Samuel was set upon, in his own words, teaching the boy a lesson.

"Easy now, Faith. Just settle down," Luke said, raising his hands, palms forward.

"Where is Colton?" she demanded. She looked around wildly. "Is he hurt?"

Luke stepped back, giving Faith some breathing space. He said her name calmly, trying to appeal to her senses. He didn't want to add to her hysteria, but dang, she was exasperating in an overprotective way.

"He was sassing me this morning. We had a little meeting—man to man. Someone's got to teach the boy some manners. You don't seem to want to do it."

Faith's flinching as if she'd been slapped was his first indication that he might have said too much. Over her head he saw Lucky's eyes go wide, and the cook retreated for cover.

"I promise, I didn't lay a finger on him," Luke added, trying to keep his voice level.

"Where is he, then?" She'd recovered from his accusation, and had come up fighting. She planted her hands on her hips and tried to face him eye to eye, despite the vast difference in their heights. Her eyes were challenging. Beautiful. He was tempted to pull her into his arms and kiss her and see just how mad she could *really* get.

"He's with Smokey," he replied coolly, trying to hide the smile brought by the image his mind was creating.

She stared at him in doubt, all the while tapping the toe of her boot. "I don't believe you."

"Smokey's taken a liking to Colton. Asked if he could ride behind him today. I said yes. Colton seemed only too happy to go."

"What?" she cried. "He's only a boy. Eight years old. He could get hurt. Or killed! I never imagined you could be so thick. What were you thinking?"

That stung. It was way too early in the morning to be called a name. "There's always a small possibility he could fall and get trampled by the cattle, but I don't think Smokey will let anything happen. He's a good hand." Luke knew mishaps like that rarely occurred, and Colton was almost as safe on the back of Smokey's horse as riding in the wagon, but he felt like teasing her a little for not trusting his judgment.

Faith's expression transformed from anger to something else. Her eyes clouded over, extinguishing that beautiful flashing light. They went cold. Dead. She looked beaten, and she turned so fast he didn't have a chance to catch her. In disbelief he watched her run all the way back to her wagon, dress flying. She showed a glimpse of her slender ankle, then disappeared inside.

Chapter Eleven

THE baby slept, blissfully unaware of the commotion around her. Francis had turned out to be a huge help, washing and rinsing the baby's clothing and blankets. He was especially good at wringing them near dry. Faith did all the diapers, knowing that chore would be just too much to ask of the youth.

"That's the last of it," she said, forcing her voice to sound happy. She'd been thinking about her encounter with Luke. She'd made a fool of herself. Called him a name. Acted like she didn't have the brains of a gnat. And after all he'd done for her and Colton. And Dawn. Especially Dawn.

While they'd worked, Francis had told her what had happened that morning at breakfast. She'd had to drag it out of him, but he finally admitted that Colton had acted disrespectfully. Luke had been forced to act or lose respect in front of his men. It sounded like he'd handled the matter with restraint . . . though she wasn't sure she liked what he said afterward.

"I'll dump the water," Francis said, tipping the bathtub she'd used last night, and spilling the water out to create a puddle. The scent of wet earth pervaded the air. "And if there's no more to do, I'll go check with Lucky. By now he'll be itchin' to pull out."

Faith stood slowly and wiped her brow with her apron. She stretched the sore muscles of her back and sighed. "Thank you for all your help, Francis."

"My pleasure, ma'am." He smiled that charmingly shy smile. "Now, why don't you just rest a while. I'll be back to drive your wagon to catch up with the herd."

She did as the young man suggested and collapsed onto her mat next to Dawn. It felt wonderful to close her eyes.

Sometime later a constant lowing passed through her fatigue, pulling her gently from her dreams. Faith rolled onto her other side, trying to block out the sound. A fly, buzzing around her head, annoyingly landed on her cheek for the fiftieth time. Refusing to open her eyes just yet, she reached up to brush it off. That's when she wondered why that animal was crying so much.

Halfheartedly she opened her eyes and blinked. Where was she? Then she heard it again. Not one cow lowing, but hundreds. And more! She remembered. And they weren't *cows*, she mentally corrected herself. Chance—a tall, rangy cowhand—had humbly enlightened her at dinner last night. "They're called steers and heifers, ma'am."

The gentle rocking of the wagon bed and the deep rumble of its steel-lined wheels told her that they were on their way. Faith pulled back the covering and carefully climbed out next to Francis on the wagon bench.

"Well, how do," he said when he saw her. "Ya feeling better?"

"Oh yes, much." Faith gasped. "Lands, we're right in the middle of all the cattle!" she said, looking around and grabbing hold of the side of her seat. She didn't want to fall into that throng of living cowhides and horns. "Are we supposed to be?"

Francis laughed. He was relaxing around her, and was a very nice companion to have. "For today it is." He pointed ahead some twenty feet at the chuck wagon in front. "We're following Lucky in the chuck wagon. He's going through the herd because the ground is too rocky along the side. He don't want to be fixing any axles today."

Turning his head, he spat a stream of tobacco juice alongside the wagon. It landed in a splat on the head of a steer. When the beast didn't do anything, Francis shrugged and smiled. "He don't mind." Faith hid her expression behind her hand, not wanting to offend. Her stomach lurched.

Flipping the long reins up, he slapped them down across the horses' backs, urging them on. "Now, normally," he continued, seeming to like having a captive audience now that they were better acquainted, "we'd pull out early, with the cattle, so we wouldn't have ta be eating all this." He gestured to the dust and dirt. "We'd be way up near the front, along one side. Sort of three-quarter front and following the trail boss."

"That's Luke?" Faith said.

"On this drive. But it could be any of the three oldest Mc-Cutcheon brothers. We never know till we start. It's the first time Luke's been running the show. That's why it was sort of amusing he showed up with you." Faith hadn't thought about how her presence might affect Luke. She'd been totally self-absorbed.

"Three *older?* There're more?"

"One more boy. Jonathan McCutcheon. But he's away at un-ee-versity, studyin' to be a doctor." Francis paused. "There's Charity, too. She's the baby, only fifteen." At the mention of her, the youth's face turned crimson.

"That's quite a family," Faith exclaimed.

"You're right about that. Mrs. Mac, that's what the ranch hands call Mrs. McCutcheon, runs it like the United States Calvary," he chuckled. "All business and boom, even though she don't come up to my shoulder. Flood—that's Mr. McCutcheon—thinks he's in charge, but everyone knows it's really his wife holding the reins." He eyed Faith nervously. "But don't say I said so."

"No, I won't."

The youth gave a sigh of relief.

"The father's name is Flood? Flood McCutcheon?" Faith asked, surprised. "That's an unusual name."

"Undoubtedly there's a story behind it, but I ain't know-ing it."

Three hours passed peacefully and Faith realized she was enjoying it very much. She felt safe, and cared for. She rejoiced at the thought of Ward losing their trail and giving up, frustrated. Two riders loped their horses from the side of the herd to the front as they began slowing the progress of the steers.

"It's nooning time," Francis remarked. "We'll just make a brief stop so the cattle won't feel rushed. Not good for the beef if the steers get nervous." He took off his hat and brushed sweat from his brow with his shirtsleeve. "Hungry?"

"Yes, I guess I am," Faith admitted. "It seems to be the only thing I am lately—hungry or sleepy."

"Understandable."

Faith shaded her eyes with her hand. Relief coursed through her. "Look, here comes Colton!"

Smokey jogged up on his horse and stopped next to the wagon. His cheek bulged with chew, and sweat trickled down the sides of his face. Colton sat directly behind his saddle, on the horse's sweaty back. Faith gasped when she saw him. Dirt, weeds and cow dung clung from every inch.

"Whooo-eee," Francis cried. "What happened to you?"

Colton beamed. "Had a small dilemma, that's all. Nothin' to get flop-eared about."

"Colton, come here. Let me have a look at you," Faith demanded.

"Ma, I'm fine," Colton said, masterfully dismissing her.

Smokey leaned his forearms onto his saddle horn and relaxed. Pulling a packet from his pocket, he stuck two fingers in and grabbed a big brown wad of tobacco. Sticking it between his lip and teeth, he added to the already existing clump.

"I'm real sorry, ma'am. We come upon a nest of rattlers and I had a heck of a time with my pony." He spit to the side and wiped his mouth with the back of his arm. "Colton here got pitched off."

Nest of rattlesnakes? Faith felt a little dizzy. "Are you sure he wasn't bitten?"

"Nah, he's jist bruised up a bit. He'll be right as rain tomorrow." Smokey shook his head and laughed. "Little bugger sure can run. Should have seen him churnin' up the dust."

Colton reached under his leg into the saddlebag and pulled out a headless rattlesnake. Blood, red as cherry juice, dripped down the four-foot-long corpse and onto the dusty ground, making little puffs of dust. Smokey's horse tossed his head and danced around anxiously. Faith couldn't say she felt much better.

"Look, Ma," Colton said excitedly, shaking the rattler's beaded brown tail, making the horse snort and paw the ground. "Smokey said I could eat it for supper!"

Chapter Twelve

RIDING toward Faith's wagon at a lope, Luke saw the growing commotion. He plunged into the herd, shouting at the cattle, trying to get through.

Faith had taken one look at the snake Colton was swinging around and collapsed onto Francis, draped across his lap like a worn rag doll. Startled, the youth fumbled to remove her, not knowing where he should or shouldn't put his hands. She moaned. As she rolled facedown into the youth's lap, he wriggled from under her like a scalded cat.

Trying to sit up, she brushed the hair from her face and looked around groggily. "What ha . . . ?" Her gaze found the snake Colton still held high in the air, and she promptly crumpled back to the seat.

"Put that thing away!" Luke shouted as he arrived. He climbed straight from Chiquita onto the wagon seat. Scooping Faith into his arms, he carried her into the back of the conveyance and laid her down.

Dawn began to cry. Faith struggled to get up, to go to her, but Luke gently pushed her back. "I'll get her," he said. "Lie here for a minute or two until your color comes back. I'll take care of her." Luke couldn't miss the I-told-you-so expression as she gazed back at him. Regardless, he was thankful the boy hadn't been hurt worse.

He looked over at the crying baby, red-faced and arms waving. Something warm snaked through him, something soft and tender. He couldn't hold back a smile. "Don't cry, little girl," he crooned. Bundling the infant in his arms, he climbed toward the front and stepped out onto the seat. The look on the cowhands' faces bespoke their grave concern.

"She gonna be all right?" Smokey asked, obviously contrite. He'd taken the snake from Colton and put it back into his saddlebag.

Luke bounced and jiggled the tiny infant in his arms, trying to get her to stop crying. Dawn just cried all the harder.

"Think so," he said over the infant's screams. "What am I supposed to do with her?"

Everyone else's eyebrows shot up in question. Smokey and Francis looked quizzically at each other. Luke realized he'd get no help from them.

"How about you, Colton? Got any suggestions?" Up until now the boy had sat quietly on the back of Smokey's horse. Now that Luke asked him for advice, he seemed to soften.

"Well, Ma always checks to see if she's wet first. Have ya done that?"

"No, I haven't. You want to come show me how?"

"No, sir." Colton wrinkled his face and looked the other way.

Luke held the squirmy, screaming baby between the crook of one elbow and his hand. Her face was beet red, and he wondered just how long she could keep this up before they all went deaf. Slowly, he lifted the diapering cloth from around one pumping little leg and peeked inside. "Well, here lies the problem."

"She bogged down?" Smokey asked.

"If that wasn't the problem," Colton professed loudly, "Ma would try feeding her." His cocky little smile had returned. "Good thing you ain't gunna try that." The boy laughed and slapped his leg, exciting Smokey's skittish mount. "I'd sure like to see you try."

"Quiet," Smokey said. "Luke needs ta concentrate."

"I'm fine now," Faith called from inside. "Bring her back. Colton's right, she needs to be fed."

"Fine, then," Smokey announced, as if he'd been the one to come up with the solution. "Everybody's hungry. Me and Colton will head over to the chuck wagon. I'm sure Lucky will be glad to see we brought some fresh meat to add to the menu."

After the evening meal, some of the men drifted off to their bedrolls early, but most lingered around the campfire, smoking and swapping stories. Colton's rattlesnake tale was a favorite and the men had him repeat it again and again.

Faith sat close to the fire with sleeping Dawn nestled in her arms. After everyone had their fill of supper, Lucky came around with healthy portions of bread pudding smothered in sweet cream. She was sure going to miss this hearty, tasty fare when she was gone.

From her seat by the fire, Faith watched the three Mc-Cutcheon brothers discussing cattle, clearly engrossed in the topics of breeding and ranching. Facts and statistics bounced back and forth, each man holding his own. The two-year-old bull the creepy Will Dickson had delivered was the topic most discussed. Matt liked the straightness of his legs, while Luke thought his height and length would be an outstanding cross with their heifers.

All three McCutcheons were attractive men with a strong

family resemblance. But something about Luke was different, and not just his black hair. It was his eyes, Faith decided. They were dark. Wild.

The tone between the men got heated, volatile, each of them taking turns spouting off. Just as Faith felt the uncontrollable urge to run for cover, laughter broke out. One brother was affectionately jabbing the other in the shoulder. It was truly amazing.

Flanked by Francis and Jeb, Chance made his way toward Faith. He was holding something in his arms. "Miss Faith," the lanky cowboy said, clearing his throat. "We heard that little Dawn was lacking blankets and such, so we took up a collection."

Faith felt her throat tighten as she took the items he offered. "Thank you all very much. That was so kind of you." She couldn't look at the trio standing there so sweetly; she'd cry for sure. She ran her hand over the stack admiringly. "Very soft," she murmured.

"'Tweren't nothin', ma'am."

She couldn't agree.

Matt, Mark and Luke's conversation had stopped. Mark looked over to Matt. "What do you make of it?"

"They're all smitten," Matt replied, watching Chance hand over the supplies. "Nothing like a little wiggle to make a man go a whistlin'."

Luke realized his brothers were watching him, waiting for his response. He nodded. "She's got 'em buggered up all right. But this job's too dangerous not to have your head on straight. I don't like it."

Mark stretched his legs. "What do you think she's really doing out here alone?" he asked, keeping his voice low.

"I've been trying to figure that out since I found her," Luke replied. "Her story just doesn't hold water." He paused. "On the run, maybe. I can't think of any other explanation for an expectant mother ready to deliver to be out in the wilderness, with only an eight-year-old boy as her help. Says, though, she has an aunt she's going to live with."

"Could be," replied Matt. "I'd feel a whole lot better if she did have an aunt. I'll send a telegram, do some checking around when we hit town."

"That won't do any good," Luke prophesied. "We don't have the name of the aunt, or even know where Faith's from. She's been pretty closemouthed when it comes to information about herself."

Matt and Mark nodded.

"She seems the most comfortable with you, Luke," his older brother said. "See what you can find out. I don't like not knowing what she's all about."

The next few days came and went without incident. Since her set-to with Luke over Colton, Faith had kept to herself, giving him a wide berth. To the other hands' disappointment, she avoided them as well. All except for Francis.

"We should reach Pine Grove by twilight," the youth told her that morning at breakfast. "Now's when we always get to spend this one night in town before reaching the ranch, as sort of a reward. The men draw straws to see who gets to go and who has to stay with the cattle." He ducked his head. "I'm shore gunna miss ya," he said sadly.

This was it. She'd known the day would come when she stayed and the others went on; she just hadn't thought it would come quite so quickly. Or that she'd feel quite so sad. Time had a way of silently slipping away. The thought of starting off alone again was daunting.

Luke hadn't given her so much as the time of day since the morning she panicked about his discussion with Colton. He was polite enough, seeing to her needs, but he kept his distance all the same. She missed him. She missed the safe feeling that just being around him brought. How lonely she would be once the cattle drive pulled out and left them behind.

Today Colton was driving and he slapped the reins across the horses' backs, urging them on. They were traveling alongside the herd following the chuck wagon again. Luke had been riding up in front and she'd been watching him for hours, daydreaming. Then he'd loped back, passing them, headed for the back of the herd. He'd tipped his hat as he'd gone by, but hadn't stopped.

Now he was back, approaching her wagon from the side. His plaid shirt, tucked neatly into his pants, and leather chaps protecting his lean, powerful legs was a welcome sight to Faith. With his hat pulled low, she couldn't see his eyes. Behind him he led a small horse that wore a saddle done up with every gadget that the other men carried: hobbles, lariat, canteen, bedroll. The only thing lacking was a Winchester rifle.

Luke fell in alongside the wagon. Looking to Colton he asked, "You want to ride back and see what Smokey is up to? I'm sure he could use your help." He offered the smaller horse's reins.

The boy's eyes lit up. "Sure."

"Just be careful," Luke added. "Remember, your horse is only as smart as you are."

"Yes, sir, I will." Colton handed the wagon reins to Faith. Copying the move he'd seen Luke execute, he climbed straight from the wagon seat into the saddle.

"Her name is Firefly. She's very gentle, so be kind to her."

Colton reined his new mount away from the wagon, smiling from ear to ear.

"Be careful not to spook the cattle!" Luke called at Colton's retreating backside. Then he turned to Faith. "She's really, really old. I'd say he can't get hurt, but the boy just might prove me wrong again. Let's just say I'm pretty confident nothing is going to happen."

Faith was a jumble of nerves. Conflicting emotions warred within her. It irritated her that Luke had taken liberties where Colton was concerned. Again. He'd never, ever, asked her permission about anything concerning the boy, just doled out orders as if Colton were one of his hired men. Still, deep down she knew this was exactly what Colton needed, a good role model, so she shoved her annoyance aside.

And, she was so glad to see Luke. Even if it was for just a few short minutes. Today was the last day she'd ever have with him.

"We'll pull into Pine Grove tonight," he pointed out indifferently.

"I know. Francis told me this morning," she replied, closing her hands tightly around the reins to keep them from trembling.

"What are your plans?"

"To rest for a few days," she said, "and then head out for Priest's Crossing. You know, where my aunt lives."

Luke pulled out a paper and some tobacco from a pouch and started to roll a cigarette. "What did you say her name was?"

She hadn't. Was he fishing for information again? She'd been very careful not to divulge too much, wanting to keep her life to herself. If Ward came around asking questions, they couldn't pass on something they didn't know. But now it would seem very suspicious if she didn't answer.

"Penelope Flowers."

Having answered, she stifled a grimace. What kind of stupid name was that? Luke seemed to agree, for he laughed. The sound was rich and inviting, so Faith smiled, knowing how silly the name sounded. It was also good to be near him again, to hear his voice.

"Really?" he asked. "That's one interesting name. And she's expecting you?"

She looked up into his face. "Yes." Oh, how she wished it were true. A relative, someone waiting for her. Someone who actually wanted her. Longing ripped her apart, so she looked away before his keen eyes saw the truth.

"From Pine Grove, Priest's Crossing is a good three days' ride north on horseback. Considerably longer in your wagon."

"Yes, I know."

"You expect to do that with the baby. Alone."

"I'm not alone. I have Colton."

Luke shook his head, then glanced away, out at the herd. Faith could feel his irritation.

"Faith, haven't you ever heard of Indians, outlaws, bad weather or a hundred other different things that could easily kill you?" His voice was angry, and she fought the urge to scoot to the other side of the wagon seat, to put some distance between them.

"Don't worry about me. I did well enough before you found me. I'd have survived that birthing, and I'll just do the same now."

"Luck. Plain and simple. It was just a matter of time before something happened."

"I'm not your concern, Mr. McCutcheon," she pointed out.

He ignored this. "How much money do you have?"

"It's really none of your business." If he knew how little she had, he'd probably fall off his horse.

He considered for a moment, then shook his head. "You're going to have to wait in town until your aunt sends someone to escort you. A lone woman on the trail is beggin' for trouble."

"That's ridiculous. I'll do no such thing!"

"How will you pull your wagon without horses?" he asked.

Oh. She had forgotten the horses were his. How exasperating. "I don't know. I'll work it out somehow."

"We'll see. My bunch won't pull out until the morning. We'll talk tonight."

Without saying another word, he tipped his hat and rode off after Colton.

Chapter Thirteen

LUKE left six men, the unlucky holders of the short straws, to watch the settled herd. All other hands rode into town with the two wagons. The men were loud and excited. Anticipation for some festivity after weeks on the trail had them singing and carrying on wildly.

Lucky pulled up in front of the closed mercantile, and Francis, who was again driving Faith's wagon, followed suit. Matt and Luke dismounted at the hitching rail and tied their horses, looking around. The rest of the men didn't stop. They continued straight down the street to the Wooden Nickel Saloon.

Since it was closing time most of the businesses were dark. The air had cooled considerably and there was a slight breeze. Here and there a lantern glowed in a window, and where the shades hadn't yet been drawn, inhabitants could be seen sweeping and straightening up. Across the street was the Imperial Hotel. It stood gleaming white and polished between the other dilapidated buildings, like a jewel among a bed of rocks.

"I'll be down as soon as I get some rooms at the hotel," Luke said to Matt as he loosened Chiquita's cinch. "Save me a spot at the poker table."

Matt tipped up his hat to get a better look at the good-size town in the fading light. Several streets connected with Main, and the town seemed to be thriving. "This is a peaceful place. No trouble ever came out of Pine Grove."

Luke stopped. Listened. "You're right about that. Still, I have a feeling."

Matt slapped him on the back. "Loosen up, little brother."

Luke nodded. "You're right. But we still have a day and a half to reach the ranch, with the Teton River to cross yet. I'd just feel better if we kept our eyes on the men. Don't let 'em get too drunk."

Matt followed after Lucky and Francis, who'd started in the direction of the saloon. Faith was looking in the store window, absorbed with the beautiful bolts of fabric. She rubbed the glass pane and leaned in for a closer inspection. Color was finally returning to her cheeks since the baby's birth. Lucky's food was filling her out and giving her a healthy glow. She seemed even more radiant every day.

Irritated with himself for noticing, and for spending yet another afternoon thinking about her, he turned his attention down the street to the Wooden Nickel, where whoops and hollers could be heard. Swinging doors burst open and a man strode out onto the street. He was tall and lean, fitting his little sister Charity's idea, Luke supposed, of a handsome fellow. His build and clothing bespoke farm work, but he had a six-gun tied to his leg.

The stranger nodded amiably to Matt and Francis as they passed. He crossed the street and strode purposely forward. "About time you got here," he said with a laugh as he approached the wagons. "I've been anxious to see you."

At the sound of his voice, Faith whirled. She'd been so engrossed looking into the mercantile window she hadn't heard his approach. Now her face went deathly white and Luke feared she might swoon again. He could see she was speechless.

It all suddenly made sense. This was the husband she was running from. The one who was supposed to be dead. And Luke wasn't the kind to step between a husband and wife, no matter the problem.

"Faith," the man called, taking a step closer and holding out his hand. "How are you?"

She looked like a cornered animal searching for a hiding

hole. Her gaze flew to Luke, begging for . . . something. Luke just stood watching the exchange.

"How? How did you find me?" she choked out.

Her voice trembled. This was a Faith Luke didn't know. He'd seen her shy with his men. Angry enough at him to chew nails. Happy and emotional at Dawn's birth, but never like this.

"Luke McCutcheon," he said, stepping protectively between the two, blocking the stranger's view.

"Ward Brown," the man replied, thrusting out his hand. He grasped Luke's and squeezed with force. But if the farmer thought he could scare Luke off with just a handshake, he was sorely mistaken.

"I want to thank you for caring for Faith. Her thoughtlessness has worried us considerably, her being in a delicate way and all." He glanced at Faith from around Luke. "Not that she might care. I see you done whelped the little one."

Damn. He wasn't one to get between a husband and a wife, Luke reminded himself again. No, he wasn't. But he sure as hell didn't like the way this man—husband or not—was talking to Faith.

"How did you know she was traveling with my outfit?" he asked, buying time.

"A little birdie told me." At Luke's dark look, Brown quickly added, "Will Dickson. I was asking around town and he was happy to give me the good news."

Luke felt Faith grab hold of the back side of his belt, and step close. At the same time, Colton looked sleepily out from the wagon bed. He quickly withdrew at the sight of the man.

"Come out here, boy! Don't you have a word of hello for me?"

Colton climbed down and stood next to Luke. His eyes were downcast and he wobbled a little. "Hello, Uncle Ward," he whispered.

"Uncle Ward?" Luke repeated. "He's not your pa?"

Colton shook his head, his previous cheekiness all but gone.

"I'll take them from here, Mr. McCutcheon. No need to bother yourself any longer. My thanks again," Ward said.

Faith's sharp intake of breath rang out like a gunshot. She was now clinging to Luke with force, and he loathed handing her over. He said instead, "Hold up, Mr. Brown. I was mistaken thinking you were Faith's husband. We should see what she wants to do."

"She's got no say," Ward said, irritated. "She's kin. My brother's wife. It's my duty to take care of her and the young'uns. Besides, Pa wants me to bring them back to the farm, where he can see to his grandbabies properly."

Luke ignored his remark and turned to Faith. She was smack up against him now, clinging like a vine. He took a small step back. "What do you say, Faith? Do you want to go with your brother-in-law?"

Faith stared at Luke, her brain numb. For the life of her she couldn't think of one thing to say. Ward had found her! Here he was now, her nightmare come true, smiling and waiting for her answer.

Luke stood firm, giving her courage. She shook her head.

"Guess that's your answer, Mr. Brown. As a widow, Faith has the right to settle anywhere she wants. You have no legal hold over her."

"That's so. Yes, I know it. She took Samuel's death hard. I thought maybe now that she had time to rethink her hasty departure, she'd be thankful to come home. Sleep in her own bed. How about you, Colton? Granddaddy sure misses you."

Colton didn't speak.

"Faith," Luke said. "Get the things you need, and the baby, and I'll get you settled in the hotel." He gave her a little nudge, jarring her out of her daze. "Go on, now. You're tired, and so is the boy."

* * *

Back in the wagon, Faith peeked out from behind the safety of the canvas cover. Ward stood there calm as could be, chatting with Luke. Who knew what lies he was telling? Oh, how she'd used to think he was handsome, him and his charming brother, Samuel. Two wolves in sheep's clothing! She'd been no match for their lying, cunning ways. And their father. At the memory of Colton's granddad she felt gooseflesh rise on her arms.

She heard pleasantries exchanged and watched Ward walk away down the now-dark, deserted street. He acted like he'd given up, like he'd just let her go on her way. She knew better.

The hotel room was beautiful, the first Faith had ever been in. Holding her sleeping baby girl, she walked around the room touching different objects and furniture. She ran her hand over the thick quilt, marveling at its downy softness. She regretted that she wouldn't get to enjoy its warmth. She'd have to run tonight. But, how? This time she wouldn't have a few days' lead on Ward.

A soft knocking sounded from the connecting room. Luke had settled her into this room and then taken the other for himself and Colton. Opening the door quietly, she saw Colton sprawled out on the big bed, fast asleep. He was still completely clothed, his boots hanging off the edge.

Faith started to go in, but Luke stepped in front of her.

"I want to undress him," she explained, looking into Luke's strong, handsome face.

"He'll be fine. Little tyke just laid down and fell asleep. Come here," he said, slipping past into her room. "I have something I want to discuss."

He reached for Dawn. Gently he took the sleeping baby and very carefully placed her in the middle of the big bed. He covered her with a blanket he took from the corner rocker. "There. I think she'll sleep for a while." He smiled. "Make yourself comfortable."

Faith walked over to the big chair and sat on the edge of the cushion, still shocked that Ward had actually found her after all this time. Luke pulled up the footstool and sat down in front of her. She felt it again: the uncanny feeling that made her seem a part of him, connected somehow. Like a thread ran from his eyes to her heart. This wasn't just excitement and daring, it was something bigger. She'd never felt anything like it.

"You settled?" he asked.

"Yes."

"Good. Because I want some answers. Honest answers. And if we have to sit here all night to get them, then so be it. First off, why are you running from your husband's family?" he asked, leaning forward intently.

Faith wanted to look away, to hide the truth. She was ashamed of her past. And, of all the people in the world, Luke was the last person she would want to know about it.

"Don't you dare make something up. The truth, Faith. I want it, now."

"After Samuel died, I wanted a different kind of life. I was tired of the farm, so I wrote to my aunt, who found me a job."

"And that would be Penelope Flowers?" He said it with a straight face and dark eyes.

"Yes."

"Damn it, Faith!" The baby stirred and he quickly lowered his voice. "I can't help you if you don't level with me."

She looked away. Oh, how she wanted to tell him the truth. It was all tangled up inside her like a sleeping ugly monster. If she ever did let it out, surely it would kill her. Moisture brimmed in her eyes, but she refused to let the tears fall.

Luke stood and pulled Faith up out of her chair. Only a small tug brought her into his arms. He was warm. He was safe. He was . . . comfortable. His hands were doing the most wonderful things to her back. Up and down they traveled slowly, working a miracle on her frayed nerves.

"Now," he murmured beside her ear, the sensation sending tingles racing down her spine. "Why were you running?"

"Samuel's father, Mr. Brown . . . he wants me to marry Ward." There, she'd said it. Taking a deep breath, she tried to relax.

"And . . . ?" Luke asked. "You don't want to marry him?"

She leaned back a little and touched the front of his shirt. His warmth stole from under the fabric into her fingertips. "No," she whispered.

"Come on, Faith, help me out," Luke said against her hair. "It may be hard to talk about, but I need a little more information. Coming between a family doesn't sit well with me, or with any McCutcheon. And like it or not, that man out there is your family. He's the uncle of your children."

Faith didn't offer any more information, so Luke decided to change directions. He'd try something a little less personal. "How long have you been running from Ward Brown?"

"Luke, please," Faith begged. "I don't want to talk about it. Just let me keep your horses for a while. When I get to Priest's Crossing, I'll send them back somehow. I promise. But I need to leave tonight."

"Whoa now!" he said, leaning back so he could see into her face. "You're not going anywhere tonight. You just get that harebrained notion out of your head this minute."

"I've got to, Luke. Ward won't give up this easily, even if he's acting like he will. He'll force me to go home with him."

"He can't make you do anything you don't want to do, Faith." He hesitated, thinking. "Our ranch is west of here, not really on your way to Priest's Crossing, but not that far out of your way either. Travel with us a little longer, until we get to it, and then if that's still where you want to go, I'll send some men on with you to help you get there safely. Or, if you'd rather, you can write to your aunt and she can come out to the ranch. Whatever you want."

Luke stared into Faith's coffee-colored eyes. They were alight, questioning. They strayed to his lips and lingered.

He must be loco, asking her to stay on. It made much more sense for her to depart before things got even more involved. Whatever troubles she had would be her own, and he could get back to business. That was the reasonable solution, the one that made sense.

She sighed and laid her head on his chest. He felt a sharp jab somewhere inside, like the first nail in his coffin.

Chapter Fourteen

THE huge hotel bed wrapped itself around Faith in a warm hug. She was burrowed deep in the feather mattress, with the colorful green and pink quilt tucked securely around her shoulders. Her cheek had never felt anything quite as wonderful as the soft pillowcase, which smelled faintly of soap and sunshine. She wished she could stay here for the rest of her life.

Reluctantly, she sat up and stretched, then checked on Dawn, who had been up every hour to eat. The babe was sleeping comfortably now, tucked into one of the drawers from the highboy dresser and placed on the floor next to the bed.

Faith took a moment to sink back into the covers, relishing the memory of the night before. Luke had said that she could stay on with him and the herd, go to the ranch and then proceed from there. A giddy excitement galloped through her, relief not to be leaving the group. Everyone had been so good to her, kind and considerate, helpful in every way.

She sat bolt upright, thinking of various incidents: Colton talking back. The men setting up a private camp for her, bringing her a tub. Lucky and Francis staying back so she could wash Dawn's things. She *had* been a distraction, like

Luke complained. She wouldn't be surprised if he'd changed his mind.

Hastily she climbed from the bed and ran a brush through her hair. She splashed her face with water and brushed her teeth. She changed Dawn's diaper, which woke the baby completely and set her howling. Done with that, Faith rushed to the connecting door and knocked.

There was no response, so she knocked a little louder. Perhaps Colton was still asleep. Opening the door, she found the room empty.

"Colton," she called, hoping he was just playing a game of hide-and-seek. There was still no answer.

Luke, she felt certain, must be with his men somewhere. Had Ward settled for Colton and stolen the boy away while she'd slept? The pair would be so far away by now she'd never catch him. Not alone. She had to find Luke. With his help she'd be able to hunt Ward down. Faith ran back into her room, grabbed up her things and bolted out the door.

Waking early, Luke, with Colton by his side, had dressed and gone out to a nearby restaurant. He was in desperate need of some brew and promised to bring Colton back and order some real restaurant food just as soon as they took a cup of coffee up to Faith.

A white china cup teetered in its saucer, sloshing hot coffee onto Luke's hand. He set it on the dresser, forgotten. Faith's room was a mess, the door was ajar, and there was no sign of her or Dawn.

Luke spun on his heel and Colton had a hard time keeping up. "Where's Ma?" the boy said.

"Don't know. She probably just . . ." He couldn't think of anything to tell the kid. His mind was too busy imagining what might have happened. "Went out."

"What about her coffee?"

"Hush now. I've got some thinking to do."

"B-but," Colton stammered, "it'll get cold."

Luke stopped. Bending down to Colton's level, he addressed him eye to eye. "To be honest, I'm a little worried. I don't think your ma would leave the room alone. I want you to run back over to the livery and tell Mark and Roady. Be quick."

Colton bolted off like a jackrabbit, his boot heels ringing down the stairs and then the old wooden boardwalk outside.

Faith ran down Main Street, dawn just barely breaking. Not a person was in sight. A horse tied to a post in front of the bank looked her way as she passed, but not seeing anyone else, she turned down one side street and then another looking for the livery stable. Where was it? That was where Luke's horses would be kept, and the wagons. The men might be there, too.

Her baby, not understanding why she was being jostled so roughly, was past hysterical. She had cried so hard Faith briefly feared she'd been hurt. Not only must her empty tummy be hurting her, but also, Faith thought, she could probably sense her mother's fear. The baby's face was still apple red and her cheeks moist with tears. Every once in a while Faith would hear her give a little sob or hiccup.

She stopped for a moment to nuzzle the child's warm, damp face. "It's all right," she whispered. "I'll find them, I promise. Then you'll have some breakfast."

Oh, how she hoped her words were true. With each passing minute Faith lost a little more hope. Why didn't she see anyone? Not a single man from the ranch. She wasn't even sure where she was anymore, or what direction she'd come from.

Spotting a lone man muttering to himself and tottering down the boardwalk, she cautiously approached. "Excuse me, sir," she said, trying to keep the anxiety from her voice.

"Huh?" His head swiveled in her direction and he tried to focus on her. He stumbled backward, caught his heel and fell to the ground.

Faith gasped. "Oh, I'm sorry!" He didn't seem to notice he'd taken a tumble and slowly climbed to his feet. He looked again at Faith.

"Could you tell me where the livery is?" she asked shakily. He smelled terrible, of stale liquor and vomit. After taking a moment to process her words, the man pointed. "That way, missy. Down the street a-ways."

"Thank you." She was off running again.

For several minutes she ran, expecting to see the livery any moment. Abruptly, the street ended. There were a few shacks, a boarded-up eatery, an out-of-business boot repair, but no stable. Not a horse or person in sight. A niggle of fear prickled her skin.

Her knapsack, full of Dawn's things, pulled heavily on her shoulder. Faith's arms throbbed from holding the baby while running for so long. Then she heard it: someone whistling. And it was a tune she not only recognized but knew by heart. It hung eerily on the cool morning air.

"Mornin', Faith," Ward called out from down the street. "Where you off to so early?" His tone was friendly, calm. There was no sign of Colton.

Darting a look to each side of the street, Faith contemplated trying to run away, but that was ridiculous. Where could she go where he couldn't find her? Besides, she had the baby to think about.

Ward was freshly shaven, his blond hair slicked back, his long curls lying along his collar. Blue eyes glittered when they looked into hers. It was like being in a bad dream and wanting to run but not being able to move.

"Why'd you run away? Pa and me were stunned when we couldn't find you, you being pregnant and all. We can work this out if you'll just be reasonable. "

Her mind was frozen. Ward was too close. All her senses screamed for her to run, but her feet wouldn't listen. Forcing herself, she answered, "You know why."

"No, I truly don't. We all thought you and Samuel were a happy couple. He never let on that there was any trouble."

Liar! She wanted to scream in his face that she knew all about their vicious blackmailing scheme to get her farm. She wanted to, but didn't.

"Let me have a look at the baby," Ward suggested, lifting the blanket back from Dawn's face. "Boy or girl?"

"Girl," Faith squeaked, inching around his tall body. He was intent on the baby and maybe wouldn't notice.

"Ain't she cute," he said, smiling. "She'll be a real beauty, just like her ma. What's her name?"

Oh, why had she taken the advice of that drunken old man? Why had she chosen this deserted, good-for-nothing street? She should have known better, and maybe then Ward wouldn't have found her. Maybe. "Dawn."

"Dawn Brown," her brother-in-law said. "Why, it has a real nice ring to it. I know Pa would be proud as a peacock to see her. He don't have any girl grandbabies yet." As if just noticing now that Colton wasn't with her, he asked, "Where's the boy?"

Faith was on the opposite side of Ward now. She took one slow, careful step back. She could feel her heart pounding in her chest.

"With the rest of the cowboys. I have to get back," she added steadily. "They're expecting me."

"Come on then, I'll walk with you."

He'd walk with her? She knew all these niceties were just for show. Just what was he was trying to pull?

He reached for her knapsack. She jerked back.

His face turned dark and his eyes flashed in a dangerous way. "I'm warning you, Faith," he said in almost a growl as the *real* Ward surfaced. "It'll be better for everyone concerned if you just cooperate." He snapped his fingers and held his hand open.

She hated to let him touch anything of hers, to help her in any way. But she handed him the knapsack and cursed herself silently for her weakness.

Chapter Fifteen

Luke and Roady rounded the corner and entered the livery just as the clock at the First National Bank chimed six o'clock. Chance, Uncle Pete, John, Lucky and Ike stood in a circle, discussing where they'd searched. The others were still out looking.

"Any sign of her?" Luke asked. "It's been a half hour since I found her room empty."

"No, boss. Sorry," Chance answered.

Lucky looked particularly upset, apprehension making him seem older than his fifty-two years.

"The others been back?" Luke asked, trying to hide his edginess. "Where's Colton?"

"He went out with Smokey. There was no stopping him."

Ike had stuck his head out the doorway and now called to Luke. "Boss, come here."

Luke hurried over, flanked by Roady and the others. From the east came Smokey, Francis, Colton and Mark. From the west strolled Ward and Faith. Her brother-in-law swaggered, toting Faith's bag and chatting amiably.

Anger slammed into Luke first. Then embarrassment at having called out a search, scaring Colton and the men. He'd thought she'd been taken by force, but here she was with Ward, happy as could be.

Everyone hurried to meet her as she approached. They swarmed around her, the men's faces etched with the same concern and questions that Luke himself was feeling.

Ward stopped and looked around. "This is quite a welcoming party!" he said, smiling over Faith's head at them. "From the looks on your faces, you were worried about Faith. No need to fret, boys, she's just fine."

Resentment burned in Luke's gut and his jaw clenched. He was damn mad at himself for falling victim to his own worry. He'd allowed Faith Brown to turn his whole cattle drive upside down. She'd not only been a distraction, but a liability. And it wasn't over yet. Smokey coughed, and a couple men shuffled their feet. He wasn't the only one feeling foolish. And perhaps angry?

Faith took her knapsack from Ward and hurried to her wagon. The men of Luke's trail drive watched her go. She climbed inside, relishing the security of the place, remembering how it had been her home for the past three months. Tears stung her eyes as she unbuttoned her dress and positioned Dawn for her morning feeding.

The baby dozed, worn out from her hysterical crying earlier. Slowly she woke, as Faith held her to her breast, but the child was indifferent to what was being offered. But she *had* to be hungry, for she hadn't had any breakfast yet.

Faith coaxed a bit more until the baby began to eat. "That's better, sweetie," she struggled to get out. She rocked back and forth and nestled Dawn close, remembering the look in Luke's eyes. In all of the men's eyes. Disbelief. Hurt. Anger. Luke believed she'd just gone off with Ward. He surely thought she wanted to be with Ward, wanted to talk with him. He probably believed everything she'd said last night was a lie, and Faith didn't see how she would convince him otherwise.

Dawn choked on a small swallow, gasped once and then began to hiccup. Each time one interrupted her, the baby would stop nursing and cry. She seemed disoriented, unable to find her mother's nipple again, even when Faith put it in her mouth.

"Here, baby," Faith offered, feeling close to hysterical herself.

"Here." She tried to interest Dawn, but the infant just kept crying.

"Missy?" It was Lucky, outside her wagon. "Let me take the young'un. Sounds like she has a bubble stuck in her belly. Gone colicky. Let me walk her a while and try an' bring it up."

"We're pulling out, Lucky," she heard Luke bellow. "Mount up, men. We'll meet the herd and start moving them northwest."

"It'll only take a minute," Lucky fired back, his tone sharp. It was the only time Faith had ever heard the cook talk in that manner. She sucked in a breath. The last thing she wanted to do was cause more trouble for Luke.

"We've lost as much time today gallivanting around as we're going to. Ask her if they're coming with us, and let's go." His tone brooked no argument.

Lucky, grumbling, followed orders and called in to her if she was sticking to the original plan. When she said they were, Colton took the reins of the wagon's hitched-up team and Francis helped him turn the horses, which fell in line behind the chuck wagon. With a jingle of harness and the muffled sound of hooves on sawdust, the wagons pulled out of Pine Grove. Dawn's persistent howling echoed down every street.

Luke scowled as he rode. Each time the baby sobbed, it pierced his belly like a hot lance. Damn it! Just what in the hell was Faith trying to pull? Ward looked like no more of a threat to her than Francis. And yet, he'd seen her fear last night written plainly on her face. Was this just some wild story she was making up so she could escape her responsibilities back home and start a new life, sashaying all over the countryside, gathering men's hearts like they were wildflowers? He scoffed and shook his head.

Roady, riding silently by his side, looked over in question. "Who's the man?"

"Ward Brown."

"Husband?"

"No. Brother-in-law."

"When did he show up?"

"Last night, when we pulled in. Dickson had ridden ahead and was forthcoming when he asked around about Faith. Says he wants to take her and the young'uns home to their farm." Luke paused and glanced back at the two wagons.

"And . . . ?" Roady prompted.

"She doesn't want to go. Says the old man will make her marry Ward."

"What do you make of it? Her out with him this morning?"

Luke shrugged. Felt duped. He wanted to help her but, without the truth, what was the use in trying?

Ward stood quietly to the side of the street as the outfit pulled out of Pine Grove. If the man were such a threat, wouldn't he try to stop them? Insist on taking Faith and the young'uns with him now? Instead he just watched Faith's wagon roll by.

"Well," Roady said. "This possibility has been in the back of everyone's mind since you found her out there all alone. Wasn't likely there wasn't a man out there somewhere. Not with a woman like her."

"That's so." At least she'd told the truth when she said her husband was dead.

Cresting a hill of waving brown grass they caught sight of the herd on the move down the Valley of Flowers, an area of Montana long traveled by Indians of all tribes. The scene stabilized Luke. It was one he'd seen many times. He was reminded sharply of what really mattered to him most, and what it meant for him to prove to his father and family that he was capable of bringing in a sizable heard without incident. They didn't want this validation, but he did. His stubbornness kept him from feeling connected to them and there was nothing he'd found that could make him believe different.

His riders rode out and joined the heard that moved slowly

west, surrounded by lofty mountains and trailed by a large brown cloud of dust. It was like one giant living creature, the all-important life's blood of his family's ranch. From early childhood Luke had been obsessed with only one thing: running the Heart of the Mountains. Now he was running their trail drive for the first time.

The Heart of the Mountains. He smiled at the silly name of the most powerful ranch this side of the Rocky Mountains. "What was I supposed to do, boys?" Flood had asked, a foolish grin on his face. "There she stood, my bride, like a willow in the wind and not yet sixteen years old. Her heart was shining right through her blue eyes. I was a man in love, smitten. I'd let her name the ten thousand acres Lollipop Lane, if she'd asked."

Now, there was a couple: his ma and Flood. Luke glanced over to the chuck wagon and then toward Faith's, which was quiet now, Dawn finally given up on her screaming. No, sir. His ma would never lie to Flood. They had a one-of-a-kind relationship. It was still full of love, respect and honesty, even after all these years. That was pretty amazing.

"What's the plan?" Roady asked, still riding alongside Luke. "Why's she still with us?"

"She's staying on until we reach home; then she'll contact her aunt"—Luke cringed inwardly, feeling again that Faith had lied to him—"Penelope Flowers, in Priest's Crossing. Says she's waiting on her."

"Sounds reasonable."

Luke shook his head. "I think she's lying."

"If she is, and I say *if*, then just maybe she's got her reasons." Roady drew to a halt. "In my way of thinking, Luke, she has a right to go anywhere she wants. Just because Ward Brown shows up and wants to cart her off to who-knows-where don't mean diddly-squat."

Luke had stopped his horse, too, and he glanced at Roady sitting easily in the saddle. The man's hat was tipped back in his usual carefree fashion, and he chewed on the toothpick that hung as a permanent fixture from his mouth. Luke wished he could be so trusting. He truly did. But something just didn't feel right. His gut was telling him someone was lying. Hell, he didn't want to think it was Faith, but . . .

"That may be," he said. "But she's risking Colton's life and also little Dawn's by this harebrained idea that she can travel across country without any help from a man."

Roady snorted. "She's got plenty of help now, ain't she?" He looked challengingly to Luke. "Any one of these men, including myself, would be more than glad to escort her to Priest's Crossing—or to San Francisco for that matter, if that's where she wants to go."

"Tell me something I don't already know." Luke couldn't keep the sarcasm from his words.

Roady's face clouded with annoyance. "Why don't you try some sweet talk? A little can go a long way with a woman. All you've done is scowl and treat her like one of the men!"

"Facts are facts," Luke shot back hotly. "That's all that matters. Honey-mouthed sayings are for fairy tales. This"—he gestured to the open countryside with his arm—"is reality."

"You might be surprised," Roady said with a scoff. "Your usual good thinking is lacking this time, Luke. Try using some of that wise red man blood you got flowing through your veins. Maybe things will become a little clearer."

Chapter Sixteen

CAMP was a quiet affair that evening. The men ate, then disappeared to their bedrolls one by one, probably still feeling the effects of the whiskey they'd consumed at the Wooden Nickel. It wasn't often that the three brothers were in camp together at the same time, because one was usually out watching the herd. The night before reaching the ranch, though, they were a bit more relaxed.

Mark, smoking a cigar, watched Matt work a frayed piece of rope. Roady and Luke sat opposite, enjoying the hot coffee Lucky had poured. Talk was small when they gave the effort; they mostly sat in silence.

Faith had not left her wagon since that morning. Lucky had taken her some supper, trying to entice her out, but she'd rejected the tempting meal.

"I'm not hungry. But thank you, Lucky," she'd added.

"You gotta eat! Think of the baby. She needs your milk," Luke heard him say.

"I have a little something to nibble on in here," she'd assured the cook, her voice steady and low. "You quit your worrying."

"At least let me take the little gal for a spell. You need some rest."

She'd refused that, too.

Ike and Will Dickson walked into camp, leading their horses. Ward Brown was by their side. Luke stood, suspicion crackling through him like wildfire.

"Found him following our trail," Ike said, motioning to Ward.

Luke looked at the newcomer, awaiting his response. Roady, at Luke's shoulder, sized Ward up.

"That's true enough," Ward replied. "Heard last night at the Wooden Nickel how you fired Earl. With a herd as large as yours I figured you'd need every hand you can get. Especially for the river crossing tomorrow. I'd like to hire on . . . if you'll have me. I'm good in the saddle and have worked my share of cattle."

Matt and Mark looked to Luke. It was true: being a man short put everyone at risk. But the decision was Luke's. The brothers respected each other's authority.

Luke felt certain that Faith was watching them from her wagon. He could feel her stare burning into his back. This just might be a good way to flush out the truth from her. Find out what was really going on.

"Grab yourself a cup of coffee. We'll use you until we reach the ranch."

"Much obliged, Mr. McCutcheon." Ward's blue eyes swung from one face to the next. "Where do I find a cup?"

As their new hire walked away, Roady rounded on Luke. "Are you loco? What's gotten into you?" He shook his head, disgusted.

Luke followed him to the edge of the campsite. "If there's a diamondback around, I want him out in the open where I can see him, not hidden under a rock ready to strike."

Roady didn't reply.

Word spread. All the men knew who Ward was, and Lucky was no exception. Luke watched the old man stand back and let Faith's brother-in-law serve himself. Normally the cook would have jumped right in to help, making a newcomer welcome.

"Where you from?" Luke asked, going over to Ward. Roady followed.

Ward raised his cup and took a sip, tasting the coffee. "Nebraska. Small town called Kearney. Ever heard of it?"

"No." Luke watched him. Ward's eyes slipped from face to face of each the camp's men, and it never once strayed to Faith's wagon half-hidden just beyond Lucky's. Curious, for a man so . . . concerned. "I suppose you know Faith's relation. The one she's going to live with," Luke probed.

"Relation? She don't have no relation. Her pa died shortly after she married Samuel. He's the only relative that I know about." Ward took another sip of coffee. "I wouldn't know who you're talking about."

"Penelope Flowers," Luke threw out.

Ward choked. Wiping his mouth with his shirtsleeve, he turned and glanced at Faith's wagon. In a sad and serious voice he whispered, "That's what she told you, then? Penelope

Flowers is her aunt?" His tone was full of concern, as he shook his head in disbelief.

"That's what she said," Luke confirmed. Though he'd expected it, he didn't like the direction this conversation was headed.

"Penelope Flowers is her *cow*. Been a good milker for years, but I wouldn't go so far as to call her kin," Ward joked, looking from Luke to Roady, his lips quivering as he tried to hide back a smile. "Although, Faith did seem quite attached to the old thing. Just maybe they *are* related!"

Luke's anger grew, but he refused to appear anything but nonchalant. He didn't know what galled him more—Faith's lie or the fact that Ward was having fun at her expense.

Ward meandered casually over to the campfire and refilled his coffee cup, a frown marring his face. "This is exactly what I've been worried about." He sat down, making himself comfortable. "Faith's always had a fanciful way about her, making things up and such. Always harmless, mind you. She's not lettin' on, but I think she's takin' Samuel's death real hard. Dreaming up things that just aren't true. It worries me—her taking care of the young'uns and all."

Roady pitched the remainder of his coffee into the crackling flames. "I'm turning in," he said curtly.

Matt and Mark, who stood quietly nearby, followed suit. They looked questioningly at Luke, then headed for their bedrolls.

"Do you want me to take a watch?" Ward asked.

The last thing Luke wanted was this man up when everyone else was asleep. But he didn't want to show his hand just yet. "You bed down with the others, I'll wake you later."

"Thanks again for givin' me a chance. I know I'm a stranger and all."

Luke watched him go. Either Ward was a damn good liar or Faith was. But then, what about her and Colton's reactions? Those hadn't been an act, he'd bet the ranch on it. So, what actually was going on here? Determined more than ever to find out, Luke looked to the wagons. Was Faith still awake? Only one way to be certain.

Faith heard Luke approaching. She waited for him to knock, but he didn't. What was he waiting for? Her temper flared. She'd heard bits and pieces of Ward's conversation about poor Samuel and how hard she was taking his death. With a pounding heart, she clasped her hands together to keep them from shaking.

"Faith, you awake?" Luke called quietly.

She sat there stewing. Colton and Dawn had been asleep for a good hour. She could pretend she was asleep, too; that way she wouldn't have to face the accusation she knew she'd see in his eyes. But, Lord. She hated not defending herself. Hated letting Ward go about spreading lies.

"I'm awake."

"Would you mind coming out here for a spell?" Luke cleared his throat. "So we can talk."

No. She wouldn't mind. But he might when she got finished with him. "I'll be right out."

Snatching up her shawl, she wrapped it tightly around herself and slipped out into the darkness. She felt his hand steady her as she climbed down the wheel to the ground. The desire to pull away was strong, but she mastered it, knowing such an act wouldn't do any good.

He steered her away from the campfire to a more secluded place beyond some trees. Her nerves were taut, frayed. Unable to hold back a moment longer, she rounded on Luke, throwing him off balance. "How could you?" she demanded.

"What?"

"How could you let that lying, cunning, sad excuse of a human being stay?" she cried. "Oh, he's so smooth. Butter wouldn't melt in his mouth."

"He hasn't lied to me—at least not that I know of."

"You believe him. Trust him. Because he's a *man*. And women are stupid, lazy, lying and . . . and . . ." She couldn't think of anything else Samuel called her. "Don't you? You don't think he's a threat to Colton or me. Or to Dawn for that matter."

His lips thinned. "Quit putting words in my mouth," he whispered angrily. "I wanted answers last night, Faith. Wanted to figure out just what was going on. But you didn't seem to have any for me. Remember?" He paced away, stood for a moment and then paced back, irritation apparent in every inch of his body.

Damnation. Why was it so hard for her to talk with him without getting worked up?

She erased any evidence of emotion from her voice. "I remember, Luke." Oh, she'd wanted to give him answers. Wanted to spill the whole ugly mess into his lap, then let him pick up the pieces of her heart and soul, one by one, and make everything right. But she couldn't. Just the thought of telling him was enough to make her stomach sour up. So, silence was her answer.

"See?" he charged, pointing his finger in her face. "You're doing it again. Right now. Shutting me out."

"You're right," she threw back, wishing she could do otherwise. "There aren't any answers."

"There aren't? Or, you just won't give them to me?" Luke stared at her. Moments ticked by. "Your aunt Penelope," he said in a much calmer voice. "She has room for the three of you?"

"Well . . ." Faith paused, thinking. "Yes, she does."

Luke crossed his arms over his chest. "And, you know her well, then, this aunt of yours?"

Each time he said the word "aunt," Faith noticed his jaw clench and release. Whatever was wrong with him?

"Why do you ask such a silly question? Of course I know her well. She's sweet and kind and gentle. She has brown hair and beautiful big eyes, and . . . I love her dearly."

"Hmm. I see," he said, his eyes reflecting dangerously the moonlight from above. "And, does she usually prefer oat, alfalfa or clover hay?" He'd dropped his arms to his side and stood glaring.

It took a moment before she realized what he'd just said. Gathering all her courage, Faith advanced on Luke and his anger. "You big"—she planted her hands in the middle of his chest and shoved with all her might—"ox!"

He didn't go flying like she hoped he would, merely stepped back and caught his balance. That made her even madder.

"'Poor Faith,'" she mimicked Ward. "'She's so upset over Samuel's death! Poor Faith, she doesn't know what she's doing!'"

Nudging up his hat with his thumb, Luke stared at her all the harder. As she tromped back and forth in anger, an amused look came to his face.

"Don't you dare look at me like that, Luke McCutcheon! Don't you dare." She stomped her foot. "I won't take it, do you hear?"

"Look at you like what, Faith?" he asked slowly.

"Like I'm a child," she said. "No, like I'm addle-headed or crazy. I'm not. Just because I'm a woman doesn't mean I don't know what I'm talking about." She sighed, tired and defeated. What was the use? She calmed herself and said, "I want to explain to you why I was out this morning with Ward. When I woke up Colton was gone and I'd thought Ward had taken him. I was trying to find the livery stable so I could tell you. I got lost and that's when he showed up and offered to carry my bag and walk back with me." She shrugged. "Ward *is* a threat to me, Dawn and Colton. That's all you need to know. If you don't want to believe me, well . . . don't." She was through fighting. She just wanted to go back to her wagon and lie down. She turned to go.

"Wait, don't go away mad," Luke said, reaching out and

catching her by her arm. He was behind her and stood only inches away. "I didn't mean to get you so worked up. I guess I just want to know more about you than I do. I think it's because I helped deliver Dawn. I'm sorry."

Those two little words flowed over Faith like thick, warm honey. Samuel had never said them. She closed her eyes and just stood there, absorbing the way they made her feel inside. He leaned in close. His mouth was just a breath away from her ear, and his hat seemed to close them both off from the rest of the world.

"You're a wildcat," he whispered, a hint of humor in his voice. "I never would have guessed it."

"And, I suppose you're a little lamb?" she replied, working hard not to enjoy his nearness.

"Depends."

There was a world of meaning in that one little word. Her feet were rooted to the spot. If Lucifer himself rose up before her, she wouldn't be able to move an inch. From behind, Luke wrapped his arms around her and pressed his cheek to hers. They stood like that, enjoying the respite.

Faith wished she could open up, but she knew that way lay disaster. It seemed like Luke already believed Ward. What if Ward told Luke she killed Samuel, or went to their sheriff? Would Luke accept it as truth? She couldn't risk the Browns getting custody of Colton and Dawn. She either married Ward, giving them her father's farm, like they wanted, and be subjected to an unthinkable life for her and her children, or they'd go to the judge in Kearney and she'd hang. If that were the case, they'd be raising her children anyway, without her being there able to shield them. Both outcomes were absurd. Escape was the only answer.

After a moment, Faith pushed Luke's arms down and stepped away from his comforting warmth, the action unmistakable. They stood for an instant in awkward silence.

"I'll walk you back to your wagon." His voice was hard, the warmth and teasing gone. Faith understood the change, and regretted having to drive him away. He wanted her to confide so he could help. Little did he know there was no help for her.

Chapter Seventeen

CROSSING the river took most of the next day. Luke came and drove Faith's wagon across early, not saying more than a handful of words the whole time. She knew he must still be annoyed with her from last night. She longed to tell him that she hadn't disliked his affection; that in actuality it was wonderful and exciting. But her memories of Samuel were hard to break. And, she couldn't take the chance of her softening and telling Luke the truth.

Safely on the far side of the river, she and Colton watched as the men brought the herd over slowly. Chance, Ike and Ward held the remuda close by, for the men needed fresh horses often. Faith looked over at Ward but whipped her attention back to the river when she found him watching her. Oh, it galled her how he'd been able to worm his way into a job! At least Luke's men seemed to be avoiding him.

The river was wide and shallow for the most part, but for thirty or forty feet in the middle it ran deep and swift. Several men atop their horses were stationed in the shallow waters, directing the cattle along the course Luke had picked out. When the beasts hit the rushing water, most got nervous and balked, refusing to take the plunge. A lead rider would have to swim his horse out across in front so that the cattle would follow; then they would exit one hundred feet downriver from Faith's wagon, and Smokey, Francis, John and Matt received the wet and frightened animals.

Colton had put up a fuss about having to stay on the wagon with her. He'd wanted to ride Firefly as soon as they were on the opposite side of the river. Luke had flat out said no. Colton was to stay with Faith and keep an eye on her and Dawn.

"I don't have a single man to spare today, Colton," Luke had said in a no-nonsense voice. "I really need you here to watch after your mother. Can I count on you to stay put?"

The boy's gaze went longingly to his small mare tied to the back of the wagon. "Yes, sir," he agreed reluctantly.

That had been several hours and many hundreds of bovine ago. Faith wondered just how many cattle were left to cross.

"Look, Ma." Colton pointed to the far riverbank. "Mark is taking the swimming spot."

Luke's brother gigged his black-and-white paint, pushing the hesitant horse forward. It shied and snorted, not wanting to go into the chilly water. Mark got him in, though, and Faith watched as he joked and teased each tired and worn-out man as he passed. She couldn't hear his words, but admiration shone from the other men's eyes.

Luke was on the far bank atop Chiquita. Faith had a hard time watching anyone else. Feeling foolish for her behavior last night, she wished again she'd had the nerve to talk with him that morning.

He crossed the river every once in a while to check the footing for the animals and the condition of his men. Moving closer, he cupped his mouth with his hands and shouted something to Mark, and his brother waved back while waiting for the next bunch to reach the deep channel. The steers plodded closer. Mark's horse pawed the water and snorted again, shaking his head. Moments later, Mark plunged him into the current.

"That looks scary, Ma."

"Yes, it does," Faith said, glancing back toward Luke. "It's plenty dangerous."

"I bet Firefly could do it," Colton said. "She's real good at everything."

Just then a shout went up from Pedro, the man stationed closest to the receiving end of the deep channel. He waved madly and pointed to the front of the herd, where Mark had been riding. He was now nowhere in sight. His horse surfaced a second later three feet downriver. Mark was still aboard but his hat was gone. He was leaning forward, giving his mount its head. Then a steer rammed him, sending both horse and rider under a second time.

On the shore, Luke sprinted his horse down along the riverbank, following his brother's path. He passed a treacherous rock bed and jumped a log before he could plunge her into the swift current. Mark's paint was there, but his brother had disappeared.

Faith stood up onto the wagon seat, grasped the wagon's bows for balance and held her breath. She watched Luke's head turn from side to side, scanning the torrent.

Jeb, Roady and Sam were on the opposite side now, spurring their horses in and swimming out to meet Luke. Roady pointed and shouted, his words lost to the thunderous roar of the icy water. Luke pressed his mare farther into the torrent. She seemed to take the challenge bravely, her head held high, nostrils scooping the air. Faith, her heart in her throat, was sure no man or animal could survive that madness for long.

Too long! It was taking too long! Luke turned Chiquita directly into the deepest part of the channel and started swimming her downriver for all she was worth. Somehow he'd missed Mark, let his brother slip by. Had Mark vanished forever?

Up ahead a flash of red caught his eye, then was instantly gone. Mark bobbed to the surface, unconscious, swirling downriver like a cork in a whirlpool, his arms outstretched, his head facedown. Luke spurred his exhausted mare onward, demanding everything from her. Her sides heaved, sucking in air. She faltered once and then steadied herself. An instant later her head went under, drenching Luke up to his shoulders.

Another ten feet and he would be alongside Mark. "Hang on, filly," he shouted above the drone of the river. At the sound of his voice he felt her gather her flagging energy and rallied.

By some miracle he found himself next to Mark's lifeless body. Luke struggled to pull him out of the water but the extra weight sent Chiquita into a panic. She almost crushed his brother with her powerful hooves, but he held tight, trying to keep both Mark up and his horse from going down.

From the corner of his eye Luke saw a horse racing along the riverbank. It pulled alongside and then, in a burst of speed, passed Luke and Mark. Without hesitation it plunged into the river and swam out to meet them. The rider reached for his brother's unconscious body. It was Ward Brown.

Luke tightened his hold, shocked. "Get a good grip," he yelled. They had to get his brother out.

"I've got him now. Let go."

It was the hardest thing Luke had ever done, trusting Mark's life to someone he knew nothing about. Beneath him he felt Chiquita floundering, and he knew she couldn't possibly last much longer.

"I've got him!" Ward yelled again over the roar of the mighty river. The three of them careened downstream and Luke had no choice but to release the grip he had on Mark's belt. Ward pulled Mark over the pommel of his saddle and turned his horse back to the bank.

In the next instant, a log smashed into Ward's horse's right side. Ward cried out as his mount went under. Luke prayed the man wouldn't let his brother fall. Roady was swimming his horse up to help.

Chiquita's leg struck something under the water and she took a nosedive, plunging Luke back underwater. Luke tried to lift himself out of the saddle, to ease his weight on Chiquita, but she was struggling wildly. The last thing he wanted to do was slip beneath her thrashing hooves.

They reached a sandbar; the mare could get her footing. Luke leaped out of the saddle and pulled the reins, trying to help her to the river's edge. It worked. At last on solid ground, Chiquita's legs gave way and she collapsed to the sandy loam, her head flopping down limply like a sack of potatoes. The cannon bone of her right foreleg was contorted at an ugly angle, her eyes wide.

Luke stood frozen, hand on his side, chest heaving. His face and hands were blue from the cold and he griped his teeth tightly together to keep them from chattering. With clumsy, frozen fingers he pushed his sodden hair out of his eyes to give Chiquita a long look; then he staggered up the river's edge and started toward the group huddled on the bank.

Chance and Smokey parted instantly to let Luke through. Luke sank to the ground by Mark's side where his brother was stretched out on the sand. "Is he breathing?" Luke wheezed, then coughed up a mouthful of water. He hunkered down and put his ear to Mark's mouth.

"Not yet," Matt answered.

The two brothers grabbed Mark's arms and hefted them over his head in an effort to rid his lungs of water. When nothing happened, Matt rolled Mark over and drove his knee into the center of his back. Mark gagged, then, and water gushed from his mouth and lungs, making him cough and choke. Several times he contorted, but at last he lay spent, exhausted. A collective sigh of relief was breathed by the men.

Faith hurried all the way downriver to where the men were gathered. She threaded her way through the throng and fell to her knees at Mark's side. Luke's brother, conscious now, looked at her and smiled wearily.

She looked up at the men, not daring yet to smile. "He's alive!"

"That he is, missy," Lucky said. "Thanks to Ward and Luke."

The men all laughed, slapping each other nervously on the backs, all talking at once, some shaking their heads, others telling what they'd seen of the dramatic rescue. Luke just stood shivering uncontrollably. He couldn't pull his eyes from Faith.

After a moment, he went and collected John's dry Colt .45 from its holster. He walked back to his horse. Chiquita lay still, unable to get up. She labored for every breath. Steam rose from her heated body, and pink foam, laced with bright red blood, bubbled from her nostrils. He knelt by her head and stroked her sodden neck several times.

He loved this mare. She'd given him her all from the moment he'd swung onto her back the very first time. She was genuine. Her eye clouded with pain. He stood and raised the gun. He pulled the trigger.

Luke stared at his horse. Matt appeared and slung a blanket around his shoulders. "Sorry about your filly," he said, rubbing Luke's shoulders and arms. "I know how much you liked that animal."

Luke nodded. He glanced over at Mark, who was now sitting up, a blanket tucked around his shoulders, too. "Yeah, I did. She was real special." His gaze continued around the group to Ward, who was having an injured leg tended by Lucky.

"Roady, Sam, Jess, Smokey! See what you can do about rounding up and settling the herd already on this side," Luke shouted. "The rest of you boys go back over and let's get the remainder of the cattle over here. I want to be at the ranch by nightfall." He went about unsaddling Chiquita and removing her bridle.

Ike rode up, leading a gelding. Luke was in the saddle again almost immediately, like nothing unusual had happened. He rode over to where Ward still sat, his leg wrapped from foot to knee.

"Thanks, Brown, for helping," he said, looking over the man's head toward the distant mountaintops. "You can ride with Lucky in the wagon the rest of the way to the ranch. We're indebted to you."

Chapter Eighteen

As the herd entered the upper pastures of the Heart of the Mountains ranch, the three McCutcheon brothers rode side by side at their head. Luke was pleased to finally be home, herd intact and each man alive and well, everything considered, though the constant lowing of the cattle attested to their uneasiness from crossing the river and then being pushed hard to their final destination.

He reined up, followed by Matt and Mark. Lifting his arm and gesturing, Luke gave the command to circle up and settle down the weary cattle.

"You did well, little brother," Matt said affectionately, giving Luke a nod and then looking to the herd. "If it hadn't been for your fast action, Ma would be heartbroken tonight. And Amy would have been a widow."

Luke grinned and looked at Mark. His brother had been unusually quiet the whole ride back, and Luke wondered what he was thinking about. There was something strange between Mark and Amy, his wife. Things weren't quite as they should be between newlyweds. He knew it troubled his ma and Flood greatly, watching the sparks fly, or not fly, between the two. Why, it troubled the whole clan, if he were honest. What affected one McCutcheon usually affected them all.

He joked, "Honestly, I was only thinking of myself. Ma would've had my hide pinned to the smokehouse door if we returned without him."

"That's a fact, Luke," Matt agreed. "And we'd have had to hear scripture from here till kingdom come." He glanced to Smokey, who was signaling that the circling had begun. "Let's let the men finish up here and get down to the house. The two wagons should be there by now, and I'm hankering to get my arms around Rachel. It's been a long drive."

Mark perked up. At the mention of his pregnant sister-in-law, a spark of humor brightened his somber face. "If you can still get your arms around her. She was pretty circular when we left. I can't picture what she must look like now."

"I'll manage," Matt said with a wink. "You don't know Rachel the way I do." And with that, Matt's horse took off like a shot. Luke and Mark rode hot on his heels.

The brothers clamored into the yard, past the bunkhouse where all the ranch hands lived and reined up in front of the barn. Matt and Mark finished in a dead heat, Luke followed by two horse lengths.

Francis ran from the barn, excitement on his face. "They're all waiting for ya in the house. You should've seen your ma's face when she spotted Faith and the baby," the youth said, smiling. He sobered, his forehead creased with worry. "I hope you don't mind, Luke. I spilled the beans about how you rescued Mark."

The ranch house door flew open, smacking against the giant log-and-chink wall with a thud. Charity, dressed from head to toe in fringed buckskin, strawberry blonde hair flying, dashed from the house and vaulted into Luke's arms. He swung her around playfully in a bear hug and set her down.

"Where's your skirt?" Luke scolded his sister. "You promised when I got home you'd be wearing one."

"I tried, Luke, really I did," she laughed "I just can't get used to all that fabric hanging around my legs. Trips me up every time."

Luke laughed, shaking his head in disbelief. "What are we going to do with you?"

Charity went over to Matt and Mark and hugged them and kissed them both on the cheek. Finished with her greetings, she shook her finger in the air. "It's about time you boys got home. You're late," she admonished. The men had handed their reins over to Francis and were walking toward the ranch house. "Ma was starting to fret and drive us all crazy. I'm going with you next time, and you can't stop me."

"We'll see about that," Matt said, chucking her under the chin. He stepped past her and hurried into the house.

Charity stopped Luke before he went inside. There was an odd gleam in her eye. "You're not disappearing on me tonight. I have so much to tell you."

"Is it about Brandon Crawford?"

"Why on earth would I want to talk about him?" Her suddenly breathless tone confirmed Luke's belief that his little sister and good friend, the sheriff, were falling for each other. She was still way too young to be thinking about marriage, but the thought had crossed his mind. They'd known each other for years, and nothing would make Luke happier. Brandon was a good man and would fit well here.

"I don't know. Maybe because before I left two months ago, according to you, he was the only man on the face of the earth worth talking about."

She slugged him in the arm playfully and ran inside.

Faith watched the reunion between brothers and sister from the large plate glass window. She'd shied away from the group of women who were making a fuss over Dawn and Colton, opting instead for the safety of the beautiful tapestry chair. Carefully holding Mrs. McCutcheon's bone china teacup, she marveled at all the beautiful things in the house and watched Luke's mother rock Dawn back and forth.

Flood McCutcheon stood in the doorway, tall and distinguished, his handsome face topped with gray-streaked chestnut hair. Beaming with pride, radiating happiness, he embraced each one of his sons as they stepped across the threshold. "Welcome home, boys," he boomed. "It's been much too quiet without you here."

"Hello, Pa—Ma," Matt and Mark both said as they entered the room. And in three fast strides Matt was smothering his wife in a powerful embrace, kissing her ardently.

"Ease up now, Son," Flood said, laughing. "Give Rachel some air. She's too close to her time for such tomfoolery."

"You're right," Matt replied, pulling back and running his hand proudly down her swollen belly. "Sorry, sweetheart."

Rachel just smiled and laced her arm through his. Her eyes sparkled happily, promising a true reunion when they were alone.

Matt looked around. "Where are my boys?"

"Off somewhere playing. They'll be along soon, with night-fall coming on," Mrs. McCutcheon said. She was carrying Dawn. She kissed Matt and Mark but stopped in front of Luke. "And how was the drive?" she asked.

"Fine, Ma," he replied. His eyes came to rest on Dawn sleeping peacefully in his mother's arms, and the corners of his lips tipped up.

"Good." She laid her hand upon his arm. "I knew it would."

Then, she turned to Mark. "Amy's waiting on a kiss," she prompted softly.

Hat in hand, Luke's brother walked stiffly to his wife. Bending, he brushed a quick kiss to her creamy cheek. "Hello, Amy," he said. "How are you?"

"Fine." The young woman's answer was hollow. She dropped her gaze and turned, hurrying into the kitchen. Everyone watched as the door swung closed.

Faith wished she could evaporate into a mist and float from the room unnoticed. This was much too personal to be watching. She'd seen Luke glance her way a couple of times, though mostly he just stood there under the massive set of longhorns hanging above the fireplace. High above that, a beautiful skinned hide of brown and white was stretched tight on the wall. It was all very masculine, and Luke and his brothers and father fit right in.

Claire McCutcheon, her trim figure clad in gray velveteen, turned to her. Everyone else's attention followed. "And I assume you've been treating our guests well, Luke?" she said, cuddling the baby close.

"As well as you can on a cattle drive," her son answered, perhaps a bit defensively.

Charity pulled her brother over to the settee. She tugged him down next to her. Faith saw that no-nonsense, leave-me-be look written on his face, the one that could freeze her insides faster than a snowstorm. His sister didn't seem to notice it at all.

"Tell us how you rescued Mark from the river, Luke," she begged, adoration shinning in her eyes.

"Later, Charity."

"Please. Francis told us some, but we want to hear it from you. How you had to ride a good quarter mile in swift water and hold onto Mark until that other man could reach him."

"I think the story is growing already," Luke said. "It wasn't near that far."

Faith saw a flicker of pain flash across Luke's face. His mother must have seen it, too, for she swooped in to the rescue.

"Charity, please go check on Esperanza and see if the water is hot yet for more tea. I know your brothers would love a cup before supper."

Charity gave her mother an I-know-what-you're-up-to look, but got up promptly to do her bidding. When the swinging kitchen door closed, Mrs. McCutcheon raised her eyes to the ceiling. "Daughters," she groaned, drawing the laughter of everyone in the room. "My sons were so much easier at this age. All they wanted to do was ride with their father and tend cattle. It was years before they discovered there was an opposite sex."

"That's true," Flood spoke up. "But then all hell broke loose." He puffed up like a proud rooster, and everyone laughed as Mrs. McCutcheon scolded him for his language.

The door banged opened, and in ran two young boys. They headed straight for Matt and wrapped their arms around him.

"Faith and Colton, these two lads are my boys. The tallest is William, but we call him Billy. He's probably just a year or two older than you," he said, nodding to Colton, who stood quietly by Faith's chair. "And this is Adam. He just turned five." Matt affectionately tousled Adam's golden hair. "Boys, this is Faith and Colton Brown."

Billy said hello, and Adam squirmed around in his dad's embrace. Adam's wide smile revealed two missing front teeth.

"Boys," Matt said, "why don't you take Colton out and show him the barn?"

Colton edge closer to Faith's chair. She reached out and nudged him. "It's all right, Colton, we'll be fine."

Her stepson looked at the boys but didn't move a muscle.

"Firefly is still tied to your wagon, Colton. Show her to my nephews. I know they'd like to see your horse," Luke said with a wink.

To this, Colton responded. He hastily met Matt's sons as they ran to the door.

"No running in the house, please," Mrs. McCutcheon admonished.

Charity, followed by Esperanza, who was carrying a trayful of teacups and teapot, entered the room. The housekeeper began pouring and passing them out.

Faith was overwhelmed. What Luke had just done for Colton in one moment was more than his father had ever done in a whole year for the boy. She couldn't tear her gaze away from him as his family's pretty housekeeper handed him a beautiful china cup that matched the one she held.

"Mister Luke," the woman said in accented English.

"Thank you, Esperanza," he replied.

The maid blushed before heading back to the kitchen. Over the rim of her cup, Faith met Luke's intense gaze.

Dawn started to fuss, so Faith set her cup down and reached for the baby. "It's her feeding time," she whispered to Mrs. McCutcheon.

The woman handed her the infant. "Yes, follow me and I'll show you where you can feed her."

Luke watched Faith's departure as she slowly climbed the massive staircase. Something about her being here in his home felt so right. He'd have liked to have gone with them and showed her the upper floor but that might look strange. He wanted to see her delight as she looked around. Maybe, if he'd just admit it to himself, he just wanted to plain be with her.

Flood came and sat on the other side of him. "Son, I hear you not only saved your brother's life but also delivered Faith's child. I'll say you've had an eventful drive!"

Luke yanked his thoughts away from what might be happening upstairs and smiled. "Yes, sir. That's right."

"I'm darn proud of you, boy. Maybe you're the one we should've sent off to medical school."

"Luke wouldn't like university, Pa," Charity said seriously. "He likes the open land and the cattle too much. Isn't that right, Luke?"

He nodded. "That's so. Doctoring wouldn't be for me. One baby in a lifetime is enough—unless it's a foal or calf, of course."

His father guffawed, slapping him on the back.

His mother glided gracefully down the stairs, smiling and humming. As a boy, Luke had always been amazed at how she did that, as if walking on air. "Faith's settled in real nice," she announced, and picked up her teacup.

"Claire, should I take her up a glass of water?" Rachel asked. "I'm always thirsty when I nurse."

"Very thoughtful, Rachel."

Rachel went into the kitchen, and then returned with a glass of water. She cumbersomely climbed the stairs, and

Luke watched her turn the corner at the top and disappear down the hall.

"I wonder where Amy got off to?" Mrs. McCutcheon said. "That girl worries me so."

Mark, who'd been quiet up until now, spoke. "You don't need to worry over her, Ma. You always seem to forget she's a grown woman."

"Hush now. 'Pride only breeds quarrels, but wisdom is found in those who take advice,'" she pronounced. "I can worry if I want. And you should, too. Mark, I'm surprised at you!" she scolded softly.

Esperanza poked her head around the kitchen door. "Supper will be ready shortly, senora."

"Fine," Flood responded, standing.

"Boys, round up the little ones and get their faces and hands washed up," Mrs. McCutcheon said. "Charity, you run off and find Amy and tell her supper will be served soon."

The men stood. Charity and Mrs. McCutcheon disappeared into the kitchen, Flood and Mark into the dining room.

Matt stepped to the door. "Billy, Adam, Colton!" he called. When there was no answer he said to Luke, "I'll be right back. Maybe they went farther than the barn."

Luke was left sitting by the fire all alone. His gaze strayed to the staircase and lingered. His homecomings had always been happy. He usually looked forward to a wonderful meal prepared by Esperanza, a little scripture quoted by his mother, and then a good night's sleep in his bed, which was much softer than a bedroll. Why, then, did it feel so strange this time?

Because his priorities had changed. Forget food. All he wanted was to bound up those stairs, like he'd done a thousand times when he was a boy, and find Faith.

Chapter Nineteen

THE seclusion in the bedroom was heavenly after the bois-
terous gathering downstairs. Faith wasn't used to such large
crowds, and she reclined contentedly on the bed, wishing she
could sink down into the coverlet and sleep for a month.

At the unexpected tap on the door, Faith's heart jumped.
"Come in," she called out, silently chastising her skittish behavior.

Rachel entered, carrying a glass of water. She offered it. "I
thought you might be thirsty."

"Thank you. I am." Faith took the glass and drank. The
cool water was refreshing.

"She's such a cute little thing," Rachel remarked as she
watched the baby nurse. "My boys were much bigger when they
were born. *McCutcheons*," she added with an affectionate
smile. "She's just so small and feminine, I can't get over it."

Faith snuggled Dawn closer, giving the woman a smile.
"She surprised me by being a couple of weeks early. Sometimes
I can't believe how tiny she is myself." The infant wrapped her
miniature little hand around a finger Faith held out.

"Do you mind if I sit?" Rachel asked, rubbing her large
belly and gesturing to the side of the bed.

"Oh, p-please do," Faith stammered, embarrassed by her
lack of manners.

"Thank you. It's just that I get out of breath easily these
days, and that tall flight of stairs is no help."

Faith modestly switched Dawn to her other breast and
relaxed back against her pillows as Rachel sat. "Are you due
soon?"

"A couple of weeks, I think. I'm hoping for a girl this time."

"That would be nice, especially since you already have the two boys," Faith surmised, helping Dawn find her nipple. The baby had hiccuped and lost it, rooted around, working herself up into a cry.

Rachel laughed. "That's so irritating."

"Oh, I agree." Faith glanced up. The other woman seemed about the same age as herself, maybe a couple of years older. How lucky she was to be part of such a wonderful family as the McCutcheons.

"This is a beautiful room," she remarked, looking around.

"Yes," Rachel agreed. "It's something, isn't it?"

Faith couldn't contain her curiosity any longer. "Do you live here?"

"Not since Billy was born. When I first got in the family way, Matt and his father started our house over yonder. It's not far off, and it gives us a little privacy."

"How wonderful."

"Yes, it is. Mark and Amy have a house, too. This is Matt's old room.

Faith nodded. "Where does Luke live?"

Rachel reached out and brushed her fingers across Dawn's downy soft hair. The baby stopped sucking for a moment as if wondering what the sensation she was feeling was. Rachel giggled. "Being a bachelor, he's still here in the main house, but he's been talking lately about building a home of his own." The woman laughed, her eyes twinkling. "His mother says he has to get married first. That's the tradition. This family is big on tradition. She says that if she didn't hold it over their heads, they might stay single, never giving her any grandchildren."

At another light tap on the door, Rachel called, "Yes?"

Esperanza was outside. "Supper is ready."

"Oh, thank you," Rachel replied, standing. "I'm so hungry I think I could eat a bear." She looked at Faith. "Do you need any help?"

Faith shook her head. "No, thanks. I'll be right along as

soon as Dawn falls asleep. You go on ahead now before it gets cold." She looked down at Dawn and again a warm sweetness filled her. "It won't be long. Her eyelids are already drooping."

At the door, Rachel turned. "Faith, I'm so glad we had this opportunity to talk. And I hope you'll still be here when my baby is born." She ran her hand down her belly again and walked back, a worried expression marring her brow. "Amy lost her child, so I try not to talk too much about it in front of her. Hers would have been born a few months after Matthew's and mine. I still think it makes her feel real bad."

"Thank you for telling me," Faith whispered, and vowed to be careful around Mark's wife.

By the time Dawn fell asleep and Faith made it down to the dining room, everyone was seated and passing around soup bowls. Mrs. McCutcheon filled them from a large cast-iron kettle and passed them back.

"Faith, dear. We're glad you made it," she called, and gestured to a seat next to Luke.

Colton was perched next to Billy and Adam at the long table, his face moist and shiny from washing and his hair slicked back. Faith smiled at him.

"Don't be worrying about your boy," Matt threw out. "He had my sons treed in his wagon."

Everyone chuckled, but Faith didn't see what was so amusing. For the last year Colton had developed a pattern of fighting, even taking on boys twice his size. She didn't want anyone to get hurt.

"Colton, you mind your manners," she scolded.

"I am, Ma," he answered. His gaze slid to Luke and then dropped to his bowl.

"The soup smells wonderful, Esperanza," Mrs. McCutcheon called out. "Creamed corn. The boys' favorite."

"I keep reminding Claire that they aren't boys any longer. They're men. She can't seem to remember," Flood apologized, looking at Faith, then at each of his sons.

"They will always be my boys, even when they're sixty-four and I'm a little old lady," she retorted, obviously happy everyone was home. She gave Flood a brilliant smile.

Again, Faith couldn't help feeling a trifle envious. She wondered if any of them realized just how fortunate they were. Ashamed for such thoughts, she picked up her soup spoon.

"Uncle Luke," Adam spoke up, interrupting Luke's meal. "Did you bring me home a horse like you promised?"

"I have one in mind," Luke fibbed. The horse he'd given to Colton was the one he'd actually picked out. Faith's boy had desperately needed something to make him feel a part of things. Like he belonged. Firefly had filled the ticket perfectly. But now he'd have to see what he could do about rustling up another old, gentle horse. Fast.

Charity eyed Colton with an inquisitive expression. "How long have you been riding?" she asked.

The whole table looked interested, and Colton's hand wobbled. Some soup splashed from his spoon onto the tablecloth. He gulped once and looked around, serious and wide-eyed. "'Bout a few days . . . I guess," he muttered.

"Hm," Charity replied, playing with her food. "Where'd you get your horse?"

"From me," Luke answered, giving Charity a look.

Adam's face clouded over, and Luke was afraid his young nephew might start to cry. He'd been promising to find him a suitable horse for the last few months.

Mark jumped in at Adam's look of disappointment. "I have my eye on a little painted gelding I saw in the remuda, Adam. He looks to be just about your size. We'll try him out tomorrow."

Luke wondered at his sister's attitude. He'd never really seen her be openly rude or hurtful to anyone before, not even the lovesick cowhands who worked around the barn. Was her question to Colton meant to stir the pot or cause friction between the boys? He was surprised.

"Charity." He directed the conversation to her. "What's new with John? Has he written lately?"

Charity's face brightened at the mention of his gregarious little brother. "Yes! I received a letter two days ago. He's having a wonderful time at university. There's just so much to do in Boston, he doesn't have enough time in one day."

"I hope he's concentrating on his studies and not all the ladies in town," Flood tossed in.

"John's a sensible young man, darling," Mrs. McCutcheon said, patting his hand. "No need to worry."

Charity smiled mischievously as she passed the gravy boat. "He said two girls were fighting over him, so he's sparking them both."

"Now, there's a sensible fellow," Flood boomed. "A true McCutcheon."

His wife cleared her throat, clearly embarrassed.

Faith intensely felt Luke's presence. He was so *close*. Every once in while his knee would accidently graze hers—or was he doing that on purpose? His hand, resting on his thigh, was so close she could touch it if she stretched out her pinky.

"Faith?"

His voice snapped her out of her thoughts. She looked at him in question.

"Ma just asked you where you're headed."

"Oh, I'm s-sorry," she stammered, feeling her cheeks burn. "I'm going to live with my Aunt Penelope—" She froze midsentence. Luke, Matt and Mark knew that her aunt was really a cow.

Luke's mother didn't seem to notice that she hadn't finished her sentence. "That's wonderful. Family is so important."

Her creamed corn soup was now as appealing as curdled milk. She couldn't breathe. All she wanted to do was run up to where Dawn was sleeping and close the door.

Glancing up, she caught Charity scrutinizing her. The girl's auburn hair draped her shoulders and elegantly framed her face. With a striking mixture of breeding and beauty, her emerald eyes snapped in challenge as they strayed from her to Luke and back again. The looks were far from kind.

"Mrs. Brown," Luke's sister said, reaching for a basket of bread and taking a slice. "Where's Mr. Brown?"

Faith sat up straighter and wiped her mouth. She returned her napkin to her lap and gathered her thoughts. She was no match for this bright, educated girl; she felt it as sure as the sun rose each morning. But that didn't mean she should let Charity trample her underfoot. When Samuel had taken his fall and died she'd vowed she was done with cowering. "I'm a widow."

"Oh, I'm *sorry*," the girl said. "How long has he been dead?"

"Charity." Luke's tone was irritated. "Faith is tired. It's been a long, hard week traveling with the herd. Why don't you save your questions for later?"

"I don't mind answering, Luke," Faith spoke up. But the piece of bread she'd been eating felt like sandpaper in her mouth. "It's been three months since Samuel's death."

With excellent timing, Dawn chose that moment to wake up. Her cries were clear from the upstairs bedroom. But when Faith started to rise, thankful for the chance to leave, Luke stopped her.

"Stay put and eat. I'll get her."

Chapter Twenty

Luke eyed the baby girl from the bedroom door. Hesitating, he watched as her arms and legs pump wildly in the air as she belted out another wail. The crying seemed much louder up here, and he was amazed again at how much noise this tiny creature could make.

He eased forward and leaned over her. "Shhh, little one,"

he murmured, sitting gingerly on the bed. Her face was scrunched and her eyes tightly closed.

The movement startled the baby and she looked his way. When she saw him, she stopped crying. Relieved, Luke went to pick her up, but instantly she resumed her wails with gusto.

"Hush now, peanut. It's not *that* bad." He carefully positioned her in his arms and tried rocking her as he'd once done with Billy and Adam. She squirmed and howled, so he lifted her to his shoulder and patted her back. She was so tiny. Certainly, though, what she lacked in size she made up in strength.

A loud burp sounded next to Luke's ear. Instantly Dawn calmed and laid her head against his shoulder, exhausted. She gave a little shudder, and he felt her body relax. A fine feeling of satisfaction welled up within him. Tender yet protective, he rubbed her tiny back.

"That's my girl," he said, smiling. "That was one fine belch—one that could rival Smokey's, and you're only eight days old. Just think what you'll be able to do in a few weeks!"

Turning, Luke caught sight of the reflection in the mirror over the chest of drawers. Walking closer, he turned his shoulder so he could see the baby's face, rosy and damp from her strenuous crying. She lay contentedly now, as her moist eyes roamed. Her hand was nestled next to her face and she sucked on it. She was pure sweetness.

Instantly Luke felt as if he'd just taken both feet of Dusty, the ranch mule, directly in the belly. Faith and Dawn would be leaving soon, whether to Priest's Crossing or back to Nebraska with Ward Brown was yet unclear. Possessiveness inched its way inside him, and giving way to its lure, he tightened his hold on the infant.

"Maybe your ma is about ready to do some talking," he said, running his hand across the baby's velvety hair. He swung her around so he could kiss her cheek, but with a jerk her little wet fist came up and bopped him in the eye. Chuckling, he shook his head. "What do you say, princess?"

He returned to the table with the baby nestled in the crook of his arm and sat. Picking up his fork, he stabbed a piece of beef and glanced around the table. The clatter of utensils on food platters ceased. Everyone was looking at him: his mother warmly, Charity surprised, and Faith . . . well, her look of longing tore at his heart. He forced himself to eat and ignore their looks.

After supper, Matt and Rachel disappeared almost immediately, leaving Billy and Adam in the big house to keep Colton company. Esperanza went about cleaning up, and everyone else retired to the parlor. The ladies took in cups of tea, while the men imbibed something a bit stronger.

"This man, Brown, the one who helped pull Mark from the river and was hurt. Who is he?" Flood asked from his big leather chair. He took a cigar from his pocket and clipped the end. Rolling it in his fingers, he eyed Luke.

Glancing at Faith, Luke sipped his brandy, taking pleasure as the warm liquor slid down his throat. "Ward. He's a farmer I met in Pine Grove, and since I fired Earl, I hired him on until we reached the ranch."

Flood's eyebrows arched up in surprise. "Earl? Why?"

"A number of reasons, the main being he was caught cheating in a game of poker the night in Pine Grove." Luke thought about Ward. The man had stepped up and risked his life today in the river. Being a stranger no one would've expected it of him. Was he really as dangerous as Faith claimed?

Flood nodded his approval. "You did right, Son. If a man will cheat his friends, he'll cheat anyone. How badly was the new man hurt?"

"His leg was bruised and he has several lacerations," Luke answered. "Not too bad."

"It was just meant to be," Claire spoke up. "I hate to think of what might have happened if he hadn't been there. Mark wasn't the only one in danger. Luke, you could have drowned, too!"

"Not likely," Luke answered gruffly. He tossed back the contents of his glass and strode into the dining room for a refill from a crystal decanter atop a large dark maple side table.

"Might he be looking for steady work, now that he's here?" Flood called out. "We can always use a good hand after his leg heals."

Faith was sitting between Charity and Luke's ma. She looked pale and tired, and a bit edgy. The baby was fussing, and she had her hands full trying to keep her quiet.

"No. He's anxious to get home," Luke answered.

"Well, before he leaves, you be sure to bring him up to the house. I want to thank him personally for what he did," his mother added.

"I want to thank him, too." Charity looked up from her knitting. "Is he handsome?"

Mark, who'd been dozing by the fire, stretched and yawned. "He's too old for you, Char."

"I'm the same age as Mother was when she first met Pa," Charity protested. "How old were you when you got married, Faith?"

Faith lifted Dawn up to her shoulder, patting the child's back in a rat-a-tat-tat rhythm. Luke wondered at the briskness of it, but the baby seemed pleased. Remembering Faith's outburst when he'd questioned her about Penelope the cow, he bit the inside of his cheek and tried not to laugh. Charity better watch her p's and q's if she was going to dig for information.

"About a year ago when I was twenty-two," Faith said.

Luke tried to keep the surprise from showing on his face. Why, he'd guessed she was about that age now. Colton was eight. That would mean she'd had him when she was somewhere around fourteen. That was awfully young. Or . . . had she been married to somebody before Samuel Brown?

Charity's eyes went wide. "Ol— *Oh?*" she corrected.

"Charity," Mrs. McCutcheon said with a sigh. "It's getting late. Please round up the boys and put them to bed in Mark's old room. I want their parents to have a little privacy tonight. Colton can sleep in there with them . . . if that's all right with you, Faith?"

Faith nodded.

"Yes, Mother," Charity said, standing. "Luke, don't you dare run off before I get back. I want a chance to talk."

"Where would I run off to?"

She shrugged. "You always seem to find somewhere," she tossed back as she flounced dramatically off into the kitchen.

"Faith, dear," Mrs. McCutcheon said kindly. "Please forgive Charity. She's very spirited."

"Spirited?" Mark rolled his eyes. "She's downright spoiled. And she's getting worse every day. Somebody needs to take her in hand." He stood and looked to Amy. "I'm tired. What do you say about calling it a night?"

His wife nodded and stood, waiting for Mark to get his hat.

"I think that's a good idea," Flood agreed. "Everyone here looks exhausted."

Luke's mother stood and set her teacup on the tray. "Come along, Faith. I'll get you settled better upstairs."

"Please, I don't want to be any trouble. I was intending on sleeping in my wagon!"

"Nonsense. I love guests, the more the merrier," the older woman answered as she led the way. "It reminds me of when all the boys were still living in the house. It was in such uproar all the time."

Faith disappeared up the stairs, and Luke fought disappointment. He'd hardly had the chance to say more than two words to her since their arrival. Shoving those feelings aside, he went back into the dining room and refilled his glass. He took the liquor in one swallow. He repeated the process. Pouring one last belt for good measure, he took it back to the fire to enjoy slowly as he nursed his unsettling feelings.

He wasn't feeling sorry for himself, exactly, it was just that he'd always been different. Never quite fit in with everyone else. Flood loved him like he were his own; Luke knew and appreciated that. It was his own stubbornness that made it tough to get past their differences.

He wasn't ashamed of his heritage; he just didn't like being different from the rest of his family. Some of the finest men he knew were Indians, and he'd even toyed with the idea of finding his real father one day. But his responsibilities didn't leave much time for anything else besides the ranch.

Bringing the heavy crystal tumbler to his lips, he let more smooth liquor slip down his throat. It pooled like fire in his stomach. Laying his head back against the chair, he closed his eyes and enjoyed the solitude of the empty room.

Faith needed to level with him. He wanted the truth. He couldn't let her go off without knowing she and her children would be safe. This fright of hers, of her brother-in-law— could it possibly be made up? Ward seemed like a pretty decent man. He hadn't done anything blatantly wrong. Hell, he'd even helped save Mark's life. He could see his sister doing something like this to get her way. Was Faith so different?

His head nodded wearily, then slowly lowered until his chin rested on his chest.

The clock chimed before Luke next opened his eyes. Rubbing the stiffness in his neck, he stretched his cramped legs. How long had he been sitting here? The fire had burned down to nothing but coals; everyone had gone up to bed and the house was dark.

"Well, Charity never made it back. Does that surprise me?" he mumbled to himself. "May as well turn in."

He banked the fire, stirring the coals and causing sparks to fly about. After everything was secure, he made his way to the stairs and slowly climbed to the top. As he placed his hand on the knob of his door, he looked across the hall. Matt's old room. That's where Faith would be.

Pausing only briefly, he stepped across the hallway and knocked.

Faith sat up in bed and pushed the hair from her eyes, wondering what it was that had awakened her. When the knocking came again she grabbed the wrapper Mrs. McCutcheon had lent her and quickly put it on. She sneaked quietly past the cradle where Dawn slept to the door. "Who's there?" she whispered.

"It's me, Luke." There was a huskiness in his voice that Faith had not heard before.

"What do you want?" she responded.

"Come out here so we can talk."

"No, Luke. Your sister and parents are just down the hall." She thought about her and Luke in the moonlight and was tempted to turn the knob. "Go to bed. We'll talk in the morning."

"It'll only take a minute."

His voice was a little louder, and Faith feared he would wake the baby and the whole house. Cracking the door open, she peeked out. The unmistakable sweet scent of alcohol wafted off Luke, setting off warning bells in her head. Samuel had been mean when he was drunk, and she didn't want to see how Luke might change.

"If you're not coming out, I'll just have to come in." He pushed open the door easily, even as she strained to stop him. He closed it behind him.

Faith reached for the knob to let him right out again, when he took her wrist and stopped her. She glared into his face.

"You look mad."

"I am!" she whispered. "What if your mother hears us and gets up to check? What will she think?"

"I don't know. Maybe that I wanted to talk and came and woke you up." He led her over to the window.

"Luke," she protested, "you've been drinking."

"A little. But I'm far from drunk."

"What do you want to talk about that can't wait until morning?" she asked, still hopeful he might leave sooner rather than later. "Besides, we can't seem to have a conversation anymore without it turning into an argument."

"You know? At this moment I can't rightly remember." He chuckled as he played with a strand of her hair. "Give me a minute."

A few seconds ticked by and Luke still didn't say anything. He just stood there staring at her. Making her feel intensely . . . what? Uncomfortable? No. Definitely not uncomfortable. Something very different.

A sudden desire to be nearer Luke surprised her. She stepped closer and saw the surprise in his eyes and the corners of his mouth curve up. Studying his lips, she realized she wanted to kiss them.

"Luke?" she whispered, nudging in closer.

Dawn picked that moment to start fussing. Disappointment bloomed. But as Faith started to go, Luke caught her arm and brought his face to hers.

Chapter Twenty-one

THEIR lips touched. At first it was as soft as a breeze, and Faith just stood there waiting for more. His lips were warm and a bit dry. She relaxed, letting him gather her closer. The kiss changed, then, deepened. She tasted the rich flavor of the brandy he'd been drinking. It was good. She shivered.

He seemed to be in no hurry, so Faith took charge. She kissed him back. She pressed gently forward, smiling at the happiness it brought. Kissing him was pure joy.

He pulled back and looked at her. "What?"

"Nothing," she whispered, fearful he'd stop kissing her and start talking.

"There's *something*," he said, not taking his mouth far from hers. "You're laughing."

Not laughing, smiling. Kissing you makes me happy. Unable to stop herself, she pressed her body to his.

There was a light tapping on the door. "Faith, dear," Mrs. McCutcheon called. "Is everything all right?" She tapped again. "Dawn's crying."

Faith pulled back, the magic spell broken. For one brief moment she stood staring at Luke, liking very much the way his gaze made her feel; then she called back, "Yes, Mrs. McCutcheon, everything's fine."

She scooted over to the cradle and picked up the baby. As quickly as she could, she went to the door and opened it. Luke ducked to the other side of the room where his mother couldn't see him.

Mrs. McCutcheon's hair was down around her shoulders, and concern filled her eyes. "I'm sorry to have disturbed you, ma'am," Faith said. "I'll try to keep Dawn quieter."

"Oh, I don't mind her crying, Faith. We're used to that. I just got a little worried when she didn't stop."

"She's fine now," Faith promised, still rattled. The fact that Luke stood just inches away didn't help matters. "I just need to change her diaper and feed her. I guess she's hungry already."

"Good night then. If you need anything at all, just call me. I'm a light sleeper."

"Thank you," Faith replied.

She closed the door and turned back to Luke. She was shivering again. Was she cold, or was it her reaction to him? He looked uncertain. She felt the same.

She laid Dawn on her bed and swiftly unhooked the safety pins that held the child's soggy diaper. Her hands moved confidently; she was getting better at it. But with the diaper off,

Dawn began kicking. Each time Faith tried to fasten a new one, the baby pumped her legs happily, partial to the freedom of a naked body.

Faith finally got a new diaper secure, but when she tried to lay her back in her bed, the child started to cry. She said to Luke, "I didn't think she'd go back to sleep on her own. I'll need to feed." She avoided his gaze.

"Right. Feed her."

He headed for the door. Faith couldn't help but feel she'd lost something.

Chapter Twenty-two

LUKE, you up there?" a voice shouted, waking Dawn and making her cry.

Faith hurried to her child's side and picked her up. Opening the door to the hall, she looked to see what was going on. Heavy steps sounded, and before she could get the door closed, Matt rounded the corner.

"Oops. Sorry about that, Faith. I forgot you were up here," he said as he looked apologetically toward the crying baby.

"That's all right. Is something wrong?"

"Just looking for Luke. Have you seen him this morning?"

"No, I haven't yet," she answered. Heat rushed to her cheeks thinking of last night.

Matt rapped hard on Luke's bedroom door and then opened it. The big bed stood vacant, atop a brown and white hide rug. A brown and blue quilt was flung haphazardly at the foot, crumpled and forgotten. Soft morning light penetrated the windowpane, making the stark white sheets glow. It looked inviting.

Luke's brother turned to leave. "Didn't think he'd still be

asleep. Sorry again about waking Dawn." He reached over and rubbed the crown of Dawn's fuzzy golden head, something that everyone seemed called to do. The caress did little to ease the babe's crying.

Faith rocked her as Matt walked back down the hallway. "Shh," she said. "You'll be fine once you have a little something warm in that tummy of yours. It's time for your breakfast."

She placed the baby on the bed and changed Dawn's wet diaper. A sweet melancholy crept into her heart as she settled in to nurse. She wished her own mother were here. Faith only had one memory of her, and she kept it safely tucked away inside. Like a well-loved picture book, she took it out every so often when she was feeling sad or lonely: They were making gingerbread in the dingy, run-down kitchen on the farm. Her mother was happy and humming a song, the tune of which Faith had been too young to remember. She stood on a chair watching her mother stir with a big wooden spoon, the tangy smell of ginger all around. Her mother smiled and handed Faith a spoon covered in sticky batter.

"Wake up," Faith said quietly, jiggling Dawn, who was trying to fall asleep. "You have to finish your breakfast."

One memory. That was all she had of her mother. Soon afterward she'd died, leaving Faith alone to work with her father on their dilapidated farm, going to school when time allowed and trying to avoid his angry outbursts.

Time passed, of course, as it always does. Life got a little easier when Toby the farm hand came to stay. This had allowed Faith to slip into town from time to time, for church or the occasional social activity. That's where she'd met Beatrice. The day Bea died, Faith had brought her crying son home, as promised, little believing the boy's father would ever return. How wrong she'd been.

Samuel showed up on her doorstep two years later. He'd said that he'd gotten a head injury and just recently gotten his

memory back. Of course, he came straight away, worried
about Beatrice and Colton. What hogwash! He said that
when he found his wife dead he started looking for his son
and found him with Faith. After that he started coming out
every week on Sunday. He'd been so sweet then, and funny,
too. He could make her laugh at just about anything. Every
once in a while, when her father wasn't around, he'd tell Faith
how pretty she was. It seemed like a dream come true when
he asked her to marry him. Not only would he be her husband but Colton would also have his father back. It seemed
perfect, a match made in heaven.

Heaven lasted about two months. Samuel returned alone
from the field at suppertime with the news that her father was
dead; he'd had an accident with the plow, and Samuel wasn't
able to save him. She'd turned to Samuel for comfort and
found only coldness. Soon afterward, his behavior changed so
drastically that even Toby ran off.

So deep was she in reflection, Faith didn't feel her tears
until one landed with a plop on Dawn's forehead. The baby
jumped, and her startled blue eyes gazed up. Faith kissed her
baby's cheek and wiped the wetness away.

It didn't matter, Faith told herself. None of the past mattered. Only Colton and Dawn were important now. Only
them. Samuel had pretended everything just to get her to
marry him, to get her father's lousy, run-down, rickety old
farm. She'd tried at the time not to believe it, but it had to be
so. He'd become even more of a monster when he learned the
farm and land were willed to her with the clear stipulation it
was never to be jointly held with a husband.

Now that Dawn was fed, Faith shoved her hurtful memories aside. She couldn't wait one more moment for the coffee
she'd smelled all the way up here in her room. The aroma
lured her down the large staircase, into the now-quiet dining
room. One place setting remained on the big table, in the
same spot she'd eaten last night.

"Why, there you are," Mrs. McCutcheon said, coming through the door in a split-skirt riding suit. "How did you sleep?"

"Fine, thank you," Faith replied.

"Good. Esperanza has your breakfast warming in the kitchen. Sit down and I'll tell her you're here."

Faith wasn't comfortable with people waiting on her. She said, "I'll get it. No need to bother her."

"It's no bother for her. Now, you sit down and pour yourself a nice cup of coffee." Luke's mother pulled out her chair. "It's only been a little over a week since you gave birth, and you've been having to survive a cattle drive! I don't know how you did it." She waited expectantly until Faith sat down and then helped her scoot the heavy chair in. "Pampering is exactly what you need." She smiled warmly, rubbing Faith's shoulder. "It's every woman's right."

Mrs. McCutcheon disappeared into the kitchen. Faith had never met a woman like her before. She was so sure of herself and her place in this family. She was confident and so take-charge. Faith could see now how Luke came naturally by such a manner.

When she'd first learned that her baby was a girl she'd been sad. She held Dawn up and placed a kiss on the top of her head. Life for a woman was hard: day after day of exhausting work, followed by abuse at the hand of some man, be it father or husband. And it was lonely, too. At least her life had been like that. But Mrs. McCutcheon was different. She was respected if not revered. And it didn't stop with her. Charity, too, was treated considerately. Not only did her parents love her, but her brothers did as well. That's what Faith wanted for Dawn, a life full of love and respect. Somehow she needed to make sure that Dawn ended up in a family like this.

Faith reached for the china coffeepot and poured a half a cup. Mrs. McCutcheon came back, her boot heels rapping on the hardwood floor. She was followed by Esperanza, who carried a platter of warm food, which she set in front of Faith.

"Thank you," Faith said.

Claire McCutcheon scooped a steaming tortilla filled with eggs, ham and other delights onto Faith's plate. She said, "That aunt of yours won't like it if we send you to her all skin and bones. So, eat up. You need to gain your strength back."

Shame crept into Faith's throat.

Mrs. McCutcheon reached for Dawn. "Give her to me while you eat."

Luke came through the door and went straight for the coffeepot. Filling a cup, he eyed Faith.

"What are your plans for the day, Luke?" his mother asked.

"I need to check progress on the covered bridge across the upper crest. After that, I don't have much on my agenda."

"Why don't you take Faith with you? I'm sure she would like to see the ranch, get a little fresh air. It would do the baby wonders to get out. Would you like that, Faith?"

Not really. Her nerves were far too raw from their encounter last night. The thought of spending hours trapped with Luke was enough to make her want to run and hide. But Luke answered before she could.

"Ma, Dawn's only a handful of days old. Faith can't sit a horse yet."

"Of course not, but she can ride in the buggy easy enough. The seats are plenty cushioned, more so than that wagon she's been crossing the countryside in. The ride would be nice and soft. I know she'd like to go with you. Isn't that right, Faith?"

What could she say? Mrs. McCutcheon might think it odd if she said no. She didn't want to appear ungrateful.

"Yes," she replied, if quietly. "Would you mind keeping an eye on Colton for me while we're gone?"

"Of course, dear, that's not a problem at all." Mrs. McCutcheon smiled at Luke and headed for the kitchen. "But don't run off just yet. I'll have Esperanza fix you a nice supper you can eat when you get there. The scenery is breathtaking."

* * *

Luke stepped closer to Faith. The rosy color of her cheeks pleased him, but he pushed such feelings away. "You sure you want to do this? It could take most of the day. Wouldn't you rather stay here and rest?"

She sounded hesitant but said, "No, I meant it when I said I'd like to go."

He was both pleased and disappointed. He must be plum loco to go off with her, especially after last night. He hadn't been able to get to sleep for hours, and finally, when he did, it was time to get up. Unbelievably he hadn't felt tired, and he'd had to force himself to stay out with the men and not return to the house for any of the several far-fetched reasons he'd dreamed up. "If you're sure, then. Be sure to grab a bonnet, and a shawl in case it turns breezy. The weather up in the high country can change fast."

"All right."

"I'll meet you in about twenty minutes out by the corrals."

Outside, he took a deep breath. Slowly releasing it, he studied the expanse of clear blue sky. He hadn't felt quite like this since he'd had that damnable crush on Martha Tyler his last year of school. How old had he been? Sixteen, maybe. He was a mess for months, always trying to figure out just where he could bump into her. He'd never gotten up the nerve to tell her how he felt. Just being around her was enough to make his stomach go squirrelly. It nearly broke his heart when the Tyler family moved to California, her pa in pursuit of gold.

Last night with Faith in his arms he'd felt the same, that familiar sweet thud of his heart. After ten long years it was back. Thinking again about Martha, he smiled. That infatuation, or crush, or whatever it was, paled in comparison to what he'd felt with Faith in his arms. She felt natural and right, like she'd been there all his life. Like he needed to keep her there for the rest of it.

He didn't know if he should laugh or cry. If he had a lick of sense, he'd run in the other direction as fast as he could.

Faith waited out by the corrals as Luke had asked. She cradled Dawn in one arm; the other held her baby satchel and brown bonnet. An overstuffed hamper of food sat at her feet.

It was quiet, not a man in sight. The bunkhouse, with its long, covered porch and decorated with old branding irons, ropes, bridles and bits, looked a welcome sight for any tired cowboy. Cuddling Dawn closer, Faith smiled at how much Colton must be loving it here.

She approached the corral fence to watch the horses. They were finished eating and now stood in the sunshine, dozing. One noticed her and came up to see if she had anything tasty to offer. The horse was brown with a white blaze running the length of his face. Stretching out his neck, he snuffled at Dawn from behind the fence. When he didn't find anything enticing, his head dropped and he ambled off in disappointment.

"Nice place they got here."

Faith spun at the familiar voice. Ward stood some ten feet behind her, leaning on a makeshift crutch.

Chapter Twenty-three

WARD," Faith whispered, looking to the house in hopes that Mrs. McCutcheon might come out. Her heart racing, she searched the area for Luke. He was nowhere in sight.

Her brother-in-law stepped closer, wincing with pain. "I've been hoping you'd come out. I wanted a chance to talk with you in private."

"We already talked, Ward. I have nothing else to say to you."

"Oh, I think you will when I've said my piece." He smiled that charming smile that so resembled Samuel's. "I want you to quit this foolishness and come home with me. You know it's only a matter of time before you do."

"I know no such thing," Faith threw back. "I'm not tied to you or your father, and I have the right to go anywhere I please."

"Not with my brother's baby at your breast—and Colton, too." He leaned over to peer at Dawn. Faith drew instinctively back, not wanting him to get too close.

His eyes darkened. "Don't make me mad, Faith, or I'll be forced to go to the sheriff and tell him what I know about my brother's death. How we found him in the barn, below the hayloft with his neck broken. Your things were still up there, along with his hat and coat. Then, a day later, you took off without telling anyone you were leaving, not even his dear old pa. Why? I'll tell you! Because you pushed Samuel and murdered him in cold blood! Pa hasn't been the same since seeing him in the straw like that."

Air whooshed from her lungs. "It was an accident." She knew it looked suspicious, like she'd pushed Samuel. "He was mad. He fell."

"Oh, I think little ol' you got tired of being a farmer's wife, bein' that's all you done all your life. You'd planned your escape and did away with poor Samuel. That's how our uncle Judge Winters will see it, too."

She'd been over the scene time and again in her head. Everything pointed to her. Perspiration broke out on Faith's skin. Dawn, picking up on her mother's nervousness, started to fuss.

"I didn't push him." Faith looked to Ward for a sign of understanding.

"Save your tears for the judge," he said. "Just remember,

after you hang for murder, Pa and me will still have little Dawn and Colton back. And don't worry, we'll tell them all about their ma. How she was strung up for killing their pa."

He chuckled, seeming to like how he had her backed into an inescapable corner. "I'm giving you one month, so it don't look too suspicious to the McCutcheons. I don't want any trouble with the likes of this family. You think up a real convincing story. Then tell them you're going home with me. You understand?" he said. "One month. I don't want to have to talk to you again. Is that clear?"

"I didn't push him," she repeated.

Ward snorted. "And just in case you're thinking about talking to anyone, just remember this is a big ranch. All sorts of accidents can happen. Luke's horse could fall and crush him. Or . . ." He paused, thinking. "Or maybe that pretty little sister will take a shine to me. If not, I'm sure a little friendly persuasion, if you catch my meaning, would change her mind." His ugly, high-pitched laughter sounded like the hiss of a snake.

The jangle of wagon wheels startled Faith. She turned to see Luke in the buggy coming around the side of the barn. Glancing back at Ward, she was relieved to see he'd disappeared.

Her emotions in tatters, she gazed down into the face of her child, gathering her thoughts. The idea of her growing up with Ward as her stepfather was unthinkable. Totally unacceptable. She'd do anything to keep Dawn and Colton from that. Which meant only two possibilities existed: she could go willingly with Ward at the end of the month . . . or she could try to outsmart him.

"All set," Luke said as he stopped the buggy next to Faith and hopped down. He hefted the basket of food into the back. "Who does Esperanza think she's feeding, the United States Calvary?"

As if it were the most natural thing in the world for him to do, he gently took the babe from her arms, and held her elbow so she could climb into the buggy and get comfortable. Nonetheless, her mind was fixed on one thing: the noose at the end of a rope.

She'd been in town one day a man hanged for robbing the bank. She hadn't watched, like many of the townsfolk, but as she left the mercantile she saw him, slowly swinging back and forth, the rope creaking loudly. She'd tried to look away, but some morbid curiosity kept her rooted in place, her gaze glued to his face, bloated like the dead frog's Colton had fetched home from the creek one Sunday afternoon. Splotches of purple and gray mottled his skin, and a stench from his messed pants floated over to where she stood.

That image had haunted her for months, popping into her head at the most unsuspecting times. Sometimes it was a man, other times, a giant lifeless frog. She'd learned his name was Frank Beans, and he'd had a wife and children in another town. She'd been glad when the memory finally started fading. But now it was as vivid as if it had happened yesterday. Would she be the one hanging there next?

"Faith, are you all right?" Luke asked. "Are you sure you want to go?"

Pulling herself together, she glanced up. Her heart swelled at the sight of Luke. His brows were arched worriedly over those expressive eyes.

"If you're not feeling up to it . . ."

"No, really, I'm fine. I want to go. I was just thinking about everything I have to get done."

"Everything to get done? Like what?" he asked, humor coloring his voice. He clucked softly to the horse as they turned around, and then he slapped the reins across the animal's back, sending the buggy bouncing down the road. "The only thing you should be thinking about is getting your strength back and gaining a little weight. If the wind starts to blow, I'll have to tie you to your seat with my rope. It wouldn't do to have Colton's ma blow away, never to be seen again. I guess

Esperanza was thinking the same thing when she packed that hamper."

"I'm as strong as I ever was, Luke," she replied.

But Faith couldn't help but be infected by Luke's good mood. She'd never seen him so happy-go-lucky. She intended to enjoy today. She'd take it as a gift. Tomorrow she'd worry about Ward and figure out an escape from this mess. She wasn't going to just lie down like a dead dog. This was her new life, her fresh start, and she wasn't going to give up easily.

Luke returned Faith's smile, then watched the landscape as they moved down the road. This was the land he'd grown up on, the land that he loved. He wondered what Faith thought of it, sitting so quiet holding Dawn as if she were afraid they'd both bounce out with the next bump.

He was trying not to stare, but damn, she was making it hard. Her eyes glowed with pleasure, and the breeze sent strands of hair flying around her face. Every once in a while a little sound of excitement would bubble forth.

He liked making her happy. Liked the way it made him feel inside. Deciding she mustn't have had too many rides in a buggy, he was glad she was enjoying this one.

"Look, Luke!" she exclaimed. She pointed over to a green meadow where a large stream gushed. Two men were clearing broken branches and small logs away from a clogged bottleneck, dragging them over to a pile to be burned. They'd removed their heavy work shirts and were dressed in only their undershirts, taking advantage of the sunshine and warm breeze. Their brightly colored bandannas stood out against the wide blue sky. Two horses grazed nearby.

"It's Smokey and Chance," Luke said.

"What are they doing?"

"Clearing out the water hole. Looks like a beaver is trying to set up house."

Hearing the clippity-clop of their approaching horse, the

men stopped work and turned. They waved as the buggy neared. Chance cupped his hands around his mouth and shouted loud and clear, "Hello, Miss Faith!"

Smokey smacked him on the arm and, laughing good-naturedly, pointed at the water hole as if chastising him.

Luke's smile faded. "Looks like Chance is still sweet on you."

"Chance? Sweet on me? That's silly."

She said the words as if she meant them, but Luke watched the small smile that curved her lips. She had to know Chance would swim the Mississippi for her, just like the rest of the men in this outfit.

"So, how come you were married a year and yet you have an eight-year-old son? Takes some fancy math to make that add up." There, that got her attention. She'd lingered long enough on Chance and Smokey.

She looked like she was about to answer when the buggy bounced in a hole, waking Dawn. The baby started crying, and nothing Faith did soothed her. Looking over to Luke, she shrugged. "Would you mind terribly if we stopped for a few minutes? So I could have a little privacy to . . ."

"Feed her," Luke finished. He tipped his hat up with his thumb and leaned close, inspecting the baby. "Sure does eat a lot." He grinned.

Chapter Twenty-four

HIS joke was a success.

"Eat a lot?" Faith smiled in return. "Yes, her tummy is so small, it doesn't take long to empty out. When she gets going like this it's the only thing that will calm her down. I'm sorry."

Luke shook his head. "Nothing to be sorry for. But don't

think I haven't forgotten the question you haven't answered. Whoa, Buttercup!"

Faith gave him an amused look. Luke assumed it was because of the name.

"He was Charity's first horse," he explained, stopping the buggy under a large stand of birch trees. The leaves rustled in the breeze and the grass looked inviting. "This spot all right?"

"It looks fine," she said, as she rocked the crying infant. She waited for Luke to set the brake, then come around to help her down.

"What do you need?" Luke asked. "I'll get it for you."

"The small blanket in my satchel and one of the soft cloths, please."

Luke set out looking through her bag, which was stuffed full with everything one might need for five infants, including a couple of clean and neatly folded gowns. The lot smelled of talcum, making his nose itch. But, it also brought a sweet tenderness to his throat. He felt like Dawn's father.

Finding the things Faith asked for, he went looking for her. She was sitting on the ground next to one of the larger trees, her back resting against it. Dawn was still crying, her face scrunched and red. The area was secluded, and Faith would have her privacy.

"Here's your blanket." He handed it over and watched her settle Dawn onto her lap. Her fingers went to the buttons on her dress but stopped. She looked at him.

"I'll just be over here relaxing," he said.

He sighed as he lowered his body onto the grass. Lacing his fingers behind his head, he used them for a pillow. It had been a long drive, and being off the back of a horse and stretched out on the ground felt good. The fragrant soil and grass molded to his body and a bee droned somewhere close by. The warmth of the sunshine made him drowsy, and without warning his eyelids felt as heavy as anvils. Faith's melodic humming reached him, bringing a smile to his face and vivid memories of her last night to his mind.

Time passed. How long did it take a baby to eat? Twenty minutes had come and gone, maybe more. Luke sat up, looked over to the buggy. Buttercup stood patiently in his harness, hind foot cocked, taking pleasure in the sunshine warming his coat. There was no sign of Faith.

Luke got up, meandered over to Buttercup and scratched the horse's neck. After checking each of the old-timer's hooves, more to kill time than look for stones, and also inspecting the harness leather, Luke began to get impatient. He didn't remember it taking Rachel this long to feed. It couldn't hurt to go check on them. If she got angry, so be it.

He walked quietly to the secluded area where he'd left them. Was Faith asleep? Inching his way forward, he peeked around the tree trunk.

Faith's head leaned against the bark of the birch, her eyes closed. Angelically serene, her face all but glowed. Dawn was cradled to her firm young breast, sleeping peacefully.

It was a beautiful sight. He was moved by its naturalness, its goodness, its sweetness. His girls.

She shifted. He withdrew and held his breath. He heard her move; she must be buttoning her dress.

Not wanting to get caught with his hand in the cookie jar, he contemplated sneaking back to the buggy. But, that seemed dishonest. This had been was a truthful mistake. It was quiet for too long, and he'd come to check. He should just tell her the truth.

The baby fussed. "Shhh, baby. Stay asleep," he heard Faith whisper.

"You about ready to go?" he asked.

She stuck her head around the tree, surprised. "Yes. I'm sorry it took us so long. I guess I fell asleep, too."

"Reckon you needed it," Luke replied.

Back in the buggy, he had a hard time keeping his mind on the road. She'd looked so beautiful. "She's settled then?"

"Yes. She should sleep for some time now."

"Will our talkin' wake her?"

"I don't think so," Faith answered, glancing down at her sleeping daughter. He almost shared the love she emanated.

"Good. Now tell me about Colton."

She looked over at him, her eyes challenging. "Why are you so interested in him? What's the difference?"

Damn, if she didn't make him feel foolish. "Just wondered, after you announced last night about being married only a year. Colton's eight years old. It just got me curious, that's all."

"He's Samuel's son. His mother was a good friend of mine. We were close, like sisters. When she got sick I said I'd take him if she died. Samuel had gone off and she didn't think he was ever coming back."

"You're telling me that Dawn here is your first?"

"That's exactly what I'm telling you."

Luke pulled on the reins, slowing Buttercup to a walk. The road had become a steady uphill climb, and the old horse was breathing hard. He needed a chance to catch his breath.

"I'm glad I didn't know that when I found you in the wagon. One of the things that kept me steady after Colton banged me on the head was—"

Faith stifled a giggle.

"I could have been seriously hurt!" he scolded, but his lips drew up in the corners. He reached up and felt the bump. "Still hurts."

"I'm sorry. Go on."

"—Was the fact that I knew second deliveries were usually easier. And shorter." He chuckled. "I was gratified at least one of us had some experience."

"No. I had no more experience at birthing than you. I was very thankful you decided to stay."

"Were you?" He glanced at her. He remembered how frightened she'd looked when he first found her crouched in the corner of her wagon, eyes like a scared rabbit.

"It was awful when our horses ran off," she murmured. "The wind was blowing and my pains were getting stronger, faster . . . I was fearful we'd never find our way back to the road. Or, that I would die and leave Colton out there alone. Or, something horrible would happen to the baby. I was very frightened."

"I know. I was, too." He wanted to ask her about Samuel. How they'd come to be married. Were they in love, or was it only for the boy? And where did Ward fit in this puzzle, if at all? The need to know only grew stronger.

"And Ward, what's his story?"

Her face looked stricken. Sorry for ruining the mood, Luke changed the subject. "We're almost there. You getting hungry?"

"I'm famished. It must be this high mountain air."

"That it is. I'm thankful now Esperanza overpacked the hamper. I'm starved, too."

Faith smelled the river before she saw it: sandy loam and the tang of fish. It gushed down through the trees and into the meadow, sending sprays of water shooting high into the air wherever it collided with a boulder. The stretch of frothy white rapids was so loud Luke had to shout to be heard.

The temperature cooled considerably, so Faith retrieved Dawn's blanket and securely bundled it around her daughter.

"Look, there it is," Luke shouted, pointing at a skeletal structure extending across the river. The bridge was three-fourths finished, with three men working on it.

One man hung freely from the side, suspended by two thick ropes. His feet were propped on the edge of the bridge as he pounded large bolts with a heavy hammer. The sight of him sent shivers crawling up Faith's neck. Heights terrified her, and the thought of him suspended like that made her insides quake.

The men turned and waved as she and Luke approached.

"Hey, Joe, the bridge is looking good!" Luke called.

"Luke, good to see you! How was the cattle drive?"

"They're a fine lot. Good and healthy. I have the five head you asked me for. Come down from up there so we can talk."

The man scaled up to the top of the tall bridge. He disappeared for a few minutes and then reappeared at the end closest to them.

"Why are you building a bridge way out here in the middle of nowhere?" Faith asked as Luke put hobbles on Buttercup.

"To save time. This river runs down the middle of the ranch, separating two important pastures. The river here is too deep for crossing. Right now we have to drive our cattle a day south, cross where the river is shallow, then take another day driving north again. This will be a lot quicker. And safer."

The memory of Mark bobbing down the river was still vivid. "Good idea."

By now the man who had been hanging on the side of the bridge was almost to where they waited. He slung sturdy arms around Luke and pounded him on the back. "How are you, boy? It's damn good to see you!"

Luke smiled when he could free himself from the man's grasp and turned to face Faith. "Faith, this is Joe Brunn. He's head foreman on the bridge job and a close friend of the family. Joe, this is Faith Brown. She's staying with us for a while."

"I'm pleased to make the acquaintance of such a beautiful guest of the McCutcheons," Joe said.

"Thank you," Faith responded. The man wasn't much taller than she was, and looked older than Luke by about ten years. He was broad-shouldered and appeared very strong. Shoulder-length dark hair was pulled back and tied behind his neck in a leather thong.

Eyes the color of the sky considered her. "And just who is

this wee little bundle you're holding? Her face is as sweet as any little fairy!"

Faith laughed. She couldn't help but like this outgoing, happy fellow. "This is Dawn."

"Have you eaten your supper?" Luke asked. "We've brought enough to feed us and the three of you."

"Oh, that Esperanza is a woman after my own heart. If she didn't only have eyes for that cocksure rooster, Roady, I'd be down at that kitchen door making a pest of myself every day. When I think about what I'd like to—"

"If you stay at the ranch long enough, Faith, you'll get used to the way men around here talk," Luke interrupted. "Mostly they speak first and think later."

"I'm sorry, miss," Joe offered. "I was just going to say she's as lovely a woman as I've ever seen."

Faith smiled. "No offense taken, Mr. Brunn. None at all." To change the subject she added, "I just can't get over how pretty it is out here." She looked around while Luke fetched the hamper to a sunny spot on the riverbank. He then shook out the blanket they had brought with them in the buggy.

Luke's mother hadn't been wrong when she said the scenery was breathtaking. The butte overlooked a huge grass-blanketed valley that was sprinkled with beautiful summer flowers of pinks, purple and white. Faith recognized columbine and lupine mixed in with an array of others.

Turning, she contemplated Luke. What did he think of her after the way she'd kissed him last night? Something had taken control of her, something she never knew existed. How wonderful she'd felt in his arms. She wished she were there right now. "Supper is served," Luke called. He gestured for her to sit, and then he and Joe found a spot on the blanket. Faith laid down Dawn, covering her.

"What about Job and Pete? You want to call them over, too?" Luke asked Joe.

"They're finishing up on the sanding. They can eat when they're done."

Luke pulled out cold roast beef and bread and handed it to Faith. She took a portion and set it in her napkin before passing the rest to Joe.

"Thanks." He grinned. "How long are you visiting the Heart of the Mountains?"

Mrs. McCutcheon had said she could stay until she felt strong enough to travel. She glanced at Luke. "For a week or two. I'm gaining back my strength. Then I'll be going on to Priest's Crossing." Out of the corner of her eye she saw Luke smile.

"Priest's Crossing? Why, my sister lives there. Do you have family there, too?" His eyes lit with interest, his food all but forgotten.

"No. But I plan on settling there and finding a job."

Clearly surprised, Joe glanced at Luke.

Luke shrugged. "I keep trying to tell her how hard it is for a woman to take care of herself and young'uns. She's stubborn. Won't listen."

"Well, it's a hard row to hoe, but it ain't impossible. My sister, Christine Meeks, raised a family of four all on her own. She never married again after William died. As a matter of fact, her youngest daughter, the one who helps her in the store, just got married. Christine may need some help." He gave Faith a broad smile. "I could ask her if you'd like."

Faith clapped her hand to her chest in excitement. "Would you?" she asked eagerly. "What kind of a store is it?"

"Just your regular mercantile. Has a little of everything. She also sells baked goods that the women bring in."

"I'm a hard worker, Mr. Brunn. I'll do anything your sister needs me to do. If she gives me a chance I won't let her down." A job in a mercantile would be an answer to her prayer! But, she had to keep herself from getting too excited because there was still Ward, and the hanging, she had to work through.

Luke took a bite of his beef and chewed slowly. He didn't like the way Joe was looking at Faith as if she were a delectable piece of chocolate cake. Joe was a longtime friend of Flood's. He'd come West with him as a young tagalong with nothing better to do than see what was over the next horizon. He'd settled close and been a part of the ranch on and off for as long as Luke could remember. Flood thought the world of Joe, who'd been like an uncle to the boys and Charity. He'd married as a young man but his wife had died in childbirth. He'd never taken another.

"I'm not planning to go to Priest's Crossing until the bridge is complete," Joe said.

"How long will that be, Mr. Brunn?"

"Three weeks, if they don't run into any problems," Luke answered.

Faith looked awfully excited about the prospect of a job. But, she would. What other alternatives did she have to going home with Ward? Only two: find work or find herself a husband.

"Two," Joe corrected. "I can't see it taking us longer than twelve to fourteen days to finish up."

Luke mentally shook himself. "Possibly. But we don't want you rushing. This is dangerous work, and we don't want anyone getting hurt or killed."

"Is Luke worried about little ol' me?" Joe flashed Faith a confident grin. "I don't think so. More likely he don't want me taking you off to Priest's Crossing before he's good and ready for you to go."

Luke didn't respond to that.

After the meal Luke inspected the bridge, and Joe pointed out all the progress that had been made since Flood's last visit. Saying good-bye, Luke and Faith both promised to return in the coming week, and then he turned Buttercup toward home.

Faith sat quietly thinking over the possibilities that had been presented to her that afternoon. If only Ward hadn't found her and the children; she'd be free to move to Priest's Crossing and work for Mr. Brunn's sister—provided that the woman liked her. But if she had the chance to work, she'd make sure she was liked. She'd be the hardest worker there ever was.

An overwhelming despair threatened to swamp her. Who was she fooling? Ward would never give up in his efforts to take her home. He and his father wanted her land. He'd marry her to get it. Samuel had married her the first time for it, now Ward thought she'd be stupid enough to make the same mistake.

What if she gave him the deed to the farm? She didn't want to give up the security the land represented, but it wasn't doing her much good on the run and she would relinquish it in a heartbeat if it meant Ward would be out of their lives forever. That he would leave her alone with the claim to Samuel's children. But she had the sinking feeling that he wanted her, too, in the way Samuel had.

"Penny for your thoughts," Luke said, breaking her concentration.

Gooseflesh rippled her arms. Her cheeks turned warm. "I was thinking about the job in Priest's Crossing," she lied.

"Thought as much. You've been pretty quiet ever since we started home." His hat was tipped back and he was relaxed against the buggy seat. His eyes were unreadable as he glanced at her from the winding road before them.

"Do you think he's serious? I mean, about me getting a job working for his sister." She knew she sounded desperate, but then, she was.

"Probably. Joe's a good man. He wouldn't have mentioned it if he didn't think he could help."

"It sounds so perfect. A job in a mercantile." Faith closed her eyes for a moment and imagined she was waiting on a customer: she was cutting a beautiful dress-length piece of blue calico, and the lady was smiling and complimenting her on her steady hand. "It's entirely too good to be true. If only . . ." She left the sentence unfinished, embarrassed at having spoken it out loud.

"If only what?" Luke was looking at her now with his dark, intelligent eyes. He seemed truly concerned. Her stomach did a flip-flop. She remembered the feel of his lips nibbling gently on hers.

She straightened her shoulders and smiled. "If only she'll hire me. It would mean everything."

"A woman alone with two young'uns is asking for trouble and heartache. I don't think you know how hard it's going to be."

"Luke, I know it will be hard. But I've worked hard every day of my life. And you heard Joe. His sister did it and so can I. Besides, if I don't . . . that would mean going home with Ward, and that's out of the question. I've traveled the route of marriage, and I'm not interested in trying it again, with him or anyone else. So it's up to me to support my children. I don't know why everyone thinks women are so weak. We're not! We just don't get the same opportunities as men. We aren't as strong physically, but we aren't helpless. I aim to prove it." She nodded her head, hoping she sounded confident, that she'd convinced him that her working for Joe's sister was all she intended on doing. "I know I can succeed."

He eyed her and shook his head. "Maybe that's what's scaring me. I think you can, too."

Chapter Twenty-five

$\mathcal{I}$T was late when they finally pulled up next to the barn. Luke looked down into Faith's face. She had fallen asleep shortly after Three Toes, the landmark indicating the halfway point, still worn out from the long journey and her recent birthing of Dawn. Or maybe she'd lain awake all night like he had. Was it possible she'd been pining away for him, too?

Her head was resting on his shoulder, and only his arm around her kept her from falling. Dawn slept like a peanut on his lap.

Luke ran his finger up the silky line of Faith's jaw and stopped just below her ear. He moved close, his mouth mere inches from hers. "Faith, we're home."

A huge harvest moon bathed her upturned face in muted white light, reminding him of peaches and cream. He could almost taste the sweetness. Thick, long lashes lay dark on her cheek. She sighed.

"We're home," he repeated, this time unable to resist brushing her lips with his own.

She came awake. Her lips trembled beneath his, her eyes opened and gazed into his.

"I've been wanting to do that all day," he admitted, smiling.

"Have you?"

"Yes. I have," he murmured, brushing her lips again with his.

"Luke, I don't think this is such a good idea."

But Luke noticed that she didn't pull away. Was she enjoying the moment as much as he? After having been in such close proximity for hours without being able to touch her, he longed to hold on a little longer.

When he kissed her again, she leaned into him. He said, "I think it's the best idea I've had in a long while."

He felt her tense, and she held him off with her hand. "I really must go in."

Knowing he was pushing his luck, he nuzzled the spot below her ear and inhaled her sweetness. "Why? The weather is nice, the moon is hanging up there, a pretty light just for us. Dawn here is aslee—"

"Luke McCutcheon," she said in a no-nonsense voice. "If I have to spell it out for you, I will. I'm smart enough to know you're just toying with my affections. You have no honorable intentions towards me whatsoever. Now let me go inside."

Annoyed she couldn't see he'd been trying to help her in every way, he attempted to ignore her statement. "How do you know what my intentions are? Could be that I'm getting the urge to settle down."

"Ha!" Faith laughed, making Dawn jump. "You no more want to settle down than I want to get married again. You're just looking to sow a few wild oats."

She fisted a hand and pushed against his chest. Luke couldn't help but smile. She looked so serious.

"My pa wasn't good at rearing children," Faith said, "but he did educate me on the things a man tries to sweet-talk a woman out of: her house, her clothes, her heart. Sweet talk is what got me into trouble last time, and I'm not falling for it again. Oh, no. I was much better off with just Colton, Pa and me. I'm much smarter now than I was." She heaved a sigh. "Let's not do anything that will only break my heart."

She'd turned his warm feelings into something altogether different, and Luke found himself more aggravated than he cared to admit. "Break your heart, darlin'? I'm not sure you have one." He scooped up Dawn and climbed out of the buggy.

The crickets stopped their chirping when the bunkhouse door opened, and Luke saw Francis coming toward them. "Evenin', Luke. You want me to stable Buttercup?"

"Thanks, Francis," Luke replied, helping Faith from the buggy and to the house. He marched her through several rooms and up the stairs, stopping finally at her bedroom door. They hadn't seen anyone, and the house was quiet.

"I don't sweet-talk anyone out of anything, Faith."

She simply stared at him.

Handing her the baby, he walked back down the hall and descended the stairs. Hell, if she wasn't one irritating woman. Just when he felt like he was getting to know her, understanding her a little, she went and stirred the pot. She was worse than the most cantankerous, barley-broke broomtail he'd ever had the pleasure of breaking. Damn it, though, if he didn't feel up for the challenge.

Chapter Twenty-six

Luke knew better than to try to retire at seven o'clock in the evening. Usually if he hadn't eaten by this time he'd go to the kitchen in search of some hearty morsel Esperanza had put aside exactly for that purpose, but he was still sated from the late lunch at the bridge and that held no appeal. He needed to get out and take a walk. Agitation rippled though him. Last night had been torture, seeming to stretch on for days. He wasn't going to go through that again, so he'd head for the bunkhouse. The people there would know where everyone else was.

He paused on the porch, appreciating being home. The soft moonlight and chilly night air reminded him why he loved this ranch so much.

The long log bunkhouse was lit up brightly, and laughter and talk could be heard from within. The heady aromas of coffee and freshly baked cake wafted on the breeze.

A moment later, a new collection of smells engulfed him, yanking him into the past, into his childhood. As he stepped through the door of the building he caught the rich scents of tobacco, grilled onions, old sweat, earthy and strong. Sandalwood soap mingled with leather. Horse manure. Mixed all together, they created the bunkhouse. He'd spent most his time down here with the other men, listening to all kinds of talk, some true, some fictitious.

All eyes turned to him. "Evening," he said—as a companion instead of the boss.

"Luke, how's the bridge on the upper crest?" Roady called. He sat at a large round table with some men in a game of poker. Most others were washed up and ready to turn in.

Ten beds ran the lengths of the room. Each sported a thick goose-feather mattress and pillow, as his ma insisted everyone at the ranch deserved the best when it came to comfortable sleeping. A rock fireplace warmed the room from one end, and on the other were the stove and kitchen supplies.

"Coming along."

Lucky approached with a mug of coffee and handed it to Luke. He looked a little out of joint, and Luke figured he was still upset over the morning in Pine Grove. The cook was loyal to a fault. The problem was, it seemed he had switched his loyalties to Faith.

Lucky eyed him, a small smile curving his lips. "Pull up a chair, boy. I'll cut you a piece of chocolate cake still warm from the oven."

"No, thanks," Luke replied, happy over the peace offering. "Coffee's fine." Taking a sip, he watched the men. "Where's everyone from the house?"

Roady, who sat with a pile of coins in front of him, smiled. "Over at Rachel's for supper."

Chance, Pedro, Uncle Pete and Ward sat around the table also, varying sums of money in front of each, every player holding five bent and tattered cards. Ward's homemade crutch leaned up against his chair.

Luke had come to the right place for a little diversion. "You got room for one more?"

Chance and Roady scooted back, making room for him to pull up a chair. Ike was reclined on his bed reading a copy of *Jane Eyre*.

"And Smokey?" Luke asked, looking around as the men anted and Uncle Pete dealt.

Chance answered. "Matt asked him to take early watch tonight."

Flood had taught Luke and his brothers how to play poker at this exact table when he was no more than five or six years old. They'd played with sour balls, and that night he'd ended up with a stomachache to end all others. He hadn't eaten one since. His mother would have raised holy hell if she'd known what Flood was up to in the bunkhouse, but playing on the hush-hush had made it all the more exciting.

"Always watch a man's eyes, boys," he had instructed his captivated sons. "You'll be able to tell if he's one to be trusted."

The men now looked at their cards, and each tossed in his bet.

"Pedro?"

"*Dos*," the man mumbled in deep concentration.

Uncle Pete nodded, sliding two cards over to the Mexican ranch hand.

"None for me, Pete," Ward said, and raised a glass of whiskey to his lips. Drinking was allowed in the bunkhouse, but never to excess. All the hands knew the rules and abided by them; Luke's ma made sure each new employee was shown the sign posted on the wall.

"These are real nice accommodations, McCutcheon. You're real good to your people. And your house is really something.

Don't think I've ever seen anything so nice." Ward took another sip and smiled.

Luke wondered if his mood had anything to do with the
smarminess of Ward's tone. Could be that, he reminded himself. Or frustration with Faith might be playing a part. He recognized himself as the least trusting of the family, and Ward
had saved Mark. He'd do well to give the farmer a wide berth
until he was gone. But there was indeed something about this
man that set him on edge. Why was Faith so unwilling to talk
about him?

Uncle Pete looked at Chance, who paused, looking at his
hand. "Better give me three . . . uh, no. Make that four." He
took the new cards and discarded the old. With a small, satisfied smile he sipped his coffee.

"You sure, uh, you don't need, uh, five, Chance?" Ward
said, mocking the other man's speech. When he saw he was
the only one amused he added, "What? It was only a little
joke, boys."

Luke scanned his cards, holding his temper. Brown was
a guest for a few more days. That's all. The hands were grown
men and could fight their own battles. Nothin' worth trying
to build on. "Fold." He slid them to the center of the table
and relaxed back in his chair.

"Roady?"

His friend's face showed nothing, no clue of what he was
thinking. "One. Luke, how was your buggy ride?" he asked,
taking the dealt card and putting it into his hand. His brows
arched and the men chuckled.

Luke should have seen it coming. Of course they'd tease
him about taking Faith on a picnic. "Fine."

Chance fingered one of his coins. With an overt look of
innocence he glanced directly at Ward. "She was about the
prettiest sight I've ever seen, setting in that buggy. You're one
lucky man, Luke."

Ward's jaw clenched several times and his face flushed.

"I'm taking two," Uncle Pete spoke up, spitting a string of tobacco juice into a rusted tin cup.

The door banged opened and Francis came in. Lucky grumbled at the boy, "How many times do I have ta remind ya not to open that door so hard. That head of yours full of feathers?"

"Sorry," the youth responded, taking off his coat and hunting for a peg on the coat rack between the ponchos, dusters and leather coats. Giving up, he threw it across his bed and headed for the coffeepot.

After the second round of betting, the only two left in were Pedro and Ward. "Call," Ward said. The man was practically gloating.

Pedro placed his cards on the table, revealing three aces, a jack and one nine. He addressed Luke at the same time. "The senorita, she like you, no?"

Damn. He wasn't a kid to be teased about his attractions! When had his every move become the concern of everyone on this ranch? "She just needed to get out," he answered.

Ward's face clouded again, and his flashing eyes challenged Luke for one instant. Then he laid down a full house and scraped the pot money over to his dwindling stack.

The cards were dealt again and play continued. Roady fared best, with Ward a close second. It didn't matter that Luke only won a couple of times, losing more than he took in; he was content just getting a chance to watch Ward. But after an hour crept by, Luke's loss of sleep the night before started to weigh heavy.

He wasn't the only one who was tired. Lucky turned in. Saying good night, the cook closed the door to his private room that opened off the side of the kitchen. Ward shuffled the cards for another hand, but before he got them dealt Pedro pushed his chair out and gathered his money.

"You ain't quitting, are ya, Mex?"

Pedro looked surprised. "*Sí*. When it's time to quit, I quit."

Luke really hated Ward's tone. He had reached his limit. Still, he knew his parents felt indebted to the man, so he satisfied himself to say, "We play for fun, Brown. Not to see how much we can fleece one another."

"I'm out, too." Roady stood and scooped up his plentiful winnings. He smiled at Pedro in solidarity.

Ward couldn't conceal his hostility as he watched Roady fixing to leave. He struggled to rein in his temper. "I'd think the winner would give the others a chance to win back some of their hard-earned wages. I was just giving Pedro here a chance to recoup his losses. I'd expect the same courtesy in return."

"Time for my watch," Roady said. He took his coat from the wall. "Luke, you better get back to the house. I'm sure Faith is longing for them pretty brown eyes of yours."

Everyone laughed except Ward.

Chance and Uncle Pete stood, slowly tossing down their cards. The friendly atmosphere had been shattered, and the men all went their separate ways. Ward stood holding the remainder of the deck, shuffling. He was fast and nimble, confirming cards were nothing new to him. Luke figured he'd been bluffing early, letting the other men win at first to gain their confidence. He hadn't counted on the game breaking up. Not before he had a chance to take everything.

"You out, too, McCutcheon?"

"That's right," Luke said. Standing, he stretched his tired legs.

"You wouldn't want to go one more hand? Bet on something, say, a little more interesting than a few dollars."

Luke shook his head. "Nope. I'm turning in."

"I guess it's not as appealing as what my dear little sister-in-law is offering you up at the house. I don't blame you in the least. No question about what I'd be taking pleasure in. As a matter of fact, maybe we could bet on—"

Quick as a rattler, Luke had Ward by the throat, pinning

him to the table. Red-faced and angry, the man bucked but couldn't loosen Luke's viselike hold. Uncle Pete's half-full cup of spittle went flying, and cards fluttered to the floor. Ward's eyes glittered with fury. A mere inches from his face, Luke glared back.

Francis and Ike sat up in bed, trying to see what was going on. Lucky opened his door.

Luke spoke quietly. "Don't you *ever* talk about Faith like that again. If you do, you'll wish your sorry hide was never born. I don't care if we're beholden to you because of Mark or anything else. I held my tongue when you insulted the men. And again the first night when you made jest of Faith's plight, because I wasn't sure where you were coming from. Now I know. Don't make the mistake of testing me. I won't tolerate you insinuating anything about Faith, ever!"

Again Ward struggled, trying in vain to free himself. The two men were about the same height and weight, but Luke's fury made him unstoppable.

"I'd expect as much from a dumb Injun," Ward muttered under his breath.

The whiskey vapors hit Luke in the face along with the insult. The man was drunk. Briefly Luke wondered how Ward had found out about his past, if one of the men had told him. But what difference did it make? A comment about punching Ward in his slimy mouth was offered by someone behind Luke. "Brown, how long you planning to take advantage of my father's hospitality?"

"Just until my leg is healed and I can ride easier," Ward wheezed. Luke didn't loosen his hold. "A couple weeks?"

"I'm real anxious to see you gone now. In the meantime, don't be harassing Faith. She's made it plenty clear how she feels about you. Understand?"

"Yeah."

"That's good, because I'll be watching—and so will the boys, just itching for any excuse to take you down. Some have been known to shoot first and ask questions later. They're loyal to me, and now to Faith. I'd step lightly if I were you."

Luke shoved Ward away. The man slid sideways, then gripped the table to keep from falling to the floor. He stood, going eye to eye with Luke, and straightened his collar. Then he turned and limped to his bunk, a small smirk curving his lips.

Chapter Twenty-seven

FAITH meandered down the staircase, feeling like a trespasser in the large, attractive ranch house. She glanced around but still everything was quiet. It had taken some time to get Dawn bathed, fed and back to sleep, but now that she had, she could no more stay cooped up in that room than sit on a bed of hot coals.

Her accusatory words to Luke kept rolling around in her mind, making her want to be sick. She wished she could run to him now and beg his forgiveness, tell him she hadn't meant a word of it. After all he had done for her, more than any other human being in the world ever had, what must he think of her crudeness?

Without any effort at all she could fall in love with him. She knew it. For the first time in her life she understood what love could be, and how it should be and how it felt. But, where would that leave her? Guarding her feelings had to be her number-one priority. She had no doubt that Ward would be livid if he thought there was something real growing here. Maybe he'd even be murderous.

Her heart hurt. It pulled like a dead weight in her chest. All those awful things she'd said to Luke made her want to scream. But, she had to discourage him for the safety of everyone, not just herself or the children. So much was at stake, and she hated the idea that Ward might try to take revenge on anyone who'd been kind to her.

When she'd awakened in Luke's arms, in the buggy, his lips next to hers, she'd thought she just might be in heaven. Anguish and regret, so intense for what might have been, made her grasp the banister for support as she slowly descended the curving staircase. Luke had said he'd been thinking about settling down. Settling down! Imagine that. He wouldn't have said it if he hadn't meant it. Would he?

She peeked into the kitchen, with its flagstone floor and big wooden crossbeams on the high ceiling. It was empty. Would anyone mind if she made herself a cup of tea? And where had everyone gone off to, anyway? Perhaps they were over at one of the other houses, Matt's or Mark's. She felt certain that wherever they were, Colton was with them, safe and sound.

Coals in the large cast-iron stove still glowed red. Faith filled a kettle from the pump at the sink and set it on top to heat. Next she'd find a cup and the tea itself.

Successfully locating and preparing everything she needed, Faith took her cup and went back into the living room to the tapestry chair she loved so much. Startled, she almost dropped the hot liquid. The chair was occupied.

"I'm sorry if I frightened you," Amy, Mark's wife, said. Moonlight streamed in the window. Its soft illumination gave the room a cozy feel and made her glow.

"I've made some tea. Would you like a cup?" Faith asked.

Amy shook her head. "No, thank you."

"Tea tastes better if it's shared."

"No, really. I'm fine."

Sadness was etched on Amy's face as clear as footprints on freshly fallen snow. Faith remembered Rachel telling her about Amy losing her baby a short time ago. Just the thought of losing either Colton or Dawn made her heart tremble.

With Amy, it seemed like more than that. The way she

never really looked at anyone, never met her husband's gaze . . . The protectiveness within Faith surfaced and she was overcome with the desire to help.

She handed Amy her cup. "Here, take this. I haven't sipped yet. I'll be right back."

She returned with another cup and sat on the sofa opposite the sad girl. Amy certainly was pretty, with her olive skin and shiny black hair. She was as thin as a willow, and the way she sat made Faith think she wanted to fade into the chair, never to be seen again.

"Your husband is a very nice man. I got to know him on the cattle drive," she said.

"Mmm," was Amy's only response.

Faith took a sip of her tea, not knowing quite how to proceed. She shifted in her seat, thinking. Amy needed a friend, someone to talk to. She didn't want to pry and it would be easier to just look the other way, but sometimes action was needed. "I heard someone say that you two are newlyweds. Is that right?"

For the first time, Amy smiled. It was brief. "Yes."

"How nice. How long have the two of you been married?"

The young woman worried her bottom lip with her teeth. "Six months. We were married on Valentine's Day."

Faith nodded. "Valentine's Day? How special! I'll bet it was a pretty wedding."

Amy's lips again curved up, but the smile never reached her eyes. "It was beautiful. Mrs. McCutcheon fixed this room up so nice. She had red hearts and white lace everywhere. It was a sight."

That had been a good icebreaker, Faith decided, taking another sip of her tea. Drumming up her courage she said, "I never really had a wedding. The justice of the peace married us and then it was back to the farm, back to work as usual. I'm not complaining, mind you, but I'd love to hear about yours. Would you mind sharing?"

Amy hesitated, perhaps deciding if Faith was serious. "Please."

"Well," the other woman began, "like I said before, it was Valentine's Day. I didn't have time to make a wedding dress of my own, so Mrs. McCutcheon let me wear hers. It fit me perfect, and she said I looked just like a princess." Her voice quavered and suddenly she buried her face in her hands.

"I'm sorry! You don't have to tell me if you don't want to," Faith said.

"I want to. Really. It just makes me sad. Everything was so wonderful then." Wiping her eyes with a hankie she'd pulled from her pocket, Amy gazed out the window. With a deep breath, she continued. "I came down the stairs slowly, and Mark was standing by the window next to the preacher. Matt and Luke were next to him. Charity and Rachel stood waiting for me. You should have seen the three men, all in their finest clothes. They were so handsome, and Mark looked so happy."

Looking at Faith, the girl stopped. Was she going to go on? Maybe it hadn't been such a good idea to bring this up. Faith didn't want to make matters worse.

"We said our vows, promising to love and cherish each other for all time. Through good and bad."

"It sounds like something out of a story," Faith said.

"Oh, it was. After the ceremony we had the grandest dinner, with everything you can think of. We even drank champagne."

"Champagne! I've never had it. Is it good?"

"Extraordinary."

Her happiness seemed forced, though, and at that moment Faith recognized herself in this lost girl. More than ever she wanted to help her, to be Amy's friend.

"It has little bubbles that go up your nose when you take a sip. I had a whole glass and started giggling at *everything*. . . ." Amy stopped again, her eyes filled with tears. "Ma and Pa didn't come."

"Why not?" Faith was astounded. It sounded like the most perfect celebration. Why wouldn't parents come to their daughter's wedding? She could see the want in Amy's eyes. The hunger to trust her. To tell her. But Amy held back.

"It's all right," she urged. "I won't tell anyone. I promise."

"They were ashamed of me. For getting in the family way. Pa said I was plain trash, and that I'd had to trap a man to get a husband. Growing up they were very strict about everything. Especially boys."

Faith went and wrapped her arms tightly around the girl. As Amy cried, Faith stroked her hair as she'd done a thousand times with Colton. "Shh, Amy. Don't cry."

"But, it's true. I am bad. That's why I lost our baby. God was punishing me."

"No, no, that's not true. You're not bad," Faith crooned. "From what I see, you're a sweet girl with lots of love for everyone."

Amy raised her head and stared into Faith's eyes. "Then why did I lose my baby?"

"I don't know why things like that happen. It's a mystery. Sometimes they just do, and there's no telling why. But I'm sure of one thing: God didn't do it to punish you. He would never do that. Why, I bet he feels just as bad about it as you do."

Several moments of silence filled the room before Amy said, "I just wish it hadn't happened. Everything is so different now. And I know Mark blames me."

"I'm sorry, Amy." Faith sat back. "But, I just don't believe that. It's true I haven't known Mark that long, but blaming someone for something they had no control over just isn't right. He doesn't seem like that kind. I think you're imagining it."

"No, I'm not. He never touches me. We hardly even talk. He's changed since that horrible day. When he looks at me now, I see the truth in his eyes. He's sorry that he married me."

"I can't guess to know what Mark is thinking," Faith answered, "but goodness, Amy, everyone in this family seems very fair." She picked up her teacup and sipped to bolster her nerves.

"Faith," Amy said with a trembling smile. "Thank you for listening. And for talking, too. Even though I didn't want to at first, I do feel better. It's as if I let some of my sadness out."

Faith felt hope. She liked this girl. She didn't know why Mark was acting like he was, but she felt sure that it wasn't because he blamed his wife for losing their baby.

"Where is everyone?" she remembered to ask. She'd been so involved with Amy's problems, she forgot to ask about Colton.

"Over at Matthew and Rachel's. She prepared dinner for everyone tonight. They were sorry that you and Luke missed it."

At the mention of Luke, Faith felt like she'd been dealt a physical blow. Again she wondered how she could she have said those things to him. And, where was he now?

"Was Colton there?" she asked.

"Yes, with Billy and Adam. Those three have become fast friends." The clock in the living room chimed ten o'clock, and Amy added, "Flood had his fiddle out, and the boys were hopping around like water on a hot skillet. But don't worry. I'm sure they'll be along shortly."

"You're right. I should relish the quiet while he's occupied. Dawn is enough of a handful."

A shadow crossed Amy's face, a trace of the old sadness. "Can we go up and see her?" she asked.

"You sure you feel up to it?"

Amy nodded. "I just want to look at her. If it's all right?"

"Of course. But if she wakes up, you're the one to hold her until she goes back to sleep," Faith teased.

They both smiled, and this time Amy seemed to mean it.

Chapter Twenty-eight

LUKE watched the girls from the shadows of the darkened hallway. They whispered and giggled over the sleeping Dawn, who was peacefully unaware that she was the object of attention. He could see by their ease with each other that they were becoming friends.

He was glad. Amy, for one, had worried the hell out of him. After she'd lost the baby, a horrible experience they'd all lived through, she withdrew into a world of her own, staying clear of everyone and everything, including her new husband. His mother was worried sick. Everything she'd done to try to draw Amy from her protective shell had been for naught. But now her laughter sounded, music to his ears, and Luke wished Mark were around to hear it.

"It's so amazing Luke delivered her!" Astonishment colored Amy's words. "Weren't you horrified?"

"When he first came into my wagon and found me, I was awfully scared. I thought he was an outlaw and that he'd slit my throat for the little money I had. He was so big, and his black eyes were frightening. . . ." Faith admitted.

Luke stepped back a bit farther into the hall. An outlaw! If he'd truly been an outlaw, Colton would have done the right thing by hitting him with that pan. Holding back his chuckle, he strained to hear more.

"Did he actually . . . you know. *Look?*"

Faith ducked her head shyly. "Yes, he did. But, by that time I really didn't care if every man in the whole territory came marching through my wagon with drums and tambourines. It was pure misery, and I was just relieved he stayed with me."

Amy giggled again. "I just can't picture him. Oh, how I wish I'd been there!"

Faith reached down and stroked Dawn's hair. "He held my hand the whole time. Imagine that, a girl he didn't even know, hour after hour." Her voice was featherlight. "I never even thanked him."

Luke stood frozen. His heart pumped so hard he felt like he'd just run up the staircase. This wasn't what he'd been expecting to hear. He hadn't foreseen it to be so personal. Swallowing, he turned to leave.

"You love him," Amy said. "I can hear it in your voice. Are you going to marry him?"

That stopped Luke dead. He waited for Faith's answer.

"No! Not him, not Ward, not the Man in the Moon. I'm going to Priest's Crossing to work and support my children and myself," Faith said. "I hated being married, and I never want to be again."

Well, that was plain enough. He'd have to be jelly-brained not to understand.

"You don't mean it," Amy said. "It was wonderful with Mark and me at first. I used to count the moments until he was home from the cattle."

"That's because you have a good husband. One who cares for you."

Amy shook her head. "I don't know about that. Not anymore."

"Yes, he does," Faith said. "I think you should just go home and talk to him. Tell him how you feel. That's what I'd do, anyway. I think you may be surprised."

"Oh, Faith, I'm scared. But I'm happy, too. You've made me see things differently." Amy wrapped her arms around Faith, and the girls embraced. "I owe you everything."

Luke hurried down the hall, not wanting to get caught eavesdropping. He heard sounds from outside: His mother's laugh. Charity's voice, low, hushing an excited Adam. Everyone was coming home.

Everyone *else*. The outsider. He was always the outsider.

Trying to shake off the morose mood that was descending, he thought of Amy. She'd had a breakthrough tonight. She seemed well along the way to recovery, and they had Faith to thank for it. Strong, independent Faith. The girl who'd seemed so fragile when he'd found her in the wagon. Was she really the same woman?

From the upper landing he watched his family come through the door. "Luke," Charity called out. "We missed you."

"Yeah. I was disappointed to miss Rachel's dinner, too. Maybe she'll do another one soon. What'd she fix?"

"Chicken and dumplings."

Luke acted like he were crushed, when actually he couldn't keep his mind on food or anything else. Like a great big dust devil, Faith's words kept whirling around inside him. "'Not even the Man in the Moon,'" he mumbled to himself, chin resting on his palm, elbow propped on the railing. It was more of a sigh than anything else.

Amy breezed by, giving him a pat on the arm. "I wouldn't bet on it."

Luke was so surprised that he had to catch himself from falling. Before he had a chance to ask what she meant, she was gone.

In came Colton, followed by Adam, who was chatting happily, trying to get his attention. Faith came around the corner next, obviously surprised to find Luke. Crimson started at her neck and slowly climbed to her hairline.

Good. He hoped she was worried about what he might have overheard. It wouldn't hurt her to fret a bit.

"Faith." He nodded.

"Luke," she answered, looking down at the people milling in the living room. "I didn't hear you come in."

"Just got here," he fibbed. Best she didn't know that he'd

heard her calling him a bandit. "Where's Billy?" he called down to his mother and Flood.

"He stayed home. He and Colton had a spitting contest. Colton won," Mrs. McCutcheon replied. She added, "I wish Smokey would quit encouraging that behavior."

"They're boys, Ma," Luke commented. "You can't expect 'em to sit around knitting doilies." Even out here in Montana, his mother was always insisting on manners and breeding. She never let it alone. She'd been thrilled beyond measure when John had expressed an interest in university. It had been good for Luke and his brothers, too, taking the pressure off.

Colton glanced up, a worried expression on his face. "Sorry, Ma. I guess I should've let Billy win."

"Never be ashamed of winning, Colton," Flood said. "Always give it your best, whatever you're doing. That way it won't take the glory away from your opponent if he wins." He ruffled the boy's hair. "Give it your all, and you won't have any regrets."

Luke looked over at Faith. She was pretending not to notice his regard, but why else would her toe be tapping nervously on the hall runner?

"Everyone to bed, it's getting late." Mrs. McCutcheon picked up the lantern she'd placed on the entry table and started up the stairs. Reaching the landing, she smiled. "You're quiet tonight, Faith. How did you like the upper crest?"

"It was wonderful! And the river and flowers were gorgeous."

"I thought you'd like it. It was one of my favorite places when Flood and I first married," she said, a secretive twinkle in her eye. "I guess it still is."

"To bed, woman," Flood said, swatting her behind as he passed. "These young people can't keep up with the likes of you. They need their rest."

"I suppose. But remember, Faith, if you need anything at all, I'm just down the hall."

Chapter Twenty-nine

LYING in bed the next morning, Faith didn't want to take the chance of getting up and have Mrs. McCutcheon send her off someplace with Luke, beautiful or not. Her nerves, worn out from yesterday, needed a respite. After everyone was gone she would venture down.

Dawn was snuggled peacefully beside her, happily fed and dry. The baby gurgled and cooed good-naturedly, seemingly content with her mother's decision of solitude. Much earlier, Faith had heard Luke rise across the hall. The squeaking floor marked his every move as he dressed and prepared for the day; then his door opened and she'd heard him leave. She'd longed to peek out for a small glimpse of him, but she refrained, remembering how she'd been caught in the hall yesterday by Matt.

Restlessness crept over her as she admired the room in the dawn light. She'd never before just lain in bed. There were always things begging to be done; the rigors of farm life didn't allow a body to luxuriate in such fashion. Even on Sundays, hungry animals waited to be fed. And, of course, there was Penelope. She got downright fussy if she wasn't milked. Sighing, Faith hoped someone was tending to the old cow.

Forcing the memories away, she played with one of Dawn's little hands. Nobody would miss Faith here. She had no responsibilities except, of course, what she was doing right now. Looking at her daughter, the same wonderment washed through her. Dawn certainly was filling out. Her milk seemed to be doing a fine job keeping the baby satisfied.

Thinking about feeding Dawn made her breasts tingle in that strange manner she was finally getting used to. Every time

Dawn cried, her body responded in that delightfully painful way, producing milk. The first time she'd felt the pinprickly heat she'd been surprised and a bit more than worried, thinking something was wrong with her. Now she understood it was just one of the funny quirks of motherhood.

Looking underneath her night rail, Faith couldn't stop a small smile from lifting the corners of her mouth. Her breasts had grown considerably since she'd given birth. She hadn't ever given much thought to her smallish breasts, but now, filled with milk, they were downright impressive.

A giggle escaped her. She marveled at their firmness, running her hand over her gown. Then she sobered, relieved Samuel wasn't here to see. She knew what he'd think of her new shape.

"Thank you," she whispered to the empty room.

Shouts from outside drew her attention. Faith hurried to the window and looked out. A group of men was herding a bunch of horses into the double corral next to the barn. Several riders flanked the gate, making sure none broke free. Billy, Adam and Colton stood well out of harm's way, jumping up and down in a wagon, hollering their encouragement.

Thundering hooves covered the area in an immense billow of dust, and the shouts of cowboys shattered the serenity of the morning. But before long, the last horse darted in the corral and Francis flung the gate closed. Rugged and wild. These looked nothing like the sleek, well-fed horses she'd seen on the ranch.

One mustang with a colt by her side pinned her ears back and lunged at the rail where Smokey stood grinning from ear to ear. Luke galloped up. His mount slid to a stop, lathered and hot. Luke threw his leg over the horse's back with the ease and grace of a dancer, and he dismounted, a grin marking his face as if he, too, had just come from the grandest adventure. Leaning his arms on the top rail of the corral, he admired its occupants.

Faith hurried to dress. She wanted to be out there, too. Excitement coursed through her as she splashed her face with water and used her tooth powder and brush. Pulling half her hair up, she hastily braided the top and let the rest hang free down her back, as she'd seen Charity do last night. It felt good. Looking in the mirror she smiled. The new look seemed to suit the way she felt inside.

Downstairs, sitting by the fire, Mrs. McCutcheon was reading. As Faith came down the stairs, she looked up and smiled. "Good morning."

Faith returned the greeting, feeling the urgency to run out to the corral but not wanting to be rude.

"You slept well?"

"Oh, yes. That's about the most comfortable bed I've ever been in." And it was by far the biggest. Her small bed back home seemed pint-size in comparison.

"And Dawn? Did she fare better last night?"

Faith rocked the baby in her arms. "Yes. She slept the whole night through."

"Good, dear. How about some tea and toast?"

"No, thank you." Faith looked longingly toward the door.

Mrs. McCutcheon laughed. "Let me hold her." She stood and reached for the child. "Go on now. She'll be fine."

"No, I couldn't impose," Faith said.

"It's one of my favorite pastimes. Ask Rachel. I can't wait for the new one, and now I have Dawn, too," she said warmly. She swayed back and forth with Dawn, smiling into the baby's face. "You best hurry before you miss all the fun."

"If you're sure . . . ?"

"I insist."

Faith didn't argue. She rushed out the door, a feeling of freedom enveloping her.

"Don't worry. She's in good hands," she heard Luke's mother call.

Outside, Faith hesitated. She wanted to run over and watch

Smokey fight to blindfold an angry black horse in the connecting corral, but Luke was standing directly in front of her. His boot, resting nonchalantly on the first rail, caused his worn leather chaps to pull snug across his strong thighs. He was laughing at Smokey, who'd just jumped out of the way of a flashing hoof. Her cheeks warmed.

This was foolishness! She wasn't going to let him run her life as she had let Samuel. If she started worrying over what he was thinking about all the time, that's just what she'd be doing.

Marching over, she looked through the rails. Chance had joined Smokey in wrestling the horse. The two men were having a heck of a time trying to get the blindfold around the colt's eyes. Chance had hold of the animal's ear with one hand and the halter with the other. Smokey, one arm slung around the black's neck, struggled with the bandanna.

"Gol-darnit," Smokey yelped when the horse's hoof nicked his leg.

"Watch yer mouth," Lucky called from the bunkhouse porch. "We got us a lady present."

All the men turned. "Mornin', ma'am," they said in unison.

Smokey and Chance, looking toward Faith, were both flung from the horse's head, and the mustang ran the perimeter of the corral kicking and bucking, the rope trailing him like the tail of a kite. Both men leaped the fence to get out of his way.

"Morning, Faith," Luke said, tipping his hat. He smiled that slow, heart-stopping smile. "I wonder what distracted them?"

She didn't speak. Nodding curtly, she focused her attention back on the men in the corral, who set about recapturing the charger. There was new purpose to their efforts now that they knew she was watching.

The blindfold finally in place, Smokey threw on a saddle and cinched it tight. The horse snorted and madly shook his head, pinned his ears back and struck out with his forelegs.

Smokey prepared to step on anyway, but Chance grabbed him by the shoulder and slipped his boot in the stirrup himself and mounted. Smokey shrugged and pulled away the blindfold.

The black vaulted into the air. Faith heard an audible snap of Chance's neck and she sucked in her breath, wondering how he could take such punishment. The horse came down with crushing force but Chance hung on, his face grim, eyes squinted nearly shut. One arm flapped wildly and the other hand gripped the lead rope as the bronco bucked. Finally, with a mighty twist, the horse flung Chance off. The cowboy landed on the hard ground with a thud.

"Chance!" Faith climbed up the two bottom rails. The unmoving cowboy must be dead.

Smokey had caught up the mustang and restrained him. Faith started to climb the remaining rails, but something stopped her. Luke had a hold of her belt and was pulling her back. "He's all right. Just got the wind knocked out of him," he said, his voice uncompromising.

"Are you sure?" Faith asked, frightened.

Chance rolled to his knees and smiled wanly up at her. He shook his head. "Just stunned me is all, Miss Faith." He winced as he stood, brushing at the dirt on his clothes. He took off his hat and beat it across his thighs. He turned back to the black.

Faith gasped. "You can't ride him again, Chance. You're hurt!"

The cowboy was playing it for all it was worth. Nothing got to a woman faster than worry, and Faith's concern was shining in her eyes. Luke rolled his eyes and taunted, "See if you can stay on that crow bait this time, Chance. I bet Adam here could fork him longer than you just did."

Crimson crept up Chance's face as the men chuckled. Faith turned on Luke, fury in her eyes.

"What?" he asked innocently.

She didn't have time to answer before Chance was again bobbing around the corral, whipped viciously here and there by the horse. His hat flew off, landing in the dirt, leaving Chance's tawny hair to fly around his face, resembling a scarecrow. The boys in the wagon whooped their approval, and Adam clapped his small hands so hard he teetered on the buckboard seat and almost lost his balance.

Then Chance hit the ground again. For a few moments he didn't move. Smokey ran out and helped him, saying, "You'd better ketch yer breath 'fore you try him again."

The black stood nearby, sides heaving, head tossing defiantly. Luke steeled himself. "Let me have a go at that mealy-mouthed outlaw." He pulled his black Stetson down snug on his head. Nothing he hated more than losing his hat.

Chance struggled against Smokey, who said, "Ah, give Luke a go. He's feeling awfully big for his britches this morning." Chance shrugged and limped out of the corral.

Smokey and Ike got the horse blindfolded again, and they held tight as Luke mounted. Nodding to Smokey, who pulled the covering off the horse's eyes . . . but the horse just stood quiet.

Luke looked to Faith, a pleased smile on his face. He shrugged. Instantly, the mustang dropped his head low to the ground and flung his hindquarters toward the sky. Luke stayed on but was thrown forward, jarred down his spine. The horse leaped again, this time almost turning over in midair.

"Look, he's 'bout belly up!" Lucky shouted out.

The men cheered and shouted. Luke thought he heard Faith gasp as the horse maliciously fell sideways into the fence, trying to crush his leg. Reacting swiftly, he had just enough time to bring his knee up out of the way.

Changing strategies, the devil spun, dropped his head again and bucked. Luke relaxed, starting to enjoy the ride. Passing a group of men on the rail, he got a quick glimpse of Chance, whose face was clouded and glum. Part of him felt like laughing in triumph, even though he knew it was a totally juvenile reaction and he should feel ashamed of himself for it.

Rallying, the mustang did a quick series of crow hops, ending with an explosion Luke had never felt from any horse. If he hadn't been trying to see if Faith was impressed with his riding skills, he'd most likely have been able to ride it out. As it was, he suddenly felt himself flying like a bird. He hit the fence, fell to the ground in a cloud of dust, then rolled until he stopped on his back.

He choked. Finding even one thimbleful of air left in his lungs would be a miracle. Damn! His body hurt like hell. From half-closed eyes he watched Faith quickly scale the fence, a flash of white eyelet lace brushing against her long, shapely calf. Running to his side, she didn't even waver as the colt, sweaty and hot, snorted at her and pawed the ground.

Hiding his smile, Luke groaned. He lay still, absorbing her concern.

"Luke," she cried, reaching out and touching his cheek. Running her hand along his face, she turned to the others. "Help me, please. Luke's hurt."

The desperation in her voice almost undid his resolve, but not quite. He would enjoy it a bit longer. Perhaps he'd been wrong. Being distracted might not be such a bad thing.

The men didn't move, just stood there smiling, so she glared at them. "What's wrong with the lot of you? Can't you see Luke's hurt?"

"He's gonna need some serious help when you figure out he's just lyin' there enjoyin' your frettin'," Lucky called from the porch. "I'm thinkin' he's found himself betwixt the ground and a hard spot, and he don't know a way out."

The men all laughed.

Faith turned slowly back toward him. Opening his eyes, Luke winked.

Chapter Thirty

"You . . . you . . ." Faith stammered as Luke watched her face change from a pretty shade of pink to candy-apple red. "I'll get you for this, Luke McCutcheon."

"Now hold on, Faith," he said. "I just wanted a little of that attention you were showering on Chance. And . . . I *am* hurt." He raised up on one elbow, dust and dirt falling from his back and arms. "You saw how I hit that fence. My back hurts something awful." He reached around and felt for an injury.

She glared at him, probably too angry for words. Standing, she brushed the dirt and horse manure from her skirt and hands and promptly marched away.

Trying to stand, Luke's knee buckled under him and he crumpled back down to his hands and knees. Hearing the commotion, Faith turned and ran back, helped him stand. This time Roady was there, too, slinging his arm around Luke's waist and helping him hobble to the gate.

Leaning on Faith, Luke snuggled her closer. Her sweet scent drifted up to needle his guilty conscience. He should feel ashamed of himself, but he didn't. The horse had punished his leg some, but not bad enough that he couldn't walk. He didn't know why he'd pulled this stunt a second time. One brick shy of a full load, his brother Matt would say. Maybe he'd just needed to feel Faith in his arms after last night and all his uncertainties.

"Sit here, Luke," she said, patting the wooden seat of a bench. "I'll get you some water." She was gone before he could tell her he didn't need any.

Whistling, Roady removed his hat and ran his arm across

his sweaty brow. His eyebrows were raised in question. "You sure you know what you're doin'?" he asked quietly. "For pity's sake, Luke, when she finds out you're bluffin' again . . . she's gonna have your hide."

"How did *you* know I wasn't hurt bad?"

"Because I know you. You'd just best hope nobody here spills the beans. I hate to think what she'll do if she finds out."

"Well, hush now, here she comes."

Luke took the dipper she offered and drank until all the cool water was gone. Wiping his mouth he smiled. "Thanks, honey. That was real refreshing."

She looked at him kind of funnylike, then turned her attention to the men who were roping another horse. The work had continued.

"Can you make it to the house?" she asked, her focus back on him, concern etching her face.

"I'm sure I can with help," he answered. When Roady reached out, he waved the man off. "The leg's feeling a bit better. Faith here can help me."

In the house Faith fluffed another pillow and placed it behind Luke's back. She'd raised his injured leg and propped it on the stool as she waited for Mrs. McCutcheon, who'd gone into the kitchen for some doctoring supplies.

"I keep trying to tell you my leg is fine. It just stung for a moment. There's nothin' wrong with it now."

"Hush. We'll be the judge of that when your mother returns." Faith sat down facing Luke. He was such a rugged man; he looked silly, out of place, sitting in such a pretty chair. His dusty leather chaps stood out against the fabric.

The moments dragged on, and Faith felt a little awkward with nothing to say. To occupy herself, she picked up the Bible Mrs. McCutcheon had left sitting open and ran her fingers down the listing of contents.

Out of the corner of her eye she saw Luke smile. "Have you ever read my book?" he asked.

Faith looked up. "Your book?"

"The book of Luke, in the New Testament."

He was talking about the Bible. "No, I haven't," she answered, amused. They shared a smile.

"Go ahead and turn to it. It's towards the back."

Thumbing through the heavy volume, Faith noticed all sorts of things placed lovingly within its pages: small pressed flowers, notes and calling cards yellowed with age. Even a small photograph. She pulled it out and looked.

"That was their wedding day," Luke said, leaning forward.

Faith gazed a long time at the two pictured faces. Most people looked so serious in photographs, but not these two. She took note of the beautiful lace dress, fine in detail, that Mrs. McCutcheon wore—the same one she'd so generously lent to Amy. Her hair was swept up, and she held a bouquet of tiny flowers.

Emotion welled within Faith. It was a wonderful picture. This was what love was like. Sweet. Simple. She returned the photograph to the place she had found it, in Proverbs, and continued.

"There it is," Luke said. "Go back a few pages."

Faith saw. The word was typed in elegant script and stood out bold on the empty page.

"'Luke,'" she read. "You were named from the Bible?"

"That's right. Here, let me show you." Reaching for it, he set the book on his lap. He looked comfortable with it, like it was the most natural thing in the world. And he must have noticed her surprise because he said by way of explanation, "Ma had us all read it when we were younger. Three pages a day, not counting Sundays. Took a couple of years, but we all finished."

Faith was impressed. She'd read from her family Bible in bits and pieces, but not nearly enough to know what all was there.

The thought of reading it through was daunting. And here, surprisingly enough, this rugged cowboy had done just that.

"Come on over here and sit with me. This chair is big enough for a herd of buffalo." He laughed at her look of surprise. "Not that you're any bigger than a mite."

She was tempted to do as he asked. There was a truce hanging between them, sweet and warm, and she felt him drawing her toward him again, against her better judgment. He patted the cushion, looked at her expectantly.

Her leg pressed his as she sat next to him, the chair molding to her shape. A slow smile stole across his mouth, reminding her of when they'd kissed. There was something remarkably exciting about sitting so close to him, but she tried to block it from her mind. She reminded herself to breathe.

"Here," Luke said, pointing. He seemed intent on drawing her attention away from their touching legs.

Looking down she read, "Matthew, Mark, Luke and . . ."

"John," he finished for her. There was a difference in his eyes, a tenderness that stole her breath. "My ma was trying for twelve, but . . ."

Mrs. McCutcheon appeared at the swinging door. Faith was embarrassed at her boldness in sitting so close to Luke, but the older woman didn't seem to notice at all. "How does your knee feel?"

"I think it's fine, Ma," Luke said. "Just getting my weight off of it was all it needed."

Nodding, she headed for the stairs. "I think I'll just go check on Dawn. She's been sleeping for some time now."

They were alone again.

Mrs. McCutcheon surely didn't want her son involved with a widow with two children. Did she? Someone running from the law? Luke had so much to offer a wife: home, protection, an extraordinary family. She had nothing. Just herself and the young'uns. A passel of trouble. Why would she leave them alone, so incredibly close?

Out of the corner of her eye she could see Luke eyeing her lips. Was he thinking about the kisses they'd been sharing all too often as of late? They possessed *her* waking thoughts. Was he feeling the same?

Faith was about to bolt out of the chair; Luke could feel it.

"Were you scared when I got thrown?" he asked, brushing a strand of hair behind her ear. Picking up her hand and lacing her fingers through his, he chuckled.

She nodded.

He said, "If I hadn't been watching you and was concentrating on what I was doing, I wouldn't have been pitched off."

"Is that so?"

"That's so. I guess I've been preaching to the choir about letting you be a distraction. Actually, I'm starting to think it's not so bad."

She giggled happily. He leaned a little closer, noticing the fawn-colored freckles sprinkling the bridge of her nose. The flecks of amber and possibly some green in her toffee brown eyes. He watched her stay her first impulse to pull away from him, saw her skittishness, watched her eyes go dark. He hurried to say, "Faith, I would never hurt you."

Her answer was barely a whisper. "I know."

It was getting almost impossible to listen to reason, which kept telling him to keep his distance from her, to watch and wait until he knew what it was exactly that she was trying to hide. For the hundredth time he reminded himself that this attraction was clouding his usual good judgment. If he got involved, he couldn't be objective.

She jumped up, pulling away from him as Colton ran through the door. "Look, Ma!" the boy said. "Look what Uncle Ward gave me!" He held out a knife encased in a leather sheath. It was covered with many different colored beads, the work intricate and extraordinary.

Luke stood and took the knife from the boy's hands, turned it over and over. It was heavy. Colton wasn't going to like him for this, but the boy was much too young to have it. Not such a dangerous weapon.

Seeming to recognize the direction of his thoughts, Colton frowned. Luke pulled the knife from its protective covering, and the wicked blade winked in the light.

"You can't keep such a knife, Colton," Faith gasped. "It's much too big and sharp."

Colton turned pleading eyes on her. "Pleeeease, Ma," he begged.

Luke saw Faith waver, so he interceded. "No. I'll find you a knife suited to your age," he promised. "Your ma will keep this one until you're older."

Glaring, Colton turned and ran from the house.

Luke reached out and stopped Faith from following. "Give him a little time. He'll come to see the truth in our words. In the meantime I'll try and hunt up a knife he can't hurt himself with."

Chapter Thirty-one

For Faith, the next several days passed in the blink of an eye. Colton continued giving Luke the cold shoulder for taking his knife, which Luke ignored. The boy was learning the rigors of ranch life, though, and seemed to be taking to it. If Faith got a glimpse of him at supper, she was lucky. Up and gone by the time she rose with Dawn, he spent a good part of the day over at Matthew and Rachel's house.

Charity had moved there also, to help Rachel with her household chores and anything heavy that needed doing. Rachel, as bighearted as she was, included Colton in Billy and

Adam's schooling. Her time was getting very near, and everyone was anticipating the new baby with excitement.

Faith had reached a decision, the only one that seemed possible. She would sign the deed for her farm over to Ward. Although the land was the only piece of security she had, and her father had warned her never to sell, it would be worth it to be rid of her past.

Finding a place to speak with him would prove to be difficult, though. True privacy was a rarity with such a large family, the ranch hands and children. She was rarely left alone.

Today was the day. Luke was going into town with his brothers and father. They wouldn't be home until late that evening. Billy and Colton were riding along. The women were spending the day canning and dipping candles, which only left Charity and Mrs. McCutcheon to worry about.

Leaving Dawn with Esperanza, Faith approached the bunkhouse. She'd watched Luke and the others ride out this morning, early, with Colton and Billy trotting behind. Soon after, the other ranch hands departed in one direction or another for their duties.

Faith stalled in the shade of a large ponderosa pine, hoping Ward would come out. She wanted to avoid Lucky. He'd surely report to Luke that she'd come around.

All was quiet. No one came out of the bunkhouse. Faith started to get nervous; Esperanza had things to get done, and she'd promised the maid to only be gone for a short while. Her gut tightened in a knot. Some chickens scratching around in the dirt and a hound lying on the bunkhouse porch, morose over being left behind, were her only company.

She approached the bunkhouse porch slowly, her palms moist, her heart pounding. She stepped around the dog and knocked.

Lucky opened the door. A big grin spread from ear to ear. "I suppose yer tired of all that prissy cookin' at the house. Am

I right, missy?" he asked, dusting the flour from his hands and then wiping them on an apron stained all sorts of colors.

"Hello, Lucky."

At her tone, his smile vanished. He came out and closed the door. "Everythin' all right? Little Dawn ain't feelin' poorly, is she?"

"No. Dawn is fine. I need to speak with Ward. Is he here?" She looked the cook straight in the eyes.

Lucky straightened. His expression bespoke surprise and disappointment. "He's here," he said. She could tell he wanted to say a lot more but was holding back. He was giving her his squinty-eye look, as the men called it.

"It'll only take a minute," she promised. Lucky stood rooted to the spot.

Turning, the cook ambled in, his limp accentuated. Faith heard voices inside, mumbling, and then a sharp word, but she couldn't make out what was being said.

Ward appeared. "Getting antsy to go?" he asked, grinning. Leaning on his crutch, he hobbled over to a chair and sat down. Gesturing to the chair next to him he said, "Set yourself down and get comfortable."

Oh, how she hated giving in to him. If there were any other way, she'd do it. There he sat, so smug and sure of himself, his hurt leg propped up on a nearby stool. She'd like to give it a swift kick.

"I have a proposition for you," she said, easing onto the chair beside him.

Ward's eyebrows arched curiously over his ice blue eyes. "Oh?"

Faith cleared her throat and fingered the bandanna she'd stuck in her pocket this morning. She'd wanted something of Luke's for courage. As she'd passed his room, his door had been left ajar and it was setting on his chest of drawers. "Yes. I think you will be very happy with what I have to say."

Lucky came out then, and, meandering over, threw a

bucket of water off the opposite side of the porch. Setting the bucket down, he stretched his back and gazed out at the corral. Turning, he eyed the two of them.

Annoyance flashed across Ward's face. "You got somethin' to say, old-timer?"

"Nah, jist stretchin' my legs." He let a long string of tobacco juice stream from his mouth, which he then wiped with the back of his sleeve.

Ward waited for the cook to go back inside before he continued. "What is it you have to say, Faith?"

Taking a piece of paper out of her pocket she held it out. "This is the deed to the farm, Ward. I'll sign it over to you today if you'll leave and never come back."

He eyed it for a moment, then relaxed back against the spindles of his chair. "Mind if I take a look?" He reached for the tattered paper. "Fifty-five acres, the house and barn. Everything?" He looked surprised. "You don't want to keep even one little acre?"

"You can have it all."

Bending, Ward picked up a small piece of twine lying on the boards. "Now I'd say that was a right generous offer, Faith."

"I mean it, Ward. You can have it all. But, I keep Colton and Dawn."

"What you're really saying is you want your freedom so you'll be able to marry that jackass, Luke McCutcheon. You got the hots for him, do you?"

Faith tried to remain relaxed. What more did he want? She was giving him everything she had of any value. Surely he didn't want the children because he loved them. His family didn't know the meaning of the word.

"Can't do it," Ward said.

"What?"

"I said no. Don't want it."

Faith sat in stunned silence. Sounds around her grew until they were an overwhelming clamor. The clucking of the chickens. A neigh. The cry of a distant hawk. Blue jays fighting over a morsel of food.

Her gaze dropped to Ward's hands. To her horror she saw he'd fashioned the twine into a miniature hangman's noose. Her throat closed.

"Why?" she was just barely able to get out.

"Because I don't like him," Ward spat out. "That highfalutin Luke McCutcheon. He don't get you. You're going home with me, like we planned. Seeing his face as you ride off with me is going to feel real good. I'll get the farm anyway when you're my wife. We're leaving sooner than I first thought. Another week at the longest."

"Ward, don't do this," Faith begged.

"It's done, sugar."

Chapter Thirty-two

THE McCutcheon men stabled their horses at the livery and walked down the dusty street of Y Knot, Montana, a medium-size town an hour's ride from the ranch. The settlement had grown in the last few years; it wasn't just cowmen and outlaws anymore. Respectable families were relocating, lock, stock, and barrel, to take a chance on this rough territory town, starting anew, like Flood had done umpteen years ago.

"I'll be down at the sheriff's office for a spell," Luke said, waiting for a peddler's wagon to pass before he crossed the rutted street.

Matt addressed Billy and Colton. "Stay out of mischief. Understood?" Both boys nodded seriously.

"I'll meet you," Luke called from the opposite side of the street, "around noon at the Hitching Post." He enjoyed coming to town every so often. He'd tried to talk Charity into riding along, but she didn't want to leave Rachel.

"Yoo-hoo, Luke," a feminine voice sang out from somewhere above. A woman leaned from the second-story balcony of the saloon and waved, her voluptuous body practically spilling from the bodice of her bright green satin dress. "What brings you to town, handsome?" she called in an all-too-husky voice.

"Business, Tilly," Luke called back. He saw his brothers down the street laughing at him. She was bound and determined to improve her standing by marrying a McCutcheon. Any McCutcheon. He was the only unmarried one left in town.

"Don't you leave without saying hello."

"Wouldn't dream of it."

Stepping into the sheriff's office, Luke paused, letting his eyes adjust to the dim interior. The room was musty and damp. Papers were piled on the desk, half of which were Wanted posters and the like. "Crawford, you here?" he called.

"In the back, McCutcheon. I wasn't expecting to see you till next month." Brandon Crawford, the sheriff of Y Knot, appeared out of the back, broom in one hand, dirty dishes in the other. A white apron was tied haphazardly around his waist.

"I wanted to let the brand office know about the new herd we brought home, and also get a few loose ends tied up."

Brandon was eye to eye with Luke and grinning broadly. "Glad you did. I'd shake your hand but as you can see mine are a mite full. Shit. This is disgusting. Jones is about the laziest piece of cow du—" He stopped himself midsentence, set the dishes by the door and tossed the broom into the corner. It landed with a clatter, knocking a half-full cup of old coffee onto the floor. "Guess I knew that when I hired him."

Luke gave the sheriff a sympathetic look. "Good help is

hard to find. I know. The Heart of the Mountains has struggled with the same problem for almost thirty years."

"How's your mother?"

"My mother?" Luke repeated with raised brows. "Don't you really mean Charity?" All the chairs in the office were piled full of clutter. He pushed a stack of papers over and leaned one hip on the desk.

"No, I don't," Brandon said with a snort. "I'm not pinin' any longer, Luke. Charity made her feelings perfectly clear the last time I saw her." The young lawman pushed his fingers through his thick brown hair. "I'm through trying to impress her. She's a grown woman now and has a mind of her own. What's done is done."

"Come on, Crawford, don't quit on me now," Luke teased. "My money's on you. That sister of mine needs a strong, firm hand. I think you're just the man to settle her down. Besides, I told you before, she's just testing you."

Brandon shrugged and changed the subject. "I'd offer you a cup of coffee but there isn't any. Jones forgot to put it on. Again."

Standing, Luke cleared his throat. "You get a chance to check on that matter I asked about the other day when we passed through?"

"I did. Couldn't find out a thing. But I'll keep checking."

"I reckon I can count on you being discreet?" Luke asked.

Brandon studied him. "You know you can."

The men were lost in thought, riding along in silence. Billy and Colton had galloped ahead in their eagerness to get home. Inch by inch, the sun meandered behind a sloping hill blanketed with aspens and pines. Shadows, long of leg, slipped along in front of each horse, vanishing slowly as evening descended. A mourning dove called plaintively to its mate and fluttered across the road, momentarily drawing the horses' attention.

"I heard Trum Edwards is looking to sell out," Matt said, breaking the silence. "That's prime grazing land. I think we should buy it before someone else does."

Flood glanced over. "Good idea. I'll send a message to him tomorrow. See what he's asking."

Luke fingered the piece of paper folded in his pocket. Indecision on when to tell Faith about it weighed heavily on his mind. Christine Meeks had replied almost instantaneously to his telegram, and she needed help immediately. The store, which had grown considerably since she'd opened fifteen years ago, was too much for her alone to handle. Faith could come anytime she was up to traveling. The sooner the better.

The sooner the better? He didn't quite feel the same. But there was one silver lining to this black cloud. At least Faith wasn't going home with Ward.

After Luke's run-in with him in the bunkhouse, he wanted the man gone. Ward was trouble waiting to happen. There was just something about the man that wasn't adding up. It was his eyes— they were shifty, like an injured wolf's. No way would Faith ever agree to marry him. If she did, he never really knew her at all.

At the fork in the road, Matt and Mark split off toward their individual houses and Luke and Flood rode for the barn.

"Something on your mind, Son?" his father asked when they were alone. "You've been mighty quiet all night."

Luke hesitated. He gazed at the ivory moon, so large in the sky. It was just poised there, setting right on the treetops. He looked at Flood. This man had been a good father to him. He'd always been honest.

"Yeah, there is." They rode on a ways. "I'm . . ." This was harder than he'd thought. "Faith seems to be hiding something from me. Holding back."

Flood kept his gaze forward. "Is there something between the two of you? Feelings?" Flood pulled from his pocket a pouch of tobacco and put a pinch under his lip.

"Reckon so. On my part anyway."

"If you give her time, Luke, she may open up."

"Maybe." Stopping in front of the barn, the two men remained in their saddles. "I've told myself since the day I found out you weren't my real pa that I was going to have honesty in my life. Come hell or high water, it was that or nothing. Like you and Ma. Nothing short. And here I find myself thinking after this girl day after day. But I can't get the same answer from her two days running." He shook his head sadly. "And still, I feel myself slipping."

"Some people got their reasons," Flood answered. "Don't be too hard on her. Besides, if it's meant to be, all your resisting won't do a thing. Some things just aren't in your control."

They dismounted and unsaddled in the dark barn. The house looked quiet, as if everyone was already in bed. One lamp burned in the window, a welcome sight for tired cowboys.

"Good night, Son," Flood said as he passed by Luke, who stood at the outdoor washbasin. "Get some rest. Tomorrow just might look a little brighter."

"G'night."

Luke washed the trail dust from his face and hands, then took a cool drink from the well. A rustling in his pocket reminded him of the peppermints he'd bought for the children. He popped one in his mouth.

Up in his room, he paced to the window and stared out. His fingers mechanically went from one button to the next until his shirt was open; then he took it off and tossed it onto the chair in the corner. Was he willing to compromise his beliefs, everything he'd thought was important to him for all these years? His heart gave a resounding *yes!* His mind told him to slow down and think this through. Frustrated, he ran a hand through his hair and sighed. Going to his dresser he reached for the earthen jug of water to splash his face but found it empty. Esperanza must have forgotten to refill it.

Pitcher in hand he headed for the kitchen. In the hallway he paused.

Whimpering—no, *crying*—caught his attention. That didn't sound like Dawn's wail that he'd grown accustomed to at all hours of the night. No, this wasn't Dawn, he was sure. But why would Faith be crying? Had she gotten hurt today while he was gone?

Wasting no time, Luke silently slipped into her room. When his eyes adjusted to the darkness, he saw her facedown in her pillow, trying to cover the sound of her sorrow. He hunkered down next to the bed and set the pitcher on the floor. He leaned close and crooned, "Faith, darlin', don't cry."

She raised her head, surprised. A small hiccup escaped as she looked into his eyes. Then, with trembling hands, she wiped the tears away with the hankie she had twisted in her palm. The look written on her face nearly broke his heart.

"What's wrong? Why are you crying?" He tucked a strand of her hair behind her ear, looking for the answer in her eyes. When she didn't respond but new tears spilled silently out, he gently scooted her over on the bed, making room for him to lie next to her. He gathered her into his arms. Up and down he rubbed her back, while her tears burned his chest.

Her sobs didn't slow but actually grew stronger the more he held and comforted her. "Shh, shh, it's all right," Luke whispered, not wanting to wake Dawn. Faith felt so right in his arms, like she'd been made just for him. She hiccuped again, then held her breath. To his relief, he realized that her tears were finally slowing.

Scooting back, he stared into her face. "Did you hurt yourself?"

She shook her head.

"Then tell me why you're upset."

"I . . . I'm just tired, the strain—"

"Don't do it, Faith," Luke interrupted. "Don't tell me another fabrication."

Burying her face in the crook of his neck she shook her head.

"What's this, you're not going to talk at all?"

"That's right," she whispered back.

Faith felt his deep chuckle before she heard it. She was too intent, marveling at how his strong bare chest, sprinkled with coarse black hair, felt beneath her fingertips. Uncontrollably her fingers skittered here and there, creating gooseflesh across his body. Grasping her hands, Luke held them tight against his chest, and Faith could feel the thundering of his heart.

No more words were spoken. His face, tender with emotion, lowered to hers. The kiss was sweet, short, the melding of souls. Oh, why couldn't Ward leave her be? Take her farm and be gone?

Slowly Luke pulled away from her. "Why were you crying?" he asked again, softly in her ear.

Didn't he know that she'd tell him if she could, if it wouldn't endanger Dawn and Colton or even him or Charity? *Didn't he?* No. He didn't. He couldn't. Because she hadn't told him.

"Tell me," he asked again, kissing her eyes, forehead, mouth.

"I can't," she choked out.

He lifted up on one arm. His eyes glittered with emotion. "No. You can but you choose not to."

"It's just that I want to make my own way, to prove to myself . . ." She looked away and trailed off, and Luke put his finger to her mouth, stopping what she was going to say next.

"Don't say another thing." He rose from the bed and walked to the door. With his hand on the knob he paused. "I was hoping you'd trust me enough to tell me the truth."

There was a different look in his eyes now, one of acceptance, regret. Faith longed to run to him, to kiss him and tell him everything, all the while begging for his forgiveness. But she couldn't. Ward was relentless. He would hurt someone here just for the fun of it. Then he would take her back to where she'd come from and turn her in. His father and the circuit judge were relatives. Ward's father had boasted a time or two of the people they'd cheated. If the judge believed he could benefit monetarily, she was sure he'd go along with his nephew. She had absolutely no doubt that she'd hang, and Dawn and Colton would be lost to her and her protection.

Chapter Thirty-three

*A*NY evidence who did it?" Mrs. McCutcheon asked from the dining room table, her voice filled with distress. Faith's pulse picked up speed while her feet slowed down. Did what? Descending the stairs with Dawn in her arms, she wondered if anyone would notice her eyes, still puffy and red from crying last night.

"No."

The one-word answer from Luke chilled every ounce of blood in her veins. *Ward!* She couldn't see him yet, but she could hear the anger in his voice. Was he still mad at her? She paused on the stairway, looking to see who else was in the room.

"It's so cruel." Luke's mother turned to see Faith descending the stairs. A wan smile crossed her lips. "I can't understand how someone could take their malicious anger out on a defenseless animal."

Faith looked to Luke and found him watching her also. "What happened?"

"A yearling bull, hamstrung and left for dead this morning," Luke answered. Anger and frustration were written all over his face.

"Sounds horrible. What is it?"

"It's when a man slices the leg tendons so an animal can't walk. Has no power over his legs. The animal usually bleeds to death in minutes. We found this particular bull lying in a pool of blood. The animal was weak but still hanging on." Luke ran a hand through his hair. Faith could feel his anger humming in the room.

"Can anything be done to save him?" she asked.

"No. We put him down when we found him."

At that moment, Smokey, Chance and Ike, with Colton and Billy in tow, thumped into the house. The cowboys politely removed their hats and waited at the door for Luke.

"Please, boys," Mrs. McCutcheon said, "make yourselves comfortable." But they just stood there.

The sight of the three brought familiarity and comfort to Faith. Dressed in their sturdy work clothes and not yet dusty this early in the day, they looked wholesome and sweetly attractive. They smiled and nodded in her direction but didn't say anything.

Colton hurried to Faith's side, clearly upset. "Ma," he said, doing his best to hold back tears. "Matt had to shoot a bull!" His shoulders shook as she drew him into her embrace. He immediately pulled back, perhaps embarrassed in front of the others. He ground one fist in the palm of the other.

"Did you find out anything new from the men?" Luke asked the ranch hands. "Did anyone see anything or anyone that looked suspicious last night?"

Smokey took a small step forward. "Not yet, but Roady, he's down at the bunkhouse just now talkin' with the boys that rode the late watch. He oughta be here shortly."

Mrs. McCutcheon placed a comforting hand on Luke's arm. "Here he comes now," the older woman said as she watched out the window. Unease tingled inside Faith: responsibility for the bull. Somehow this was her doing.

Roady joined the group inside, his brow furrowed in thought. A stony mask covered his face, in sharp contrast to his normally easygoing nature.

"Well?" Luke said.

Roady didn't answer. Looking at Billy and Colton, he seemed apprehensive.

Luke caught his meaning. "Boys, run out to the barn and unsaddle your horses. They've had enough of a workout for one day."

"But . . . Okay, Uncle Luke," Billy said, heading to the door. He looked over his shoulder. "Come on, Colton, reckon they got things to discuss we can't hear."

With the boys gone, the men, along with Mrs. McCutcheon, crowded around Roady. Faith stayed back.

Roady turned his hat in his hands, rolling the rim. "No one saw anythin' definite."

"What *did* they see?" Luke asked.

Roady looked around at Smokey, Ike and Chance. "I think we'd better discuss this in private, Luke."

"Come on, men, we've just been dismissed, too," Smokey said. "We'll be in the barn with the boys if you need us."

The men shuffled for the door, heading out single file. That left Faith, Luke's mother, Roady and Luke. Faith, feeling like an intruder, headed for the stairs.

Roady cleared his throat. "You might want to stay, Faith."

Fear crackled through her. No, she didn't want to stay. She didn't want to be involved in this. But somehow she knew she already was.

Roady looked apologetically toward Mrs. McCutcheon. "Pedro was coming in around two. Said he heard something in the barn." He cleared his throat again.

Faith noted a look of pain on Luke's face, as if he already knew where this was leading. She wished Roady would just hurry up and spit it out. The suspense was making her sick.

"When he crept in, he saw Ward Brown. Him and Charity . . . well . . ."

Mrs. McCutcheon sank into the welcoming cushions of the tapestry chair, her face pasty white, her eyes closed. Luke was almost out the door when Roady caught his arm.

Luke shook off his grip. "I'll kill him."

"Just a minute! They were only talking . . . and getting a mite friendly. Pedro broke it up before . . . well, he escorted Charity back to Rachel's. Ward took off and wasn't seen till morning."

"I'll kill him," Luke repeated, pacing in front of the fireplace. He stopped and turned on Faith as if just remembering that she was there. His eyes were unreadable. They seared Faith from head to toe.

Apparently deciding he didn't want to reveal to his mother the connection, at least not yet, he turned his gaze to her. She still sat quietly.

"I can run him off or even escort him home," Roady offered. An unsure expression made his handsome face somber.

Mrs. McCutcheon stood, her back straight, her blue eyes snapping. "We're not running him off. That just won't do." She ran a hand across her swept-up hair. "Charity's growing up. Like it or not, it's a fact. The surest way to send her falling into his arms is to tell her she can't. The more we say no, the harder she's going to say yes. Besides, let's not forget that he did help save Mark from a sure death. That has to count for something."

Luke stood frozen, like a predator ready to pounce on some unsuspecting critter. Muscles in his jaw clenched. "We're not going to do anything about this?"

"That's right, Luke." Mrs. McCutcheon smiled a little, regaining her composure. "I was her age when I first met Flood. As you know, my papa was a preacher and as strict as they come. His constant ravings about the no-good saddle bum that was showing his only daughter a little interest only fueled the fire that was burning inside me."

"She has a point, Luke. Just like that old mule you got hanging around here. The minute he gets out he always heads for Esperanza's garden—the one place he's not allowed to be."

"Are you comparing my sister to that flea-bitten mule?"

"No, I'm not!" Roady chuckled mirthlessly. "I'm just agreeing with your ma. I think she has a point. If Charity has taken to Brown," he said distastefully, "then running him off won't do any good. She's an expert tracker. She could find him faster than most men in this outfit."

"Thank you, Roady," Luke's mother said. "We'll leave this be until I have a chance to talk with Flood. He'll know what to do. Luke, give me your word you'll stay clear of that man."

Luke grimaced and nodded. "Where's Charity now?"

"She hasn't come home yet from Rachel's," his mother answered.

Luke snorted. "Knowing Charity, she did her very best sweet-talking Pedro last night and thinks he won't say anything. But she won't be sure. Right about now the waiting will be driving her crazy." His eyes glittered, and a slow smile replaced his scowl. "We'll just let her stew until Pa gets back from the east range. Roady and I'll ride out and meet Matt up north. See what he's found out."

His hat back on his head, Roady turned to leave. Luke glanced at Faith and said to him, "I'll catch up in a minute. I'll find you."

"Sure," Roady replied.

Mrs. McCutcheon was already halfway up the stairs. Luke gestured to Faith to come have a seat on the sofa. She didn't want to talk to him then, not when he was so mad, especially after last night, but she approached, Dawn snuggled to her breast as if the baby were her protector.

Dawn gurgled in delight at the closeness. She had filled out. Her little cheeks were now plump and rosy in color, and she seemed to have transformed overnight into a happy baby instead of a wrinkly newborn.

"Luke, she just smiled!" Faith pointed out excitedly. All her worry over Luke's mood was forgotten. "Did you see?"

"No." Luke stood ramrod straight. His stance bespoke anger but his pupils darkened. Adoration shimmered in his eyes when he looked down at the baby.

"It was a real smile, and she was looking right at me."

Luke ignored her comment and sat. He waited for her to do the same. "Is he capable of slaughter?" he asked.

"Ward?" she clarified, feeling all her joy disappear. "Yes. He is. He's capable of anything." Again she felt ashamed for bringing this mess to Luke's doorstep.

"And compromising Charity?"

How did an honorable man make sense of the ways of the immoral? Luke would never compromise a woman for his own gratification. He didn't have it in him.

She nodded.

Luke sighed. "I felt pretty sure that he was, but I wanted to hear it from you."

"I'm sorry for bringing this trouble to your ranch. And, to you. I wish Ward never found me, never followed after we left."

Luke glanced down at a Bible that sat open on a footstool. His face softened. "You know, last night when I found you crying . . . I thought just maybe you'd open up, tell me what's eating at you . . ."

She couldn't let him go on. Quickly she pressed her hand to his mouth. "Don't, Luke. Please, just let it go."

"Fine," he whispered. "It's done." He stood and walked to the window that looked out over the ranch. He seemed to be struggling with something. Returning, he handed her a piece of paper. "This is for you."

Faith opened it and quickly scanned the telegram's words. "It's true, then? About the job?" She sucked in a breath. "And, she wants me as soon as possible."

"That's right. As soon as you feel up to the trip."

Ward, her mind shouted. *What do I do about Ward?* She looked up to find Luke analyzing her.

"What?" she asked.

"Nothing. I was just thinking."

"Well, that's plain enough. I want to know what you were thinking."

Luke left the question unanswered. "I need to get back to work." Pulling his hat on, he made for the door.

"Luke?" she said.

He turned.

"Thanks for this," Faith said, holding up the tattered paper. "Contacting Christine Meeks for me."

"I reckon it was the least I could do for a guest staying under our roof."

He made it sound so impersonal. Darn him, anyway. Stubborn must be his middle name. Luke Stubborn McCutcheon. She'd tell him, if she could. Confiding the whole darn mess would be a blessing. But she couldn't. And that's what she had to remember, strengthen herself to not give in to the temptation.

Chapter Thirty-four

WARD Brown was probably still asleep, exhausted from his nocturnal activities.

Luke untied his horse's reins from the hitching rail. Across the worn leather of his saddle, he glared at the bunkhouse. Wanting to kick himself for not seeing this coming and allocating one of the men to watch the stranger day and night, he sighed. He should have trusted Faith's initial comments about the man, explained or not. He shouldn't have been so caught up in trying to discern her other motives.

A firm knot formed in his chest. *Charity.* She'd been his constant and all-adoring shadow forever. As soon as she was able to ride on her own she'd been tagging along after him. Rain, snow, it didn't matter. Kindred spirits, she'd called them. And he realized that he hadn't given her much of his time since he'd returned from this drive.

Lucky stepped out of the bunkhouse. The cook limped

around back, slop bucket in one hand and kitchen cloth hanging over his shoulder. His limp seemed more pronounced this morning, and Luke realized just how old his friend was getting.

Returning, Lucky spotted him. He waved and started over, shaking his head. "Just a shame. About the bull, I mean. I jist can't cotton to any feller who'd do such a thing. Can't understand it."

"None of us can, Lucky."

"It's truly a shame. Any idea who dun it?"

"I have my suspicions, but nothing we can pin down yet," Luke said. "But I won't rest until we know."

Lucky looked away, clearly not able to meet his gaze. "I almost forgot to tell ya," he said slowly. "Yesterday, when you all rode inta town, missy"—his voice caught—"came by. She was looking for Ward."

Luke's stare drifted from Lucky to the house, stopping on Faith's upstairs window. More secrets?

"They sat out on the porch for a spell, talking. I went out once to check on 'em, and missy, she looked white as a sheet. I'm thinkin' that polecat is stickin' around for more reasons than his injured leg."

His next move was clear. Pulling his horse around, Luke stuck his foot in the stirrup. In one easy motion he was mounted. "Thanks, Lucky. Keep your eye on Ward today, will you? I want to know if he leaves the bunkhouse. Send Francis to get me if he does, but don't let him know he's being watched. I'm going out to where the bull was killed."

The old man nodded in understanding, and Luke galloped off.

The bull had been of superior breeding and worth a small fortune, but the cruelty of the act was far more serious. Unfortunately, the perpetrator left no evidence. After an hour came and went, Luke wasn't any closer to knowing anything more.

Frustration ate at him as he rode back. And annoyance at not being able to pin the bull's crippling on Ward wasn't the only thing gnawing at his insides. Faith's visit with Ward mystified him. And Charity, his sister's lack of judgment. He couldn't believe that she'd actually gone seeking the man out. In fact, he *wouldn't* believe it. It had to have been the other way around. Didn't Charity know if they'd gone too far Ward could end up her husband?

"I want to marry you, Luke. Then we can be together always," Charity had said once, when she was not any older than Colton. Her sweet words had touched his young heart, grounding him in her love.

He'd laughed, of course. "You'll think different when you're older, half-pint. Some handsome man will ride up and steal your heart. He'll take you away to some faraway place."

"No, Luke," she'd promised. "Even if I can't marry you, I'm always staying here. I want to live here and work the ranch all my life. Just like you. I'm never leaving. I promise."

Too many things to think about in one morning.

Circling back to the barn, Luke saddled up Charity's palamino. Ponying the horse behind his, he rode over to Matt's, determined to do what he should have done when he'd first gotten home: be his sister's friend.

Her huge belly preceding her, a mixing spoon in one hand, a smile on her face, Rachel answered the door. "Luke, what brings you out so early?"

Luke was always amazed at his sister-in-law's pleasant disposition. Never was she angry, impatient or sullen. A sweet smile now graced her face that went clear to her eyes. It was obvious she hadn't heard about Charity or the bull.

"Mornin', Rachel. I'm looking for Charity. Is she here?"

"She sure is. Come on in while I fetch her for you." Halfway to the hall she stopped. "Would you like a cup of coffee, Luke? It's freshly made."

Luke waited in the entry, not wanting to muck up Rachel's clean floors with his dirty boots. "No, thanks."

In moments, Charity, dressed and as fresh as a spring rose,

came waltzing out of the kitchen as if she hadn't a care in the world. Luke's heart twisted. On the outside he saw what he always did: a beautiful young woman just coming into her own. Confident and sharp.

As she smiled, his temper flared. Damn it, she knew better! She'd heard the family's conversations from time to time about women who were loose, not caring about their reputations. What could happen if she wasn't careful.

"Brought your horse around," he said calmly. "I'm riding out to Three Forks to check on the cattle there. Hoped you might want to go with me."

Her eyes lit eagerly before suspicion clouded them. "I really don't want to leave Rachel alone this close to her time. She could need me at any moment."

Luke glanced at his sister-in-law over Charity's head, his eyes beseeching.

"Don't be silly," Rachel said. "Go with your brother for a ride. The fresh air will do you good. You've been cooped up here with me for days." She placed her hand on her belly and stretched. "I have Adam here. He can run for your mother if I need anything. You go on, now."

Luke flashed Rachel a smile of gratitude. To Charity he said, "I'll be waiting outside."

He'd had a plan but, miles from the house, he still hadn't gotten past polite conversation. From the corner of his eye he could see his sister sitting her horse, propped straight in her saddle, pretty as a picture. Someone who didn't know her true explosive fire, her great love of adventure, would think she was a demure young lady.

He had to change his impression of her, accept the reality that she'd grown up. She wasn't a child any longer. That, he realized, was the heart of the problem: she wanted to be noticed and, if it wasn't going to come from her family, she'd get her attention elsewhere. Like the hayloft of the dark barn.

They needed to talk. But why was it so darn hard to get

started? He'd never had a problem talking with her before. For that matter, Charity had never held back from him, telling him the most intimate of things. Granted, those things had never included men. She was growing up and he hadn't seen the signs.

Hell. Who was he kidding? She was *grown*.

"Saw Brandon yesterday," he said nonchalantly.

Charity was relaxed in her saddle, watching the billowy clouds in the sky. "How is he?"

"Better now. He's finally over you breaking his heart."

She straightened in her saddle just a hair and, reaching down, fingered her mare's silvery mane.

"There's a new girl in town. The schoolmarm's niece. Heard he's been stepping out with her." He hoped Charity wouldn't go to town anytime soon. It was true about Miss Langford having a niece, but she'd make the rankest of men run for cover.

Charity's response was a smile. Enthusiastically she replied, "I'm so glad."

Luke had always known Charity was a good actress, but this performance was truly outstanding. His sister cared for Brandon, he was positive. They'd had an attraction for years. She was just too confident in the young sheriff's love for her. Luke felt in his bones that Charity would snap to, if ever given some true competition.

"Saw her myself," he continued, giving a low whistle. He was intent on getting a reaction. "Too bad I didn't see her first, before Brandon had a chance to stake his claim. She's from Boston. Hope she won't miss her family too much if they decide to marry."

Charity turned in her saddle, looking over the grass-covered meadow. "Who knows, Luke? Maybe Brandon will want to go back and see the city. Maybe he'll even want to settle there."

"Don't count on it. He's a Western man through and through. Hell, he hates cities. Whoever ends up taking him on is going to be stuck out here. The way I see it, a wife follows her husband—or should—living where he wants, leaving her family and friends, clinging to him through good and bad. Just like Amy and Rachel. And, of course, Mother."

That seemed to give her pause. They rode on in silence for some time. He'd just let her stew. The Heart of the Mountains without Charity? That was a sad thought. She'd said for years she was *never* moving away.

She was pretty quiet for about an hour. When they stopped at a stream to let their horses drink, Luke looked her over and admitted, "So, you're quite grown. That's a fact. You planning to attend that finishing school Ma thinks so highly of?"

A look of horror crossed her face, and then she studied him as if trying to figure out if he knew about her shenanigans last night.

Luke smiled. "Just wondering."

"You know my plans, Luke. I'm staying right here. I can ranch as well as any of my brothers, including you," she bragged.

"Oh? I just hadn't heard you say it for a while and got to wondering." He dismounted and checked his mount's right hind hoof for a stone. Setting it down, he leaned against the horse's hip. "I reckon I just needed to hear it again."

"I'm not a kid anymore, Luke."

"I know, Charity." He affectionately slapped his horse on its hindquarter and remounted. "That's what has me worried."

Chapter Thirty-five

RETURNING to the ranch, Luke saw Charity to Matt and Rachel's house and offered to take her horse back with his. Arriving at the corrals Luke found Francis sitting in the entry of the huge log barn, polishing glass chimneys from lanterns used to light the bunkhouse and yard area. He had the pear-shaped globes lined up on a sturdy table, sparkling in the sunshine. Luke dismounted as Francis came forward. The boy reached for the reins of both horses.

"Thanks, Francis, but I'll do it," Luke said, shaking his head. He needed time to think. With Charity occupied for the time being, he needed to ponder on Faith.

He looped both sets of reins around the hitching rail inside the barn's dim interior and threw his stirrup over the saddle of his mount. He unbuckled the back cinch, letting the leather swing, and reached for the front. The bay gelding he'd picked as a replacement for Chiquita gave a deep sigh.

Luke lifted the saddle and pulled off the pads. The aroma of warm horseflesh and sweat floated up. With ease he carried the heavy, hand-tooled saddle to the saddle rack and laid the pads upside down atop the seat so they could air out and dry; then he ran a brush over the bay and turned the horse out in a freshly bedded stall. He repeated the process with Charity's palomino mare and gave each animal a small scoop of grain, as a reward.

Lucky had said Faith came looking for Ward. Luke would've thought it would be the other way around. What had Ward done or said to make her cry as if the whole world were coming to an end? He had been sure her tears were because of him.

"Hear any more about the bull?" he asked Francis on his way out.

"No, it's been real quiet around here."

Luke looked first to the house, glancing at Faith's window, then to the bunkhouse, weighing which situation needed his attention first.

"Faith. Have you seen her?"

Francis shook his head. "'Bout the only folks I've seen are your ma and pa. Flood rode to town this morning to tell the sheriff about the bull. Your ma went with him."

That settled it: he'd see to Faith just as soon as he had a talk with Ward. He'd waited as long as he could.

He opened and closed his fists as he strode toward the bunkhouse. It was going to feel real good planting his fist in the middle of that man's smug face. Injured or not, he should've thought before he messed with either Faith and Charity.

Lucky was skinning an onion over a pail, and tears streamed down his weatherworn face. He glanced over as Luke entered, then lifted the lid off a giant cast-iron kettle and tossed in the vegetable.

Ward, sitting at the table, was playing solitaire. Seeing Luke in the doorway, he smiled.

"Stand up, Brown."

Gathering the cards, Ward held them in his hands. He didn't look quite as relaxed. "McCutcheon," he said, standing.

In the blink of an eye, Luke had him by the shirtfront. Ward's startled eyes grew black with anger. He tried to shake Luke off, but his attempts were useless.

Adrenaline shot through Luke. "You dare touch my sister?"

"Nothing happened," Ward answered. "She's been giving me the eye ever since I arrived. I find it a mite convenient she was just hanging around out at the barn, too. I got the distinct impression she was waiting for me."

Luke slammed his fist into Ward's stomach, and the man's air expelled in a whoosh as he doubled over. Luke threw him to the floor. Ward slowly stood, his arm pushing into his hurt abdomen.

"You'd hit an injured man?"

"Injured?" Luke scoffed. "You're nursing that leg to stay on longer than necessary. You're as fit as any man here." He held back, knowing his mother was going to be madder than a wet cat when she found out he'd taken the matter into his own hands. Still, he couldn't help but say, "Come on, Brown, let's see what you're made of."

Faster than Luke thought possible, Ward picked up a chair and swung. Luke ducked. The chair leg glanced off his temple, sending him reeling. Ward next hurled his full weight on top of him, knocking the air from Luke's lungs.

The man was able to get one good punch into his face before Luke rolled over, taking Ward with him. The stinging in his right eye didn't stop Luke as he threw blow after blow to Ward's face. Soon the other man wasn't fighting back but lay limply on the floor. From far away, somewhere behind his raging anger, Luke heard Lucky's voice screeching to lay off.

Luke stayed his fists. He shook Ward until the man opened his eyes. "Don't ever even look in Charity's direction, understand?"

Ward nodded.

"And, what the hell did you say to Faith to make her cry?" Ward didn't answer, so Luke shoved him, knocking his head against the floor.

"Nothing. She came looking for me. I guess she just wanted to talk." He panted a couple of times, then continued. "She was reminiscing about Samuel. Guess she's missing him some."

Luke didn't believe it for a minute, but he didn't think he'd get anything truthful out of Ward. "You're scum, Brown," he said. "If you think because you saved Mark you can do whatever you like, you're mistaken. As far as I'm concerned, me not killing you right now makes us even. Furthermore, if we find out you're the one who crippled our bull, we'll hang you. It's the law of the range. No one will question it. So my advice to you is get the hell out of here before I decide a beating isn't enough for you."

Standing, Luke brushed the dirt from his hands and looked to Lucky, who held out a thick chunk of raw beef. "Put this here to your eye. Looks like it's gonna be a real shiner."

Luke just waved him off.

Ward struggled to his feet and then wobbled outside to the washbasin. His face was bloody and bruised, but the sight gave Luke little comfort.

"Make sure he doesn't leave the bunkhouse," he said to Lucky. "I don't trust him around anyone."

Lucky sighed. "Reckon you're right."

On her way to the kitchen, Faith ran smack into Luke, filthier than Colton the day he was bucked off the back of Smokey's horse.

Lifting her gaze to his face, she couldn't stop her gasp. "Your eye. Your poor face!"

Luke just stood there. The injured eye was streaked with blood the color of molasses, and the skin around it, red and angry, was swelling with fluid. "Hurts bad," he said after a moment.

"It must. I've never seen one so bloody. Sit over here and I'll get you a cool cloth." She led Luke to the sofa and sat him down. "Would you rather lie on your bed? Does your head hurt, too?"

"That sounds like a good idea," he admitted.

"Fine, then." She helped him stand, then ushered him upstairs and fluffed his pillows before he sat down and lay back. "Comfortable?"

He nodded.

Faith hurried back down the stairs, and in the kitchen she found a clean cloth. Working the pump until water gushed forth, she caught it in a pail. Next she filled a glass and started back up the stairs.

When she returned, Luke's eyes were closed and his long legs stretched out on the bed, his feet crossed. She softly called his name. "Luke?"

He didn't open his eyes. "Yeah."

"What happened?"

"Had a little run-in with someone's fist. Nothing to worry about."

She didn't want to pry. She had the sneaking suspicion that the fist was Ward's, but she'd find out later, after he felt better.

Gingerly she pressed the cold cloth to Luke's eye, and he flinched.

"Sorry." She waited until he seemed to relax, then continued her cleaning. Several other scrapes and cuts on his face were angry and red, so she dabbed at them with the corner of the cloth.

Unable to stop them, she watched her fingers lightly smooth his soft black hair back from his forehead. Unexpectedly a long lump rose under his hairline, quickly turning an ugly purple and brown.

"You've been hurt worse than your eye. This looks really bad."

Almost asleep, his answer was a whisper. "Just a bump. Nothing to get your skirts in a knot over."

Faith couldn't help but smile, amused. But her heart trembled at the thought of him fighting Ward. And Ward wouldn't even be here if it weren't for her! How much would this family suffer because she'd been thrown into their lives? First Charity and now this. It was too much.

"I'm so sorry," she said.

Luke opened his eyes. "Why are you sorry? You're not responsible for what that man does." He looked deep into her eyes. Funny, she felt like he didn't blame her. He really didn't. And, oh, how his eyes did strange things to her insides. What would loving be like with Luke? She knew in her heart that the union wouldn't be like it had been with Samuel. It would be wonderful and sweet.

The beginnings of a slow smile tipped up his lips. The look in his eyes made her wonder if he'd been able to read her thoughts. She felt her face heat.

"It feels real nice," he said.

Flustered, she wondered if he was talking about the cool rag or something entirely different. Her thoughts galloped back to last night as they'd lain together on the soft bed, his body melding with hers in the most natural way. Again she found herself wondering why she couldn't just tell him the truth. Then when she left he wouldn't hate her. He would know at least that she'd had to go. That she'd had no other choice.

If she looked into his eyes a moment longer she would tell him; she wouldn't be able to stop herself. So she stood. "I'm going to check on Dawn. It's her feeding time. Will you be all right alone for a little while?"

He nodded and closed his eyes. "Only a little while, though."

Nodding, Faith went to see her baby. In the room across the hall, Dawn slept peacefully. Faith paced back and forth, telling herself that she only had herself to count on now, but she'd get through this. She was strong. It was best if Luke hated her when she left to supposedly work in Priest's Crossing. Then he wouldn't follow and find out she was really with Ward. That secret she'd do anything to spare him.

Anything.

Excited voices woke Luke from his deep sleep. Confused, he tried to remember where he was and why he was lying in his bed when there was daylight streaming through his window. The motion of turning his head made him wince and feel like he needed to throw up. He lay back until the feeling passed.

His head and neck were painfully sore, and his eye was another matter. Gingerly he explored it with his fingers as he remembered the fight. He might be hurting some, but he'd give a buffalo nickel to see Ward.

Faith materialized out of thin air. She rushed through his doorway, excitement brimming in her eyes. She cradled Dawn, who was wrapped in a blanket. The voices continued.

"What's all the commotion downstairs?" Luke asked. With everything else that'd happened today, he wouldn't be surprised if she said the sun had fallen from the sky.

"It's Adam. He says his ma is going to have her baby now."

"As if she has a choice," he mumbled tiredly.

Faith smiled, then gave a quiet laugh. "You're right about that, Luke McCutcheon. Our babies make the rules, don't they?" She glanced down at Dawn, placed her finger in the baby's tiny fist and wiggled it around.

The look of adoration and love on her face was a sight to see. Did she wish her dead husband could see his daughter? Luke wondered. Was she missing him, as Ward said? He pushed the jealous thought out of his mind and asked, "So. Did you get her fed?"

Faith glanced up. "Oh, yes. Why, that was some time ago. You've been asleep for a couple of hours at least."

Luke struggled to sit up. He'd had no idea he'd been resting that long. He had things to do; the men must be wondering where he'd made off to. A wave of dizziness swept over him, and he closed his eyes.

"You don't look too good, Luke. Maybe you'd better lie back down."

"I'm getting up and going to Matt's. Has he been told yet?"

"Yes."

Luke stood. Feeling better now that he'd gotten his balance back, he stepped close to Faith and looked down at her child. "You want to come?"

"Do you think she'd mind?"

"No. I'm sure she'd be glad to have your help. Being that you're an experienced mother and all. Gather what you need and I'll wait downstairs."

Faith was down shortly, and the three of them headed for Matt's. On the way they saw Chance, Roady and Smokey on the bunkhouse porch, eating their noon meals. Seeing Luke, they broke into earsplitting grins.

"Boys," Luke acknowledged.

They just nodded and kept eating. But their smiles proved Ward looked a sight worse than he did.

They took a footpath that would join up with the road that led to his brother's house. It was well-worn from constant use of the family going back and forth. Its sides were lined with rocks, and there was a little bench under some trees along the way.

"Won't she get a mite warm dressed like that?" Luke looked again at the baby, who was bundled in a dressing gown and also wrapped snugly in a blanket. A beanie that his mother had knitted and given to Faith topped her head.

"I don't want her to catch a chill."

Luke laughed. "For God's sake, Faith. It's nice out."

"You think she's too warm?"

"She must be roasting, wrapped up like that." Luke pointed to the infant's shiny forehead. "I think she's sweating."

"You're right." Faith pulled the little hat from Dawn's head and opened the blanket.

The baby, with her sky blue eyes, looked right up into Luke's face, interested. She was much more alert now, compared to when she was born. Completely aware of the things around her. Luke smiled down at her as they walked.

"Howdy there, perdy little gal," he said, accentuating his Western drawl. Faith giggled. "You don't think I'll scare her with this eye?" he added, pointing to his face. She laughed again and shook her head.

Matt's house sat atop a little knoll. When he went to build his own home, Luke planned a place with a little more privacy. Especially if he had a wife like Faith. Why, he'd take her off to a spot like the upper crest. A place a man could feel the land around him there, all-encompassing and grand.

Faith went about collecting anything that was even remotely connected to the flower family. Most of her treasures were wild grasses or weeds, but she did manage to find a late-blooming pink primrose to add to her makeshift bouquet. It occupied her as they walked.

Luke knocked softly on Matt's door. Swinging it open, he let Faith step in before him.

Charity was the first to greet them. She blanched when she

saw Luke's face and hid her mouth behind her hand. "What happened to you?"

Matt gave a long whistle, stepping out from his bedroom. His brows shot up in question.

Luke answered with a knowing look. A moment later he asked, "Find out anything more about the bull?"

"No. Nobody saw anything, and the one you're wondering about has an alibi of sorts. Said he was playing cards with that Cheyenne scout who lives in the area, Eagle Gray. I wasn't able to find Eagle this morning, but I have word out for him to report in."

Luke nodded toward the bedroom. "How's Rachel?"

"Just getting started. I'm going to ride out and inform Mark." At Luke's surprised look, Matt laughed. "Don't worry, little brother, he's not far. Besides, if the delivery goes like the other two, I've got lots of time."

After Matt's departure, Amy came hurrying out of the bedroom. "I thought I heard your voice!" She gave Faith a hug. "How are you?"

"Fine. How are *you?*" Faith replied.

Amy smiled and turned, pulling her off to the side. "I'm just fine . . . No," Luke heard her whisper, strangely excited. "I'm better than fine."

"I'm just going to poke my head in and say hello," he said to no one in particular. Neither Faith nor Amy answered; they were too busy chatting, so he took Dawn from Faith and went into Rachel's bedroom.

"Luke," Rachel said breathlessly on the tail end of a contraction. "Your poor, handsome face. What happened?"

"Got into a fracas, but I'll live."

"I thought you gave up your fighting ways." She smiled affectionately and patted the side of her bed. "Is that Dawn you have there?"

He nodded.

"Bring her here so I can see her."

Next to the bed Luke bent down so Rachel could see the child. The baby stared back, blue eyes shining.

Rachel held her breath. "Isn't she beautiful? Like a little angel."

Luke laughed. "You're just used to boys."

"May I hold her?"

Luke handed the baby over. Within moments Dawn started to fuss and Rachel said, "Here, take her back. I don't want to upset her."

Oddly, as soon as Dawn was back in his arms, she quieted. Her eyes were brimming with tears ready to fall, and her little lower lip was shaking. As silly as it felt, Luke was moved that she seemed to want to be held by him.

Faith watched from the doorway as Rachel handed her crying child back to Luke. Tenderness shone from his one good eye, an expression which you'd only expect to see from a new father.

She rapped gently on the doorjamb. "May I come in?"

"Of course," Rachel said.

Approaching the bed, Faith stopped next to Luke. She suddenly felt a little foolish for gathering the bouquet she held behind her back. "I brought these for you," she admitted, producing the scraggily bunch of greenery.

"You're sweet. Thank you."

"How're you feeling?"

"I'm fine. My pains are coming about every ten minutes or so, and Matt's going to send one of the men to town to fetch Dr. Handerhoosen."

Faith eyed Luke. "A doctor? How wonderful. I'm glad to hear you're going to have plenty of help."

"He was here to help with Billy," Rachel informed her, "though I had Adam on my own, with the help of Claire and Charity. The doc was tied up and came out the following day." She lay back on her pillow, a smile on her lips. Soon her smile faded and she closed her eyes, a contraction rippling through her body and making her stomach stretch taut. After a few tense seconds, though, her smile reappeared.

"She's so good at this," Faith exclaimed. "I was so out of control."

"You weren't out of control," Luke replied, rocking Dawn. "As a matter of fact, I was quite impressed at how in control you seemed to be. Particularly considering that you were alone apart from Colton in the most hellish downpour I've seen in fifteen years."

"Well, I'm just glad it's over," Faith said. "It's one experience I don't—"

Rachel interrupted before she could finish. "Yes, you will. Because what you get in the end more than outweighs the pain and worry you have to go through."

"Come on, Faith," Luke said. "Let's let Rachel get a little sleep before her labor sets in." He touched her arm while giving Rachel an encouraging smile. "We'll be waiting in the front room."

Chapter Thirty-six

$\mathcal{J}$T was well past six o'clock. Luke had taken Dawn back to the main house so Faith could stay and help with Rachel, whose labor was now very active. Both he and Rachel had assured Faith that Esperanza had plenty of experience looking after infants, and that Dawn would be in expert hands.

"I'm warming some soup for the men," Charity called from the kitchen. "Would you like some?"

Faith's stomach knotted. She could no more eat than run naked through the house. Rachel's contractions were powerful. Sweat was running down the sides of her face, and the bedsheets were soaked. The woman's eyes, clouded with pain, were dull with exhaustion.

Soon after Matt had ridden off to find Mark, Rachel had switched from calm and comfortable to full-blown labor, a reaction forceful enough to indicate the whole process was starting in earnest. Since then, Matt had returned, saying Roady was on his way to fetch Doc and would be back just as soon as possible. Amy had become withdrawn and nervous when Rachel's labor became hard, and she had taken the children over to the big house. Luke had also returned.

Mopping a cool rag across Rachel's forehead, Faith squelched the impulse to shiver. Soon it would be time for Rachel to push, and she'd feel better if Mrs. McCutcheon would hurry up and get back from town. Faith couldn't shake a niggling feeling eating away at her insides.

Where was that darned doctor, anyway? Luke had said he would be arriving anytime. He was no doubt tied up with someone else, because he'd been expected long ago.

"Push," Rachel gasped out. "I need to push."

Faith was jarred from her thoughts. Adrenaline shot through her. She wiped Rachel's face and smiled. "That's good. Just wait for one minute. I'll be right back." She doubted Rachel even heard, for her eyes were closed and she was in the middle of another contraction.

Trying to calm herself, Faith hurried into the other room. The men were eating, discussing the possibilities of the new herd of cattle and what it was going to do for their existing breeding program. The lantern on the table cast a warm golden light and also the men's shadows onto the rough log walls.

Mark ripped off a piece of bread and passed it to Luke. Both men were totally absorbed in their conversation, as if Faith and Rachel were just in the other room having a tea party. Faith suppressed the urge to kick them in the shins.

"She's wanting to push now." She knew her voice sounded

panicky, but that was the least of her concerns. "Where is the doctor?"

Matt smiled up from his seat at the table. "Relax, Faith, Rachel is an expert at this by now. She pops 'em out like kittens."

Luke didn't look quite as sure. He stood. "Anything you need me to do, Faith?"

Yes! Hold me and tell me everything is going to be fine. But she couldn't say that.

His very presence was enough to give her courage. She wished he could come in the other room with her; he was the one with the experience at delivering. She'd been something of a reluctant participant.

"Let me wash up and I'll help," Charity said. "I'm plenty old enough now."

Faith couldn't help taking the opportunity for a jibe. "If you do that, who will keep the men busy, so they won't worry?" She directed her remark at Matt, who was clearly enjoying his bowl of soup.

Luke smiled.

Faith and Charity exchanged a knowing look, then returned in haste to Rachel's side. Faith took her hand. The woman cried out and grasped her belly. Her eyes searched the room wildly. "Is Dr. Hander . . . ?" She groaned and panted, leaving the name unfinished. "Is he here? I need to push."

Faith stroked her face. "Not yet, Rachel, but he will be any minute. You just hang on, all right?"

Faith hurried back into the kitchen. "We're going to have to deliver this baby on our own."

Matt stood and wiped his hands on his pants, Mark and Luke following suit. "You sure?" he asked. The words were hard, his face a mask.

"Yes. She wants to start pushing. I can't help but be worried. I'd feel better if the doctor were here."

Mark crammed his hat on his head, heading for the door.

"I'll go get that damn doctor myself. Do what you can till I get back."

At Rachel's moan, Faith returned to her bedside and brushed the woman's hair from her face.

Matt followed, throwing all sensibilities to the wind. He came into the room to be with his wife, and upon seeing him, Rachel's eyes widened; she was frightened what his presence might mean. Crying out softly, she reached for him, and he took her in his arms.

"Oh, Matt." Her lips formed the words but her voice was barely a whisper.

"Shh, sweetheart. It's going to be fine. I promise." His agonized gaze met Faith's over Rachel's head. "It's just like . . . the other times, with Billy and . . ." Matt's voice cracked and he was unable to finish his sentence. Faith kept her eyes trained on Rachel's limp hand that she held in her own.

Silence loomed between contractions like a big, ugly monster just waiting for Rachel to run out of energy and give up. Faith could hear Luke pacing from the front of the house to the back, stopping briefly each time Rachel cried out. And poor Charity was scared to death; Faith could tell the girl wanted to help but there was nothing she could do.

Faith lifted the sheet and glanced underneath. She stifled a gasp in her throat. "You're doing fine," she encouraged Rachel. "But see if you can hold off pushing just a little longer. The doctor will be here soon." Voices signaled someone's arrival. Faith ran out with Matt following. Charity stayed with Rachel.

Roady stood talking with Luke. Their conversation was heated.

"Where's the doctor?" Matt barked.

"He's out in his buggy," Roady replied. "But he's drunk as all get-out."

"He's not a drinking man!" The fear in Matt's voice stilled Faith's heart.

"He lost one of the Whipple girls two days ago. The family's taking it hard. So is he. I took him over to the bathhouse and dipped him in a few times trying to sober him up. That's what took us so long."

Matt swiped his hand across his face, desperation radiating from every inch of his body. "Bring him inside."

Within moments, Luke and Roady returned with the doctor hanging between them, his head drooping forward and his feet stumbling. They set him in a chair in the kitchen, with Roady holding him steady by the back of his collar.

Luke patted the man's cheeks briskly and gave him a shake. "Doc, wake up," he demanded.

Nothing.

"Damn it, Doc," he tried again. "Wake up!"

"Luke, zzzsat you?" he slurred.

Faith pushed past. She had to do something. The baby could die. "Doctor! Please!" She shook his shoulders hard. "We need you!"

"It's no use," Matt said. "He won't come around for hours. We need to handle this—"

"We can't," Faith said in a panic. "We need the doctor!"

Luke took her by her shoulders. "Why?"

"I saw the baby's cord. It's coming out first. All I know is that time is of the essence and if we don't—"

Rachel cried out, stopping her in midsentence, and Charity ran into the room.

Matt's face was white with fear. "How? How do you know this, Faith?"

Dread gripped Faith. Her first impulse was to run to the main house to check on Dawn. Anything to keep from saying what she needed to say. "Because when my friend Beatrice gave birth I was there. The midwife told me about what happens if the cord comes out first. If the weight of the baby pushes on it, the oxygen and other things get cut off." Luke was staring at her and she didn't want to go on. "It's very dangerous for the child."

Luke gripped her shoulders tightly. "Then we must act quickly. Do you remember what she said?"

Faith nodded. "Get the weight of the baby off the cord. Just keep it from getting squashed during the delivery." That sounded impossible, and by the looks of everyone's faces they all felt the same.

Luke turned her to the sink. "Then let's get you to it."

At the sink, Faith scrubbed her hands quickly. "Come with me," she begged, taking a deep, unsteady breath and looking to Luke.

Luke seemed to consider. At last he sighed. "I suppose under the circumstances Rachel won't mind."

Chapter Thirty-seven

In the bedroom, Rachel was barely conscious.

Faith looked under the sheet, which was now stained red with blood, and examined the situation closely. The baby was crowning, the little head covered with brown hair, slick with moisture, was easy to recognize. The cord, pulsating and pink, snaked out beside the baby's head and protruded out about a quarter inch. Faith took a deep breath and tried to calm her fright.

Matt hadn't even flinched when Luke came in, and for that she was grateful. Luke's brother seemed beyond caring, and with the next contraction his wife's face contorted in pain and she screamed.

Faith reached down and carefully pushed the birth canal away from the baby, trying to make space for the cord. It pulsed several times, then stopped. "Oh!" she cried. She looked up at Luke. "It's a little purple."

"Go on. You can do it." His voice was steady. Resolved.

When the contraction passed and Rachel relaxed back onto Matt, Faith gently pressed on the baby's head to try to get it to recede a tiny bit. With trembling fingers she wiggled and pulled to bring the cord up, to release pressure. It looked like it would have more room on the top of the baby. With a little more force she tried again. She needed to get this done before the next contraction.

"Good job, Faith, keep working." She heard Luke's encouraging words, but they sounded a thousand miles away. She glanced up to find Luke watching her. He nodded, never taking his gaze from hers. It gave her a modicum of strength.

Oh, Lord. Be with me now, Faith thought. *I need your help.*

As she worked, Faith realized with horror it would soon be time for another contraction. She must hurry, but she didn't want to do anything that might hurt the baby. Up she moved it, but it slipped back down. The baby rotated and the umbilical cord was flattened.

Rachel cried out. The sheet covering her belly moved, her muscles contorted and Rachel bore down. Moments seemed like hours. The cord turned dark, and Faith felt that must be a very bad sign.

"Luke? I'm not sure what to do."

Then Rachel relaxed again, wheezing out a small sob that was barely audible.

"Breathe," Luke whispered.

Faith looked up at him, realizing only then that he'd been speaking to her. It gave her courage. With a little more force she pushed back on the head and with determination finagled until the rubbery tube slipped up and turned pink.

"I think I've got it! Now we need to get Rachel to push for all she's worth."

* * *

As Faith spoke, Luke was sure she was unaware of the tears that coursed down her face. She was so beautiful, so strong. She had no idea what a wonderful and compassionate woman she was. His heart felt full to overflowing with want, and he knew then he'd never love anyone else.

With the next contraction they all encouraged Rachel to push. The baby slipped halfway out. Faith gasped. "Almost there, Rachel, almost there. Keep it up!"

The baby fell into Faith's hands a few minutes later. It was blue. Luke reached for the infant and gave it a quick smack on its bottom. The babe sucked in a breath and let out a cry. It didn't take but a moment before its face was as pink as a ripe tomato.

Luke grinned like everyone else. "A filly of your own," he said, looking at Matt and Rachel.

Charity hopped up from her chair and threw her arms around Faith. "You were wonderful!" Her face showed nothing but delight.

Extracting Faith from his sister's arms, Luke lifted her into his own. He carried her into the other room and laid her on the sofa. She struggled to sit up, but he captured her lips with his, tasting their sweetness. Desire flashed through his body.

Nibbling at her lips he whispered, "See? You *are* the bravest woman on this earth. I'm proud of you."

Roady cleared his throat, making Faith struggle all the harder.

"You should have seen her, Roady . . ." Luke's voice trailed off as he sought to hide the thunderous emotions rumbling around inside him. "She was truly a sight to see."

Several days passed, and Luke couldn't stop thinking of what had happened with his sister-in-law and Faith. Not until to-day. Now he relaxed in the saddle and surveyed the new herd. This rich Montana grassland had once been home to thousands of buffalo, animals that had grazed just like his own were now.

Pride filled him as he watched the crimson-colored Herefords with their characteristic white faces. It had been a long time in coming, this addition to his family's stock. It had taken months to locate and purchase a herd appropriate to crossbreed with their previous mild-mannered red shorthorns and rangy Texas longhorns. If things went as expected, breeders would soon be coming from all over the country to see the result.

Luke heard a shout. Turning, he saw Charity riding in his direction. He hid his surprise when he saw Faith following very slowly on Buttercup. Not two days earlier she'd told him she was frightened of horses and didn't want to learn to ride.

Seeing Faith with his sister reminded him again of the episode with Rachel. His sister-in-law continued to grow stronger, though she was still confined to her bed by Dr. Handerhoosen. Thank God things had turned out well. When the doctor had sobered up and heard everything that had happened, he'd been sick with remorse. He was having a hard time forgiving himself.

Luke had visited several times and marveled over the tiny baby girl whom Faith had delivered. Still astounded by the turn of events, he shook his head and couldn't keep a smile from forming.

The situation with Ward was at a standstill. Without the testimony of Eagle Gray, Luke's hands were tied. He'd lost the debate with his family of running him off, but it wouldn't be long before he was healed enough to be able to ride on. That's what Luke was waiting for.

Charity had said nothing about him and had not been seen with Ward again, and Luke hoped his words had sunk into that thick skull of hers. She didn't seem particularly interested anymore, but would she be more careful where her reputation was concerned? Only time would tell.

"Mornin'," Luke greeted the women. "Nice day for a ride."

"It's beautiful." Faith fairly beamed with pleasure. Her eyes sparkled as she looked his way, and Luke had the urge to snag her off the saddle and roll her in the soft grass.

Charity looked down at the cattle in the valley. "I thought Faith needed to get out and enjoy the beauty of the ranch. Do you like it, Faith?"

"It's breathtaking. I had no idea."

Her words warmed Luke's heart, feeding the hope he fought to keep at bay. This land was part of him. A very big part. She couldn't want him without wanting the land, too. Then Luke mentally chastised himself. She hadn't said anything about wanting him. Other than the kisses they'd shared, he had no more idea of what she was thinking now than a week ago. Plus, she was purposely making sure that they were never anywhere alone together. Still, with each passing day Faith stayed and didn't go off to Priest's Crossing and her job waiting there, Luke was a little more hopeful.

"These cattle look quite different from the others I've seen on the ranch," Faith said.

"You're right," Luke answered, proud that she'd noticed. "This breed is entirely different from what we've bred in the past. They're called Herefords." He pointed. "See how that calf is strongly built at such an early age? This breed matures faster than the others. An animal that weighs the most at market time brings the most money."

Charity smiled, too. "They are a sight, aren't they? I especially love watching them graze." Dramatically, she popped her forehead with the heel of her hand like she'd just remembered something important. "Silly me. I promised Rachel I'd help bathe the baby!" Then, wheeling her horse around, she loped off with the ease of an experienced horsewoman.

"Wait for me," Faith called, fear crossing her face.

"Just ride home with Luke," Charity shouted over her shoulder.

Luke could see Faith was gripping her saddle horn with white knuckles as Buttercup danced around. The horse tossed his head twice, then started off in the direction Charity had galloped.

"Pull the reins," he told her.

Faith tried, but the reins were long and droopy and made no contact with the gelding's mouth. Buttercup, sensing his rider had no control, was soon trotting after his companion as briskly as his old bones would go.

"Luke!" Faith screamed.

Luke loped up easily alongside her. He made no effort to stop her horse, just grinned.

"Stop him," she begged.

She was in no danger of falling, not with him right there to grab her, so he continued riding alongside. "Promise me first."

"What?"

"You'll share the snack I have in my saddlebag."

The old horse suddenly increased its pace, and Faith's eyes grew as round as saucers. Luke grabbed her reins and brought both mounts to a stop.

Faith laughed, her eyes sparkling. "I never promised!"

"Darn it. I know. But, when you really got scared I couldn't just let him keep going."

She smiled. "All right. I'll admit I am a bit hungry."

Luke hid his feeling of good fortune. He'd have to thank Charity for bringing Faith out. Ever since Rachel's difficult birth, she'd shown a new and friendly interest in the other woman. She was a good ally.

"How's that spot look?" he asked, pointing back to where they'd first stood watching the herd. A cool breeze played with his hair and the sky was as blue as he pictured the endless ocean.

She shrugged. "Looks fine."

Luke dismounted first and then helped Faith to the ground. They walked back in companionable silence until they reached the grassy spot. After taking his canteen from the pommel and saddlebags from the saddle, Luke slipped the bridles free from both horses to let them graze.

"Won't they run off?" Faith asked.

"They're trained to stay put. At least mine is." He gave her a wink. "If Buttercup decides to run home, I'll let you ride with me." He waggled his eyebrows, and Faith laughed.

Cross-legged on the ground, he waited for her to take a seat. He pretended to be looking around at the contents of his saddlebags, when truthfully his awareness of her was driving him loco. Sitting out here with Faith by his side, under the endless expanse of the sky, just the two of them, felt perfect. His blood fairly hummed through his body, making it difficult to concentrate.

"Here." He handed Faith a strip of dried beef. Her expression was one of bewilderment as she looked at the withered morsel. "Go on. It's good."

Taking one himself, he ripped off a healthy portion and chewed with vigor. He smiled. She was trying to get a corner of the tough meet to rip off, but she wasn't having much success. The harder she tried, the more he chuckled.

"Give it to me," he finally said, purposely grazing her fingers with his own. He gripped her jerky with his teeth and ripped off a section, then placed it in her mouth. His fingers lingered a smidgen too long, and he watched as her eyes dilated.

"Tasty?"

She nodded, all the while chewing and looking out at the grazing cattle. The sight of her fueled his blood. She was his. Dawn was his. Why couldn't she see it?

Taking his canteen, Luke unscrewed the cap and held it out to Faith. "Thirsty?"

"Yes, I guess I am."

She took the canteen and enjoyed a small sip before handing it back. Luke held it to his mouth and took several long gulps, all the while never taking his eyes from hers. He let his gaze drop to her lips and then lower.

He set the canteen in the grass next to him. Scooting closer to Faith, he tried to read her expression, her mood. As always, she was a mystery. Did she want him as much as he wanted her? Did the sight of him set her blood to coursing?

He had to know. Without words, he slowly laid her back in the soft, fragrant grass. He pulled free the pins that held her hair and let it flow around her shoulders.

Chapter Thirty-eight

Luke?"

"Shhh, don't talk," he said. "Just let me feel your hair free from its bonds. I've been wondering about it for a long time."

Faith closed her eyes as he slowly feathered her long hair over her shoulder and ran his fingers through it. Picking up a section he held it to his nose. The lowing of the cattle in the distance could be heard over her breathing. He felt the pulse at the base of her throat with his thumb and stared into her eyes. He saw what he needed to see.

First he brushed his lips across hers, as if testing their softness. Getting no resistance, he lowered his head, letting his mouth meander slowly over hers, barely moving, reveling in the closeness.

His hand moved down her side, then back up past the curve of her waist, stopping just below the fullness of her breast. She was strong. Even for just having had a baby, her body was firm and beautiful.

He waited for her to tell him to stop, to show any sign she didn't want him to take such intimate familiarities, but she lay by his side, kissing him back. She sighed and pressed her lips more firmly to his, answering his unspoken question.

"Luke," she whispered against his lips, "I like lying in the grass with you."

He slid his arm around her body and pulled her closer, leaned back and touched her nose with a finger. "You know what I thought when I found you in that wagon, pouring rain all around?"

"What?"

"I thought you were a little girl, lost." He pulled again, and their bodies meshed together as only a man's and woman's can. "Not a vixen."

It seemed she was having a hard time paying attention to what he was saying. She finally responded, a bit breathlessly. "I'm no vixen, Luke McCutcheon."

"Oh, I might argue with that. Every cowhand in the outfit is in love with you." He cleared his throat. "But, I can't blame 'em. You're by far the prettiest woman I've ever known. And sweet, too."

"Oh, Luke . . ."

To his utter amazement, this time she initiated the kiss, gently, sweetly, but with an undercurrent of passion that set his head spinning. Embracing her, he rolled until she was on her back, the high fragrant grass making a wall around them.

He deepened their kiss until they were both breathing heavily. When he attempted to draw away, to give her some air, she protested and pulled him back, frantic.

"Faith?" he whispered against her temple. He'd felt the change in her body the moment she tensed. Her deep, dark secret was back building the wall between them. Whatever it was, it wasn't going away. Her thoughts were elsewhere. He smoothed the hair from her forehead and looked down into her eyes. "Faith. Talk to me, sweetheart."

* * *

Faith tried to push everything from her mind except the joy of being with Luke, safe and secure in his arms, enjoying the closeness and wonder of him. She wanted to remember every tiny detail: his taste, the way his cheek rubbed against hers, the timbre of his voice when he said her name, the feel of his hands as they ran the length of her body. Her senses fairly hummed with acute awareness of everything around her. She was finally, truly and unbelievably alive.

But now the world was trying to intrude. She wouldn't let it. No. She wanted—*needed*—this memory to keep with her in the years to come. She reached for his hand and placed it between them on the bodice of her dress.

When he didn't move, she began releasing the tiny buttons. They ran down the front of her dress, from her chin to her waist. She peeled back the fabric until a thin cotton chemise was the only barrier between them.

"What's this about?" he whispered.

"I want . . ." She rolled her head to the side where he couldn't see her face. She didn't have the nerve to finish her sentence.

Bending close, he slowly nibbled at her lips, sending fire coursing through her veins. He lightly touched the swell of her breast and said, "Faith, honey, this is very sweet of you but—"

"It's the only thing I have to give you, Luke," she interrupted. "You've done—"

"Hush," he whispered, as he took her face in his hands and turned it so he could see into her eyes. "Don't you know I don't want this unless I can have what's *here?*" He tapped softly on both of her temples. "And this, too." He leaned down and kissed the spot where her heart beat wildly in her chest. "It would mean nothing to me without the rest of you."

Luke rolled onto his back, taking Faith along with him, snuggling her into the crook of his arm. He looked up into the blue sky and pointed to a bird flying high on the breeze. "See the hawk?" he asked, all while his fingers were lightly tracing, barely touching, slowly moving back and forth over her heart.

She ran her hand across his chest in answer, sneaked it inside his shirt. At his intake of breath when she actually touched his skin, she smiled. "I see it."

His horse nickered loudly. Lifting his head up above the tall grass, Luke looked around. His mount issued another shrill call, sides heaving and eyes bright, looking to the west. Luke followed his gaze.

"What is it?" Faith asked.

Luke looked down at her open bodice and quickly pulled it closed.

"What?" Faith asked again, her voice an octave higher. She struggled against Luke, trying to see.

"Rider. Coming this way. Looks like Roady."

Faith pushed Luke's hands aside and, with flying fingers, began doing up all the tiny buttons of her dress.

Luke took another quick peek. Roady had stopped. He sat halfway down the draw, studying their two horses grazing peacefully side by side. Without a word he reined his horse around and loped back in the direction he'd come.

"He's gone," Luke said, pulling Faith to her feet. With her hand in his, they walked through the tall grass to the edge of the bluff atop the rim rock. "Careful now, darlin', don't slip," he cautioned.

To his delight and amazement, Faith wrapped her arms around his middle and hugged him tight, her face buried in his chest. In return, he circled her in his arms and stroked her hair. They stood that way for a long time, looking out over the herd, him just enjoying the feel of her. It was a perfect day—a day that could turn into thousands just like it if she'd consent to becoming his wife.

He kissed the top of her head, which was warm from the

sun. Her hair sparkled with golden and amber highlights as it moved in the breeze. "Are you happy?" he asked.

"Yes," she said.

But her sorrow was so deep it couldn't be hidden. With his hands, he tilted her face up so he could look into her eyes. "You don't sound too happy."

"I am," she insisted breathlessly. "How couldn't I be?"

Not knowing what else to say, he said, "I'm glad."

Faith turned in Luke's arms to look out over the valley. *Please God, not now.* The day had been too sweet, too good, something she'd remember forever. But . . . *Don't let him ask me to stay.*

"Faith," he said, bending to whisper in her ear. "We belong together. I feel it as sure as I see that herd out there under God's blue sky. And I know you feel it, too."

Feel it? She lived it, breathed it, and it would kill her when she left. What could she say to deny feelings that were written so clearly in her heart?

"Faith?"

Pulling herself from his protective embrace, she turned and walked back toward the horses. Within moments, he had her by the shoulder and turned around. His face was angry with frustration. His injured eye, a dark purplish brown made her heart constrict.

"For God's sake, Faith," he gritted out, "you're not going to start that nonsense again about working in Priest's Crossing. I can't believe that after today. I just can't." When she didn't say anything, he went on. "If you're waiting for the right words . . . then you may be waiting an awful long time. My words, they just come out plain and simple. Just like me."

"Luke." She steeled herself against her longings and looked him in the face. "I want to work. I want to be on my own. How many times . . ." She almost choked. "How many times do I have to tell you before you accept it?" She looked away. "I don't want you." She glanced back, but his stunned expression was just too much. She turned away so she couldn't see his face.

It was a long time before he spoke. When he did, he said, "I finally understand. It took me a while to get it through my head, but . . . you don't want to be tied to a half-breed. That would make your children breeds, too. I'm surprised at you. I didn't figure you for that type, Faith."

"What are you talking about?" His accusation shocked her. She spun around and looked him in the eye. She knew nothing about what he was saying.

"Don't tell me you didn't figure out Flood isn't my father. Or that you never noticed I was the only one in the family with black hair, olive skin . . . You'd have to be blind not to."

She stared at him, silent.

"Now if it were Mark or Matt doing the asking, wouldn't your decision be a mite different?"

She shook her head, unbelieving. Race would never make a difference to her. She loved him! Every itsy-bitsy part of him. Indian or not, red, green or blue, he'd always be the love of her life.

His eyes blazed with anger, his expression a mask she couldn't read. For the first time she recognized the Indian heritage he was talking about.

"You see it now, don't you?"

His anger was frightening. She took a step back.

"What's wrong? Afraid I'll lift that beautiful head of hair? It would make a notable trophy." He took a menacing step in her direction.

"Stop it," Faith said. "I can't believe you're talking crazy like this. Stop, stop, stop!" She put her hands over her ears and squeezed her eyes shut.

When she opened them, Luke wasn't standing where he'd been. She saw him putting the bridles on the horses, getting ready to ride out. She hurried over to Buttercup and, lifting her skirt, stepped into the stirrup.

"Ready?" he asked as she lifted herself onto the saddle. His voice was emotionless.

"Yes."

"Let's go."

Chapter Thirty-nine

Back at the house, Faith paced from one side of her bedroom to the other, the crumpled telegram from Christine Meeks in her hand. She couldn't stay much longer. Things had become too tangled, too involved; people she truly cared about would be hurt when she left. Her image of Luke as she swore she didn't want him tortured her mind, piercing her heart just like a knife.

The inevitability of her leaving was a fact. She'd find Ward and tell him they needed to leave as soon as possible. She'd get him to agree that leaving with Joe Brunn—for cover purposes—would be best. Then she'd meet up with him on the trail. She couldn't bring herself to let the family know she was leaving with Ward; he would just have to understand. But when was Joe going to be done and come to fetch her? Waiting any longer didn't seem like a good idea. Especially not after today.

Collapsing with a sigh onto her bed, Faith crossed her arms over her chest and stared at the ceiling. She closed her eyes and relived the kaleidoscope of feelings Luke had created inside her. She remembered the hardness of his chest and how wonderful it felt pillowing her cheek. The wonder of it set her blood spiraling through her body. With a sob, she reached for Dawn, who was sleeping by her side, and held the baby tight until she squirmed for release.

Faith relaxed her hold. "Things will be fine," she said,

looking into her child's face. "Somehow this will all work it-self out, and then . . ."

A knock sounded on her door.

"Yes?"

"Mrs. Brown?" Esperanza called. "The mistress says dinner will be at six o'clock tonight."

"Thank you."

"Would you like the tub brought up?"

"That would be lovely."

The maid's footsteps retreated down the long hall.

Maybe the hot water would help her wash away memories that kept haunting her. Memories of angry black eyes, reaching for the bottom of her soul.

Faith waited for the last possible moment to descend the stairs. She'd heard voices for some time now, talking and laughing, but she just couldn't summon up the courage to face Luke.

Luke! Part Indian? Now that he'd pointed it out, she was surprised that she hadn't noticed it herself. He'd always seemed different from the rest of his family, and yet she'd been unable to put her finger on just what that difference was. In her opinion, he was definitely the most handsome of the three boys. And the wildest. Faith wondered what had happened to Mrs. McCutcheon for Luke to be born in between her other children, sired by a different man?

She checked on Dawn one more time, making sure her baby was still fast asleep, then forced herself to the stairway. She'd tried to spruce up one of her simple dresses, but it wasn't much use. She felt drab. The only thing that lifted her spirits was the flower Esperanza had placed in the room. She'd fastened it in the back of her hair, which was now styled like Charity's, half up and half down.

From the upper landing, Faith surveyed the main room. Everyone was there. Rachel sat on the sofa with Matt by her side. He proudly held their family's new arrival. Colton, Billy and Adam walked around the long dinner table, sneaking bits of roast meat from the platter. Esperanza was having a time shooing them away.

Faith spotted Luke lounging next to the stone fireplace. He was staring straight at her, and she suddenly knew what a sparrow felt when it came face-to-face with a hungry cat. His gaze scorched her from head to toe. Form-fitting buckskin breeches hugged his muscular thighs like a second skin, disappearing into delicately beaded, knee-high moccasins. Fringe swayed slightly as he crossed one foot over the other. Never taking his eyes from her face, he slowly lifted his glass tumbler to his lips and drank.

Swallowing hard, Faith straightened her shoulders and stiffened her spine. With determination, she lifted her chin, plastered a pleasant expression on her face and descended the stairs. He was even more stunningly handsome in his native clothes. She tried to keep her eyes from his face, his body, his all-too-sure-of-himself expression. Surely someone must notice how strangely the two of them were acting!

"Look, everyone, Faith's here," Charity called out, skipping over and gathering Faith in an enthusiastic embrace.

Luke raised his glass. "A toast to the guest of honor," he said, light sarcasm lacing his voice.

Faith glanced at the others, who clapped and cheered, people who had become so very dear to her. Confusion held her immobile.

"What is this?" she finally managed to say.

"It's a party for you. In honor of you, and to thank you. We wanted to wait until Rachel and the baby could join us before throwing it," Flood explained. "We're very grateful and indebted to you for what you did for Rachel. For all of us."

A hush descended over the group as Matt stood and approached, carrying his tiny little baby girl. "Would you like to hold Faith Elizabeth McCutcheon?"

The baby, who was sleeping in her father's arms, woke when he handed her over. She fussed a little and then started rooting around at Faith's breast, looking for something to eat. Everyone laughed.

Everyone except Luke. As she glanced his way, pain, regret and something akin to anger stormed across his face. He got up and strode to the small table with the decanter and refilled his glass.

"What do you think of her, Faith?" Amy asked, looking down at the baby. "Isn't she sweet?"

"Yes, she is." Faith barely got the words past the lump in her throat. "Adorable. But you really shouldn't have named her after me."

"Nonsense. It's because of you that she's here right now," Rachel said. Her eyes were filled with tears of gratitude. "I'll never, ever, be able to thank you enough. We're going to call her Beth for short."

To Faith's relief, Billy and Adam started arguing, and most everyone's attention turned to them. Colton made his way through the group to stand at Faith's side.

"How are you, Colton?" she asked. "This is the first I've seen of you all day."

"Fine, Ma," Colton said, standing on tiptoe so he could see Beth. "I stayed out at the corrals with Smokey and Roady. They was teachin' me, Billy and Adam ta throw a rope. I was almost gettin' the hang of it, too."

He was thriving here, her little boy with the giant chip on his shoulder. All the attention from the men was good for him, making him happier than she'd ever known him to be. Colton's smile had returned a few days ago, and now that it was back, he wasn't selfish with sharing it. How would he hold up when they made the trip back to their old home, and how would he feel about the change? Everything the future held for them was just so uncertain.

"What's wrong, Ma?"

Faith knelt down and hugged him with her free arm. "Nothing's wrong. I'm just happy you're enjoying our visit so much."

"I am. I like it here a lot. I don't even mind Luke so much no more."

"You don't?"

"Nope. He's usually right with whatever he tells me, and Francis said he learned everything he knows from Luke. I guess he ain't so bad."

Faith nodded and stood.

Flood appeared. "Here, let me take Beth from you. You have enough baby-holding every day, what with Dawn," he said, smiling.

Faith carefully placed the infant in his large arms. Here was the man she'd thought was Luke's father. Now, as she looked a little closer, she was amazed she'd ever thought that, because they looked nothing alike. Feeling uneasy, she glanced over her shoulder to find Luke watching. His expression was clear: he knew that she'd been comparing them.

"That Luke, he's a handsome lad. Don't you think so, Faith?"

Her heart felt as if it just might pop. Did Flood know about the two of them? Had Luke said something to him? "Why, yes I do," she admitted. What else could she say?

"He'll make a fine catch one day for some lucky young lady. Why, it's a nuisance to take him to town, what with the women and all. Makes no difference if they're married or not. He's an attention-getter, all right."

Flood was sweet. But Luke would be furious if he knew what his father was up to.

"Is that so?" she said, laughing a little, smiling at Flood brightly and then glancing purposely over her shoulder. She made eye contact with the subject of their conversation, who frowned.

"Yes, it's been that way since he was just a boy," Flood continued, warming to the subject.

"Tell me, Mr. McCutcheon, what was he like as a child? I wonder at his moods sometimes."

This clearly threw Mr. McCutcheon. A tiny line of worry creased his brow, and Faith almost regretted asking.

"He does have times when he's in deep thought, but that's all that they are. Why, he outgrew his temper and fighting days years ago." Seemingly a bit embarrassed, Flood cleared his throat and went on. "That is, except for this last fracas with Mr. Brown. Got a worthy heart, he does."

Luke appeared. "What are you two so deep in conversation about?"

Faith looked innocently to Flood. The older man actually beamed. "You, Son."

Luke's eyes narrowed. "That so? And just what exactly were you saying?"

"Your father was telling me—"

"Dinner is served." Mrs. McCutcheon clapped her hands as she called them all to eat. Everyone moved eagerly to the dining table, which was laden with all manner of dishes.

Luke pulled out Faith's chair for her, and she couldn't help but notice his fluid grace as he himself sat. He was like some kind of wild animal, dangerous and hard, especially in this dark mood. Her hand itched to reach out and test the softness of his lovely buckskin pants, which clung to his body indecently, and the contrast between his white shirt and the darkness of his skin . . . well, she was ashamed at the way her thoughts kept running wild.

Grace was said and the food passed around. Luke was quiet, but if anyone noticed they didn't mention it. The most talkative were the boys, who entertained everyone with their stories of their day learning to rope and trying to ride some of the motherless calves kept close to the barn.

A knock on the door interrupted Billy, who had them all laughing. Flood stood and went to see who it was.

"Come in, come in," his voice rang out. He came back with

a young man Faith had never seen. Mrs. McCutcheon smiled brightly and gestured for him to sit.

"I'm sorry to interrupt," the man said.

"Nonsense, Brandon. There's plenty here. I'd be hurt if you didn't join us."

Faith noticed the look that passed between the newcomer and Luke, after the fellow's first shock at seeing Luke's black eye. "Thank you, I'd love to," he said with a smile. "It's been too long since I've had Esperanza's cooking."

The maid quickly set an extra place while the broad-shouldered fellow hung his coat and hat by the door. When he took a seat across the table from Faith, she couldn't help but smile a welcome.

Flood made the introductions. "Faith, this is Brandon Crawford. He's the sheriff in town. Brandon, this is Faith Brown, who's staying here at the ranch for a spell. And that tough-lookin' hombre down at the end of the table is Colton, her son."

"I'm pleased to make your acquaintance, ma'am," Brandon said politely. He nodded to Colton.

Faith wondered what the handsome lawman and Luke were up to. "The pleasure is mine."

She watched Brandon's eyes skim down the row of faces and stop on Charity. He nodded slightly. Charity's cheeks turned rosy.

Matt took a heaping scoop of potatoes and passed the dish along. "So, Brandon, what brings you out our way this evening?"

"I have a little news concerning your dead bull calf." He took a drink from his water glass. "But it can wait until after dinner. Nothin' urgent."

Faith wanted him to go on. She felt it would indeed concern her. Or was she just being foolish? The men seemed to accept the lawman's appeal to wait for later, dishing up food and eating heartily.

"Congratulations on your new young'un, Matt," Brandon said. "Doc says you got yourself a little girl this time."

"I sure did. She's over there sleeping by the fire. You'll have to take a look when you're done eating."

Luke broke apart a biscuit and popped half in his mouth. He glanced at Charity, who ate slowly, the picture of refinement. What a time for Brandon to show up! How would Charity receive Brandon after what he'd told her a few days ago about the sheriff being involved with the schoolteacher's niece?

She looked at him now, a silent challenge in her eyes. Luke slowly shook his head. A smile he knew all too well appeared on her face. Trouble was brewing.

Chapter Forty

WHAT's the news in town, Sheriff?"

Charity glanced at Brandon with the most innocent, beguiling look, and Luke cringed. Brandon just seemed taken aback that she'd addressed him. He wiped his mouth on his napkin, and swallowed.

"Not much new in town, Charity. It's been mighty quiet this past month."

"I'm surprised to hear you say that." She let her statement dangle, leaving not only the sheriff wondering what she meant by it, but also everyone else at the table. Everyone except Luke.

"Well, the new dry goods place did finally open up for business. They had themselves a little shindig commemorating the occasion."

"Ah, good," Flood commented. "Someone needs to give old man Swanson a little friendly competition. He's had it too easy for too long. I don't like the way he treats some of the people in town." The family all nodded in agreement.

Charity said, "Oh, I wish I could have gone. It's been so long since I've had a party to attend." The statement, and the way it was gushed with gooey sweetness, drew many surprised looks. "I suppose *everyone* in town was there?"

Brandon looked to Luke in silent question. Luke shrugged. "I reckon."

"And Miss Langford. She was there and brought her niece?"

Brandon swallowed his food. Again he politely wiped his mouth. Thinking for a moment, he nodded. "Yes, they were both there."

"I'll bet she was just the belle of the ball," Charity continued, as if unable to stop herself. Most at the table had now guessed that she was in some sort of jealous snit, but poor Brandon hadn't a clue. "With her beautiful flaxen hair"— Luke's eyes went wide at the fanciful description he'd not given her—"and charming smile. Did she flash her baby blues your way, Sheriff?"

Brandon almost spit his water all over the table.

"Charity, mind your manners!" Mrs. McCutcheon scolded. "Mr. Crawford is our guest tonight, and you'll treat him accordingly."

"Well?" Charity pressed, as if she hadn't heard her mother.

Irritation flashed in Brandon's eyes. "Yes, as a matter of fact, she did."

Resembling the trial lawyer the family had once seen in Bozeman, Charity seemed to be satisfied with his answer and let the subject drop.

The women settled in the parlor with little Beth, leaving the men to venture outside for a smoke. Flood lit his cigar and puffed a few times, creating a cloud around his face. "So, Crawford, what have you learned about the calf?"

Brandon took the cigar that Flood held out, rolled it

between his fingers. He smiled. "I think you'll be pleased to know I have two men in custody for maiming your bull."

"What!" the three McCutcheons said in unison. "Who?"

"Do the names Earl Morton and Will Dickson ring a bell?"

"Earl? That no-good bastard," Luke growled.

Flood shook his head. "I'd expect something like this from Will Dickson, but Earl? You sure? We were pretty certain we knew who did it."

"Heard it with my own ears. Tilly overheard them laughing about it in the saloon. I stood in the liquor room and listened through the wall. By the way, Luke, Tilly said she'd have my hide if I didn't remember to tell you hello. She misses you." He chuckled a moment, then continued. "When she heard Earl murmuring the McCutcheon name to some of his cronies, she got suspicious. That's when she came and got me."

"Well, I'll be damned," Matt said. "I suppose he was taking his revenge for being fired off the drive."

Brandon's face was serious, so Luke asked, "What else?"

"That's it."

"I know you better than that," Luke said. "There's something you're not telling us."

Brandon hesitated a moment. "By the time I arrested him, he'd had a snout full. He said no half-breed was going to fire him and get away with it."

Luke shrugged, unaffected. He was through feeling different. From now on he'd wear his heritage proudly, for all to see, whether they liked it or not. That's why he was wearing his buckskins tonight. And because he wanted Faith to know full and well who he was. Eagle Gray had dropped them off at the bunkhouse years ago, encouraging him to embrace his heritage, but he'd never before felt compelled to wear them.

"Well, I guess a half-breed *did* fire him and get away with it. But then that poor bull had to suffer. That's a crime I won't forgive. What was Will Dickson's part in this?"

Brandon shook his head. "Since when does Dickson need a reason? Seems he was just out for some sport."

Mark spoke up. "When will the judge be through town?"

"Possibly next week."

"Good. Let us know when they have their hearing. We'll be there," Luke promised.

Matt dropped his cigarette and ground it out with his boot. "I'm for joinin' the women. How about you?"

Nodding, the men went inside.

They hadn't missed much. Luke was always amazed at how long women could stare at a baby. First the females of his family had stared at Billy, then Adam. Now they acted just as excited about Beth.

"Here, Sheriff, you hold her," Charity suggested as she handed the child to Brandon.

Luke chuckled as his friend took her, a look of terror on his face. "Charity, take her back. She looks like she's goin' to cry," Brandon said.

"Don't be silly. She's as content as can be." Then Charity flounced away, leaving Brandon with the four-day-old squirming in his arms.

"Take her, Luke," the sheriff said, trying to hand the baby over.

"No, sir. I've done more than my share of baby-holding these past three weeks. You need a chance to catch up."

The lawman made a face. "I guess you don't want to hear what I know concerning . . ." He let his statement go unfinished but looked at Faith, who was chatting with Rachel and Amy. Dawn lay contentedly in her mother's lap, her head resting on Faith's knees.

"What did you find out?"

"Take this little tyke first and I'll tell you."

His insides humming with anticipation over what information his friend might have for him, Luke took Beth from

Brandon's arms and gave her to Rachel. He led Brandon to a secluded part of the dining room, where they wouldn't be overheard by anyone and prompted, "So?"

"From what I've learned, there is some question over how Samuel Brown, her husband, died," Brandon explained softly. "There's a possibility she killed him."

"Impossible." Luke's heart slammed in his chest. This wasn't what he wanted to hear.

"Not so," Brandon argued. "They had a troubled marriage. It was thought that maybe he beat on her on occasion, when he'd had too much to drink. But, from what I gather, a real investigation hasn't happened. For whatever reason, I'm not sure. It's more rumor and speculation from certain individuals."

Despair for Faith's circumstance washed over Luke. He couldn't stop himself from looking over at her as she laughed with his two sisters-in-law. He was mad at her, and she was as stubborn as a mule, but there was no way she could kill a man and not have it eating her alive.

But, what if the man were beating Colton? He'd seen her protectiveness over the boy. What then?

"I have a few more leads I still have to investigate," Brandon admitted, interrupting Luke's thoughts. "The marshal from China Gap is heading over in that direction this week. He owes me."

Hell. Should he call off the investigation? If she had killed Samuel and was on the run, did he want to inform the law where she was? They wouldn't just let her off scot-free. Females were prosecuted under the law same as a man. He'd never considered that she'd done something like this, if indeed she had.

"Call off the marshal," he said.

"What?"

"I said to call him off. I'll go myself and investigate."

Luke's friend gave him a long, hard look, then gazed around the family gathering. He shook his head. "Not advisable,

Luke. You could be getting yourself into a lot of trouble. Aiding and abetting is a serious crime."

Luke jammed his hand through his hair. Frustration vibrated through him. "Dammit, Brandon, look at her. You tell me she killed her husband."

At that moment, Dawn began to cry. Excusing herself, Faith ascended the stairs with the infant in her arms. At the top she paused and for a brief moment looked back down. Luke saw the questions in her eyes. Then she turned the corner and was out of sight.

"We've been through a lot together, Luke. I don't want to see you makin' the biggest mistake of your life. You know better than anyone else I can't look the other way if a crime has been committed. Especially murder. Not for you, not for any of the McCutcheons or anyone else."

Even though it angered him, Luke knew his friend was right. "How long do I have?"

"A week."

"Fine. But wire the marshal and call him off. Tell him you're sending someone else to look into things, that you'll let him know if he's needed. Just make darn sure he knows that you'll be handling this yourself. And we *will* handle it. I promise you."

Brandon shook his head. "I hope she's worth it, Luke. I really do."

Chapter Forty-one

*F*OR the hundredth time, Luke went over the facts that Brandon had delivered. Each time he did, the same feeling of sick helplessness consumed him. Leaning back against the corral post, he looked at the night sky. The vault of the heavens enveloped him, all-consuming, and the sight that usually filled him with wonder now only turned his insides cold and black.

Was it possible that Faith really did love him but with so much at stake was afraid to trust him or let her feelings show? Yesterday, lying in the grass, she'd shown her desire, and he believed she'd meant it. But, what if she were guilty? What if she had killed Samuel and skedaddled out of town before anyone found out? What then?

He'd cross that bridge when he got there. *If* he did. He still felt that this was one hell of a mix-up and that she was what she said she was: a woman on her own, out to start fresh, not wanting or needing a husband.

Not wanting or needing him.

"Luke?"

He turned at the sound of his mother's voice. She was making her way toward him in her night wrapper, her hair unbound. She was still a very beautiful woman, with her petite size and ageless skin. But it was her gentleness, her goodness that made her the special woman that she was.

As she got closer, he could see the question in her eyes.

"What is it, Ma? What brings you outside this time of night?"

"You do, Son. I got up to get a glass of water and noticed your door ajar. I wondered where you'd gone off to."

"I just needed a little fresh air is all."

She smiled that smile he remembered well from his childhood and stroked his cheek, letting her hand linger. "Such pain in your eyes, Luke. What is it?"

"Just something I have to work out on my own." His voice was hoarse, his throat tight.

His mother surprised him by climbing up on the corral rail and sitting down. She had to go slowly so she wouldn't catch her wrapper under her feet and fall. Luke chuckled and climbed up next to her.

"You comfortable?" he asked.

"It's been a while since I've sat up here. I used to love to watch Flood as he rode the wild mustangs."

"You should have seen me the other day," Luke said, shaking his head. "I let a mediocre ringtail throw me into the dust."

"I was going to come out when I heard the commotion and cheering, but then I noticed that you already had yourself an audience."

Luke gazed at the dark sky, remembering. Had it been only a week ago? "I reckon I did."

"She's a lovely girl," his mother said softly. "I watched as she ran out when she thought you'd been hurt. Even that angry horse wasn't going to stop her." Her laughter sounded like bells. "Really, Luke. You should be ashamed for scaring her."

Luke smiled at the memory. Then he looked at his mother's profile as she gazed out over the tall pine trees toward the mountains. "How did you know I wasn't really hurt?"

"Flood. He used to pull that trick on me all the time. Whenever he was feeling that you boys were getting all the attention he'd let himself get pitched off a horse, then wait until I came running. I never let on that I knew his game. I just kept fussing over him when he needed the fussing. It's a natural thing, you know."

Luke sat in silence, just absorbing the bigness of his surroundings.

"So, what are your plans?"

Startled, Luke looked at his mother. "What do you mean?"

"Faith. You're not just going to let her slip away, are you?"

"She has secrets. A past she won't share. Every time I ask her about it, she lies." He snorted. "It's complicated."

"How complicated can it be for two young people in love? I see it in both your eyes. The question is, how much are you willing to bend?"

Bend? His temper flared. He'd been bending ever since that night he found her in the dilapidated wagon, about to give birth. What more could he do if she didn't want his help? "I would bend if she'd be honest with me. But she's hiding things that are big. Things that she needs help with but won't ask. I want a marriage like you and Pa have, one built on honesty and trust. Without that you got nothing."

"Fear's a funny thing, Luke," his mother said, placing her hand on his thigh. "It can change things around in your head until you believe them wholeheartedly. Maybe she's scared."

Maybe she was. If she was innocent, he'd go to Kearney and clear her name if it was the last thing he did. But that didn't mean they were suited. If she had come to him in the beginning and been truthful, maybe they would have stood a chance. But now, he just didn't see it.

"Look at me," his mother scolded. She took his chin and twisted his head in her direction. "You are definitely the stubbornest man on this ranch. You come by it naturally, though, from the Cheyenne blood flowing in your veins. They didn't come any more hardheaded than Netchiwaan, your real father."

Shocked, Luke stared at her. Never before had she made reference to the fact that he was different because of his Indian blood—or even mentioned his father's name.

"As you know, I was very young when I married Flood. By the time Mark came along, I was still only nineteen years old. This ranch was just a small cabin, a couple of corrals and as many steers as Flood could afford to buy. Wilderness surrounded us on all sides." Her voice took on a dreamy quality, as if she were reading a novel of the most wonderful adventure. Luke would have thought memories of the abduction would haunt her. But that didn't seem to be the case.

"I won't go into detail, but one day when Flood was out and I was here with my two little boys, a band of Cheyenne warriors came through the yard. After I'd pushed Matt and Mark into the cabin but before I could lower the bar, one grabbed a hold of my hair, dragging me onto his pony. I scratched him up real good but was unable to get free."

Luke held up his hand. "Ma, you don't have to tell me this," he said, his head reeling. He'd never before asked for any information because he'd wanted to spare her the pain of remembering.

"Oh, yes I do. I'm sorry Luke, I should have told you years ago. I didn't realize how much you needed to hear."

And then she told him everything.

When she got done, he was speechless. Luke had expected to hear an account of rape, hardship and torture. But that hadn't been the case at all. Although her heart was broken when she'd been ripped from her husband and children, and she never gave up trying to escape, the months in captivity hadn't been all bad. After one month of living as a slave to the chief's oldest wife, and unharmed in any physical way, she'd been given to a young brave named Netchiwaan. He was kind and they grew fond of each other . . . and a small part of her still loved him. Luke had been a very special gift.

She'd been Netchiwaan's second wife, and since he was a warrior of great standing, the other Indians treated her well. After she'd been rescued and she realized that she was carrying the warrior's child, she'd worried over what it would do to Flood. But Flood, being the man that he was, accepted Luke as his own, loving him exactly like his other boys.

"You were and still are very special to me, Luke," his mother whispered. "When I see you, with your flashing black eyes, your pride as big as a Montana sky, and even your stubbornness . . . I remember. Please don't misunderstand, I was beyond happiness when I returned home to my husband and family, but I carry guilt about something: if I'm completely honest with myself, I have to admit that I did, in a way, love Netchiwaan."

It was unbelievable, what his mother was telling him so calmly. All these years, she'd loved a man other than Flood.

"So, Luke. Do you think I could have been completely honest with Flood, telling him my Indian captor was sweet and charming, with a wonderful sense of humor? That he was a passionate young man who loved me fiercely? That he has his own little spot in my heart that I cherish? Flood's a very understanding man, forgiving to a fault. But would he forgive me for what I feel? Could he live well knowing that truth?"

"No," Luke responded thoughtfully. At least, he couldn't imagine himself being that understanding where Faith was concerned.

"So you see, things are not always easy. They're not always what they seem. The human heart is a complicated and mystifying thing; as hard as we try, we can never fathom its depth and capacity. Faith may have something so frightening in her past that she thinks she can't share it with you—and maybe she's right to do so. Don't shut her out because of it. Give her a chance. And if she doesn't ever tell you, let it go. If you get together, focus on the love you share. That's all that matters."

They sat silently for some time. Astounded, Luke couldn't picture what his mother had just confided. Was she thinking about his Indian father now as she sat beside him?

"I'm getting a mite chilly," she said at last. "I think I'll go back to bed before I'm missed."

Luke hopped off the rail and reached up, taking his mother by the waist and lowering her to the ground. "Thanks, Ma." He laced her hand into the crook of his arm and covered it with his own. They walked silently back to the house.

"Get some sleep," she suggested. "Things will be brighter in the morning." Then she disappeared into the dark doorway.

Sleep? He'd not get any of that tonight. His mind whirled from what she'd just told him about his biological father. Sweet and charming? A man with a wonderful sense of humor? Fiercely passionate! Everything he'd ever believed had been shattered in the blink of an eye. The secret his mother kept was not one of shame, but of love.

Suddenly, Luke's heart spread its wings and soared like a mighty eagle. For the first time in his life, he didn't curse the

Cheyenne blood that made him different but yearned to feel it strong and true. With a mighty war cry he bolted through the yard. Throwing a bridle on his horse, he vaulted astride bareback and galloped off into the night.

Chapter Forty-two

FAITH and Mr. and Mrs. McCutcheon were finishing up breakfast when Luke stepped through the door. She jumped. His wind-tousled hair and a day's growth of dark whiskers caused him to appear even wilder and more foreboding than usual. He still wore his buckskins, but his chest was bare and dripping with water as if he'd just bathed. Eyes that fairly crackled with energy sought her face first, before moving to the other two at the table.

Mrs. McCutcheon beamed. "Would you like something to eat?"

"I'm famished," Luke replied, shrugging into the shirt he held in his hands. "Do we have a steak out there somewhere?"

Flood laughed. "This is a cattle ranch, Son. I'm sure Esperanza can find you a whole side of beef if you want."

Luke pulled out the chair next to Faith's and sat. "Sleep well?" he asked.

"Yes," she lied. What was the cause of this complete turnabout in mood, she wondered. He'd been civil to her last night, but just barely.

Mrs. McCutcheon circled the table, put her arms around Luke and hugged his back. The look on her face brought tears to Faith's eyes. Oh, how lucky the people in this family were! Were they even aware of how rare their fortune was? Looking away, she sipped from her cup of coffee.

His parents visited and shared their plans for the day. When Esperanza set a two-inch-thick T-bone steak in front of Luke they excused themselves and went out to saddle their horses. Luke sliced into the tender meat, took a deep whiff and appreciated its aroma. Popping the wedge into his mouth he chewed. His eyes closed. "Mmmm." The sound was a purr. He took a sip of his coffee and sliced off another bite.

Faith nibbled at the food on her own plate, but everything had lost its appeal.

"I'm going to take a trip," Luke spoke up, wiping his mouth with his napkin.

"You are?" Alarmed at the thought of Luke leaving, Faith frowned. "When?" She'd done nothing but hurt him since coming into his life. He probably just needed some time away from her.

"Soon. Today. Just as soon as I can get ready for travel."

Today? How could she bear it? She'd more than likely be gone by the time he returned. Her heart fluttered wildly, like a bird caught in a trap. She fought against the urge to cry and whispered, "I see. How long will you be gone?"

"Don't rightly know." He forked in another huge piece of meat, and Faith watched the ripple of his jaw as he chewed. "Will you miss me?"

He said it so casually that she thought she might not have heard right. "What?"

Luke turned and laid his fork on his plate. Taking her hands in his, he held them to his lips. "I asked if you'd miss me while I'm gone."

His tenderness was exactly what she didn't need, not if she wanted to maintain her composure. Squeezing her eyes closed, she nodded. A tiny unwilling moan escaped her.

"Shhh," he crooned. "Don't cry. Everything is going to be all right." Reaching out, he stroked her hair. With a small tug he had her in his lap, and she buried her face in the warmth and safety of his neck.

Breathing in his wonderful scent, she circled her arms around him.

"That's better," he said, rubbing her back. "Now, stop your crying." He handed her his napkin. "Blow."

She did and then reined in her sad feelings. Luke, tipping her face up with his finger, looked into her eyes. "Tell me you won't leave until I return," he commanded. When she didn't answer, he quickly went on. "Stay and wait for me. Then, if you still want to go to Priest's Crossing, I'll take you there myself. I promise."

She didn't know when Ward wanted to leave, but she figured it was going to be soon. Luke looked so hopeful. She wanted him to stay happy. Would it matter much if she added one more lie to her list?

"All right."

He squeezed her so hard she feared she might faint.

"Where . . . ?" she started to ask, but he put his finger to her lips and stopped the question.

"Just wait till I get back."

She nodded.

Standing, Luke set Faith on her feet. "I have a lot to get done before I go." He turned to leave.

"Luke?"

He looked back at her. "Yes."

"I'm sorry about yesterday," she said. Oh, how she wished she could go back. She'd do so many things differently. In her mind she'd tell him all the things she felt in her heart. How she longed to be his, only his, forever.

He grinned, confusing her again. "So am I," he called, then bounded up the stairs.

Faith stood there long after Luke rounded the hall out of sight. Something was driving him, something that had dramatically changed his mood. She wished she knew what it was. Did it have something to do with the sheriff?

Instantly, she went cold inside. But if the sheriff knew

about her past, surely Luke couldn't be happy about it. No, Brandon Crawford had come with news about the bull that she'd learned this morning at breakfast: Earl Morton, one of the men on the cattle drive, and Will Dickson, the awful man with the scar, had maimed the bull.

Cruel. So cruel. They reminded her of Samuel.

Luke shoved a shirt into his saddlebag, which was the last of it. He was traveling light. He'd take two fast horses to alternate between, Pony Express—style, switching whenever one got tired. In Waterloo, he and his horses would board the train traveling east. He should make it to Kearney in a couple of days at the most.

Confidence that he'd be able to get to the bottom of this nightmare had him hopeful. What worried him was what Faith would do with the information upon his return. There was a good job for her in Priest's Crossing, if she were really set on being alone. But was that what she really wanted? He couldn't believe it.

Luke caught a glimpse of himself in his bedroom mirror. He paused, studying his reflection. Looking back at him was not the man who'd been there yesterday. He was the same height, had the same smile, but inside he'd changed. The fact that his mother had been carried off all those years ago was still wrong, a dark spot in her life, in all of their lives, but knowing that she hadn't suffered every moment, like he'd believed, meant a great deal. His mother's comments had given Luke pride in his other self, the self he could never before acknowledge.

Back in his ranching clothes and boots, he tossed his saddlebags over his shoulder and stepped into the hall. Startled, he found Colton waiting by his bedroom door. When the boy caught sight of him, he turned and hurried away.

"Wait, Colton. Hold up," Luke called.

The boy whirled, staring up at Luke with fearful eyes. "I didn't do it," he yipped.

Luke hunkered down eye level with him. The youth's hair was dusty and he looked everywhere else. "Didn't do what?" Luke asked slowly.

Colton, seeming to have realized his mistake, shrugged. "Nothin'."

Luke didn't want to press the issue, since he was leaving so soon. He and Colton were working on a truce, and it felt good. Besides, if he hadn't heard about something amiss by now, whatever the boy had done, it must be minor. "I reckon you'll tell me when you're ready," he replied. "You think?"

Again, Colton just shrugged.

The boy clearly had something he wanted to ask, but he was having a hard time getting it out. Luke slowly stood. "Why were you waiting at my door?"

"Wasn't waiting."

"Oh?"

Colton fidgeted under Luke's scrutiny. "Just wondering . . ." he began. "Heard you was leaving. Are ya?"

Luke hid the warm surprise that flowed through him. Maybe Colton didn't dislike him as much as he'd thought. "I am."

The boy raised his eyes, longing and confusion both written plainly there. "When?" His voice had lost its bravado, and he jammed his hands into his pants pockets.

"Just as soon as I can. But I won't be gone long," Luke assured him. This was a new role for both of them. Instead of being his adversary, Colton was actually reaching out.

"Can I go?" The boy looked miserable.

Luke shook his head. "Sorry, son, I have to make good time. It's very important. Any other time I'd say yes."

"I won't hold you up," Colton begged.

Damn. He couldn't take him. Not with so much at stake. But for some reason Colton had had a change of heart concerning him, and he hated to let him down. He turned and headed back into his room. "Come here, Colton, I have something I want to give you." At his dresser, Luke pulled open the top drawer and began rummaging around. Turning, he held out his hand. "Here, I want you to have this."

Colton eyed the knife Luke held in the palm of his hand. It was small, and the handle, carved from a deer horn, was shiny from use. "Go on, take it," Luke said with a smile.

Slowly Colton took the knife. He turned it from side to side, looking solemnly at the object, then up at Luke. He didn't say anything.

It was Luke's turn to shrug. "I was just about your age when Pa gave it to me. Be careful not to hurt yourself or anyone else. A knife is a big responsibility, but I think you're man enough for it."

Without warning, Colton threw himself into Luke's arms, almost knocking him off balance. In return, Luke wrapped the boy within his embrace, marveling at how good it felt. A tremble racked Colton's body, causing Luke's throat to ache with emotion.

"Hey, what's all this," Luke whispered gruffly.

Colton turned his head and hid his face in the crook of Luke's neck. His breath and the warmth of his tears tickled Luke's skin as he squirmed to get closer. "I want you to stay."

"I can't, Colton. That's impossible. But I do need you to keep an eye on your ma for me. And that little sister of yours. Think you can do that?"

Colton nodded.

"Good. I'm counting on you."

Struggling from Luke's arms, Colton raced off down the hall. Luke shook his head and smiled as he again hefted his saddlebag and left the room.

Faith's door was open a couple inches, and he could hear Dawn fussing and crying in her crib. "Faith, you in there?" he called through the door. Opening it a little, he stuck his head in, anticipating finding Faith in the room or possibly resting on the bed. He didn't. The room was empty except for the crying baby.

Tossing his saddlebags onto the bed, he ventured over to the pinewood cradle where the baby cried and peeked inside. Here was the trouble. On her belly, Dawn had scrunched herself up into the corner of the bed. Her head, fussing from side to side, couldn't get comfortable. Arms as small as chicken legs flailed unhappily.

Luke looked around the room and then back at the infant. "Here now, little Dawn, you're all right," he said.

When the fussing baby heard his voice, she let loose with a gut-wrenching sob and worked herself up in a rhythm that he would recognize as hers even in a roomful of young'uns. She bellowed in outrage.

Surprised, he took a step back and analyzed the situation. He didn't have the heart to just let her cry endlessly until Faith came. Why, that could be some time. No telling where she'd gone off to. So, with ringing ears, he lifted Dawn up to his shoulder.

Her sweet powdery smell, mixed with the aroma of dried milk, brought a smile to his face. Patting her back, he started walking around the room and singing. That's what they did out on the trail when the cattle were edgy, so it sure couldn't hurt to try.

"Come along boys and listen to my tale . . ." he sang, patting her back as he walked around the room. Her sobs continued, but he could be just as stubborn as she was being. "I'll tell you of my troubles on the old Chisholm Trail . . . come-a ti, yi youp-yea, come-a ti, yi youp-y youp-y yea . . ."

When he got to the chorus, Dawn actually hushed for a moment as if listening. "That's a good girl," Luke crooned. But the minute he quit singing, she started up again.

"On a ten-dollar horse and a forty-dollar saddle, and I'm goin' to punch Texas longhorn cattle . . . come-a ti, yi youp-yea, come-a ti, yi youp-y youp-y yea . . ."

He could almost hear his own voice now. She was calming down just a bit, like a restless steer would do. Pleased, Luke couldn't help but experience satisfaction at the job he was doing.

"I woke up one morning on the old Chisholm Trail, rope in my hand and a cow by the tail—" Turning, he came face-to-face with Faith. Her broad smile went from ear to ear, exposing her delicious-looking dimple. He finished up, "Come-a ti, yi youp-yea, come-a ti, ye youp-y youp-y yea . . ."

He handed back her baby, who snuggled up next to her breast but kept wide, tearful eyes on him. "Please, Luke," Faith whispered, "don't stop."

He leaned over, bent down close to Dawn. "Stray in the herd and the boss said to kill it, so I shot him in the rump with the handle of the skillet . . . come-a ti, ye youp-yea, come-a ti, ye youp-y youp-y yea."

"More," she mouthed as he let his voice trail off low and slow until he could stop. He shook his head and gestured to the sleeping baby. He pointed to the cradle and then to the door. He watched with a full heart as Faith laid Dawn back into the cradle; then he left the room and waited for her in the hall.

She pulled the door closed with a soft click. He waited for her to speak first, interested in what she might say. Instead, she slipped her arms around his waist and laid her head on his heart. A moment slipped by.

"Luke, your voice . . . It's beautiful," she whispered. "Why, when I came up the stairs and heard that deep, rich singing I couldn't imagine who it was. Why wouldn't you sing a few more lines?"

"That particular song has numerous verses, Faith, so we can sing for hours if we need to calm edgy cattle. I didn't think you really wanted to hear all that."

"I did. I loved it."

He pulled her close. Even though he knew he was pushing hard, asking for things she wasn't ready to give, he threw caution to the wind. "First thing when I get home I'll sing you the whole song start to finish. We'll take a moonlight buggy ride and I'll serenade you for hours."

Her face clouded over. Just by watching her expression, he knew she cared.

"When are you coming home?"

"As soon as I can, darlin'. Don't you get impatient and run off to Priest's Crossing. I'll send a telegram to Christine Meeks telling her you'll be there soon. She'll hold the spot for you. I'll make sure of that."

"Oh, Luke," Faith said, playing with the buttons on his shirt. "I wish so many things could be different."

"Like what?" He thought he knew what she was referring to. He'd bet it was the mess she was in at home and her resulting fear that kept her from him. He was still hopeful that she'd open up and share her past with him, but that didn't matter so much anymore. He was banking on the future, on her actions, not on her words any longer. He was counting on the way her eyes went dark when she looked at him, the longing he could see in her face, her warm response when he kissed her. Those things a person couldn't fake.

She shook her head and leaned into his embrace. "Just . . . things."

He inhaled her scent and stroked her hair, committing its silky feel to memory for the days he'd be away. Between worrying over her running off and Brandon finding out unfavorable things, he'd be home in record time.

Faith looked up at him expectantly, her breath coming faster. He took her face in his hands and kissed her mouth briefly, softly, lingering for a moment. Then he gathered her against his chest and kissed her hard. His urgency surprised him, and he longed to carry her into his room across the hall and close out the world. Instead, he released her.

"You take good care of that peanut while I'm gone," he said as he looked into her eyes. She nodded. "And if you need anything, anything at all, you know you can go to any of the family. They love you."

Again she nodded. Her face, even dark with despair, gladdened his heart. He couldn't be wrong about her feelings. She was his. She just didn't know it yet.

Chapter Forty-three

FAITH watched Luke ride out. Her mind screamed and pleaded, making every argument it could think of against his leaving. She didn't voice any of them, and anguish, anger and heat ripped her insides apart. When he returned she'd be long gone. She wanted to fall to the ground and beat her fists against the hard, dusty ground for the unfairness of it all.

That day, the only thing that kept her from falling into a pit of despair was the fact that Joe Brunn rode in, greeting everyone with a cheerful hello. He had no idea that her heart was breaking, that her world was falling apart, that her life would never again be the same. He simply arrived with the news that the bridge was complete, which Faith took as just another indication that she had to get busy. She'd known all along she was going to have to leave Luke eventually, that her stay here was temporary. Well, "eventually" had reared its ugly head.

Joe planned to leave immediately. He intended to get to Priest's Crossing just as soon as he could. He didn't go into any details, but he let Faith know that if she still wanted it, he was happy to escort her. Now she had to find Ward and convince him to let her ride out with Joe before meeting him somewhere along the way.

She found Francis in the barn. It had been a while since she'd talked with the youth, and she gave him a little hug.

"Francis, it's good to see you! How have you been?" she asked, causing his cheeks to color.

"Just fine, ma'am. And you?"

"I've been fine, too," she lied. She felt anything but.

"What are ya doing out here?" He gestured to the barn.

"I came looking for you."

His eyebrows rose.

Faith forced herself to relax. The last thing she wanted to do was arouse any suspicions. "I was wondering if you'd hitch my old wagon. I'm making a trip into Priest's Crossing."

Doubt flicked across his face. "You are? Does Luke know?" The boy's loyalty to Luke was heartwarming.

"Why, yes he does." Faith held out the telegram from Christine Meeks. "He knew I'd be going, but I wasn't sure when Mr. Brunn would show up to take me. Well, Joe arrived today and wants to set out as soon as I can be ready."

Francis glanced at the note. "You sure?" When she nodded, he said, "It'll be ready by the time you're packed."

"Thank you, Francis," she said.

Turning, she saw Ward in the barn doorway, leaning on his crutch. He smiled as she approached. "Thought I saw you going into the barn."

His appraising gaze made her skin crawl, and it also fanned a flame of anger that was slowly burning inside her. This poor excuse of a human being, this lowlife who preyed on creatures weaker than he was, who caused pain and devastation without thought to the lives that would be destroyed, was ripping her world apart. That's just what she felt like doing to him.

"I'm getting ready to leave, Ward."

His face turned ugly. "What do you mean? You ain't going nowhere without me." His unflinching gaze filled her with a sense of foreboding.

"You told me to think up a plan so the McCutcheons wouldn't question my leaving, and I have. Do you want to hear it?" she asked, gathering her courage. "Or not!" Even this tiny bit of defiance made her feel good.

"My, aren't you the sassy one." He stepped closer. "Just what did you have in mind?"

Faith lowered her voice so Francis, who'd set about gathering harnesses, wouldn't hear. "If the children and I ride out of here with you, everyone is going to know something is up. That in some way you forced me to go. No one is going to let that happen." She paused, glancing around to see if anyone was watching them.

"Go on."

"It will be much more convincing if I leave with Joe Brunn, a friend of the family who offered to take me to Priest's Crossing to work for his sister. You wait for us on the road. Since he doesn't know you, when I tell him I've changed my mind and want to go home with you he'll think nothing of it."

She held her breath as Ward mulled over what she'd just suggested. Finally he nodded. "Fine. Even though I'd like to make that high and mighty Luke McCutcheon eat crow as he watches you ride away with me, this does make more sense. And since Luke will know you're with this other fellow, this friend that he trusts . . . What did you say his name was?"

"Mr. Brunn."

"Since he thinks you're with Brunn, he won't come looking." Ward tossed down his crutch. "I'm leaving as soon as I get my horse. I'll see you, Faith, honey, on the road to Priest's Crossing. Don't keep me waiting long."

Faith realized as Ward strode away, just a slight limp slowing him down, that he didn't know that Luke had already left.

As she made her way back to the house, she heard her name called. Turning, she saw Amy waving to her and running in her direction, eyes glowing and step light.

"Faith," the young woman said, taking Faith's hands in her own while struggling to catch her breath. Her joy was contagious, making Faith forget her problems for the time being. "I still can't believe it. You were right. The other night I got the courage up to go home and start talking with Mark. At first he didn't want to discuss anything and avoided me all the more. But I didn't give up. I wanted to be strong like you, so I followed him around and just kept talking. I talked up a storm. You would have been proud of me." She squeezed Faith's hand. "The more I told him how I felt, the easier it got."

"Why, Amy, that's wonderful." Faith hugged her. "I'm very happy for you."

"But that's not all. After I told him that I was sorry for losing our baby, for getting in the family way, for forcing him to marry me, he opened up, too. He's been thinking that I was sorry for marrying him. Without the baby, he thought I didn't want to be his wife anymore. Can you believe how silly we both were?"

Faith was shocked how much her friend had changed. With her long hair and shining eyes, her cheeks tinted prettily pink, Amy was beautiful, love radiating from every inch of her.

"So," Faith asked, "things are better then?"

"Everything's wonderful. It's just like when we first met and Mark was coming into town almost every other day to see me. We couldn't stand to be away from each other for more than a few hours. That's how it is now." She laughed and twirled around. Moving closer, she whispered, "Sometimes he comes home in the middle of the day." She covered her mouth with her hand. "I just love him so much." She linked her arm through Faith's. "Let's go have a cup of tea."

Faith shook her head. "I can't. I'm packing."

"What?" The girl pulled back in dismay. "What do you mean, you're packing? Where are you going?"

"To Priest's Crossing. I've a job waiting for me," Faith said quietly.

"What about Luke? I know you have feelings for him, and Mark says Luke's in love with you. You can't go."

Oh, the unfairness of it was enough to make her start crying and never stop. She hadn't killed Samuel, hadn't been mean and ugly to him though he'd treated her like an animal. Would she have to pay for marrying him for the rest of her life?

Flood and Joe's laughter emanated from inside the house, which reminded Faith she had to get moving. Joe wanted to leave as soon as possible. She didn't want to anger him before they even got started.

She gave Amy's hand a squeeze. "Don't be upset with me on my last day here. Come and help me pack my things. You can hold Dawn while I gather my belongings."

Chapter Forty-four

$\mathcal{F}$AITH looked over at Amy, who sat forlornly in the corner of the big bedroom holding Dawn. Mrs. McCutcheon had found the two girls packing in Faith's room and wanted to know what was going on. For the past half hour she'd been trying to talk Faith out of leaving.

The woman wrapped Faith in her arms and held her close. "Are you sure there's *nothing* I can do or say to make you change your mind . . . just until Luke returns? I know he's going to be extremely unhappy when he learns that you've left without saying good-bye."

Faith closed her eyes and enjoyed the comfort of the woman's embrace. She smelled of roses, and her arms were warm and soft. Oh, how she'd longed for someone just like this all her life. Her heart throbbed painfully in her chest. This was the mother she'd dreamed about all those lonely years on that godforsaken farm.

Determinedly, she pulled herself together. "I'm very sure. He'll understand. Besides, Luke knew I was going soon and he left anyway." She marveled at how confident her lie sounded.

"So you see"—Faith shrugged—"he's probably relieved that I'm finally on my way."

Mrs. McCutcheon shook her head in disbelief.

"Please." Faith reached into her satchel and drew out a sealed envelope. "Would you give this to him?" Faith handed Luke's mother a small brown envelope.

The older woman smiled, her expression a bit wobbly. "Of course I will. I keep trying to remind myself that it's not like you're going far, far away. Why, Priest's Crossing is a lovely town! I'm sure we'll see each other from time to time, and once Luke gets here he'll spirit you back before we even start to miss you."

"You mustn't let him come after me." The fear of him learning that she was with Ward was just too much. Too hurtful. She wouldn't be able to bear it if she thought he'd know the truth. "I need to do this, to take care of myself and my children on my own for a while. I need to prove to myself that I can."

"You, my dear, are just about as stubborn as Luke himself." Mrs. McCutcheon plastered on a smile. "No wonder he's so taken with you. You're kindred spirits. If you're set on going and you're sure there's nothing I can do or say to change your mind, then I have a few things I'd like to send along with you." Seeming to read Faith's mind, she patted her hand. "And don't worry about Joe leaving without you. He won't go until I'm good and ready to let him." She hurried out of the room with the note Faith had given her, promising to be back in a few minutes.

"That's about the last of it." Faith finished stuffing her things into the old trunk that had made the trip all the way with her from Nebraska. It seemed a lifetime ago since Luke had carried it in, setting it on the stand by the window. Each morning she'd gathered the things she needed from it as she looked out on the most beautiful view she could ever remember seeing.

Colton bolted into the room. He was dusty from head to toe and sheer panic was written on his little face. "Ma," he cried, "why is our wagon out front and getting loaded with stuff? Are we goin' somewhere?"

This was the lie she hated most of all. When Colton found out the truth, he'd never forgive her. He'd probably never trust her again. No matter how logical she made it sound to go back to the farm, he'd never understand.

"We're moving on to Priest's Crossing. We have someone to take us now, so we can't wait."

"But Ma," he said defiantly, "I like it here. And so do you. Let's stay. I don't want to move anymore." The desperation in his voice ripped at her insides. His hand reached out and grasped her skirt, clinging with a vengeance. "Please, Ma!"

"We can't stay, Colton. We were only visiting. Now run into the next room and put your things into your knapsack. Hurry now, we can't keep Mr. Brunn waiting."

Colton backed out of the room, disbelief and anger clouding his face. He shook his head. "I don't want to go. I *don't*. Luke said I didn't have to go if I didn't want to. I don't want to!" He ran from the room, slamming the door behind him.

At the loud bang, Dawn woke up and started crying. Amy approached and handed Faith the infant. It was apparent that the baby wanted to eat. "You take her now, Faith," she said. "I have something at home I want to give you. Don't you dare leave until I get back. You promise?"

"I won't."

"I'll be back quick." Amy hurried from the room, too, and Faith soon heard her footsteps on the stairs.

Sitting in the chair by the window, she slowly unbuttoned her dress and placed the crying infant to her breast, but the comfort that nursing the baby usually brought eluded her. Her mind raced ahead to her coming time with Ward. Dread was pitted in her stomach, fear making her skin crawl. How long, she wondered, until he felt he could take her body like Samuel had? How long?

After suckling for a moment, Dawn tossed her head to the

side, fussing. Whimpering, she latched on again, sucking hard. Faith winced. The baby kicked her little legs in protest. Her frustrated mouth formed an O as she cried around Faith's nipple.

Distressed, Faith looked down. "What is it, sweetheart? What's wrong?" The hot prickling that usually accompanied feeding time hadn't been present, and Faith realized that her milk had not let down. She had to relax somehow, think of something nice.

Closing her eyes, she drifted back to that morning on the bluff: the warm sun on her skin, the hawk flying high above her head . . . She held her breath, recalling the feeling she'd got as Luke gazed into her face with his dark, expressive eyes, questions written on his face that he'd never ask.

She was sure now that he loved her. She didn't need to hear the words from his lips, for she could read them in his eyes every time he looked at her. Warm tingles careened through her body at the thought. Her breasts prickled. Dawn latched on for all she was worth, nursing greedily.

This would be the last time she fed her baby here in this spot. She looked around the room, taking in every detail so that she could remember them once she was back on the farm. Back with Ward and his father.

There was a light tap on her door.

"Who is it?" she called.

"Francis, ma'am. I've come for your things."

"One moment, please." Faith grabbed a clean cloth and draped it over her shoulder, hiding the nursing infant. "You can come in now."

Francis stepped in, accompanied by Smokey. The men kept their eyes trained far from Faith. Without a word they hoisted the trunk up on Smokey's shoulder, and he hustled out of the room. Francis gathered her odds and ends, knapsack and anything else he could find. He quietly closed the door and left.

* * *

Colton was doing his best not to cry, but Faith could see the wet streaks on his cheeks that he kept wiping away. He stood behind Joe Brunn, who sat in the seat next to her, long leather reins in his gloved hands. Tied behind the wagon was Joe's horse, along with Firefly, Colton's little mare. Flood had assured Faith that a man needed his horse, and it wasn't like they didn't have a few to spare around the ranch.

Everyone in the family had come to see them off. Rachel and Matt, holding little Beth, stood with Mark and Amy, Mrs. McCutcheon and Flood. Charity was on her horse and planned to ride along for a while.

"You be sure to get time off around the holidays so you can come and visit," Mrs. McCutcheon said. "I won't take no for an answer."

Faith held Dawn close as she forced a smile. "I will." Another lie. They'd all hate her when they learned she'd gone off with Ward. After everything they'd done for her, that's how she would repay them, by throwing it all in their faces.

And Luke. She couldn't think of him. Every time she tried, her heart froze up and nothing seemed to matter. But, no. Her children were what mattered. Nothing else.

"Good-bye, Joe," Matt called. "Take good care of your cargo. You don't want to have my little brother on your tail."

"Little brother. I wouldn't call him that." Joe barked out a laugh. "I am a tad worried about when he gets home. Tell him I didn't coerce her into going. He already thinks I'm after her."

Faith felt heat rise to her cheeks but kept the smile plastered on her face. "Thank you, Amy, for the gift." Faith held up the pretty bonnet that Amy had gone to get her. "It's charming."

"That's so you don't forget me," the girl said shakily. She turned into her husband's arms and started crying.

Rachel's eyes met Faith's meaningfully as she brought Beth to her lips and kissed the baby's cheek. "Thank you," she mouthed.

"Haw," Joe shouted to the horses, slapping the reins over their backs. "Get up."

A chorus of good-byes rose. Tears were wiped from sad faces and wobbly smiles bloomed all around. The jingling of the harness and squeaking of the wagon wheels drowned out most of what was being called out.

The cumbersome wagon turned, making a wide circle and pulling up alongside the bunkhouse. Word had spread, and the hands who weren't far from the ranch house had come in from their duties to say their farewells. Stepping off the porch, they walked single file past Faith's side of the wagon.

Francis was first to step forward, a bashful smile on his face. "Good-bye, ma'am. I'm sure gonna miss you and Colton and little Miss Dawn."

Faith smiled in return but couldn't find words. Francis seemed to understand that she was too choked up to speak, and he moved aside to make way for Smokey.

The wrangler spat and wiped his mouth. "Sorry about that rattler. I hope I ain't got hard feelin's 'bout it."

Faith couldn't stop her smile as she remembered the day she'd fainted onto Francis's lap. "Of course I forgive you. I was never angry about that." The smile that split Smokey's face made her laugh. He turned away, lightness in his step.

Pedro was next. His dark eyes were somber as he waited for his turn to say good-bye. "*Adios, senora.* May the Lord go with you, *sí*," he said in his accented English. He made the sign of the cross, then kissed his fingertips.

Chance and Lucky were the only two left, and Faith didn't know if she'd be able to get through without breaking down. Taking out her damp hankie, she wiped at the corner of her eyes, willing herself to stay in control. Her chest felt as heavy as a load of bricks, and her eyes burned.

Chance, in his charmingly shy way, stepped forward and took her hand. His eyes were unreadable. "Good-bye, Faith." Her name, without the Miss attached, spoken softly in his slight Texan accent, felt like a caress. Surprise filled her as she realized that it was how he intended it to sound.

"I'll miss you more than you'll know." He gazed into her eyes more boldly than he'd ever done. "You take care of yourself and baby Dawn. All of us here, in some small way, feel like her pa. If you ever need anything at all . . ." That was all he could get out; he quickly turned and walked away. After a few steps he turned back, hope shining in his eyes. "I'm coming to Priest's Crossing next month."

She whispered his name so softly that she doubted he heard. These men were the most wonderful friends she'd ever had in her life. When she was sad, they'd cheered her up. When happy, their eyes danced with shared merriment. Homesick, they'd sing her a song. She didn't want to leave! Maybe she hadn't tried hard enough to outsmart Ward. What if she'd just told Luke the truth? Would he have been able to help her?

Lord, her mind screamed out, *don't send us back to Samuel's father. Please!*

"Don't look so sad, missy," Lucky said. Faith could tell he was wrestling with his feelings. "Can I hold her fer one minute?" he asked, gesturing to the baby. As she handed over the blanket-wrapped child, he marveled and played with a golden puff of her hair. "She sure is still such a little thing."

"Thank you, Lucky—for everything."

He looked up, startled.

"Don't look so surprised. You helped me beyond measure, even standing up to Luke when he was angry with me. I'll never forget you."

"Don't talk like I ain't never gonna see ya again. We've got a bet goin' on how long it'll take Luke to cart you back once he gets his tail end home." He handed Dawn up and gave her a wink. "I'll be seein' ya soon."

But, he wouldn't. He'd never see her again. Ward would see to that. This was the last time in her life she'd be with any of these people. And what about Colton? She looked back at his dejected little face. Heartbreak was written there plainly for all to see.

Joe looked over. "You sure you want to go?"

"I'm sure," she said.

"Then we best be on our way. Good-bye, everyone," the builder called, waving.

"Good-bye!" The clamor went up again. "Be good, Colton. Good-bye, Faith. Take care of the children. We'll miss you. See you at Thanksgiving. Take good care of Firefly."

That was all she could take; Faith's manufactured smile crumpled and with a sob she buried her face in her handkerchief and cried. Nothing mattered anymore. She didn't care what Joe thought of her.

Luke? She hadn't even been able to tell him good-bye. Not really. Her love. He'd asked her to wait for him, not to run off before he got back. Here she was, leaving on the very same day.

Thinking of the note she'd left with Mrs. McCutcheon made her wince, and grief surged within her so strong she thought she just might swoon. Joe reached over and laid his hand comfortingly on her back. On she sobbed, regretting, regretting, regretting. Forcing herself to write a note that would be sure to keep him from trailing her was the hardest thing she'd ever done in her life. She'd been cruel. So cruel that it took her breath away. But she'd had to be. Under no circumstances did she want Luke coming after her. She wouldn't be able to stand to see the look on his face if he found her with Ward. It was better if he learned the truth later from Joe, months afterward she hoped. By then he probably would have forgotten she'd ever come into his life.

Atop a bluff, Charity reined to a stop. "Good-bye," she called, waving. "I'll see you soon." Her hair was loose and blowing in the soft breeze, and she wore the buckskin clothes she'd worn the first night Faith met her.

Faith and Colton waved back. Faith was thankful for one thing: she might be leaving, but she was taking Ward away.

She'd never forgive herself if he'd done anything to compromise Charity. Thank heaven it hadn't happened already. Faith knew firsthand just how attractive the Browns could be, with their charming ways and handsome faces. And as deadly as scorpions.

Chapter Forty-five

LUKE made good time in spite of the weather turning stormy just hours after he left the ranch. His horses carried him for twelve hours straight, with only short breaks to eat and drink. Their bold, unflagging courage was a credit to the ranch's breeding program. Several generations of handpicked mares crossed with the ranch's two breeding stallions had resulted in what the McCutcheons considered the perfect animal, with intelligence, heart, stamina, strength and courage. The two he'd brought were proving to be champions.

Arriving at his first destination, he rubbed their legs with liniment and checked carefully for splints that could cause lameness. Both horses were sound. He looked at them now as they ate, heads low, breathing steady, and knew Flood would be proud to hear of their performance.

Pulling his hat low, Luke leaned against his saddle and tried to get comfortable. The rocking motion and the rhythmic clickety-clack of the boxcar lulled his weary mind. Just a few more hours and he'd arrive in Kearney.

Idly Luke fingered the deputy's badge he had in the pocket of his sheepskin coat. Brandon had insisted he take it: a little extra ammunition was always a good thing. Also in his saddlebag was an official-looking document with Samuel Brown's name neatly printed on the envelope and secured with a wax seal. The paper sheets inside were blank.

He tried to relax. Still, his gut tied up tight like a wet rope when he considered what the next stop held in store. There was the possibility Faith had truly killed Samuel. If she had, he was sure it was in self-defense, but that was something that would have to be proved. He lay there going over every possible scenario.

An hour passed. His eyelids drooped. He was tired and he should try and get some sleep, he realized. He yawned, swiping his hand across his face, and thought about Faith and wondered what she was doing right now at the ranch.

"Kearney!" the conductor bellowed in a deep voice loud enough for Luke to hear. The whistle blew and the brakes screeched in protest, steel grating against steel. The train car rocked strongly as it slowed, upsetting their balance, and the horses braced themselves.

The train jerked a couple of last times, then slowly rolled to a stop. Luke stood, stretched the sore muscles in his legs and pushed open the long wooden door, welcoming the breeze into the hot timber box. He saddled both horses as they peeked out the door with curiosity, and then mounted the dun.

The gelding only had to be directed once. Lowering his head, he eyed the small distance from the train car to the ground, and hopped out, and the bay Luke held by the reins followed suit. Once outside on a grassy knoll, all three enjoyed a deep breath of cool, clean air.

Kearney was not much to look at. It was small and, from where he stood at the depot, only a handful of businesses looked like they were thriving. The rest were dingy, unkempt and in desperate need of paint. A group of young women sat in the park, covered top to bottom in calico and bonnets to protect them from the late-afternoon sun. One read out loud from a book. A chorus of giggles issued forth as Luke rode by, drawing a scowl from their teacher as she tap, tap, tapped her pointer on the back of the bench.

This was Faith's town, he thought as he studied the landscape, buildings and people. The place where she'd grown up. Had she liked it here? Had people been good to her? The townsfolk looked at him with open curiosity, taking stock of the newcomer.

Spotting a bathhouse, Luke stabled his horses at the livery and spent time cleaning up and gathering information. The Brown farm, which had been the Duncan place for years, wasn't more than a mile out of town. Mr. Duncan's daughter married Samuel Brown, from over Trinity Hill Way, Luke learned from a barkeep with nothing to do but talk, and Duncan himself was killed in an accident shortly afterward. There was someone living out there now, he believed, possibly kin to Mr. Brown, but he didn't know for sure.

"Are there any other places out that way?" Luke had asked the man.

"Just one a bit east of it."

That's where, first thing in the morning, Luke planned to start. First he'd wire the information he'd gathered back to Brandon.

The next day, Luke approached the shabby little farmhouse slowly. An old wooden board tacked crookedly on the gatepost read THOMAS FARM. Three dirty-faced children ran about, chasing a handful of clucking hens. One disgruntled, sharp-eyed rooster stood watching. Each time one of the children turned his back, the rooster would make a run for them, sending the children shrieking with laughter as they dashed to safety.

"Quit pestering them hens or I'll whup your bottoms, ya hear?" a female voice shouted from the barn. "Get 'em so worked up they can't lay worth squat for days. I mean it!"

The children hadn't spotted him yet, as they worked quickly to bury some eggs they'd broken in the game. They'd been so busy they hadn't heard him ride up. He was sure that the person behind that voice wasn't one to issue a threat and not follow through.

"Howdy," he said, startling them. "Is this the Brown residence?" he asked, knowing full well that it wasn't.

A dark-haired girl, no older than three, ducked behind her older sister. Luke noticed that a shoe was missing and her dress was inches too short, outgrown long ago. The other two children, a boy and girl, who looked relatively the same age, stared at him wide-eyed.

Gathering his courage, the boy spoke up. "No, sir, it ain't."

Just then their mother, haggard and weather-beaten of features, came from the barn hauling a bucket of milk. Pushing the hair out of her face she looked Luke up and down.

Her son ran to her side. "He thinks this is the Brown place. Guess he can't read."

"Hush now, Harvey. You and Hannah take this milk into the house before it spoils here in the sun. Be careful now not to spill it if you want sweet cream tonight." The children lumbered away with their burden, working together not to spill a drop.

The mother turned her attention to Luke. "What do you want, mister?"

"I'm looking for Samuel Brown," he said, pulling his fake document from his saddlebag. "I have something for him."

Her inquisitive gaze moved from the document back up into Luke's face. "That's gonna be a mite hard," she said, giving him a shy smile.

"Why so?"

"He done up and died some months back. His place is the next farm over."

Luke faked surprise. "Does he have a wife or some other kin close by?"

"Faith Brown, his wife. But she ain't around. They say she left the day after he died, without telling a soul." She shook her head.

Finally, he was getting somewhere. This woman probably

knew Faith as well as anyone. "Do you mind if I give my horse a drink?" he asked, gesturing to her watering trough.

"Help yourself."

Dismounting, he led his horse to the trough and the gelding dipped his muzzle into the water. Tongue between his lips and the bit, the horse sucked noisily, bringing a giggle from the smallest girl, who'd stayed behind with her mother.

Luke looked at the envelope he held. "I suppose I should give this to his wife. You say you don't know where she is?"

"No." The woman's expression darkened. "I wish I did. She was a nice neighbor and friend. I miss her. Things around here can get a bit lonesome with only children and animals to talk to."

Luke missed Faith, too. Trying his best at nonchalance he asked, "Why'd she run off without telling anyone?"

"Now, mister, that's hard ta say. I wouldn't blame her if she had given that nasty man a push out the loft, but I don't think that's how it happened. Don't reckon anyone thinks it is. No one who knew her at any rate."

Now, why would Faith run off if she wasn't considered a suspect? The bartender hadn't hinted at any such thing, and here this woman, her closest neighbor, said she wasn't a wanted criminal. For some reason Faith believed that she and Colton were better off on the trail, away from her family home where she'd grown up. But why?

"My boss will want to know why I wasn't able to deliver this. Do you know anything more? How he died? If anyone else worked for them at the time?"

The woman shooed away the child who was hanging on her skirt, and she walked over to the shade of a cottonwood, Luke following. "All I know is he fell from the loft in the barn," she said. "Broke his neck. It was rumored that a few of Faith Brown's things were found up in the loft when the sheriff came out to look," she admitted, "but that don't mean she pushed him."

"No, you're right," Luke agreed. Pulling some peppermints from his pocket, he held them out to the little girl. Her smile beguiling, she came forward and plucked the candies from his palm. "There's enough for you and the others," he said. Off she ran into the house, calling excitedly to her siblings.

He looked back to the woman expectantly. "What about anyone else being out there on that day? Perhaps a witness? Any farm hands?" he prompted.

"No true farm hands. But before Mr. Duncan died a year ago, they used to let an old black man live in their barn. He was partly crippled, I think. Anyway, he'd help around the place in exchange for food and a place to lay his head at night. But after Faith married, Samuel Brown pretty much run him off. But Ol' Toby kept coming back every so often, drop in now and then to check on Faith."

Excitement coursed through Luke. This man might know why Faith was so frightened, or even the true circumstances of what happened the day Samuel died. He needed to talk to him.

"Any possibility that you might know where he is?"

The woman thought a minute. "His name was Toby Johanassey. About fifty-nine, or maybe a little older. He brought me over the cow, late one night after Faith left. Said nobody over there would milk her."

Penelope! Luke looked to the barn at the mention of the cow, his mind racing. Penelope Flowers, Faith's charming aunt with the big brown eyes. She must have felt very desperate indeed to make up such a story. At the time, her lies had seemed so contrived, so unnecessary. But maybe they weren't. Shame filled him, and he wiped a hand over his face. He was going to make it up to her. If only she'd let him.

"He just wanders around from farm to farm looking for food and odd jobs, but I ain't seen him for a spell," the woman continued. "Maybe he's moved on."

Luke pushed away his disappointment. He didn't have

much time to find out the facts and get back to the ranch. If Toby were still around in the area, come hell or high water he'd find him.

"Would he go back and stay at the Browns' now that Samuel is dead?" he asked.

The woman's eyes got big. "I reckon not! That pa of Samuel's, he moved in after he put his son in the ground. I don't think Toby would go back there now. If Samuel Brown was ornery, then his pa"—she paused, thinking—"why . . . he's the devil himself."

Luke looked over the weed-strewn fields with the broken-down fence, past the barn and over to the homestead closest in the distance. A row of apple trees ran along the road, leading to a small house where he assumed Faith had grown up. Had she climbed in those trees and eaten that fruit? A bird dipped and turned across the sky until it was out of sight.

"If I go back, he'll make me marry Ward." Faith's words echoed loudly in his mind. He recalled the night Ward had met them outside the mercantile in Pine Grove, and the following night, after he'd hired him on and she'd been so upset. *"Ward is a threat to me, Dawn and Colton. And if you don't want to believe me, well . . . then don't."* She had basically told him all he needed to know—that is, if he'd been listening. He'd been too busy condemning her for the things she wasn't saying.

The woman in front of him's words played back in his head. *"If Samuel Brown was ornery, why, his pa is the devil himself."* It wasn't the law that Faith had been running from, but the family she'd married into.

Dread ripped through him like a hot knife. He'd gone off and left her right there in the palm of Ward's hand. The bastard was likely holding something over her head, threatening her with some kind of danger. If only she'd come to him. He was sure that the charges Ward must be using were false. But,

f he didn't get this straightened out now, once and for all, it
would always be haunting her; she'd never be free. She'd
promised to stay at the ranch until his return. That was the
only thought that gave him peace.

He stood there so long, so deep in thought, the woman
cleared her throat to get his attention.

"Sorry," he said. "I was just thinking about everything you've
told me." Turning, he stuck his boot in the stirrup and swung
into his saddle.

Looking up, Mrs. Thomas shielded her eyes against the sun
so she could see him on his horse. "What's in the letter?"

"I didn't write the contents, ma'am," he replied. "I'm just
the messenger, bound to deliver. If Toby happens to stop by,
tell him I have a reward for him in exchange for talking with
me. He can find me at the hotel." Luke pulled a small leather
pouch from his saddlebag. Withdrawing several dollar coins,
he reached down and placed them in her hand. "And this is
for your trouble."

A look of disbelief crossed her face, and she tried to hand
the money back.

He wouldn't take it. "Much obliged for the information."

"Are ya goin' over to the Brown place now?" she asked.

It was his turn to nod.

"Just watch your back," she said, looking in the direction
he intended to ride. "That bull ox is not to be trusted."

Luke tipped his hat and rode out.

Chapter Forty-six

AFTER speaking with Mrs. Thomas, Luke went back to his hotel room and made another sealed document, an envelope with blank paper. This one had "Toby Johanassey" written on the front. Now he sat atop his horse at the split in the twisting little road that led to the Brown place.

The branches of the trees lining the lane were heavy with shiny red apples. A sign stood off to the right of the road, a few feet inside a wooden fence that had seen better days. The name Duncan had been scratched out with coal, and Brown was written in over the top. Pulling his gun from its holster, Luke quickly checked its chambers, knowing full well that it was loaded. He holstered the weapon, pulled his hat low, then nudged his horse forward.

The house sat atop a slight rise, giving its occupants a nice view of their land and the approach of any visitors. The barn was between several massive trees. An outhouse, well, smokehouse and storage shed graced the farmyard, and a large chicken coop was partially hidden around back. Although run-down, the farmstead was appealing in a disorderly way and might yet be a nice place with a little care.

Luke stopped just short of the well, where a cat spooked by his horse darted from behind the stone foundation and careened toward the barn. An eerie silence followed. A slight breeze puffed by, bringing with it the smell of fallow earth baking in the hot sun.

The door creaked open and a man stepped out, a very large man who must have been a head and a half taller than Luke himself. Faith's father-in-law. His face showed neither greeting nor hostility.

"Howdy," Luke called, real friendly.

The man nodded. "What can I do you for, stranger?" He moved a few steps closer and placed his ham hock of a hand on the porch rail. His fingernails were so black Luke could see their filth from where he sat his horse. His clothes were dirty and his hair unkempt, the complete opposite of Ward. Luke also noticed how the man's eyes roved, assessing the quality of his horse and clothes.

"I'm looking for some information, if you can spare the time."

"I'll help ya if I can," the man replied. He hawked and spat off the side of the porch, his spittle landing in a flower bed overgrown with weeds. One that Faith had most likely planted. "Tie your horse up and come on in."

Luke corralled his temper. "Thanks, but I'm in a hurry." He shifted in his saddle, looking around. No telling whether someone was in the barn.

"I'm listening," Brown said.

Luke drew the fake envelope from his saddlebag. Wiping the moisture from his brow with the back of his arm, he again took stock of his surroundings. "I'm looking for a man. Older gentleman with a lame foot. Heard he's been working out here for you, off and on. Toby Johanassey."

Mr. Brown's face changed subtly, a tiny spark of suspicion crossing his eyes. "Why you want him?" Luke noted that the man's eyes never once strayed to the letter.

A twig snapped behind him, and instantly Luke swiveled in the saddle, gun drawn. When he turned back, Mr. Brown slowly smiled.

"A mite touchy?"

Slowly releasing the hammer with his thumb, Luke slid the gun back into its holster. He ignored the man's question.

"There's a reward if I can find him. It's yours if you'll tell me where he is."

"How much?"

This was a cagey fellow. He wouldn't endanger himself

unless the bait was good and tempting. But Luke wanted to get this resolved and get back to his family ranch. He was worried about Faith. Something inside was telling him to hurry.

"Fifty now, and another hundred after I deliver." It was more than most farmers made in a couple of good years. The offer was sure to get the man's attention.

Mr. Brown laughed, a harsh sound that made Luke tense. "That's a hell of a lot of money, son. What did the bastard do to be wanted in such a bad way?"

"Don't rightly know," Luke replied, putting the document out of sight in his saddlebag. "I'm just hired to deliver this document and be on my way. It's the party on the other end with all the money. Have you seen the man I'm looking for?"

"Could be. Let's see the money."

Without taking his eyes from Mr. Brown, who'd walked to the well and was pulling up the water bucket, Luke reached into his saddlebag and felt around. His fingers touched on the small satchel he'd brought with over fifty dollars. Settling back in his saddle, he held it up for inspection.

Mr. Brown held out his huge hand. "Let's see the other hundred."

Did this man think he was a fool? "I need information, solid information, before I hand this over. The other hundred is in town."

Mr. Brown's eyes narrowed. So did Luke's. All pleasantness was gone.

"How 'bout if I fetch him for you? But it'll take a while. You ride back to town, get the money and come back tomorrow. Then we'll finish the business."

Luke didn't like putting Toby in danger, but without his testimony he had no hope of wholly clearing Faith's name. "I'll be back this afternoon, but the remainder of the reward stays in town until I've delivered my letter. Those are my instructions. You can ride back with me and pick it up at the bank."

Chapter Forty-seven

$\mathcal{M}$ORE coffee?" Faith asked as she lowered three tin plates into a bucket of warm water and began washing them. Joe shook his head. Standing, the brawny man stretched his legs and set about harnessing the team.

Quietly, where Faith had left him, Colton carefully held his little sister. He wasn't allowed to walk with her yet, being that she was still so young. His eyes, darkened by worries not meant for someone his age, studied the baby. His brow was furrowed, his lips thin.

Three long, tormenting days had passed since they'd left the Heart of the Mountains ranch, and still there was no sign of Ward. The road though the countryside had been desolate and was traveled uneventfully. Faith had let herself become hopeful that somehow a miracle had happened and Ward had changed his mind and gone home. Then she'd come to her senses. She was edgy, expecting to see him around each corner they turned—or perhaps sauntering into camp just in time for breakfast or supper.

Closing her eyes, she let herself daydream about other hopeful outcomes to the predicament she and her little family were in: Luke would come home, read her note, not believe it, come find her in Priest's Crossing at the mercantile and insist that she return with him to his ranch. To marry him? Of course.

"Ouch!" Faith yanked her hands from the bucket. She inspected the index finger she'd just jabbed with the pointed end of a knife. A small drop of blood beaded on top. Wiping that away, she stuck the finger into her mouth.

"I want to go back," Colton announced matter-of-factly, for the thousandth time.

"Shh, you'll wake Dawn," Faith said, in a weak effort to change the subject. The moment that Colton stopped crying he'd begun pestering her day and night to turn the wagon around.

He drilled her now with a sullen stare. "Mr. Brunn can go ahead on his horse and we'll take the wagon back. We done it before. We can do it now." His nostrils flared. "I know the way."

Faith shuddered. What was he going to be like when he found out they weren't going to Priest's Crossing at all, but back to the farm? Back to his grandfather.

"Colton, please. I've explained before that we were only visiting. We have to make a home of our own."

"Colton," Joe called. His patience with the boy was inexhaustible. "Leave your mother be. She's doing what she feels is best for all." He came around the wagon and started loading their belongings, getting ready to pull out.

Conceding, Colton waited for Faith to take the baby. "Can I ride Firefly today?" he asked. A measure of hope flickered in his eyes, and Faith didn't have the heart to say no.

"I think that's a fine idea. Just stay close to the wagon. No riding ahead."

With drooping shoulders, Colton made his way over to the tree where his mare was tethered, and he began saddling her. His downcast mutterings to the animal could scarcely be heard.

Faith found Joe assessing her. "Don't worry so about the boy," he said. "Young'uns are buoyant. He'll get to town and meet some friends. He'll forget all about that ranch." He reached for the dishpan and tossed the water onto the fire. "Can even start school."

"Yes, school," Faith repeated. "I would love Colton to go to school."

Joe's attentive gaze made Faith uncomfortable, especially as his eyebrows lifted. He'd taken to talking with her every opportunity that arose. She'd liked him better when he was more on the quiet side, like when they'd first started out.

"How much longer will it take to get to town?" she asked. With Dawn in one arm, she went about the best she could picking up the rest of their belongings. A couple more things and they'd be ready to leave.

"I'd say about three more days. We're doing pretty well on time and covering a lot of ground." He grinned broadly. "Anxious to be rid of me?"

"Heavens no," she stammered, embarrassed that he'd read her mind. Being alone with a man—any man, besides Luke—rekindled uncertainties. Fears. In her mind she knew Mr. Brunn would never hurt her, that he was a good man who had the faith of the McCutcheons, but that didn't stop her overactive imagination.

"Well, good. I'm awfully glad to hear that. Being that you're goin' to be working for Christine, I'm sure we'll be seeing a lot of each other," he said, his expression meaningful.

"I'm sure you're right, Mr. Brunn."

"It's Joe. The least you can do is call me by my first name."

She swallowed. "All right . . . Joe."

Morning came and went. A strong breeze picked up and covered them all from head to toe with a thick coat of trail dust.

Still no Ward. Was there a chance that somehow he'd gone and gotten himself killed? Oh, for heaven's sake! She'd turned into a wretched woman, hoping for a man's death. But that was exactly what she was doing.

Stretched out on his stomach, Luke watched the farmhouse from the top of the ridge, his field glasses pressed to his eyes. The sun, which was creeping west, had slipped behind a large cloud, cooling the air considerably. He rolled to his side and eyed the canteen that hung from his horse's saddle some ten feet down the far side of the bluff.

He'd stay out all night if he had to, and track Brown when the man went to fetch Toby. But not much was happening down there now. Nor had it been for the past two hours. He was getting restless.

"Come on, you cow dung," he said under his breath, "make your move. Enough lollygagging, already. Let's get this over with."

He set the glasses down in the grass and ground his thumb and forefinger into his eyes. Faith had said she'd wait. She wouldn't leave until he'd returned, would she? Her dead husband's brother and father and her past cast a whole new light on things. With Luke being over in Kearney and off the ranch, would Ward just up and pack her off? Luke was afraid of that. But surely his brothers wouldn't let that happen.

With a knuckle Luke nudged the brim of his Stetson up and scratched his scalp. The warmth of the sun was making his head sweat. And the ants . . . He slapped his neck. This waiting was maddening. Could be he hadn't made the bait tempting enough.

Picking up the glasses, he looked down at the house. Movement caught his eye. Brown crossed the porch and was heading for the barn. Finally!

Luke lay still until Brown reappeared with a horse and rode off in the opposite direction; then he jogged over to his horse and quickly followed. He tried to stay off the road but there were some places rocks and brush made that impossible.

After a good three miles, Luke spotted Brown's horse tied behind a little shanty where a dried-up streambed crossed the road. He tied his own horse behind an outcropping of trees and waited. Soon he heard Brown's angry voice, though he was too far away to actually hear what was being said. Luke edged closer.

"Toby, you skinny old goat, get your ass up," Brown bellowed. "I'm gonna beat you within an inch of your life if you don't get on your feet."

"I can't. I's sick," came the reply.

"You ain't sick. You're coming with me," Brown ordered.

"I's sick." Toby went into a bout of coughing that had Brown cussing a blue streak.

Luke plastered his body to the wall, holding his breath as Brown stomped out. Through narrow eyes, he watched the man mount and ride off.

Luke cautiously entered the shanty. When Toby saw him, he struggled in fear, trying to sit up. He held a cloth to his mouth and was hacking so hard his eyes were watering. Splotches of red stained the handkerchief as he wiped his mouth.

Dropping to his knees, Luke helped the man lie back. "Can I get you anything?"

The old man shook his head, clearly miserable.

"You're Toby." It was more of a statement than a question, but the man answered anyway.

"Yes, sir."

"I'm Luke McCutcheon. I need some information. Do you think you can talk?"

Toby started coughing again, and Luke looked around for a cup for water. Finding nothing, he ran out to his horse and retrieved his canteen. He held it to the man's cracked lips, helping him drink. The anguish on his face was gut-twisting.

"I'm a friend of Faith Brown. I'm here on her behalf."

The man transformed immediately. His expression became something of a smile. "Miz Faith," he said on a sigh. "How is she? And Master Colton?"

"They're fine," Luke said, hoping his words were true. "But I need to find out about Samuel Brown and what happened the day he died. Do you know anything about that?"

Toby was quiet so long Luke feared maybe he'd get nothing out of him. Desperation fueled him to say, "Please. She may be in trouble unless I get the truth. Was she responsible for Samuel's death?"

Toby took a breath and struggled to speak. "They said they'd kill me iffin I told. Now it makes no matter. I's dying anyway. No. She didn't push him like somes think. He was beatin' on her like he liked to do, drug her up to the loft cuz she was skeered of heights. Liked to frighten her."

As Toby launched into another coughing fit, Luke tried without success to be patient. Fury at Samuel and how he'd abused Faith raged within him. If the man weren't dead already, he'd have been dead shortly. "How did he die?"

"I was on my way up ta try ta stop him when he lunged at Miz Faith. But she rolled away. He fell over the edge and broke his neck. I guess you could say he done killed hisself."

Finally! All he had to do was keep this man alive to tell the sheriff what he knew.

But Toby grabbed his arm as he went to stand. "Dey's more."

"Go ahead."

"Soon after Miz Faith married that scoundrel, he went out to work with her pa. Another man showed up, and the two off an' put him under the plow. Dey killed him." Toby squeezed his eyes shut and stopped speaking.

Luke gave him a minute before prompting him to continue. "Do you know who the other man was?"

"His brother."

A deep and sharp dread filled Luke. He'd been a blind fool! Ward was more desperate than he'd ever thought. And much more dangerous. He tried to keep the anger from his voice as he asked, "Why didn't you go to the sheriff and tell him what you knew?"

"Dey said they'd hurt her more—and the boy, too. The judge and Brown are relatives. It wouldn't do no good to try nothin'. I's the one who told her of the plan they was making to blackmail her. I heard 'em talkin' the day after Mr. Ward proposed, and helped her get away. I sneaked in and put tainted meat in their stew so deys would get awful sick. I didn't care iffin dey died, dem blackhearts deserved it . . . but dey didn't. It gave Miz Faith a good head start. I wanted ta go wif her, but I have a sista I look after, too."

The slow, deafening click of a gun's hammer being drawn back reverberated through the room. Luke spun around to see Brown standing in the doorway. The man's pistol was aimed at his head.

"Thought them tracks were fresh, might belong to you," he said, his voice raspy like he needed a stiff shot of whiskey. "Just what are you *really* after, boy?"

Luke never took his eyes off Brown. No way was he going to end up dead here, not with Faith needing him back home. Not in this lifetime. Not in the next.

Brown gestured to Toby. "What have you been tellin' him, old man?"

Toby didn't answer, and Luke could see Brown's anger building, smoldering, getting ready to erupt. In the blink of an eye, his face turned ugly. "I should've killed you a long time ago." He swung his gun from Luke toward Toby. Brown's finger flexed.

Luke grabbed the end of the cot, dumping Toby to the floor. Brown fired. Luke dropped and rolled to the left, drawing his gun. The big man swung back, and both men fired at the same split second, the sound exploding through the room and filling it with the acrid smells of smoke and blood.

The smoke cleared. Luke found himself crouched in a corner, holding his right shoulder. The blood seeping through his fingers was surprising, for he felt no pain.

He looked around. The bulky body of Ward's father was lying on the floor, faceup, eyes wide. Even in death, he had an evil look.

Toby lay still as well, so Luke scrambled over to the old man and felt for a pulse. Struggling to right the cot took a major effort, and with only one arm Luke strained to get the aged black man back atop it. Toby was shot in the side. It was a flesh wound, but it was bleeding heavily. He needed to get to town quick if his life was to be saved.

"Toby, can you hear me?" Luke ground out, an edge to his voice. The pain in his shoulder was kicking in and soon it was going to hurt like hell.

"I . . . hear ya."

"I'm taking you to town. To the doctor. So just try and hang on."

"Don't ya worry none. I's hangin' on till I talk ta de sheriff."

Luke looked into the old man's face. "You're a good man, Toby." Giving a final look at the corpse on the shanty floor, he gritted his teeth against the pain and hoisted Toby onto his good shoulder.

Chapter Forty-eight

LUKE tried to get comfortable on the hard wooden bench, but the throbbing in his shoulder pounded through his body, making him queasy. The rocking motion of the train didn't help either. With each tiny move, pain coursed wildly through him, and he closed his eyes, wincing.

It'd taken hours for the doctor to get him patched up. The bullet had lodged deeply in his shoulder, and because of that he'd lost quite a bit of blood, leaving him as weak as a day-old kitten. The wound had forced him to take the train the remainder of the way home, which was costing him an extra day. According to the doctor it was suicide to travel so soon after surgery, but waiting wasn't an option.

Damn Brown! If he hadn't gotten shot, he'd be home now. Able to tell Faith all he'd done to exonerate her of any guilt in

Samuel's death. Though, maybe he was kidding himself. Possibly she'd still want to go to Priest's Crossing. Her first marriage had been so horrible, she might not want to risk trying over again. That's what she'd told Amy, wasn't it?

Luke tried to rest, reminding himself he was in a weakened condition. With head leaned back against the wooden slats he reached up to cradled his wounded shoulder. The landscape sped past the boxcar's opened door as his mind went over and over each possible scenario.

Thankfully, Toby hadn't let him down. Just like he'd promised, he'd hung on until Luke could get him to the doctor—and also until the sheriff had a chance to talk with him. After the sheriff learned Luke was acting as a deputy for Brandon Crawford, and of Ward's part in the killing of Faith's father, he'd given Luke a warrant for the second Brown's arrest. Toby, recovering from his wound, was also being treated for consumption. Luke had left the doctor plenty of money to ensure that he would be properly cared for. He'd also made arrangements for a stay at the boardinghouse while the man healed and recuperated.

Frowning, Luke slowly reached with his good arm for his saddlebag. He felt around until he found one of the willow branches he'd packed before boarding the train. He stuck the twig in between his teeth and chewed, trying to be patient.

The landscape had changed from desolate isolation to occasional signs of civilization. Every so often they'd pass a farmhouse or ranch with families who'd call out greetings to the little wagon making its way toward Priest's Crossing.

Faith was becoming more than hopeful. Ward would have shown up by now, wouldn't he, if he intended to follow through with his scheme? She couldn't imagine what had changed his mind or what had happened, but she wasn't going to question this blessing. Joe said they'd reach town by tonight. That in itself was a welcome miracle.

"You'll need a place to stay," Joe remarked, looking over at her from his spot on the wagon seat. "Maybe I can help out with that."

"Oh, please. You've already done enough for us, Joe. I can't ask any more of you."

"Nonsense. I know the owner of the boardinghouse personally. Actually, I stayed there from time to time before I bought my own place. I'll check and see if she has any rooms open."

Faith hated being so indebted to Joe, but what could she say? She did need to find lodging, since Ward hadn't shown up. Maybe she really could start a new life with a job with Christine Meeks. "Thank you," she said.

With a rustle of skirts, she climbed back to check on Dawn. She also needed some space and time to think. The wagon slowed and then came to a stop. She glanced out in question.

"Rider coming," Joe called back.

A rider? No! Don't let it be Ward! Not now. Please, God, not that.

It was Ward. He was slumped in the saddle, disheveled, several days' growth of whiskers on his face. He must have been gambling and drinking for several days because he looked like he felt horrible. A rider could go cross-country to Priest's Crossing so much faster than staying on the road, and that's what he must have done and spent his time waiting for her in the saloon.

"Howdy," Joe called when he was close enough to hear.

Ward nodded but didn't take his eyes from Faith. "Hello, Faith," he said tetchily. "You 'bout ready to come home and stop all this foolishness?"

This was it. She needed to be convincing for Joe's sake. He'd become quite possessive of her, protective, and now she worried about his reaction.

"Ward," she said.

Joe's head snapped around at her declaration. "You know this man?"

"Yes. He's my brother-in-law. Family." Her mouth went dry and she couldn't look at him.

"I'm glad to see you, Ward," she said with fake enthusiasm. "I've tired of this traveling and the silly idea I had of working for myself and putting down new roots. I miss home," she added, choking back a sob.

Ward reined up alongside the wagon. He nodded. "Thought you might."

Glancing at Joe, Faith saw his angry expression. "Just what are you saying, Faith—that you're going off with this man? This stranger?"

"He's no stranger. He's Colton's uncle. I *am* sorry, though, to have been such a problem to you and the McCutcheons. I never should have run away after my husband was killed. But I thank you for all that you've done for me, Mr. Brunn. And for the children."

She held her breath. Would he believe her?

Clearly unhappy, Joe turned his attention back to Ward. "You're planning to just up and take this wagon back the way we've come? You don't have enough supplies!"

Ward nodded. "I've purchased supplies in town. We'll pick them up tonight and then head out tomorrow." As if annoyed at being questioned he added, "This is Faith's—or should I say my deceased brother's—wagon."

"These are the McCutcheons' horses," Joe shot back.

"I'll buy a new team in town," Ward said. "I wouldn't want to have anyone accuse me of horse-stealing."

He'd certainly thought of everything. Joe looked like he was wavering. Even if he didn't approve of the choice, he wouldn't stop her if she had a mind to go home.

Home? The word made her heart beat fast. Home was Luke's ranch, Luke's arms. Home was the afternoon they'd spent in the grass.

Clearly just having awoken from a snooze, Colton popped his head out from inside the wagon to see what was going on.

His gaze flew from Ward to Faith and back again, astonished. He looked too scared to say anything. Thankfully, Joe didn't notice.

"Time's a-wasting," Ward called, and he turned his horse in the direction of town.

He rode alongside Faith. The scent of cheap perfume and whiskey wafted up to the wagon seat. Ward began whistling.

"Preacher's waiting, too," he said just loud enough for her to hear.

Chapter Forty-nine

LYING on his back, Luke solemnly studied the cracks of his bedroom ceiling. The scowl that seemed permanently etched on his face was carved into his heart. Faith hadn't waited. She'd run off the very day he'd left the ranch. And on top of that, the telegram he'd sent from Kearney, telling his family to keep an eye on Ward and Faith until he returned, had been misplaced at the sheriff's office and reached the ranch four days late. That damn deputy! Brandon ought to fire his . . .

His shoulder wound was still very painful. He'd hidden the injury from his mother, knowing she would all but chain him to his bed if she knew the extent of it. He'd never seen her so hysterical as when he'd arrived. She'd gotten the telegram only hours before, when all the men besides Francis and Lucky were two counties over at a barn raising. The women had stayed home on account of Rachel and the new baby.

Cursing to himself, he looked at the side table and the note from Faith. He'd read it fifty times, knew it by heart. Still, he reached over and unwrinkled it to read one more time:

Dear Luke,

    I know I said that I would wait until your return, but that just was not possible. Joe Brunn came the day you left and that was my chance to get to Priest's Crossing.

    Please believe me when I tell you that I really do want a new life. One where I am the provider for my children. You have a wonderful family and are very blessed, but to be a part of that is not my dream. Please respect my wishes and let me go. Don't make this harder than it already is. I don't want to have to tell you to your face that I don't want you or any other man. I especially don't want a half-breed for my husband. Or to be the father of my children.

    Thank you for all your help with Dawn and everything.

—Faith

It wasn't quite the homecoming he'd envisioned. In fact, the more he thought about it, the less he believed it. He felt sure his suspicions were right: Ward was blackmailing Faith. So he had to concentrate on summoning the strength to get out of bed and back on his horse.

There was a rapping on his door. "Luke," Charity called softly as she poked her head inside his room. "I've gathered all the things you wanted, and a fresh horse is saddled." She entered with a tray. "I brought you food. You hungry?"

"Thanks."

As he picked up a slice of beef, he winced. Charity's eyes went wide. "You're hurt?" she asked. Instantly she was trying to see inside his shirt, but he waved her off. He had a time of convincing her, but finally she sat back and held her hands in her lap.

"It's nothing. Just a flesh wound," he promised.

Charity's brow twisted in a frown. Clearly, she was upset. "Have a sip of milk. It'll help fortify you," she said, handing him a full glass.

He cringed. "I don't drink milk. Can't stomach the taste."

Her expression turned hard as nails. "I don't care. You're hurt, and you need something in that belly of yours. Just humor me, please. Now drink it."

He did. Then he asked, "Will you do something for me?" He knew full well she would, though her eyebrows rose in speculation. "Don't tell Ma about my shoulder. I don't want her to worry."

"Worry? You're just afraid she'll not let you go."

"I'm going. She can't stop me." Cramming his meal into his mouth, he took one last drink of milk, just to get on Charity's good side, and stood. "When the men get home from that barn raising, send them to . . ." He paused. Hell. He didn't know where to send them. "Just tell them what happened and that I'm going to Priest's Crossing to fetch Faith back."

Charity's eyes went dark and she hugged him, being careful not to hurt his shoulder. "Be careful, Luke. I love you."

Her voice had a little catch in it, and Luke was afraid that she might start crying. He tipped her face up to his. "I love you, too."

"I know you still think of me as a little girl," Charity whispered.

"You *are* a little girl," he interrupted with a growl. "A special little girl. My sister."

She rolled her eyes and tried again. "I just wanted to tell you that I understand what you were trying to tell me the other day when we went riding, about a woman following where her husband goes. I was foolish meeting Ward in that barn. It was just that . . ."

He soothed the hair from her face, realizing that indeed she had grown up. "I know, Charity. We all get hankerings. But . . . your time will come. Just be sure that, when it does, it's with the right man—*and that you're married first.*"

"I know. I know!" Her eyes were instantly filled with tears.

"Shhh, don't cry." Luke drew her closer, ignoring the discomfort in his shoulder.

"Was it true about Brandon and the schoolteacher's niece?" she whispered.

He didn't dare tell her she had Brandon wrapped around her little finger; it would surely send her running for more adventure. Instead he said, "To tell you the truth, I'm not sure. I reckon you'd best ask him yourself."

She leaned back, wiping the tears from her cheeks. "I can't," she said, mortified. "What would he think?"

Luke hid a smile. "You're right, that would be pretty revealing. Still, I'm sure you'll figure out a way of attracting his attention. Subtly, of course—and definitely not alone in the barn."

She caught his arm as he was going out the door. "There's the old road to Priest's Crossing. Don't forget about that. If I was on the run, that's exactly the route I'd take."

He kissed her again. "I can always count on you."

Colton retreated to the back of the wagon and refused to come out. He'd been shaken when Ward showed up on the trail. Now that he'd learned they were returning to their old home, he'd reverted to suspiciousness and hostility.

Ward picked up supplies and purchased some new horses from the livery. He made arrangements to board the McCutcheon team until they were picked up. Now they drove up to a little building on the far side of town.

The undertaker's? Surprised, Faith kept quiet.

"Jackson Bennett, sheriff and undertaker," Ward read aloud. "He's agreed to marry us."

Anger bubbled up inside Faith. She'd never expected this to happen so soon. Ward was robbing her of a future, throwing her back into the nightmare she'd so recently escaped. And what was in it for her? Her children would indeed suffer when they returned to Kearney, regardless that she'd be there to buffer them. What in heaven's name was she doing?

She took a deep breath. "No. I'm not going."

"Don't start this, Faith. You don't want to make a scene, do you?"

"Take the farm, Ward," she pleaded. "It's worth some money. Sell it. I don't care. Just leave me here." Her insides had seized up, but Faith was determined to talk some sense into him.

Several onlookers from the street stopped and watched with curiosity. Ward leaned close, so that only she could hear. "Don't make me tell you again. Get your butt off that seat and get inside. I've already made arrangements with the sheriff. He's expecting us."

"No."

Ward hopped down from the wagon and circled around. With a jerk he pulled Faith out, leaving her sprawled in the street. Her breath was knocked from her lungs and her thigh stung, and Ward's eyes glittered dangerously. But though Faith's limbs shook and pain radiated from her legs and up her back, she'd not marry him without a fight. She shook her head defiantly.

Ward grabbed the collar of her dress and pulled her to her feet. He shoved her back against the wagon with force. Dizziness enveloped her, and from far away she could hear Dawn screaming. Also, what sounded like the whimpering of a small animal. Colton.

She turned her head and stared at the building. Her resolution remained unchanged. She'd not step a foot inside. She'd make her stand here and now.

"Colton, bring me that baby," Ward called.

Faith craned her neck to see the boy rocking Dawn in his arms, fervently trying to calm the screaming babe, fear etched on his face. And a hint of challenge.

When Colton didn't move, Ward strode to where the boy stood and took the infant. "Now," he chuckled, "we'll go inside."

Panic like she'd never known welled up in Faith's throat.

She reached for Dawn, who was squirming in Ward's arms. What would he do if she refused to go inside? One toss could cripple or kill her.

"Let me take Dawn, Ward. Please, she's crying," Faith said as she reached out.

Ward turned, bouncing the baby in his embrace. "Nope. I've hardly had a chance to get to know my little niece. I think I'll just keep hold of her until she settles down."

Faith gave in.

Within minutes it was over and they were back in the wagon, Mr. and Mrs. Ward Brown. Townspeople watched as the conveyance rolled off down the street. Faith willed away her memories, telling herself it was not the time to think of them. Memories of dark, concerned eyes. Eyes that could make her insides go soft with just a glance. Luke's strong arms, arms meant for comfort not causing pain. Luke, the night Dawn was born, crooning in encouragement.

"Quiet now, little one." She choked back tears and kissed her baby's wet cheek. "Things will be fine."

Chapter Fifty

Luke made it to Priest's Crossing in record time. His horse was spent, and he felt guilty about using him so hard. At the livery he rented a fresh one and asked around. The fast pace also took its toll on Luke. His shoulder wound had worsened, broken open and oozing, leaving him in an appallingly weak state.

Fear and anger coiled deep inside him as he learned about the scene Ward created outside the undertaker's. It was clear that Faith desperately didn't want to marry Ward. So, why hadn't somebody stepped forward and helped her?

"Hang on, sweetheart. I'm coming," he whispered as he gripped the saddle horn with his free hand and rode onward.

After a short distance he reined up and pulled his hat lower to shade his eyes from the probing rays of the setting sun. It was getting harder by the moment to keep his seat and he swayed in his saddle. Touching his throbbing shoulder, he drew back his fingers and gazed at thick red blood.

He should have found them by now, he admitted. It made him worried. He had no trail to follow, since the comings and goings of the townspeople had wiped it away. Guessing at Ward's destination and route was the best he'd been able to do. And now . . .

"You can't do her any good if you bleed to death before you figure it out," he chastised himself.

The old road Charity had mentioned was a handful of miles south, and it was, as she'd mentioned, the best option for Ward if he wanted to stay out of sight. If he cut cross-country, Luke would meet up with it. He wouldn't know if he was behind or in front of them, but he'd just have to leave that to luck. Right now he had to concentrate on staying atop his horse. On finding Faith.

He rode on.

Something skittered across his cheek. With a swat Luke sent it flying and opened his eyes. It was pitch-black, the clear night sky shining above with millions of bright stars. What the hell was he doing on his back in the middle of nowhere?

Slowly everything came back to him. He must have passed out and fallen off his horse. Barely able to summon the energy to turn his head, Luke struggled until he did. His horse was several feet away, still saddled, reins loose on the ground. The beast was eagerly cropping at the grass.

Luke extended his arm in the animal's direction. He stretched, wiggling his fingers as if he might reach the reins from where he lay. "Come here, boy," he croaked out, eyeing the canteen that hung from the saddle pommel. "Horse!" he called again, impatience with his own weakness curling inside him.

The horse didn't budge. What the hell was it the man had said its name was? He'd be damned if he could remember.

"Sam?" His voice was raspy and weak. The horse ignored it completely. "Saint? Striker!"

Seemed as if he recalled the name starting with an S. The effort was making Luke dizzy. He rolled his head back and closed his eyes.

He swallowed, and the dryness of his throat made him wince. Frustration swept through him like a tidal wave. If he didn't make it to the horse, he could easily die out here. Not only would that be letting Faith and the children down, but Charity would nail his hide to the barn door. Not that he'd feel it, he thought humorlessly.

With enormous exertion, Luke rolled to his side and looked at the horse. "Stupid." The horse stopped grazing and raised his head.

"Good boy! Now, come on over here."

But, the horse wasn't looking at him. It was listening to something far off to the west, and it snorted.

Alarm hummed through Luke's body. If he didn't get to that animal soon, it would run off.

Luke forced himself to roll to his stomach. He couldn't stop the grunt, a result of pain that radiated out from his shoulder and coursed through his body. He squeezed his eyes shut and for a brief moment thought of Faith's pretty smile, and the memory dulled the pain. He took a few hurried breaths. "Easy, boy. Easy now."

Dragging himself with his elbows, he focused his mind's eye on the way she'd said his name their first night as they walked to her wagon, and it buoyed him enough to keep going.

He was closer to the jittery flea-bitten gray. "Silver . . . ? Is that your name? Keep eating that nice grass." Luke kept talking. He didn't know if it was to calm the horse or his own tremulous feelings. He actually smiled when Faith came to mind again as she tried to talk him into believing she had an aunt named Penelope. No doubt she'd been a distraction to him—in the very best of ways.

"Salty! That's it. Here, Salty. Be a good old boy, Salty, and stay there until I can drag myself over to you."

The horse's head came up again, and this time Luke heard the distinct jingle of a harness and the crunching of wheels on dirt. The old road must just be over the rise! And who else could it be, if not Faith and Ward?

Necessity fueled Luke, giving him the strength to pull himself the last few feet to the horse. He gripped one rein, closed his eyes and groaned. Salty, agitated with excitement generated by the approach of other horses, danced around and almost stepped on him.

Through sheer force of determination, Luke heaved himself up and caught hold of the stirrup and crawled into the saddle. Between huge gulps of air and bouts of nausea he rode toward the sound, wondering how he was going to keep Ward from seeing he was wounded. The cover of darkness could help. Possibly Ward wouldn't see his weakened condition.

He positioned himself behind a scrub oak but made sure he had a good view of the road. The moon shone softly on the lane, and he could make out a wagon, distant yet approaching at an even pace.

Luke didn't have to check his weapon. It was loaded and ready, and he took it from its holster so he wouldn't have to be doing any fast-drawing in his condition. But he wavered in the saddle. Gripping the horn and gritting his teeth, he swore softly at the effort just sitting there took. That wagon had best hurry.

"Brown!" Luke bellowed when the wagon was within fifteen feet. He could see Faith wrapped in a quilt next to Ward. Instantly, both figures straightened. Luke thought he saw

Faith mouth his name, but his vision, blurry as it was, might be playing tricks. Ward dropped his hand to the edge of the wagon seat.

"Keep your hands where I can see them," Luke warned.

Ward brought his hand back up and laid it on his lap with the other. "What do you want, McCutcheon?"

"I think that's pretty obvious. I told you to stay away from Faith."

"True enough. But, things have a way of changing. Faith is my wife now, so you don't have no claim on her."

A cold chill descended on Luke, frosting his insides. A few moments passed while he wavered and fought the weakness that was threatening to overtake him, threatening to topple him from his saddle.

"McCutcheon?" Ward called.

"Yeah?"

"McCutcheon, you just sit back and let us pass. I'm taking my family back where they belong. I don't want any trouble."

Again Luke had to catch his breath, and it was a moment before he could answer. "You're not taking her anywhere. Now climb down off that wag . . ." Damn. He had to clench his eyes shut, and his gun barrel wavered. Lances of hot fire flashed through his shoulder and radiated up his neck. He stammered, "G-get off the wagon."

Ward spotted his weakness. His hand darted under the wagon seat and pulled out a pistol. Seeing as Luke had cover behind the bush, he made a more sinister move. "Drop it, Mc-Cutcheon, or I kill her." He had the gun pressed to Faith's side.

Luke squinted and tried to steady his gun. Would Ward actually kill Faith? A drop of sweat rolled down his forehead and stung his eye.

"Drop your gun. Now!" Ward shouted.

It was too risky. He couldn't shoot and take the chance of hitting Faith. Not now, when there were four of the man on the wagon seat. Which was the real Ward Brown?

Chapter Fifty-one

$\mathcal{T}$HINGS were looking bleak. But then something dark hovered in the wagon opening just behind Ward, and instantly Luke knew what to do.

"Haw!"

He spurred his horse forward, bolting out from behind his cover. As he did, Ward swung his gun around and fired at him. But not before a tremendous clang rung out in the night air. A moment later, Faith raised her foot and shoved Ward's unconscious body from the wagon seat.

"Luke!" she screamed. Climbing down off the wagon, she ran to where he hung slumped in his saddle.

Ward's shot had grazed his thigh, but Luke didn't feel a thing. All he knew was Faith was alive and steadying him, helping him stay in the saddle as he struggled to speak. "Ward . . . ?"

There suddenly came the sounds of a multitude of horses' hooves, mixed with the clicking of pistol hammers being drawn back in a moment of serendipitous fortune.

"Don't worry about Brown," Roady called out. "I'm watching him real close."

"Me, too, Miss Faith," Chance called from the west side of the road.

"*Senora*, I'll be *very* happy to shoot him between the eyes for you. *Sí?*"

Faith looked around, clearly astonished as the shadows came alive, and the cowboys from the Heart of the Mountains rode forward. They stopped and remained where they were, with the exception of Flood, Matt and Mark, who barreled up next to Luke and Faith and dismounted, lifting Luke down and carrying him toward the wagon.

"Oh my God," she whispered when she saw the blood covering his chest. "You're hurt very badly."

He looked down and saw his whole side drenched in blood. "It's an old wound." Still, he clutched it with his hand. His leg was nothing.

As they approached the wagon, Luke nodded. "Good work, Colton. I was praying I wasn't seeing things when you held up that frying pan. You did well, boy. I'm proud of you."

Closing his eyes, he gave himself up to the darkness.

When they laid him in the wagon, Faith made Luke as comfortable as she could. He was so still, it sent chills through her body. Now, as she wiped his face with a cool, damp cloth, she gave a sigh of relief. He was coming around.

The light from the lantern played across his face. His eyes, midnight black, centered on her face and never wavered. As the moments ticked by, she became increasingly uneasy under his scrutiny. Dawn was fussing in her bed, upset since the shot had awakened her.

"You said you'd wait," he ground out, over the baby's cries. The accusation in his voice was thick.

Knowing what she knew, fearing what she feared, she still couldn't tell him the complete truth. Not when Ward could still implicate her in his brother's death. Not when Ward was still a threat to the safety of her children.

"I changed my mind." When Luke struggled to sit up she said, "Stay down. You've lost a lot of blood."

"Just get me something to put behind my back so I can lean against the sideboard."

Faith quickly folded a blanket and helped him get comfortable. Colton came and looked at the two of them, flanked by

Luke's father and brothers. "Uncle Ward is still out cold, and he's tied up good and tight."

"Good," Luke said in approval.

Matt stuck his head in. "What do you want to do?"

"I'd like a minute to talk with Faith before we do anything. And, thanks for showing up when you did. Who knows how this would have turned out. Charity?"

"Yeah. I don't think any of us would have remembered this thoroughfare without her reminder."

Luke's mouth pulled up at the corners. "Her and Colton's quick thinking saved the day."

Saved the day? Why, when Ward woke up he was going to be mad as hell. Faith shuddered when she thought of what he might say or do.

They were alone again. The quiet was almost louder than Dawn's cries had been when Ward first fired his gun. Now she was quieting and would soon be asleep, unaware of the commotion going on around her.

"Why'd you run off?" Luke finally asked.

The question was so soft, his eyes so full of tenderness, Faith wasn't quite sure she'd heard him correctly. Maybe it was her imagination, but he seemed to still care. He sounded more concerned than angry, as he'd been moments before.

"Didn't you get my note?"

"Found it a little harsh," he admitted.

"Then you know why I left."

As she shrugged, he stared at her. "Possibly, but why'd you marry Ward?"

She grazed her fingers across the top of Dawn's head, trying to find an answer, an anchor in her storm of emotions. She finally decided on, "I realized I was being foolish. I wanted to go home to the farm I'd grown up on. I missed it."

Luke sighed loudly, his exasperation pushed to the limit. "Don't think so," he said, in his deep-timbered voice. Faith watched him subconsciously reach up and press on his shoulder. His normally tempting mouth, the one that could make her insides twist with want, was now pinched with pain. "Try the truth, Faith. Maybe I'll have a little good news for you."

What was that supposed to mean? Whatever he had to say couldn't change the fact that Ward lay bound just outside the wagon, a man whose testimony might see her hanged. Worse, they were married, and he had a piece of paper to prove it. She was doomed now, and there was no escape.

She glanced down at Dawn, finding momentary comfort. This was right: being with the man who'd brought the child into the world. Oh, God, how she wished it were Luke who'd married her. He felt like part of her family already.

"If you had the choice of working in Priest's Crossing or going home with Ward, which would it be?" Luke asked.

"That's a fool question. I'm Ward's wife," she replied.

"Go on, answer. Which would it be?"

She swallowed, lifting her eyes to him. His eyes implored her for the truth. She owed him that much, no matter what Ward would say. "I'd work."

Luke sat, head tilted back, resting on the wagon sideboard, causing Faith to wonder if he was too weak to hold it up on his own.

"And," he continued slowly, "if you had a choice of working in Priest's Crossing"—he paused and took a breath—"or going home to the Heart of the Mountains and having to put up with my family for the next seventy or so years, what would your answer be, then?"

Faith sucked in a breath. Was he serious?

"Faith?" Luke pressed.

"That's a cruel question. . . ."

"I'm not being mean. I want your answer. Your *honest* answer."

"I'm married to Ward," she repeated. She tried to keep her voice strong and steady, but it wavered.

"You're *not* married to Ward. He forced you under duress. It's not legal."

She shook her head, surprised he was pushing the point. Turning back, she saw he was deadly serious. So it was time for her to come clean. "It's not just that. It's that back home, when Samuel died. We were in a hayloft and—"

"Praise the Lord," Luke said. "The truth. And the truth is, I know all about Samuel. I've been to Kearney. You didn't kill him. The sheriff there knows it now, and so does Brandon. No one will ever bring any charges against you. And, just in case you're wondering, Ward's going to prison—that is, if he doesn't hang first."

Faith was thunderstruck.

Luke sighed. "I guess the important question really is: how do you truly feel about my Indian blood? I know what your note said. Was it the truth, or just something to push me away? I'd like to think it was just an afterthought, something to hurt me, so I wouldn't follow. There are reasons beyond understanding why we end up the way we are, though. I'm done questioning."

Faith blanched. The truth. She could finally tell the truth. "No! Your blood is good and honorable. I've never known another man like you, Luke." Ashamed of all the hurt she'd caused him, embarrassed of her weakness and inability to stand up to Ward, Faith turned away.

"Look at me," Luke said.

She shook her head. "I can't."

"Please, honey?"

The anxiety in his voice surprised her. She turned back to him to find his mouth tipped up and his expression not what she'd expected.

"I'm asking you to marry me, Faith. Do I have to spell it out?"

"Marry you . . . ?" she whispered, unable to believe what he'd just said. Unable to believe everything he'd just related. "Yes, say it again. Spell it out."

His lopsided grin widened across his face. "Marry me, Faith. I love you. I have since the first time I saw you, and will until the day I die."

They were the sweetest words she'd ever heard. Scooting in carefully, she brushed his hair back from his face. He brought his good arm up around her, and she gazed into his eyes.

"Don't keep me waiting, darlin'. You're killing me." His tone was hushed, his lips just a murmur away.

"Oh, Luke . . . Yes, I love you, too. I want to be your wife more than anything in this world."

Chapter Fifty-two

THE evening was cool and lovely, three weeks since the confrontation with Ward. Men, women and children alike wore their finest clothes, and Esperanza fixed a meal fit for royalty. Tables were set up in the meadow next to the house, the only place large enough to cater to the enormous crowd; white linen tablecloths, flowers and bows adorned each. Children ran here and there in a game of hide-and-seek. A dance floor was set up under the pines, complete with a bandstand and hanging lanterns for when the sun went down.

Luke gazed at his new bride, who danced protected in his father's arms. Her cheeks, bright from the champagne she'd been sipping, reminded him of rose petals from his mother's garden. He laughed, enjoying her happiness.

Roady arched a brow. "What's so funny?"

Luke threw back the remainder of the champagne in his glass. "Just enjoying the scenery." Lucky, Ike and Smokey were providing the music, but they also, one by one, had been demanding a break every so often to swing Faith around the dance floor.

His friend gave a long whistle. "She is a sight. I'm still trying to figure out how you got so lucky."

It was a moment before Luke answered. Then he winked and punched Roady playfully in the shoulder. "Good living . . . and lots and lots of sweet talk."

The man just laughed and shook his head. Over in the corner, a taciturn Chance stood dejected, disappointed he hadn't gotten a chance at winning Faith's heart away from Luke. He made polite conversation with Doc Handerhoosen, who'd been completely forgiven and had sworn off whiskey for life. Joe Brunn was there, too. He'd been more than understanding after he'd heard the story about why Faith had so abruptly left with Ward. It turned out Christine had found another willing helper in Tilly the saloon girl, who had decided to change her ways and move out of town since Luke was now taken. Brandon approached, and Luke remembered the relief he'd felt when Faith told him Ward hadn't consummated their illegal union. She'd kept Colton and Dawn practically glued to her side, not wanting to give Ward a chance. The sheriff reached in his pocket and pulled out a piece of paper.

"What's that?

"Telegram. Thought you'd like to know Ward, Earl and Will all got their maximum penalties. It'll be years for the two who killed your bull calf to be eligible for parole. And Ward," Brandon said solemnly, "will hang."

"What are you waiting for?" the lawman added, as Luke glanced at his watch for the tenth time in the past hour.

"A surprise. I'm expecting a delivery, and I hope it gets here before this shindig is over."

The sheriff, sipping from his crystal champagne flute, smiled roguishly. "Ah, what a mysterious bridegroom. What could it be?"

"You'll just have to wait to find out like everyone else, Crawford."

Charity appeared at their side. She was garbed in a beautiful blue dress that fit her slender figure perfectly and accentuated her tiny waist. Luke almost laughed at her obvious overture. On her head was the beat-up old Stetson that Brandon had given her when she'd been just a girl following him around like a puppy dog on his trips out to the ranch. Luke hadn't known she still owned the old thing. By his expression, Brandon hadn't either.

She stood there twisting back and forth, hands clasped behind her back and beautiful young face exuberant. She threaded her arm through Brandon's and said, "Aren't you *ever* going to ask me to dance, Sheriff?" She gave a pout, all mock wide-eyed innocence.

"Well, I guess I'm asking now." And with that, Brandon skillfully guided Charity to the center of the dance floor, his hand on the small of her back.

As he turned her, Charity glanced at Luke. He winked. She smiled.

Colton and Billy burst into the center of the crowd, followed by Adam, scattering the dancers and bringing the music to an abrupt halt. "A wagon's coming!" they both shouted excitedly.

Luke smiled. Looked like he'd gotten his wish.

Dressed in his Cheyenne wedding clothes, her new husband was a sight to behold. His dark hair ruffled in the breeze, and the small feather Charity had attached at the nape of his neck fluttered. Faith thought she'd die at the sight of him. Never could there ever be another as handsome as he. Even with his bandaged shoulder and remnants of the bruised cheek he'd gotten falling from his horse, he stole her breath away.

He came to her and took her hand possessively in his, and they both watched the approach of a tall freight wagon. It was boarded up on all sides, making it impossible to see inside. Anticipation hummed through her body.

Everyone hushed as Luke turned to her. He grinned mischievously, and then he brushed his lips across hers. "It's your wedding present, sweetheart."

"A present?" she repeated, surprised. Warily, she glanced at the wagon. Seeing her worried expression, everyone laughed. "What on earth could it be?"

A loud moo sounded from the wagon interior.

"A steer? My wedding present is a steer?"

The freighter, who'd gone back to unload the wagon's contents, led a dark brown and white cow down the tailgate. Luke was laughing.

"No, not a steer. We have enough of those around this ranch. A milk cow. A very special milk cow." He grinned.

Shocked, Faith covered her mouth, adoration shining in her eyes. "Penelope!" The name came out as a whisper. She ran to the cow's side and slid her hands lovingly around the docile animal's neck and kissed the top of its head. Penelope, calm of demeanor and wide of eye, looked curiously around at all the spectators.

"Penelope," Faith breathed again.

"Hold on now," Luke protested good-naturedly. "Don't be giving all your kisses to her."

Faith threw herself into Luke's arms. "How did you find her? I mean, I can't believe . . ." She stopped, unable to go on, and buried her face in his chest.

"Shhh. This is your wedding day," he replied, tipping her face up to his and gently wiping the tears from her cheeks. "Don't go about crying."

"Oh, Luke." She shook her head, overwhelmed. "I love you . . . *so much*. I only wish I had something to give you, too."

"You do, honey, you do." He gestured to Colton, and then to the upper bedroom window where Dawn slept soundly. "You've given me more than any man rightly deserves."

He gently pressed his lips to hers, kissing away her tears.

"One small favor," he asked with a crooked smile.

"Yes?" she whispered, enjoying the contact of his body pressed next to hers, the feel of his lips on her face. It didn't matter that his whole family and the townsfolk were watching; this was now her family, too. They wouldn't judge her. There wasn't *anything* she couldn't share with Luke. He was her champion and would love her through thick and thin, and then some! Her heart, secure in his hands, was sheltered by his strength. It was a magnificent feeling.

He cleared his throat. "I'm all for having your aunt here for the wedding, her being your closest relative and all . . . but maybe we should skip inviting her anywhere for tea. It might be a trifle hard to explain to the neighbors."

INTERACT WITH DORCHESTER ONLINE!

Want to learn more about your favorite books and authors?
Want to talk with other readers that like to read the same books as you?
Want to see up-to-the-minute Dorchester news?

VISIT DORCHESTER AT:

DorchesterPub.com
Twitter.com/DorchesterPub
Facebook.com (Search Pages)

DISCUSS DORCHESTER'S NOVELS AT:

Dorchester Forums at DorchesterPub.com
GoodReads.com
LibraryThing.com
Myspace.com/books
Shelfari.com
WeRead.com

☐ **YES!**

Sign me up for the Historical Romance Book Club and send my FREE BOOKS! If I choose to stay in the club, I will pay only $8.50* each month, a savings of $6.48!

NAME: _____

ADDRESS: _____

TELEPHONE: _____

EMAIL: _____

☐ I want to pay by credit card.

☐ **VISA**   ☐ **MasterCard**   ☐ **DISCOVER**

ACCOUNT #: _____

EXPIRATION DATE: _____

SIGNATURE: _____

Mail this page along with $2.00 shipping and handling to:
Historical Romance Book Club
PO Box 6640
Wayne, PA 19087
Or fax (must include credit card information) to:
610-995-9274
You can also sign up online at **www.dorchesterpub.com**.
*Plus $2.00 for shipping. Offer open to residents of the U.S. and Canada only.
Canadian residents please call 1-800-481-9191 for pricing information.
If under 18, a parent or guardian must sign. Terms, prices and conditions subject to change. Subscription subject to acceptance. Dorchester Publishing reserves the right to reject any order or cancel any subscription.